The Storm Within Her

AMI SPENCER

GW00503625

First Edition February 2023

Published by Ami Spencer

Copyright © 2023 Ami Spencer

ISBN: 9798355370886

Editor: Charlie Knight

Cover Design: Ami Spencer

CONTENT WARNING: Depression, anxiety, self-harm.

ACKNOWLEDGEMENTS

There are so many people who without their support and input this book would just not be possible.

To my beta readers; Shell, TJ, Monna and Jayne. This one has been a tough one, but your support, encouragement and feedback has been invaluable as ever.

To my editor, Charlie, for pushing me to make sure this book is worthy and truthful, and reminding me that it is a story which needs to be told, and helping me in making sure it is told in the best way possible.

To Lindsey and Melissa, those friends who I can send a simple "I'm not okay" text to, and know that they will be there to listen to all my irrational, muddled thoughts and talk me down when my mind wants to trick me into thinking the worst.

And to Kim. Thank you for loving me and standing by me through the past ten years when things have got too tough for me to handle, when I didn't think I was worth it, when I thought I'd never get out of that black hole. I'm not one for public displays of affection, I'm grumpy and sarcastic, and a little bit of a nightmare to live with, but you're still hanging in there despite it all.

And finally, to all those out there who struggle with their mental health; keep fighting. Keep going. Fight for another day. Because the sun will rise tomorrow, and the day after that, and the day after that. And one day the burden will lessen, your shoulders will ache a little less with the load you carry, and life will become brighter again. It might not be permanent. It might come back, and drag you down into its inky depths again. But there is always someone out there to listen. It's okay not to be okay. You are not weak. In fact, if you wake up and keep going, even when the odds feel stacked against you, you are one of the strongest people alive.

Mental health matters. And so do you.

CONTENTS

Prologue	1
Chapter One	4
Chapter Two	7
Chapter Three	18
Chapter Four	30
Chapter Five	36
Chapter Six	42
Chapter Seven	46
Chapter Eight	51
Chapter Nine	62
Chapter Ten	71
Chapter Eleven	77
Chapter Twelve	82
Chapter Thirteen	90
Chapter Fourteen	98
Chapter Fifteen	103
Chapter Sixteen	112
Chapter Seventeen	125
Chapter Eighteen	131
Chapter Nineteen	139

Chapter Twenty   145

Chapter Twenty-One   157

Chapter Twenty-Two   164

Chapter Twenty-Three   169

Chapter Twenty-Four   173

Chapter Twenty-Five   179

Chapter Twenty-Six   185

Chapter Twenty-Seven   191

Chapter Twenty-Eight   198

Chapter Twenty-Nine   206

Chapter Thirty   215

Chapter Thirty-One   221

Chapter Thirty-Two   228

Chapter Thirty-Three   232

Chapter Thirty-Four   240

Chapter Thirty-Five   245

Chapter Thirty-Six   249

Chapter Thirty-Seven   253

Chapter Thirty-Eight   258

Chapter Thirty-Nine   262

Chapter Forty   268

Chapter Forty-One   278

Chapter Forty-Two   288

Chapter Forty-Three   292

Chapter Forty-Four   296

Chapter Forty-Five   301

Chapter Forty-Six   311

Chapter Forty-Seven   315

Epilogue   320

Also by Ami Spencer   328

About the Author   329

PROLOGUE

*J*uly, *the previous year*

The sun was beating down on Seph's skin, her exposed lower legs showing the unexpected tan which the mini heatwave they were experiencing had graced her with. She closed her eyes behind her sunglasses and tipped her head back, resting it on the slim, sculpted shoulder behind her. Warm, comforting arms came around her waist, bracketing her in a cocoon of security, but the teasing manner in which fingers brushed across the sliver of bare skin on her stomach caused a wave of desire to flash through her body.

"Mmm, that feels good," she muttered, allowing herself to relax further.

"Yeah? You look good," Kate murmured in reply as she started to trail soft butterfly kisses up Seph's neck. "Wish I could whisk you away right now. A beautiful, sunny beach, just me and you."

"Hmm, sounds amazing." Something about Kate's kisses, the way her fingers were seductively stroking up and down her skin, and the low tone of her voice as she spoke directly below her ear, ebbed away those final few cares Seph had this afternoon. "Where would we go?"

"Oh, there's this beautiful place in Portugal. The hotels around there are amazing, but the best bit is there are all these hidden, secluded beaches. We could take off, find a little quiet beach somewhere. Somewhere where no one else could find us. We could just be on our own."

The idea of a corner of the beach to themselves sounded incredible. Not only could Kate and Seph be by themselves, but she suspected Kate had picked somewhere where Seph would feel comfortable. Too many people unnerved her, and she much preferred to be out of the crowds. Plus, she could be with Kate in a bikini, without staring judgemental eyes. To her, that was perfect.

"We could find a little bar that does amazing local food and cocktails, spend the evening just talking and laughing without a care in the world, then walk back down the beach together, holding hands. The next day we'd be exhausted from making love all night because it would have been a *huge* struggle for me to keep my hands off you. So we would spend the day just sitting by the pool, and I would catch a sneaky look of you in your bikini over the top of my book—"

Seph laughed, interrupting Kate's vision.

"What's so funny?"

"You are never that subtle."

"Oh, really? Well, I guess you're right. I find it hard not to stare at you even when you're dressed. You're just too fucking gorgeous."

The compliment was accompanied by another trail of kisses, this time partnered with the gentle nip of Kate's teeth over her pulse point. Her hands had started to roam further under Seph's vest, spanning the skin underneath it. Seph loved how Kate made her feel desirable, how much she admired and almost worshipped her body, as if it were perfect. With Kate looking at her and touching her in the way she did, almost with a reverence, all Seph's fears and self-doubt washed away.

Kate snapped her out of her musings. "Where's your favourite place to go on holiday?"

"I love Greece. The islands. I love the history, all the mythology and stories." Seph's voice was becoming breathier, softer, her eyes growing heavier with each passing minute. Kate surrounding her and her voice were pulling Seph into a state of almost meditative calm.

"Of course you do. Did your parents take you when you were younger?" Kate asked with a smile.

"Yeah, Mum used to drag us round to see the sights. Helena hated it, but I always loved learning about the history. Mum would always make a special point of telling us the myths and legends we were named after."

There was a moment of quiet while the two women just savoured being in each other's company, the only sound coming from neighbouring gardens and families enjoying the hot summer weather.

"Have you always been known as Seph?" Kate asked, clearly having spent a moment thinking about the origins of Seph's name.

"No. When I was a kid, I was Percie, but that was a boy's name to me. Unless I was in trouble, and then I got Persephone. But I didn't like that either; it felt too long and tricky. It was only when I moved out and went to uni that I started using Seph."

"I like it. I think it suits you." Kate smiled, resting her face against Seph's hair and inhaling deeply. Outside of these four walls, or fences as it was this afternoon, life was chaos. Business meetings, client calls, and too many other factors which complicated things and just caused stress for both of them. Seph knew it was the same for Kate; her brain was always whirring, making everyone else happy, putting everyone else's demands first. But here, when she was just with Seph, she hoped all that faded away.

There were no other people. No other demands. Just her and the woman whose arms were wrapped around her, who settled her racing mind while simultaneously making her heart pound with excitement and desire. This was her happy place, she thought, as she felt Kate's thighs grip tighter around her hips, dragging them even closer than they already were, tangled up within each other.

"I love you," Kate whispered softly in Seph's ear. Seph smiled as she reached back to find Kate's lips.

"I love you, too," Seph mumbled into a kiss.

CHAPTER ONE

January, present year

Seph Graves tapped and lit up the screen of her phone for the sixth time already that evening. When she saw, unsurprisingly, that there were still no messages since she'd checked five minutes ago, she sighed and shoved her phone into the back pocket of her trousers before taking a long gulp of her drink.

She looked around the room. She hated these types of social events at the best of times, being forced to socialise with people you only usually see at work. She had begged Fiona to come with her, but she'd declined, stating that it was far more fun to think of Seph squirming and making small talk than to actually help her friend.

Seph also thought it was strange that her new firm had their Christmas party in January. But she wasn't going to complain too much since she only had to pay the usual inflated prices for a hotel glass of wine rather than the overly inflated Christmas prices. The cost was only adding to her discomfort about being there.

She glanced at her watch—8:16. She again wondered how long she needed to stay before it was acceptable to vanish. And whether she could slip out or if she had to make it known and say goodbye to someone.

She smoothed her free hand down the side of her jeans. She felt a little out of place. She'd only been at Bailey, Bradshaw and Haynes for four months and still didn't feel like she fit in entirely. At times, it felt like she was back at high school, the clever studious kid surrounded by the clique of popular girls. Looking around the room now in her black skinny jeans and blue and white pinstripe fitted shirt, she knew she stuck out amongst the cocktail dresses the other women were wearing.

Her fingers drummed against the small box in her pocket, and she contemplated finding the smoking area. She had just swallowed down the last of her drink, though, so she decided to head to the bar first. She was just accepting her drink and change from the barman when a voice behind her called for her attention.

"Seph!"

She took a deep breath before turning around, grinning a hopefully not overly enthusiastic smile at her boss who was sauntering up to the bar.

"Hi, Tim."

"I'm glad you could make it. I hope you're having a good evening?" he greeted her with an overly friendly hand on her shoulder. She tried not to flinch at the gesture; he was just trying to be amicable, and it wasn't his fault she was touch-adverse at times.

"Yes, thanks. It's lovely."

"Good, good. You know, I've heard some good feedback about you. The clients seem to like you, and I think you could really carve yourself a reputation with us."

"Oh, well, thank you. I really hope that this year, I can start to make my mark."

"I'm glad we got our hands on you. You've shown you're a hard worker, and I think we'll make the most of your talent."

"Me, too."

She had always wondered how much of an interest Tim Bailey actually took in his law firm. Apart from dealing with the odd influential client, she suspected most of his time was spent enjoying the benefits of being a senior partner, if his car and the set of golf clubs which sat in the corner of his mezzanine office were any indication. Aside from her interview, she had rarely seen him around the office; according to his personal assistant, he was working from home more often than not.

She supposed he had earned it, though. From what little she had seen or heard about him, he was a good leader, one of those bosses who liked to be a little more casual with his staff than traditional employers perhaps would have been. But she sometimes felt like he was trying a little too hard to portray that image. It didn't sit so well with the expensive watch and designer shirts he wore.

"I'm not sure that you've met my better half yet," he said, as he looked around, then tapped on the arm of a woman who was standing behind him. He pulled her from the conversation she was having with someone else. Seph was mid-thought about how it seemed rude to interrupt his wife's conversation when the woman turned, and a sudden wave of nausea hit Seph. She swallowed, hoping her reaction was not been visible as she felt the blood drain from her face and the strength disappeared from her legs.

"Kate," Tim began, "I'd like you to meet Seph Graves. Seph, this is my wife…"

Chapter Two

*M*arch, the previous year
"Kate Earnshaw."

The room rippled with light applause as the guest speaker was introduced and moved behind the podium. She was the last one before lunch—not an entirely enviable position, thought Seph, since she could already feel her stomach grumble.

But her appetite aside, she found the woman speaking captivating; she clearly knew she had to fight against growing hunger within the room to win some attention, making her discussion light-hearted and informal. Before she knew it, the hour was up, and the hall was beginning to empty. Seph joined the throng filtering out of the room and heading towards their complimentary lunch.

Lunch quickly moved into the afternoon sessions, and Seph was grateful when she could go back to sitting in the crowd, anonymous within a sea of people. Despite her somewhat striking appearance, her bright copper hair standing out amongst the blondes and brunettes in the room, she was an expert at going unnoticed; her natural disposition was to blend into the background rather than make herself known.

She sighed, rolling her head on her shoulders as she thought about the amount of work she could be getting done if she weren't here. It wasn't that the talks and guest speakers weren't useful or interesting—some she was finding extremely beneficial. But it was all the other stuff in between she could do without. The breakaways and activities and group work were making her social anxieties spike.

Tonight, she would eat her dinner and go straight to her room to try and catch up on some of what she was missing from the office. She wasn't really fussed for the final evening networking and drinks event; she couldn't honestly think of anyone she had crossed paths with that she wished to network with. And she was terrible at small talk or starting conversations. A quiet night alone in her room was just what she needed.

The current guest speaker finished, signalling another break in the schedule, and seats emptied as everyone headed towards the instant coffee and tea urns at the back of the hall. Seph stayed seated, avoiding the crowd and instead opening her laptop and spending the brief interlude checking her emails. She tapped out a reply to the most urgent before she looked up to see how the crowd at the coffee table was progressing. But instead, her view was filled with the slim, subtle curves of a woman's hips.

She quickly diverted her eyes upward in an attempt to discern who the hips belonged to. From her sitting angle and with the woman's natural height, she seemed remarkably tall, and Seph had to crane her neck up to see clearly.

"Hi. I thought you might like one of these," the woman said as she handed Seph one of the cardboard cups filled with hot coffee. Seph recognised her instantly as the guest speaker from this morning, but just in case she hadn't, the woman held out her hand as Seph took the coffee cup and introduced herself properly. "Kate Earnshaw."

"Umm, hi. I'm Seph Graves."

"I saw you wisely avoiding the crowds, so I thought while I was there, I might as well get you one," Kate explained, nudging her head towards the coffee stand.

"Thanks."

"Can I?" She pointed to the empty seat next to Seph.

"Oh, sure." Seph mentally shook herself, thrown by the woman coming over and introducing herself. She felt the rising panic of having to try and hold a conversation, already aware of how eloquent and accomplished Kate was. She took a moment, staring down into her coffee and trying to calm her rapidly racing brain.

"I really hate having to network. Pretending you're interested in whatever they're interested in just to get to the business after twenty minutes of small talk. Maybe you've got the right idea in ignoring the crowds."

"Oh. I—" Seph looked up, about to try and deny that she was practicing some serious avoidance techniques, but stopped when she saw Kate's soft, knowing yet non-judgemental smile. She smiled back, helpless in her reaction. "Yeah, I'm not a fan of these things."

Now Kate was sitting down, Seph had the opportunity to study her properly. She was older than Seph, mid-forties or maybe even early fifties, but Seph could only garner that from her impressive resume which accompanied her presentation, otherwise she would have put her nearer her own age. Her shoulder length white-blonde hair fell in loose, messy waves, and her bright, sparkling blue eyes were perfectly framed and enhanced by the thick rectangular glasses she wore. Seph noted that Kate's smile was wide, warm and inviting, instantly calming any worries which anyone, Seph included, may have. She tucked her hair behind her ear, and Seph noticed the silver ear cuff which glinted in the light and was linked to a small stud by a delicate silver chain.

"How are you finding it apart from the forced niceties?"

Seph blinked, bringing herself back into the conversation. "Yeah, okay. Really interesting," she quickly replied, glancing down at the cup in her hands. Her social awkwardness was already showing enough as it was without being caught staring as well. "I mean, the talks are interesting. It's just all the other bits. Some people are just a bit...you know."

"Hmm. I saw you were about ready to throttle that curly haired woman in your group earlier." Kate gestured to where one of the women who Seph had spent the afternoon with stood. Janice was mid conversation with a man who currently resembled a rabbit in headlights.

"Yeah, well. She had some very...unique views." Kate chuckled softly, and Seph noticed how her whole face smiled, her eyes wrinkling slightly in the corners. "What about you? Are you having a good time? I enjoyed your presentation earlier," Seph said shyly. Her talk on how the workplace thrives with women in leadership roles was inspiring, most definitely the most interesting session of the past two days. Seph had found herself a little in awe afterwards.

"Thank you." Kate ducked her head slightly, clearly touched by the feedback. "I'm very passionate about women in the workplace. I think, where men are often seen as ambitious, women are labelled as cold or hard faced. Women should be encouraged to push as far as they can go; they have a lot to offer."

"I still see a lot of cases where women are discriminated against just because of that fact. Usually once they have had children, they are viewed differently because they are mothers as well as women. They are considered not as committed because they have other priorities or focuses, when in reality, they tend to be holding together a family and a job and doing both better than most other people would be able to do either."

It was the most Seph had managed to say since Kate had joined her, but she found it easy to talk about something she was so passionate about. The fact that Kate's very presence was ebbing away at her nerves with each passing second also didn't hurt.

"You work in employment law, right?" Kate asked before taking a sip of her coffee.

"Yeah, mainly. It's a lot of corporate HR stuff—unfair dismissals that sort of stuff. It's not very exciting most of the time." She shrugged.

"But you're good at what you do. Or so I've heard."

Seph looked at her, surprised that someone had supposedly been talking about her. Although thinking about it, she should have known when Kate knew her area of expertise.

"Umm..."

"Sorry," Kate apologised with a small laugh. "I didn't mean to put you on the spot. I was just asking around earlier for some advice and someone from your firm"—she pointed to one of Seph's colleagues—"said you might be good to speak to."

"Oh."

Something she couldn't identify sank heavily in Seph's stomach. She knew this was too good to be true; people like Kate Earnshaw didn't speak to her without a reason. She pushed away whatever sense of disappointment had washed over her, instead focusing on what she was being asked while clearing her throat.

"Well, someone's been inflating my ego. There are far more knowledgeable people than me." She wished she could say her self-deprecating manner was a joke, but she really didn't think herself knowledgeable enough to be recommended by anyone.

"In this room?" Kate had a look on her face which was starting to soften her barriers, and Seph couldn't help but smile.

"Well, maybe that narrows it down."

"Between me and you?" Kate asked, raising a perfectly styled eyebrow in a quizzical fashion.

Seph chuckled, the last remaining sense of that lead weight lifted with Kate's own self-deprecating humour. "Then I'm assuming definitely yes, you've come to the right person."

"Well, in that case, I was hoping I could pick your brain..." Kate flashed a smile so wide, it made Seph's stomach flip.

Kate saw Seph sitting at the bar. It wasn't the first time she had spied her that evening, but it was the first chance she'd had to make her way over. She steeled herself, taking what was supposed to be a calming breath before walking over.

She wasn't entirely sure why she felt so nervous about approaching her, but she hadn't been able to stop thinking about Seph since they parted ways earlier in the day. As she got closer, her gaze drifted to what Seph was wearing: skinny black jeans, tucked into chunky black leather ankle boots, and a simple white t-shirt. Never had she seen something so understated look so sexy. She caught herself checking how those jeans hugged Seph's curves in all the right places, quickly stopping herself when she realised what she was doing.

With a final exhale, she reached the bar and slid onto the empty stool next to her, taking a second to watch as Seph slowly turned her glass in her fingers. Again, just like earlier, she looked lonely, almost despondent, and painfully uncomfortable.

"Hello again." She hoped that approaching and talking to her again was the right thing to do. She'd noted how awkward Seph looked earlier in the day when Kate had introduced herself, and although she slowly relaxed a little throughout their interaction, the tension was obvious. Any fears she had were alleviated, though, as Seph turned to her, her smile wide and genuine.

"Hey."

"Can I get you another?" she asked, pointing to Seph's glass.

"I was only planning on staying for one..."

"Oh, that's a shame." Kate tried to hide her disappointment.

"But I could be tempted into another," Seph said, voice wavering slightly. "I-if that's okay?"

The sudden burst of uncertainty mixed with the fact that Seph had agreed to have a drink with her made Kate smile. She shouldn't have been so happy over such a small thing as Seph accepting an offer of a drink, but she was quickly realising that she wasn't entirely in control of how she reacted around Seph.

"Of course. Otherwise, I wouldn't have offered." Diverting her eyes to the bartender, she swiftly ordered her drink and another for Seph. She then turned back to Seph. "I'm glad I bumped into you again." She hoped her admission seemed as nonchalant as she intended, but she feared it came across slightly more desperate than planned.

"More ulterior motives?" Seph gave her a glance over the top of her wine glass, and Kate's fears settled at the remark. There was a glint in her eye which made Kate smirk in response. When she wasn't worrying about talking to people, Kate suspected Seph could be a little mischievous.

"No, not this time." Kate leant in a bit closer, as if she was divulging some deep secret, trying to encourage and validate Seph's own attempt at a playful nature. More than anything she wanted Seph to feel safe and comfortable to be herself. The fact that being flirty with her came easily was just an added bonus. "I bloody hate these dinners, so a friendly face and some half decent conversation is very welcome."

"Half decent?" Seph laughed, lightening Kate's heart. "Steady on. I'll be getting an ego if you keep on complimenting me like that."

"I know you find these things just as painful," Kate quipped, tilting her head as she picked up her glass. She took the opportunity to study Seph a little deeper. Her look somewhat jarred with the impression she gave; her copper shoulder-length hair stood out, especially when scraped up into a messy ponytail that showed off her undercut and the exquisite line of her neck. Her left arm was decorated with a beautiful, classical style tattoo of a woman, as if a sculpture had been traced upon her skin. Her ear was dotted with three—no, four—silver studs. Seph was beautiful, and Kate was starting to realise why she hadn't been able to stop thinking about her all evening.

"Honestly, I think they're fucking excruciating." Seph leant in, mirroring Kate's actions and snapping her out of her trance. "Unless you have some half decent company," she added, smiling playfully.

Kate felt her breath hitch with Seph's look this time. It may have been years, but she still knew flirting when she saw it. It eased her nerves slightly, if anything, her fear of being obvious with her own physical attraction calmed by the confirmation that it was not entirely one-sided. She also felt an odd sense of pride and happiness that Seph felt so content, so at ease around her that she could behave in such a way. Her anxieties were so obvious that for her to relax was a joy to see. And Kate wanted to see so much more of it.

A thought crossed her mind, buoyed by Seph's own admission of disliking their current situation. Kate looked around, before ducking her head and lowering her voice. "Fancy finding a quiet corner to hide?"

"Yeah, sure. Hang on..." Seph gestured to the barman. "Excuse me. Can we just get the bottle please?"

"A girl after my own heart."

Seph flashed Kate a grin which made Kate swallow hard, and she felt her cheeks heat as they flushed. Not wanting to dwell on the reaction more than necessary, Kate stood as Seph grabbed the bottle and they moved, finding themselves a small table tucked into the corner by the patio doors. Without a second thought, both slid onto the small two-seater sofa which sat against the wall, effortlessly continuing their conversation.

It flowed easily all evening, punctuated with laughter throughout, and with each passing moment they became even more relaxed in each other's company. After a while, Kate noticed they had gravitated even closer to one another without either of their conscious knowledge. Kate's touches became more deliberate and frequent—a gentle hand on an arm, a brush of fingers across a knee. The feel of Seph's leg pressed against her own was intoxicating, the heat burning through her trousers and scorching her skin. For each lingering touch of Kate's, Seph reciprocated, and when Seph leant in to say something, so close that her lips almost brushed Kate's cheek, Kate nearly lost her composure.

After a while, when the heat and the noise of the bar became too much, Seph suggested stepping outside for a cigarette, and Kate was grateful for the respite. She may have been guilty of encouraging the flirting but sitting in such close proximity to Seph was rapidly becoming a difficult task. The cool dusk air was a welcome respite to her flushed skin.

"Didn't have you down as a smoker," Kate commented, watching Seph's nimble fingers slide a cigarette between soft lips.

"I'm not. Not really. Only when I've been drinking or I'm in anxious situations."

"And which is the cause this time?"

"Little of both." Seph smirked, offering Kate the box.

Kate slipped a cigarette out, leaning in to light it when Seph offered her the flame. She blew the smoke of her first exhale into the air.

"Seph is an unusual name," Kate said, ignoring the fact that something was making Seph a little anxious.

"It's short for Persephone," she answered. "My mother is a Classics professor. My sister is called Helena."

"Does that mean there's a story behind it? Some myth of gods and goddesses?"

"Kind of." Seph chuckled. "Persephone was the daughter of Demeter, the goddess of fertility and the harvest. She was beautiful and wanted, by many but she continually turned down all the men who tried to marry her. Until one day, Hades, the god of the underworld, decided to abduct her and keep her for himself. Demeter, who didn't know where her daughter was, fell into a great depression and the land suffered as a result. Crops failed, and the land was barren. Zeus, worried about the earth dying, found Persephone and told Hades to return her. He agreed but not before tricking her into eating pomegranate seeds, which is the fruit of the underworld; she was then tied to the underworld eternally. So a compromise was made between the two gods: Persephone would spend half her time on earth, during which Demeter was happy and the land flourished; the other half of the year, she was in the underworld, during which the land dries up and nothing grows. And that's how the Ancient Greeks explained the seasons."

"Oh, wow. That's kind of beautiful. Tragic, but beautiful."

The silence settled between them, heavy with something which neither wanted to acknowledge but neither could ignore either. Kate, for the first time that evening, was at a loss for words. Instead of speaking, she marvelled at the sight of Seph in the gentle glow of the patio lights, taking in the way that the shadows highlighted the contours of her face. As her gaze rose to Seph's eyes, she realised the younger woman was looking back at her. Embarrassed at being caught, she was about to apologise when a shriek cut through the air. Kate found her body being yanked and spun, her back hitting the cold brick of the wall with a gentle thud, a warm and very welcome body pinning her in place.

"It's Janice," Seph hissed, explaining where the ear-splitting noise had come from. "The bloody woman collared me at dinner. I'm not getting stuck with her again." Seph peered around the patio area.

Kate, failing miserably at trying to be stealthy, desperately tried to stifle a giggle at the situation.

"Shush!" Seph hushed urgently. She put her hand over Kate's mouth, clearly trying hard not to laugh herself.

Kate mumbled something, but even she struggled to make out her own words, sniggering against the palm of Seph's hand, feeling her breath bounce back towards her. Seph gave her an adorable frown, clearly not having a clue what she said either.

"What?" Seph asked, dropping her hand from her face.

"I said, you should be careful who you drag into shadowy corners."

Kate saw the realisation of their situation dawn across Seph's face. Kate's back was still pressed against the wall, and Seph was very much within her personal space. Her hand was still bunched in Kate's shirt where she had grabbed it, her free one now holding herself up against the wall beside Kate's head. They were so close, she could feel the rise and fall of Seph's chest as it brushed against her own, the rhythm seeming heavier than before. Soft huffs of air tickled over her cheek. Her eyes momentarily flicked down, attention caught by Seph's lips, then back up. Kate was stunned by her eyes, which appeared dark and stormy in the shadows.

Suddenly, as though the spell had been broken, Seph swallowed and took a step back, releasing Kate's shirt as she did so. Kate thought she saw her eyes shoot downwards to her own lips but dismissed it as her imagination, her slightly inebriated and overactive mind playing tricks on her.

"Sorry," Seph muttered.

"No, don't be," Kate murmured, unable to stop looking at Seph's mouth. She'd never wanted to kiss anything as much as she wanted to kiss those lips at this moment.

Almost without thought, she let her body lead, her fingers finding Seph's by her side and curling her own around them, stopping her from increasing the space between them any further. Her other hand reached out, bridging the gap, tentatively resting on Seph's stomach. Again, they locked eyes, and Kate lost herself in the swirl of excitement and anticipation which rolled through her. She couldn't remember the last time she had felt so wildly, instantaneously attracted to someone.

She found herself again focusing on those soft lips, wondering what it would feel like to run her tongue across them, what Seph would taste like. She sensed rather than saw Seph leaning into her slightly, and in response, she twisted her hand into the fabric of her t-shirt, tugging her closer.

Emboldened, Kate leant in even further and let her lips brush softly against Seph's, Seph mirroring and reciprocating the action. It was brief, fleeting, and timid, and as Kate felt Seph pull her fingers out of her grip, for a second, she panicked that she was pulling away entirely. That was until the gentle caress of Seph's fingertips ghosted across her cheek, and she cupped Kate's face in her palm.

Kate, swept away by their first, tentative touch, kissed her again, this time more confidently and more sure of herself. She allowed her hands to do what they had been itching to do all evening and skimmed around Seph's waist, settling on her hips and feeling the curves she knew sat underneath her clothes. Her fingers toyed with the hem of her t-shirt, her mouth moving in harmony with Seph's, a soft sigh escaping as they continued in perfect rhythm. It was full of the thrill of a first kiss yet seemed so natural, as if they had been doing it for years. *For years.*

Suddenly, reality hit her like a truck, her stomach lurching, and she pushed against Seph's hips, pulling her lips away. Seph stumbled back a step, gaze instantly casting to the ground.

"Oh, God. Shit! Sorry. I totally got that wrong," Seph offered.

Kate took a moment, guilt and regret swirling alongside excitement and arousal, before realising what Seph had said.

"Oh, no. No. No you didn't. I...I kissed you. And I've been wanting to all evening," she admitted, swallowing hard, her fingers ghosting across her lips where she could still feel the phantom sensation of Seph's kiss.

"Oh," Seph said, clearly confused. "Then, what—"

"I'm married."

CHAPTER THREE

January, present year

Kate sat at her parents' kitchen table, her tea untouched and long cold in front of her, her eyes glazed as she thought back to the night before. The last person she had expected to see was Seph. And ironically, the only person she had wanted to see for months was Seph. She'd been so strong, so resolute in her belief that Seph was better off without her, that she had spent every day fighting her desire to call or see her. And then, at last, there she was.

She thought of the look on her face. How hurt she was. How confused. How *terrified*. She felt overcome with the need to just wrap her up in her arms and tell her everything was going to be okay. But she couldn't, and instead, she choked her way through the interaction. Luckily, Tim had never been one for long conversations at social events, and he quickly moved on to the next person. Despite selfishly hating watching Seph walk away, she was grateful for Tim's short attention span on that occasion. She could see the strength drain from Seph the moment Tim moved on, turning and practically running away.

By the time she had gotten away from the crowd and followed in the direction she had seen Seph leave, she had gone. Where, she didn't know; she assumed Seph left the party all together since she didn't see her for the rest of the evening. Or at least for the hour or so she remained there herself before feigning a headache and leaving as well. She argued with herself what the best thing to do was; should she go to Seph's house? Should she call? Should it be then, or later, when they had both had time to process what had just happened? Or should she leave her alone for good, safe in the knowledge that she had definitely done more than enough hurt to the woman without inflicting any more pain on her. No choice seemed any better, any clearer, than the other.

Sleep was never going to come easily, and by the time she heard Tim return home in the early hours, she hadn't even tried. She couldn't bear to be anywhere near him, and luckily for her, he didn't question or care too much when she made her excuses for sitting in the dark on the sofa in her home office, the radio on low, as her mind replayed every touch, word and moment with Seph.

"Katherine?" Kate snapped out of her memory and looked up at the mention of her name. Unable to bear being in her family home any longer, she had slipped out and found refuge at her parents' house before Tim had even risen. Her mother looked at her, and Kate realised that she was expecting something. An answer, maybe? She couldn't honestly say she knew her mother had been speaking, let alone the question she had been asked. Her mother's forehead crinkled as she realised she hadn't been heard. "Did you hear what I said?"

Kate shook her head, trying desperately to focus. "Sorry. What were you asking?"

"I was saying, your father's talking about having a retirement party later in the year."

"Sounds nice."

"He wanted to know about the hotel for Tim's party last night. Was it any good?"

"I guess so," Kate replied, not really knowing or remembering many of the details about the hotel, the food, the company...anything but Seph.

"Do you think you could get the details for me?"

"Sure."

A few moments passed before Kate became aware of her mother studying her. She knew she must look tired; she'd seen it herself in the mirror this morning when she first got up and dressed. When she had stood in the bathroom, studying her reflection, she could see the glassy look in her eyes that betrayed her lack of focus, the dark circles which accompanied them, making it clear that sleep had been lacking. She could have tried covering them up, but really what was the point?

"Katie?" The use of her childhood nickname, usually only now uttered by her father, drew Kate's gaze up from where she had been staring into her cup. "Is everything okay, my darling? You seem distant this morning."

"I..." She sighed, unsure how to continue. The way she was gnawing at her bottom lip in a nervous tick she'd had since childhood portrayed the weight of her thoughts. With a final huff, she threw out a question. "When you met Dad, how did you know that he was special?"

"What do you mean, darling?"

"Well, you were both engaged to other people. How did you know it was him over Brian?"

Her mother pulled out the stool opposite Kate, her brow furrowed at the topic of conversation. "Why do you ask? Has this got something to do with why you've been miles away all morning?"

"Just..." Tears started to well in her eyes, a lump forming in her throat. She swallowed it down, pondering her words carefully. She looked down, her fingers fiddling with the handle of her mug. Her thumbnail had found a blemish in the ceramic and scraped over it in repetitive grounding motion.

"Kate? What is it?" A warm, comforting hand on her arm reassured her of her mother's presence.

"I've really messed up, Mum," she choked out.

"Come on now, it can't be that bad. Just take a deep breath, and when you're ready, tell me what's going on." Kate couldn't help but be reminded of when she was a child, and her mother would calm her in exactly the same way. Except, back then, it was usually because of a fight with a school friend or an exam she thought had gone badly. This was a whole other dimension of pain she wasn't even sure the love of a mother could soothe.

"I...I met someone." It sounded so puerile, so immature, and yet she didn't know any other way to say what she needed to say.

"Who? Why's that a..." Kate cringed as her mother made the connection. "You mean—"

"I had an affair, Mum," Kate confirmed, her tone slightly shorter and snappier than she planned, her anger at herself seeping out.

"You know I'd never judge you, Katie."

Kate nodded slightly, further calmed by another gentle squeeze of her hand. Maggie Earnshaw had always been supportive, never overly judgemental or critical. Even now, she felt it, that undeniable sense of there being no right or wrong answer, as long as it was the one truthful to herself. It was how she had been raised and an attitude which she hoped she'd passed to her own children. Right now, the only person she was judging was herself for hurting Seph in such a devastating way.

"I know. Sorry, I just..." Kate petered out, unsure how she was feeling let alone what she wanted to say. She was grateful when Maggie spoke up.

"You said you had? It's over now?"

"Yes. It has been for months," Kate answered, her voice shaking as she tried to hold back the tears. Answering questions was simpler than forming her own thoughts but still wasn't easy.

"So if it's been over for months, why say something now?"

"Because I saw her again. I saw her, and everything I had been trying to push down for the past few months just came flooding back like this tidal wave." Her voice broke, and the tears flowed freely, streaming down her face in a torrent of repressed emotion. "I love her. I love her so much, but I've hurt her so badly that I don't think she'll ever forgive me."

"Oh, my darling. Come here."

Kate dropped her head onto her mother's shoulder and felt her wrap her arms around her, letting her cry into her. Maggie stayed there for a few long minutes, not moving or asking for anything, which Kate was appreciative of. Instead, she just let her cry, let her release all the emotion she had tried so hard to ignore and bury over the past few months. Once Kate felt her sobs begin to calm and her breathing settle slightly, she loosened the grip she had on Maggie's jumper. Maggie took it as a sign that it was safe to pull back a little. Once she did, she wiped the tear-dampened hair from her daughter's cheeks, holding her face in her hands so she couldn't escape her gaze, just as she did when she was younger.

"I think this calls for a fresh cup of tea and breaking into your dad's secret bourbon biscuit stash. Go on. Go make yourself comfy, and we can have a proper chat."

Kate sniffed, giving her mum a small smile, before being ushered towards the sofa which sat in the corner. She slumped down onto it and grabbed a tissue from the table beside her, wiping the tears from her cheeks. Taking a moment to try and compose herself and her thoughts, she picked at the tissue as she nervously awaited Maggie's return. After a few minutes, she came in with the promised mugs of tea and a plate of biscuits.

"So," she started, sitting beside Kate and passing her one of the mugs. "Why don't you tell me all about her?"

Kate looked up at her mother. This was the difference between Maggie and other women, certainly of her generation. While others may have wanted to know the details of the situation, how their daughter came to be in this circumstance, and quite possibly, how they could have been so foolish to do so, Maggie had always been more liberal in her views. All she wanted to know, first and foremost, was about the woman who had clearly won her daughter's heart because she knew this wasn't something that Kate would enter into lightly. Kate swallowed before starting.

"Her name's Seph." Kate smiled, unable to hide the joy that just thinking about Seph brought her.

"Where did you meet?"

"At a conference. We started speaking about work, but instantly, there was something else with her, Mum. I've never felt anything like it. As soon as I saw her, I was hooked. It felt like I needed to be around her. But I told her I was married, and nothing happened..."

Well, almost nothing. That first kiss they'd shared still blew Kate's mind. She'd never experienced anything like it.

"Then, a few weeks later, we bumped into each other again." She shrugged, hoping the rest was self-explanatory. "At first, I thought it was the idea of something I couldn't have, you know? Something exciting and new. And that was why I was so enamoured with her. But then when I saw her again..."

April, the previous year

It was three weeks after the conference when she heard the familiar sound of her voice. It was odd, Kate thought, how despite only having spent that one evening together, her voice seemed to carry over and find her way to her. Kate turned around to confirm what she was almost certain of. Standing a few feet away, she spotted Seph immediately, deep in conversation with a man. She looked her up and down, the action almost involuntary. Her grey chequered suit trousers and waistcoat fit her perfectly along the curves of her body, the sleeves of her black shirt rolled up to her elbows, showing the tattoo which spanned the length of her forearm. She felt herself blush, her body temperature rising as she realised what she was doing. Something out of her control commanded her to go over when the person she had been talking to walked away, and as she did, Seph turned around. Instantly, a smile spread across her face, which sent warmth through Kate's body.

"Well, hello. This is a surprise."

"A good one?" Kate asked with an air of levity, despite feeling a wave of guilt about their last encounter. Even though they had left each other that night with a tentative understanding, Seph had every right to still be angry at her.

"Of course," Seph reassured, her smile warm and genuine. "What are you doing here?"

"Messy divorce with child custody issues. You?"

"Unlawful dismissal."

They stood there a second, both with soft smiles on their faces. Kate studied the way Seph anxiously fiddled with the strap of her satchel, the same nervous energy she had displayed on that first day when she noticed her.

"How are—"

"How have you—"

They both started at the same time. A gentle bout of laughter fell between them at their failure to be able to hold a conversation, both stumbling over their words, stumbling over each other's words. It washed away that last lingering tension between the pair of them.

Kate spoke first. "How have you been?"

"Yeah, good, thanks. You?"

"Yeah, I'm okay," Kate replied, not entirely sure of herself. She was, for all intents and purposes, being honest. However, for the past few weeks, she had been feeling a strange sense of unease. As if suddenly, her life wasn't so solid and sure anymore. But she shook off the feeling, not wanting to burden Seph with the details.

"Good. Well, I better..." Seph started, gesturing behind her, and Kate was aware that they were now just staring at each other in the middle of the corridor, something unspoken and unknown hanging in the air between them.

"Yeah. Me too," Kate choked out reluctantly, a sudden sense of loss cascading over her. "It was good to see you."

"Yeah, you too," Seph responded, shuffling slowly but not fully turning away as if she was expecting something. After a second, she did turn, clearly leaving the conversation, and Kate had an epiphany about what was causing her to hesitate so much.

"Fancy lunch?" Kate called after her.

Kate watched Seph fidget as she paid the bill, wondering if she now regretted accepting Kate's lunch offer. While the conversation had been easy, there were moments when Seph seemed conflicted, as if she was struggling to know what to say or how to react. But Kate couldn't deny the happiness she was feeling at spending time with Seph again.

She was worried that the whirlwind of their first meeting had clouded her memories, rose-tinted Seph and the way she made her feel. But then Seph would give her a smile, or she laughed at something Kate said, or just looked at her with those deep, impossible eyes and... Yeah, Kate wasn't sure lunch was a good idea anymore. Her attraction to Seph was growing by the second, and she wasn't sure it was something she could control. But if this had proved difficult for Seph, she would step away. As much as she felt pulled towards her, she would never want to make her feel uncomfortable.

"*Are you okay?*" *Kate plucked up the courage to ask when they walked out of the restaurant.*

"*Hmm. Yeah, I'm fine.*"

"*You sure? Because you don't seem fine. Or very convinced of it yourself.*"

"*It's nothing,*" *Seph tried to reassure her, but Kate saw right through it.*

"*You're a terrible liar, Seph,*" *Kate replied with a grin.*

Seph looked up ahead, avoiding eye contact with Kate, and blew out a breath. She was clearly warring with herself about what to say, and Kate felt a panic engulf her at what it was that Seph was feeling. Maybe it would be easier if Kate was the one to deal the final blow. "*Was this too weird? Because you could have said no, I wouldn't have minded.*" *Seph couldn't help but smile again, a breathy chuckle escaping her lips. Kate's forehead creased, confused about what was funny.* "*What?*"

"*I don't think I could have said no even if I wanted to,*" *Seph replied.*

"*What do you mean?*" *Kate asked, pausing in her stride.*

Seph looked back at Kate who was now a step behind, grabbing her arm gently and steering her to the far side of the pavement out of the flow of foot traffic after a passer-by tutted at her sudden stop. Reaching the railings which overlooked the canal, she let go of Kate's arm, and looked at her, taking a deep breath.

"*Seph?*" *Kate questioned.*

"*Sorry, I...*" *She leant forward on the cool metal railings which ran in front of them, focusing on the murky water. Kate moved to be next to her, mirroring her position. Side glancing, she saw that Seph was still looking straight ahead, and Kate was grateful that she wasn't looking at her. If this was going the way she suspected, she wasn't sure she could handle seeing the hurt in Seph's eyes.*

"*Thing is, I've been thinking about you a lot. And I know I shouldn't. You're married, and I respect that and your honesty that night. A lot of people wouldn't have said anything. But I don't often find people who I get on with so easily. You've got into my head, Kate.*" *She turned and smiled timidly at Kate. The soft smile reassured Kate that she hadn't stepped out of line with her invitation.* "*So when you asked if I wanted to go for lunch, I'd kind of answered before I even knew what I was saying.*"

Kate's grin transformed into something altogether more pleased with herself, watching as Seph relaxed, bumping shoulders with Kate playfully. "Don't look so fucking smug!"

"Who? Me?" Kate grinned, pointing a finger at her chest.

"Oh, fuck off. Wish I'd not said anything now," Seph mumbled, clearly embarrassed at her admission, looking back down the canal.

"Don't say that." Kate's voice dropped slightly, and Seph looked at her. Kate was taken aback by the look in her eyes. It was something she couldn't quite place, but it took her back to that night at the conference. "I've thought about you a lot as well."

Seph's eyes were focused on her, almost burning into her with the intensity of her stare. Kate felt her heart quicken, and she swallowed the lump which had appeared in her throat. Kate chanced a touch, brushing her fingers over the back of Seph's hand timidly.

"Kate..."

"I'm not sure what's happening to me, but I've not stopped thinking about you since I left you that night." Kate looked up at Seph. "And I don't want to mess you around. I'm not a person who plays fast with someone's emotions. But if I'm being completely, brutally honest with you, no-one's captured my attention like you have for years. I'm not sure if anyone ever has."

"You've got a husband. And a family. What about them?"

"I don't know. I don't want to hurt them either but..."

Without realising, they had found themselves in unbearably close proximity to each other. She could feel Seph's chest rising as her breathing got heavier. God, was Seph really as affected by her as she was with Seph? The charge between them was palpable.

Kate's eyes flicked down to Seph's lips, the memory of the last time they kissed still playing in her mind like a video on repeat. She'd thought about that kiss too many times in the past few weeks, replaying how Seph's lips felt against hers, the taste of her, how her hands felt on her body. She felt Seph's thumb brush against her skin, the smallest of touches, nothing too forward, nothing too great, but enough to grant her a flash of bravery.

"I can't stop thinking about when you kissed me. About how it made me feel..." *Kate whispered, her breath ghosting over Seph's lips. "I haven't felt like that in years."*

Kate couldn't resist, closing the gap between them so their mouths finally met. Her touch was tentative, a part of her still believing that she had mis-read the situation, that this would all go the way their first kiss went, ending with a feeling of dread and regret. Within seconds, though, any doubts were banished; Seph reciprocated with a searing kiss filled with three weeks of what if's.

Caution was thrown to the wind, as soft and slow gave way to unresolved tension and desire. Kate grasped the material of Seph's suit jacket, pulling her even closer, before sweeping her hand round to the small of her back. Seph broke the hold of their fingers, her hand moving to Kate's hips, pushing her body closer, her tongue swiping across her lips. Kate let out a soft moan at the intensity of the moment, and Seph pulled back, suddenly reminding Kate of their public setting. A fire had been stoked within her but she still had a tenuous grip on reality around her, despite Seph filling her view.

"Shit," Seph breathed, reminiscent of their first kiss, but this time for an entirely different reason.

"Seph..." Kate moaned, breathy and desperate.

"Do you want to stop?" Seph asked, dropping her gaze to her feet.

Kate tilted her face back up to look at her with a single finger underneath her chin, greeting her with eyes dark with desire. They both knew they had reached the point of no return.

"No," Kate affirmed, "but we need to go somewhere else."

"I fell so deep and so quickly. I just couldn't stop myself. Every second I could find to be with her, I would. When I wasn't with her, I would be thinking about when I could see her next. I was like a teenager, just so incredibly smitten with this wonderful person I'd met. And God, she made me feel so special—like I was the only person in the world. I can't remember the last time someone made me feel like that. I'm not even sure Tim ever has. She showed me nothing but love, and I just broke her heart."

"What happened?"

"I got scared. I hated leaving her. I hated seeing her when I left, what it did to her. Slowly, I could see her becoming less and less happy because there was already a part of her missing from when I last had to leave. She wanted to give me everything; she wanted to be with me. But I couldn't do it. I couldn't walk away from Tim and the kids."

"And is that what you wanted? To be with Tim over her?"

"God, no. I know that sounds awful because I should want to be with Tim. He's my husband...but I've always wanted to be with her. From the first moment I met her, I just wanted her."

"So what stopped you? If she was willing to go through all of that to be with you, why did you not take the leap?" Again, there was no judgement in Maggie's voice, only the need to understand where Kate was coming from, the rationale behind her actions.

"I could imagine a life with her. I could imagine doing all those little domestic things, which we couldn't do because I was forever watching the clock or sneaking away. But when I thought of the reality of how to make that happen, what decisions I would have to make, who that would affect, the enormity of it all...I got scared. I was terrified of the kids hating me, of what Tim would do, of what it would mean for everyone involved. What if I made that decision and it all went wrong? What if I lost everyone? Seph was right. I took the easy option."

"I don't think there was anything easy about the decision you made, Katie," her mother continued, leaving the explanation as it was. Kate was grateful she didn't probe further, unsure as to whether she was ready to unpack anymore at this moment. "Was it the simpler of the two choices? Yes. But it still took a lot to allow yourself to deny what you really wanted. And it's not made you happy, has it?"

Kate looked at her mother, the question hanging for a few moments before she shook her head quickly as more tears came. She sobbed into her hands, another wave of emotion crashing over her at admitting the truth.

"I've tried so hard to put her out of my mind and move on, but I can't. I always end up thinking of her. And then last night, when I saw her... Mum, she looked so tired and broken. And it hurt, it physically hurt, to see her like that."

She grabbed at the material of her shirt over her chest, emphasising where the pain had hit her, as more tears came at the memory of seeing Seph, the look of broken horror that flitted across her face.

Maggie took a moment to digest what her daughter had told her, allowing her to let her emotions spill over some more before speaking. "Well, I guess to answer your question, when I met your dad, it felt like everything was so easy. It wasn't that it was difficult with Brian; it just felt effortless with your dad. Conversation was easy, and the silences were comfortable. He made me feel like everything I did, however small, was extraordinary. When we were together, it didn't matter that there were people judging us or talking about us. The only two people that mattered were me and him. And I'm guessing, by the way you speak about her, and how your face lights up when you do, that it's exactly the same as when you and Seph were together."

She brushed some hair away from Kate's face, tucking it behind her ear. "My darling, there is nothing wrong with going for what will make you happy. Twenty years of marriage is nothing to be sniffed at, especially with two beautiful children to show for it. But if your heart is really that taken by this woman, you will never be content in your relationship with Tim anymore, and it will make you miserable. Maybe now is the time to do what you want to do instead of putting everyone else first."

Kate looked up at her mother, eyes stinging from her tears. "What if she doesn't want me anymore? What if I've pushed her away for good?"

"Surely it's better to try and know for sure rather than live with a lifetime of what-ifs?"

Kate thought about it. As much as it would hurt to be rejected by Seph, she had to know if she still had a chance. Her mind was made up. She had to see her.

Chapter Four

S eph sat on the sofa, curled up within herself, staring into space. The television had been playing non-stop all day, but she couldn't honestly recall a single thing that had been on. Her eyes were tired and itchy, and every time she blinked, they scratched and stung. She closed them in an attempt to let them rest, but as soon as she did, all she could see was Kate. Her stomach knotted again, forcing a lump to rise up her throat. She had spent the day in much the same state, and it didn't look like it was going to subside anytime soon.

She had, she hoped, managed to make a fairly inconspicuous escape the previous night after enduring a short yet agonising conversation when Tim introduced her to Kate. She could feel Kate's eyes on her at all times, although she couldn't bear to look at her herself, the fear of breaking down too imminent and real. The few times she did dare to meet Kate's eyes, she didn't know what to make of what she was seeing. Shock? Confusion? Pain? Concern?

Seph was grateful that Tim quickly moved on as she'd felt her legs start to buckle with each passing second, her energy draining with the effort of holding the inevitable anxiety attack which was about to come crashing down upon her. Once she was certain that Kate was out of sight, she rushed towards the toilet, slamming the cubicle door behind her and dropping to her knees, her stomach threatening to heave its contents. She could feel her heartbeat in her throat, hear the blood rush through her ears, the hiccupped sobs as she tried and failed to hold back the emotion.

She had somehow made it home, got changed, and climbed upstairs into bed. She wasn't sure how; there was a whole chunk of her memory missing as if she hadn't pressed record on a tape. It wasn't until later she even knew where she had shed her clothes, finding them in a pile in the bathroom. She felt exhausted and depleted, but she knew sleep would be hard to find, if at all. She existed in some strange state of limbo, brain over-active and processing but unable to retain anything it witnessed or thought.

It was somewhere in the early hours when Seph decided to move from the bed to the sofa, her legs wobbly and weak, her head still fuzzy. Burying herself under a blanket, she switched on the television in the vague hope of finding something to distract her. She must have fallen asleep at some point, only apparent by the jumps in what was playing, but it wasn't for long.

And so the cycle continued until she found herself sitting there nearly twenty hours later. She felt sick, her body weak and aching, her head pounding. A soft knock drew her out of her reverie, its gentleness still enough to reverberate through her skull. She glanced at the clock; five-thirty. Another knock, this time a little louder and more insistent. A little more painful.

Dragging her heavy legs across the room, she went to open the door. If it was Fiona, she wouldn't give up, but she might be able to get rid of her quicker if she told her she had a migraine.

"Hi."

The air from Seph's lungs was sucked out in one excruciating gasp. Kate was standing in front of her, sheltered from the wind on her porch, scarf pulled up to keep the rain from her neck. Her voice cracked, even under the single syllable she had uttered. Seph couldn't think, couldn't formulate a sentence, her jaw dropping open in anticipation of words that never made it. She stumbled back, her legs suddenly feeling as though they had been taken out from under her.

"Wh..." Seph managed to croak out, throat dry. She was struggling to see past the black dots which were edging into her vision.

"Seph? Seph, look at me."

Seph could hear Kate's voice, echoing as though being shouted down a tunnel towards her. She tried to focus on it, knowing it was an escape from the hole she was falling down, but simultaneously it was triggering so many reactions within her. There was so much in her head she wanted to say, but she didn't know where to begin. It was like her brain was firing at a hundred miles an hour but into the fog with no idea what its target was. She could feel her chest tightening, her breathing becoming more rapid. She squeezed her eyes shut. She could hear something, but everything was as if it was being played through cotton wool, fuzzy around the edges. There was a sensation as if she were drifting, being pushed through water, before the final specks of light were engulfed by the blackness.

Seph's eyes flickered open, the light instantly assaulting them and causing a piercing pain through the front of her head. She quickly squeezed them shut again before a shadow appeared, dulling the brightness. Cautiously opening them again, she saw Kate's worried features swim into view. She tried to speak, but all she did was croak out some unintelligible sounds as her brain started to reboot.

"Hey, hey. It's okay. Take your time." She heard Kate quietly reassure her.

She felt a familiar four-beat tap on the back of her hand, concentrating on her breathing to try and get it to match. Nothing was said by either of them for an indeterminable length of time until Seph opened her eyes, and the room had stopped swirling in front of her. After a couple of long blinks, she looked up, taking in the concerned crease of Kate's brow.

"What—" She cleared her throat. "What are you doing here?" she asked quietly, gaze now turned down. The words were still hard to choke out.

"I had to come. I had to make sure you were okay. I'm so sorry. I had no idea..."

Seph still offered no response. The kindness in her voice, the concern, was just too much to bear, and she felt the emotion rise up in her throat. She must have taken longer to compose herself than she thought because Kate broke the silence again.

"Seph..." Kate moved her hand, gently resting it on her arm to bring her into the room. Seph shrugged it away, the speed of the action forcing Kate to retreat, wobbling backwards as she crouched in front of her. "Sweetheart—"

That was enough to snap Seph out of her trance completely. Anxiety temporarily overtaken, all she felt was anger.

"Don't," she stated, cold and hard, as she scrabbled to unsteady feet, bracing herself against the wall behind her. As she steadied herself, her head still swimming, her eyes made their way up, finally looking at Kate. "You don't get to call me that."

"Please, don't be angry at me. Not for last night. I had no idea you worked for Tim. How could I?"

"Know a lot of people called Persephone, do you?" Seph spat.

"He never spoke about you. We don't talk about work. We don't talk a lot about anything—"

"Oh please, don't give me the whole *we practically live two separate lives* thing. You looked pretty solid as a couple last night."

"We do. Live two separate lives, I mean. It's just a front. We're both so busy with work—"

"And having affairs." Now she had opened the floodgates, the words were pouring out. Months of hurt and pain thrown in the face of the person she blamed for it.

"Please don't. Don't reduce what we had to just some sordid secret," Kate pleaded, her face crumpling with the insinuation.

"Why not? I mean, that's what I was, wasn't it? I was your dirty little secret. And double points for ticking the lesbian fantasy box at the same time!"

"You know it was more than that."

"Do I?" Seph felt her legs shaking beneath her and stumbled slightly. She was grateful when she saw Kate start and then change her mind about helping her. The last thing she needed in this moment was Kate's touch.

"Yes. What we had... You know it meant something. You know it meant something *to me*. You know how I felt about you. It wasn't easy for me to walk away."

"It looked fairly easy from where I was standing," Seph retorted, not wanting to believe Kate's pleas.

"It broke my heart to leave you—"

"And yet you still did it! You still went back to your husband—"

"Because I couldn't bear to see you hurting! And every time I left, every time I walked out that door, it broke me to see what it did to you."

"You didn't want to *see* me hurting?" Her voice returned to a cold and calm tone, the anger of before giving way to something deeper and more primal. "As long as you didn't see it, it was okay? Because it still hurt, Kate, even when you weren't looking."

"I know. It hurt me too. I thought, in the long run, it would be better for you, for both of us, if I walked away."

"Who are you to decide what's best for me? I'm a grown adult; I can make my own decisions," Seph threw back, with a hint of a sneer in her voice.

"But we were in too deep. It wasn't going to get any easier."

"It was never going to be easy! We knew that! But I thought...I thought you wanted to be with me. We were so worried about getting into something we couldn't handle at the beginning. Where did you think it was going to go? How did you think it was going to end?"

"I know, and I did, I wanted to be with you, but..." Kate paused, her next words falling into the silence.

"But you're a coward," Seph finished for her. "Just admit it, Kate. Stop lying to yourself."

Seph watched as Kate swallowed, nothing more to reply with as she resigned herself to the cold hard truth she'd clearly been avoiding for the past five months. Kate let her head drop, unable to look at Seph, shame filling her features.

"You have no idea what it's been like," Seph continued quietly. "Everything has been horrific. I've had to hold it all together for everyone. And to begin with, it was a blessing, as twisted as it was, because it gave me something to think about other than how much I hated you. Except I didn't hate you, not really. I wanted you. I wanted you there at the end of the phone so I had someone to talk to, someone to cry with when it all felt too much. Because it was, it was suffocating me. And I felt angry with myself that the only person I really wanted, really needed right then was you. Even after everything, I just wanted you."

Anger and frustration made way for heartache and sorrow. Months of holding it all together came unravelling in a matter of seconds. She'd told herself she'd never let Kate see just how much she had hurt her, just how hard she had found it. But in that moment she needed Kate to know just how hard the past five months had been. Unshed tears were finally released, cascading down her cheeks. Her fingernails dug into her palms, trying to give her something else to focus on rather than the suffocating silent tension which surrounded her. Kate stood, her face flashing with...what? Concern? Pain? Heartache? Seph wasn't sure, but tears that matched her own stained her face.

"Seph...I'm so sorry."

She stepped forwards, and Seph was slow to sense the arms lifting up in order to bring her close.

"No." She pushed Kate away, disregarding her embrace. "You don't get to do that now."

"I'm sorry." Kate stepped forward again.

"No, no..." Although her words were resisting Kate's attempts, her voice wavered with each refusal, emotion lodging in her throat.

"I'm sorry, sweetheart."

"No..."

Seph took a step backwards in her attempt to escape Kate's sympathy, hitting the wall and finding herself pinned in. Bracing her hands against Kate's chest, she tried pushing her away, but her muscles were screaming and depleted from the adrenaline drop in her body. All the while, Kate resolutely refused to give up, attempting time and time again to bring her into her body. With each repetition of Kate's insistence, her own resistance grew weaker and weaker, and slowly, her resolve crumbled, and her tears started to fall once again.

Kate, with all her patience and love, stood there, taking each shove, each denial, until, with one final weak shove, Seph slumped against her chest. Kate instantly curled her arms around her, cradling her head and shushing her as the stress of the past five months came flowing out in a torrent of ugly, heaving tears.

"I'm so sorry, sweetheart," Kate said again, this time whispering softly into her ear.

CHAPTER FIVE

K ate ran her fingers through Seph's hair, inhaling her scent. She was just as she remembered—a mix of cigarette smoke, vanilla, and apple. She dared to place a soft kiss against her temple; it was a risk, but she couldn't resist the urge to comfort her.

Seph was clearly exhausted; she could tell the moment the door had opened. And on top of that, she had just had an anxiety attack. Kate was shocked when she mustered enough energy to stand, let alone try and fight back. Her body was heavy in her arms, muscles slack as she took her weight. Slowly, Kate felt Seph's sobs subside, and she mourned her loss as Seph gently and slowly pushed out of her embrace. Kate let her arms fall, reluctant to sever the contact between them but aware she didn't want to push things too far and break the tentative connection she hoped they had made.

She watched as Seph leaned back, putting some space in between them, and her heart ached again at the sight before her; Seph's eyes were red and swollen from crying, her face a little thinner than Kate remembered and paler, and her shoulders slumped with an unbearable weight. Seph leant back against the wall, letting the solid surface take her weight, her face dropping down to the floor, chest heaving. She looked as though she could sleep for days. Kate ignored all her hesitations and reached out to run her fingers across Seph's cheek, brushing away a tear with her thumb. Her hand lingered, her palm cupping her cheek and cradling it softly. Seph didn't pull away.

"I'm sorry, Seph. I'm sorry I walked away. I'm sorry I hurt you. You were right; I am a coward. You deserve so much more than me, than this." She felt Seph lean slightly into her palm. She leant forward, closing the minuscule space between them. "There's not a day that's gone by when I've not thought about you and about coming back. I wish I'd been braver and walked away from him and back to you. I wish I'd been there for you when you needed me."

Her other hand found Seph's down by their side, and her fingertips gently clasped around hers, her thumb rubbing over her nails, rough and bloodied from her nervous biting habit. Everything about her screamed of a broken soul, and Kate so desperately wanted to start piecing it all back together again. She could see Seph had no more fight left in her, and Kate was ready to be here to hold her up while she rebuilt herself. Kate tried to gauge if Seph was being receptive to her pleas, if she stood a chance of being able to be here for her, but as she continued the stare down at the floor, Kate wasn't sure that Seph had heard her at all.

"I know I've got a lot to do before you trust me again, but I promise that if you give me a chance, I will spend every second working to restore that. I will be the person I should have been these past few months. I will be the person *you* need."

She leant in a little closer, buoyed by Seph's lack of resistance. She brushed her nose gently against Seph's, Seph's lack of energy resulting in her swaying slightly at the force. As their foreheads rested against each other, she heard Seph sigh into the touch.

"Can you forgive me, Seph? Can you give me another chance?" Kate pleaded.

"It hurt so much..." The tremble in Seph's voice broke Kate's heart.

"I know. And I know it's a huge leap of faith, but I promise I will not let you down this time. Let me be here. Let me be the person you need right now, the person I should have been for you before. Please, Seph..." Her voice drifted off, the unasked question hanging in the air between them.

She almost didn't believe it when she felt Seph's fingers push further into hers ever so slightly, gently intertwining at the tips. Scared she was imagining it or that it would disappear as quickly as it had appeared, she took a chance, closing the gap and brushing her lips timidly against Seph's. There was still a part of her that expected Seph to pull away, to tell her she had missed her chance, that it was too late. She thought it was coming when she felt Seph hesitate into the kiss, but after a second, she felt Seph return the gesture. The touch was gentle, a whisper of lips, but it was there. Spurred on by her response, Kate twisted her fingers fully with Seph's. Winding her other hand more certainly around the back of Seph's neck, she kissed her properly this time before pulling herself away.

She wanted to keep kissing her, to sweep her up and worship her like she deserved to be, but the woman in front of her was a shadow of the person she knew, and the link binding them was tenuous and delicate at best. Seph exhaled, any last shred of strength from her body dissipating as she gave up her fight. Kate felt her wobble, her legs wavering beneath her as she swayed in towards her, and quickly released her hold on her hand to grip her shoulders, steadying her before she fell.

"Woah, okay, sweetheart. It's okay. Let go. I've got you," she muttered softly, bracing herself to take Seph's weight. Seph slumped forward, her head resting against Kate's shoulder, Kate pressing a soft kiss to the top of it. She could feel Seph's body growing heavier against her. "Come on, baby. Let's get you on the sofa before you flake out on me completely."

Guiding Seph to the sofa, she sat her down, taking her own coat and scarf off before disappearing into the kitchen. She returned a moment later with a glass of water, perching in front of Seph on the coffee table. Handing her the water, Kate gestured for her to open her hand, dropping two white tablets into its palm. Seph looked up at her.

"You'll have a splitting headache soon if you don't already."

Kate had seen the after-effects of Seph's anxiety attacks, although she wasn't sure how severe they would be, considering this was by far the worst attack she had witnessed. Either way, the next few hours would be filled with exhaustion, headaches, and hopefully some rest to solve both of them. She watched Seph greedily swallow the tablets down with a gulp of water.

"Have you been taking your meds?" Kate asked. There was no judgement to her questions, purely concern at how far gone Seph was. The small nod confirming that Seph had been taking her medication made her exhale with relief. Kate waited for Seph to finish the glass of water, not wanting to rush her.

Once empty, Kate took the glass off her, putting it down before scooping her hands in her own.

"Look at me." A pair of tired eyes looked upwards, and her heart tore at the sight. "Take your time; it's okay."

They sat, Kate patiently waiting until Seph came round a little more, her thumb rubbing reassuringly across the back of her knuckles. She watched as Seph closed her eyes, breathing rhythmically, counting along with her in her head, so she was ready if Seph stuttered and needed guidance.

"Kate?" The voice was so small and unexpected, Kate almost didn't hear it. She couldn't even judge if her lips had moved, her head still hung low.

"Yes, sweetheart?" Seph's voice breaking the silence put her on edge, ready to run and execute her every request, however menial.

"Do you mean it?"

"Do I mean what?"

"That you want to be with me?"

Kate sighed, her chest aching with the doubt Seph had about her intentions. "More than anything. I've been so unhappy without you."

"Because I can't do this if you don't mean it. It hurt so much when you left…" Tears started to track down Seph's already blotchy cheeks. Kate moved so she was sitting on the sofa next to her, knees and thighs pressed together in an attempt to get as close as possible.

"I know. I made a massive mistake, and I know I hurt you, and you have every right to tell me to leave. But when I saw you, God, I just thought of all the things I've denied myself. Everything which I've spent the past five months trying to ignore just came flooding back. I just knew I had to see you again, ask for your forgiveness. Ask if you could give me, *us*, another chance."

"I want that more than anything, but…" Seph swayed, letting her head drop. Kate guessed another wave of pain or lightheadedness had washed over her. Kate gently ran her hand up and down her spine, feeling the bumps of her vertebrae through her hoodie. She leant in close, resting her chin on Seph's shoulder so she could whisper directly into her ear.

"Let me take care of you."

"I needed you so much," Seph admitted, her voice cracking again.

"I know. I'm sorry I wasn't—"

"Dad died."

Seph's voice was quiet, barely a whisper, but the words cut through the room like a knife. Kate felt her heart shatter. This is what Seph had to deal with without her. She'd been holding her family together. Kate's brain frantically searched for words, but nothing came up which seemed anywhere near adequate for the situation. So instead, she did the only thing she could think of and pulled Seph into her, tucking her head into her chest and squeezing her impossibly tight into her body. As she did so, she felt Seph's body start to shake as another flood of tears erupted from her.

"Oh, sweetheart. I'm so sorry."

If sorry seemed inadequate before, it was outright insulting now. She pushed down her self-scolding at leaving Seph to focus on the small sobbing form in her arms. She could feel her own tears running silently down her face, the physical ache in her chest only becoming more crushing with each passing cry from Seph. Kate combed her fingers through Seph's hair, scratching lightly at her scalp, remembering how it soothed her. Kate swallowed back her own tears to speak.

"What happened?" She was aware that maybe Seph didn't want to talk about it right now, but she had to ask, had to give her the option of speaking to someone about it. She guessed that maybe she hadn't had much opportunity, considering her earlier comments about being there for everyone else.

"He had a massive heart attack. Just collapsed in his office. By the time they'd got him to the hospital…" Seph choked out another cry, shaking with the overwhelming emotion in Kate's arms.

"I'm so sorry, baby." Again, it seemed pathetic, insulting almost, that that was all she had to offer, but she genuinely didn't know what else she could say.

"It was two weeks after you left."

Kate was wrong. *That* was the sentence that shattered her heart. Anything left of it was smashed into a million more pieces. Two weeks after she had walked out on Seph, Kate was still spending hours in her car, sitting at the end of Seph's street, arguing with herself about whether to go back and beg for forgiveness. If she had done it, if she had just stopped being so foolish and admitted to herself what she knew, she could have been there for Seph during her darkest hour.

"I...I just...I..." Seph stammered, clearly feeling like she needed to say more, explain more, but unable to find the words. To Kate, she needed to explain nothing.

"Shh. You don't have to say anything. Not now. We can talk later, but right now, you don't have to say anything." She looked down at the shrunken person curled into her lap. "You don't have to be strong anymore, Seph. I'm here."

Chapter Six

Seph woke, her eyes sticky and tired, but her mind already whirring. As her focus slowly returned, she recognised her living room. It wasn't the first time she had fallen asleep on her sofa. More often than not recently, sleep had crept up on her, and she had woken up here. But this time, there was something different.

The cushion beneath her cheek was warm, and there was a heavy, unfamiliar, but not entirely oppressive weight resting in the curve of her waist. The familiar scent of a perfume she used to cherish filled her nose. She pushed herself up, her foggy memories being confirmed. Kate was there, head rolled back uncomfortably, sleeping on the sofa as well. Just the flicker of the memory from earlier exhausted her, but she pushed through what she could remember, replaying every word, trying to make some order of her thoughts. Kate had come over, apologised, begged for forgiveness, for a second chance. Seph had cried, had broken down, had told her about her father. Kate had said she would be there, that Seph wasn't alone anymore. And here she was, still here. Maybe this time, it could be different. But then again, hadn't she heard all this before?

Seph shifted again, sitting up fully, suddenly feeling unwelcome in the cocoon of warmth and security she had felt a few moments previously. The movement woke Kate with a start, snapping her head up, concern creasing through her features as her eyes flitted to Seph.

"Seph?" Kate asked, worry lacing her tone.

"Sorry," she mumbled, pushing herself away. "Must have fallen asleep."

"It's okay. What time is it?" Kate asked, sounding disorientated herself.

"Don't know. Late." Seph rubbed her hand down her face.

Kate hummed in agreement as she studied her watch. "Why don't you try and get some more sleep?" she suggested as she reached forward and tucked a strand of hair behind Seph's ear, letting her fingers linger against her cheek. Seph tried to ignore how good the touch felt.

"Maybe."

"You need to sleep, baby."

Seph stayed slumped forward, her head resting in her hands, fingers scratching back and forth along her scalp. She was still trying to process everything, trying to work out what was going on. Which was made even more difficult by the cotton wool filling her head at the moment. Every thought seemed to be getting snagged on its way to the front of her mind, dragged down into a pit of confusion. She attempted to ground herself, to focus on what she knew to be real and tangible; the feel of the oxygen inhaled through her nose, the blood pumping behind her eyes. A warm palm settled in between her shoulder blades and rubbed gently, bringing her back into the room.

"Seph?"

"Hmm?" She looked up, finding Kate studying her with inquiring eyes.

"I said, why don't you go to bed?"

"I won't sleep."

"You should at least try," she said, her fingers finding their way to her hair again, brushing through it in a soothing manner. "Now I'm here, I can take care—"

"Are you?" Seph interrupted, pulling further back from Kate's fingers, leaving them lingering in mid-air. The sudden movement made her head pound again.

"Am I what?"

"Are you here? Because that means you've left him, and you haven't said that. Have you left him?" The sensation of Kate's touch disappearing altogether as she let her hand drop answered Seph's question. It was all the response Seph needed. She scoffed. "You're unbelievable."

"No, please," Kate begged as Seph shakily stood. "I haven't seen him—that's the only reason why. I nearly came here last night, but I didn't know if it was too much. I didn't know what to do. But I couldn't sleep thinking about you, I was so worried. And I needed to talk to someone, to tell someone about you, so I went to my mum's, and then I came straight here. I promise. Please, Seph…" Seph turned to see Kate standing behind her, tears once again rolling down her face. "One thing I do know is whatever happens between us, my marriage is over. I can't be with Tim; I don't want to be with Tim. I don't love him anymore. I love you."

There was a delicacy in those words which Seph couldn't ignore, something other than just the words themselves which told her that Kate was being sincere. But she couldn't unpack it and analyse it now, her headache was already raging behind her eyes again, and she was scared that too much thinking would only trigger another attack. Instead, another small morsel of Kate's speech made itself known within the noise.

"You told your mum about me?"

"Yes. Everything."

Seph couldn't help but let out a tired giggle, the absurdity of the statement providing much-needed relief to the tension in the room.

"What's so funny?" Kate asked, smiling back.

"Why does it feel like we're teenagers sneaking around?"

Kate stifled a laugh and dropped her head, Seph watching as she took her hand in her own.

"There will be no more sneaking around. I promise."

Seph sighed a great big heaving breath which utterly deflated her. She wanted so badly to believe Kate, to throw caution to the wind and believe her. But she'd been promised this before. Or she had at least convinced herself she had. But she was broken, snapped in two by the world's cruel tests, and as easy as it would be to give in, to just say *yes, let's do this,* she knew that she needed to be selfish. In this one moment, she had to say *it's my way or nothing* for her own survival.

"I can't do this again—" she started, abruptly shut off by Kate's pleading.

"Please, Seph, don't do this."

"Wait," she said, holding up her hand. "I can't do the sneaking around and lying again. I don't have it in me." She pulled her fingers out from between Kate's and took a few shaky steps. Her legs still felt weak, and she could sense Kate following her, but she needed to gain some space. Otherwise, she would never think clearly.

She turned to look at Kate, her eyes watching her, full of sympathy and sorrow. She wanted nothing more than to fall back into her lap, into the security of her arms, and stay there, but she knew if this wasn't resolved now, it would only be harder as time went on. Kate was so consumed with ensuring Seph's well-being it was heartwarming, but it wouldn't address the elephant in the room.

"If you really want this, us, you have to be available. You have to make yourself available. And that means leaving Tim."

"I know."

"Then I need you to leave while you do that."

Kate stepped forward, reaching out to Seph, but Seph took another wobbly step backward, knowing how tentative her resolve was. One touch, and she may just crumble entirely. Kate looked dejected, confusion crossing her face.

"I can't leave you. Not like this," Kate begged, stepping forward and clasping her hands once again.

"You have to, Kate. You need to do whatever it is you need to do." Seph could feel the tears starting to well again, and she had to swallow them back in order to finish what she needed to say.

"But what if something happens? What if you have another attack—"

"Then I'll call someone."

"Me. Call me. Please, Seph."

"Fine, I will call you. But if you're serious about being here—"

"I am, I'm serious. I want to be with you."

"Then you need to go." Seph looked into her eyes, full of disappointment, pulling her hands free before turning away. She could sense Kate behind her before hearing her collect her things, keys rattling as she picked them up.

"I love you," Kate said quietly.

As the door clicked shut, Seph screwed her eyes shut as another wave of tears threatened to pull her under.

CHAPTER SEVEN

K ate shut the front door, falling against it in exhaustion. Home was undeniably the last place she wanted to be for a number of reasons. She
wanted to be back in the warmth of Seph's home, making sure she was sleeping
and resting, offering the support she had been absent in offering before. But
she understood why Seph had told her to leave. She understood her need for
certainty and reassurance.

She followed the sound of the television, which drifted down the hallway
from Tim's den, breathing deeply as she reached the doorway. She spotted the
glass of whiskey on the table in front of him, his bare feet propped next to it, the
light of the television the only thing illuminating the room.

Just being in his presence irritated her irrationally. It wasn't his fault she no
longer loved him. Or was it? Was he to blame, if only partially? Maybe they both
had given up on their marriage. If the last few months had told her anything, it
was that her situation—because that was what her marriage felt like—was more
for show and convenience than anything else. But now that convenience, for
Tim at least, was coming to an end.

Bracing herself for the conversation to come, she cleared her throat, announcing her presence. Tim shifted around, looking over his shoulder as he
acknowledged her.

"Hey. Where have you been?" he asked, not really interested and already
turning back to focus on the television.

"Mum's." It wasn't a total lie, but she hoped it was enough to quell his
curiosity. It seemed to be, as he gave a grunt of acknowledgement. The sound
caused a wave of annoyance to rise in her chest.

"Tim…"

"Uh huh?" he muttered while still watching the screen.

Yeah, I can see where we went wrong.

"I think… We need to…" She took one final deep breath. "I'm leaving."

"Mmm."

Kate realised she wasn't even bothered by his lack of interest. Instead, she was more annoyed at the fact she was going to have to repeat herself as if she was talking to one of their children.

"Tim? Did you hear me? I said I'm leaving."

"Yeah, I heard. When are you going to be back?"

This was becoming more infuriating by the moment.

"I'm not. I mean, I'm leaving *you*."

"Yeah, I heard…wait." He shot around to face her. "What?"

"I'm leaving you, Tim." She was strangely calm as she said the words. She thought she would feel some sort of emotion, some sort of loss or mourning for her relationship, but it was as if something within her had finally come to terms with what she was doing. With what she really wanted.

"You're kidding?" He laughed, but the sound was hollow and unconvincing. His face hardened when she didn't react. "You *are* kidding, right?"

"No, Tim, I'm not." She swallowed, a little unnerved by the look which flashed over his face. "I think it's time that we admit our marriage is over."

"What are you talking about?"

"I'm not happy, Tim. This, us, hasn't been working for me for a while."

"Hasn't been working… What the fuck?" Tim was standing now, still on the opposite side of the sofa to Kate, but his body was intimidating in its posture, shoulders hunched and tensed. Kate steadied herself as she continued.

"Let's face it. We're not a couple anymore. We spend most of our time apart, we only spend time together when we go out—"

"Yeah, we both work busy jobs! And when we go out, it's our downtime. That's what couples do, Kate! They go out, they socialise!"

"But the difference is, couples do it because they want to be out together. We do it because it's expected, so we look like the perfect couple."

"*Look* like the perfect couple? I do it because you are my wife, and that's what we do!"

"Exactly! That's what we do, Tim! You should do it because you want to, not because I'm your wife, and it's expected! But for you, it works. You have me on your arm while you wine and dine your fancy clients. It looks good for you to have me as your wife—"

"That's not true!"

"Please, Tim, don't insult me. I've heard you say it. Heard how you use my firm's success to bolster your own ego. Claiming it was you who put up the starting capital and handed us clients when we first started?"

"That's not... It was just a little exaggeration to seal a contract." He shrugged, trying to downplay the accusation.

"A little? Tim, you put exactly nothing into the business. In fact, when I left my old firm to start up with Sarah, you told me I was making a mistake."

"I'm not sure I said it was a mistake," he muttered.

They were starting to veer off topic, and Kate really didn't want to spend all night discussing the finer details of what happened seven years ago when she decided to take the leap on her own. She absolutely still remembered Tim's mockery of her suggestion when she first said she was considering leaving the profitable law firm she had spent the best part of a decade at, to set up her own firm, which specialised in helping women with their legal issues.. Maybe she should have paid more attention to why he was being so dismissive, instead choosing to prove him wrong and throwing her all into making the business a success. Maybe that was when her relationship had really started to disintegrate.

"Tim." She sighed, pinching the bridge of her nose and bringing the conversation back around. "The point is, our relationship has been merely a front for a while now. A show because it's what we are used to, and it's easier to just carry on than rock the boat. But the past few months, it's just become too much..." *Because I fell in love with someone else.*

"Too much?" Tim stalked around the sofa, coming to a stop in front of her. "What's that meant to mean?"

"It means that this is becoming tiring. And I think it's time that we stop just coasting along and move on with our lives. I'm going to stay at Mum's tonight."

She turned, walking out of the den and towards the stairs in the hallway. She knew it was rude to walk away from Tim, but she wasn't sure what to say next; he looked dumbstruck, and she really didn't have the patience to stand there while he processed what she had said. She was exhausted, the past twenty-four hours being some of the most stressful and draining she had ever experienced.

She heard Tim scramble behind her, his bare feet thudding on the carpet. "Don't walk away from me, Kate!"

"I'm packing a few things, and then I'm going to Mum's. We can talk—"

"Like hell you are! Kate! Kate, come back here!" He lurched forward, grabbing her arm as she walked further away from him.

"Get off me, Tim!" she demanded through gritted teeth, trying hard not to lose her temper.

"Is there someone else? Who is he?" he spat, his grip tightening. She wasn't sure he even knew he was doing it, but it was starting to hurt, and she suspected it was going to bruise in the morning.

"There's not another man, Tim," Kate said honestly. She could tell him the truth, but she wasn't prepared to put Seph into the firing line. Especially since Tim hadn't loosened his grip, let alone let her go at all. "Let go of my arm, Tim."

There were a few moments when they faced off with each other, Kate staring down Tim, until he finally loosened his grip. Pulling her arm back out of his hand, she turned away from him and continued up the stairs.

"Are you seriously just walking out tonight? Twenty years and you're just going to your mother's?" he spat behind her.

Kate paused again, sighing at his persistence.

"Yes, Tim." She turned to face him, "I really thought that this wouldn't come as such a shock to you, but obviously, I was wrong. And in the meantime, until you're calmer and have had time to process things, I think it's best that I stay somewhere else."

She turned away from him again, finally reaching the top of the stairs before he spoke.

"The kids will hate you. They'll never understand. And you can think again if you think you're getting anything from this house or the business. I'll fucking ruin you if you walk out now!"

"I don't want anything from you."

If he was trying to guilt her or hurt her into staying, it wouldn't work. Because nothing could be more painful than the look on Seph's face when she left tonight. She was already ruined.

CHAPTER EIGHT

Kate found a quiet corner of the coffee shop and slid into the booth seat, satisfied about how much privacy she could have here. She was tired. She really hadn't slept at all last night, having spent most of the night relaying her visit to Seph's to her mother after turning up on her parent's doorstep with a suitcase. As she packed and left, Tim stayed in his den, the television turned up obnoxiously loud, no doubt finishing the bottle of whiskey he had started.

Once alone in her parents' spare room, she had lain in the dark staring at the ceiling, the image of a shaking and sobbing Seph laying on her knee ingrained into her mind. She longed to be able to reach out and take a hold of her pain, wrap her hands around it, physically remove it and run as far away from Seph with it as possible, throwing it into the ocean to wash away.

Kate let her eyes close, tired and raw with tears, her head dropping into her hands as she tried to process what Seph had revealed last night. Not only had she been dealing with Kate leaving, but then her father had died. Kate thought about her own father; she had only seen him this morning before she had left. She hadn't paid much attention, too preoccupied with her own issues, only vaguely aware of him moaning about something he had bought on a whim, being too complicated or not working like it should. What if that was the last time she saw her father? What if the final time she saw him, she didn't even pay him any attention? Fresh tears tracked down her cheeks at the thought.

"Hey. What's going on? Your message sounded urgent. Especially for this early on a Sunday." Kate looked up at the comforting voice of her best friend as she pulled out the chair opposite her, concern suddenly painting her features as she registered Kate's tears. "What's happened? Is it the kids?"

"No, the kids are fine," she replied, wiping her face with a napkin.

"Then what is it? You look like shit," Sarah said, ordering herself a drink from a passing waitress.

Sarah had been her best friend for nearly ten years. She was never one to mince her words, which worked well in the courtroom, but could often leave people thinking she was abrasive outside of it. Kate, however, knew her softer side. It helped that they had met with a mutual understanding of being golf widows; Tim and Sarah's ex-husband had both golfed at the same club before Sarah decided she had had enough of being under-appreciated and walked out. But before that, they had shared numerous bottles of wine at a golf club function, finding they had more than just husbands with a love of the green in common. Seven years ago, Sarah approached Kate with the business proposition that they should open a firm of their own, which specialised in representing women in legal matters. They quickly found their services were highly sought after, to the point that both were now considered experts in the field.

"Thanks." Kate huffed a laugh. "I didn't sleep much last night."

"So what's happened?" Sarah blew over the hot tea in her cup, sipping it gently to test its temperature. Just as she decided it was cool enough to drink, Kate spoke.

"I've left Tim."

Sarah choked as the tea shot down the back of her throat, drawing the attention of the few other customers who were also out early on a Sunday morning.

"What? When?"

"Last night." Kate sighed before taking another sip of her own double-shot coffee. She was really going to need the caffeine today.

"Shit. Are you okay?"

"Yeah, I'm fine. Tired. It was late when I spoke to him, and to be honest, we didn't talk a lot because I stayed at Mum's."

"What happened?"

Kate paused, then admitted, "I had an affair."

"Shit! With who?"

"You don't know her. Or I don't think you do. Maybe you do, I don't know. I thought I'd never see her again, but then after Friday night..." Kate drifted off, her head still a jumble of everything that had happened in the past forty-eight hours.

"You are literally making no sense right now. Hang on...her?"

"Sorry." Kate rubbed her hands up and down her face. "I'm so fucking confused."

"You're not the only one. Her? Really?"

"It's not the first time, you know. I know you only know me as being married to Tim, but I'm actually bisexual. Just no one bothers to ask once you're settled," Kate snapped, slightly incredulous that such a huge part of her adult life had been defined by her marriage to Tim. She had somehow lost herself along the way.

"Fair enough." Sarah shrugged. "Doesn't bother me, hun."

"Sorry. I'm just..." More guilt settled on top of what she was already feeling, this time at snapping at her friend who had only voiced a reaction to finding out something previously unknown about her.

"Hey, it's fine." Kate felt Sarah place a hand on her forearm and looked up. She felt the gentle, silent reassurance of the action. "How did Tim take it?"

"Not brilliantly. Apparently, he couldn't see anything wrong with our relationship."

Kate watched as Sarah sat back, lifting her cup to her mouth and taking a sip. She knew that look. She'd been in enough meetings and enough drink and dinner events to recognise Sarah's tell signs. And right now, she had something to say.

"What?"

"Hmm?" Sarah acted oblivious.

"Oh please, Sarah, I know that look. Say what it is you want to say. Don't worry about hurting my feelings. Trust me, they're already battered and bruised enough."

"Okay. Thank fuck you've left him, and he's a moron if he thinks there was nothing wrong. But really, I think he's just been hanging on because you give him credibility. If he's playing the wounded husband, it's only his ego that has been damaged."

"Wow." Kate sat wide-eyed. "That's what you think?"

"Yeah." Sarah shrugged like her big reveal was nothing big at all. "You did ask."

"I know, but...how long have you felt like this?"

"Years. He's been riding on your successes ever since we opened the firm. He barely does any work anymore from what I hear, more business lunches up at the golf club and looking cool around the younger associates than actual caseload." She leant forward, placing her hand over Kate's. "I'm sorry I didn't say anything sooner. I know we tell each other everything, but there's a line, and I honestly thought things were okay. However, if I'd known you were having an affair..."

"It's not exactly something I wanted to shout from the rooftops."

"No, I know. But..."

"You're pissed I didn't tell you?" Kate could feel the residual anger she had at Tim starting to flare up again, this time directed towards her best friend. What she needed right now was an ear to listen, not a judgement about the fact she kept something to herself. Sarah must have sensed her rising irritation.

"No, of course not. Not really. I just hate the fact you've been struggling on your own. That you felt you couldn't tell me."

"It wasn't like that, not really. I just got so swept away...my time with Seph was so precious and short. And every moment felt like we were in a bubble and no one could burst through. I guess I just wanted to keep it that way."

"How did Tim take the bit about this Seph being involved?" Sarah grimaced.

"I haven't told him about Seph. I just said that things weren't working out between us anymore." Sarah gave her a look, and Kate put her hands up in defence. "I know, but it's true. If things were good between us, then I'd never have even contemplated having an affair."

"Fair enough, but—"

"I'm not telling him. Not yet."

"But don't you think he should know? I mean, I'm not the bloke's biggest fan, but—"

"I think Seph doesn't need to be dragged into this right now!" Kate snapped before dragging her hand down her face, instantly regretting it.

Seph's well-being was undoubtedly the primary reason for not telling Tim everything last night. If Kate could shield her from any more pain or stress, then she would do whatever it took. She wasn't sure how much more Seph could take, how much more pressure she could be put under before she would snap. And Kate wasn't planning on letting anyone or anything conduct that experiment to find out.

She closed her eyes, the tears pricking behind her eyelids as an image of a broken Seph telling her to leave flashed into her mind.

"Kate? What's going on?" Kate looked up, her tears now making their way down her face. Sarah covered her hand with her own and gave it a comforting squeeze. "Hey, hey, it'll be okay. What is it?"

"I'm so scared, Sarah. The Seph I met... She had this understated, quiet presence to her. She was nervous about who she was and how she fitted in, but when you got her alone, God, she shone. But last night, she was just a shadow of that. Her eyes were so empty and dark. And that's partly because of me. What if I can't get her back, Sarah? What if I've broken her forever?"

"Hey, come on." Sarah pulled her chair closer and wrapped an arm around Kate's shoulder. "I'm sure everything will work out. How did you leave things with her?"

"She told me I had to leave while I sorted things out. That if I was serious, I needed to show it and make a choice."

"And you chose her?"

"I can't imagine the next ten years with Tim. But I can with her."

"Then you've made the biggest step. Jumping into the unknown is scary, but it's a million times more courageous than settling for second best because it's easy and safe." Sarah gave her a reassuring smile. "What can I do to help? What do you need?"

"I need somewhere to stay. I can't be at the house. I stayed at Mum's last night when I finally left, but I can't be there all the time."

"Done. Move in with me."

Kate relaxed. She knew Sarah would offer, but actually hearing those words lifted one of the many weights which were hanging around her neck at the moment.

"It'll only be until I find somewhere else."

"Doesn't matter. Stay as long as you need. What else?"

"I need to get my stuff. And a lawyer." She huffed a teary laugh at the irony before deflating again. "And I need to speak to the kids."

"Okay. So ring the kids and get them to meet you at your parents' house this afternoon. Then afterwards, we'll go to the house and pick up whatever you need for the next few days. I can come with you in case Tim is there and causes trouble. And I've got a friend who's an excellent divorce lawyer. I'll give her a ring."

"Thank you. I honestly don't know what I'd do without you."

"It's what best friends are for, right? Besides, if Seph is having a rough time, she needs your undivided attention. So let's get you sorted as much as we can before you see her again."

"Thanks for coming. I know you're both busy, but I needed to see you together." It sounded so formal, but Kate honestly didn't know how to start this conversation.

She'd texted both Cam and Meg while still with Sarah earlier, asking them to come round to her parents' house because she needed to speak to them. She hoped and assumed, judging by the lack of questioning messages she hadn't received, that Tim hadn't said anything to either of them. Kate, on the other hand, had been on the receiving end of Tim's messages and phone calls since she left the house last night, each one becoming progressively angrier and demanding as he undoubtedly worked his way through another bottle of whiskey.

She knew she deserved a lot of it; she had tipped his world upside down, despite her belief that their marriage was all for show. Maybe he was hoping Kate would come to her senses, change her mind and come back home, say it was all a mistake. Or maybe he was just sleeping off the hangover he would no doubt have. Whatever the reason Tim hadn't contacted the kids, Kate was relieved that telling her children was left to her. She wanted the opportunity to try and talk to them both rationally before Tim and his rage started to bleed through and taint everything.

"Mum?" Cam's voice brought her out of her thoughts, and she looked up at him, his face a picture of concern.

"Hmm?"

"I said is everything okay? Are Grandma and Grandad okay?"

Oh. She'd not thought about the fact she had asked them to come to her parents' house instead of the home she shared with Tim would ignite this direction of concern. "Yes, yes they're fine," she quickly replied, trying to extinguish any worry they might have about their grandparents before it spiralled further.

"Then what's wrong?"

Kate looked into Cam's eyes. Deep green orbs stared back at her, full of quiet concern and love. Cam shared her eyes and her heart, her compassionate nature and love for others. His chiselled features and mousy brown hair were inherited from Tim. She looked at Meg, a perfect mix of Kate's blonde hair and Tim's brown eyes. Her stare had always been a little harder, her emotions more carefully guarded, her nature a little more brusque and stand-offish than Cam's, a fiery temper and passion always just simmering below the surface. But even now, they were tinged with something which softened her, and Kate was suddenly reminded of the little girl who hardly ever cried, always trying to suck up her weaknesses even as a small child.

Her heart cracked a little at the fact she was about to change everything for them. Even though they were adults with their own lives now, she was about to irrevocably alter the one constant that remained throughout everything in their lives up until this point.

"I..." She choked back a lump of emotion which threatened to engulf her and drown out her words. "I'm leaving your dad."

There. She had said it. Four simple words which had the power to change everything for so many people. She closed her eyes, waiting for the storm to hit, but was only met with a stony silence. Long seconds passed before anyone said anything.

"You're what?"

It was Meg who broke the silence. Because who else could it be. Meg, with her fire and passion and slightly näive outlook on the world.

"I'm—"

"Yes. I heard you. What the fuck?" There it was. The anger she had anticipated rose within her daughter, spilling out. "What do you mean you're leaving Dad? Are you fucking crazy?"

"Meg, if you'd let me explain..." Kate sighed sitting down on the stool by the kitchen island. "I know it's a shock. But there's no other way to say it. Things haven't been right between me and your dad for a while, and I can't carry on anymore. Something needs to change."

"Then change something! Don't just give up on your marriage!"

"This is what needs to change. There's no amount of rekindling our relationship or re-discovering our love for each other that will change that."

"Who says? You? I mean, have you even given Dad a chance to do anything?"

"It's not about giving your dad a chance. This is something within me, and nothing he or anyone else can do is going to change that."

"So you just decided, and he doesn't even get an opportunity to make things better?"

"Yes! As harsh as it sounds, yes, I have! Because I know that nothing he does is going to make a difference!"

"Because you don't love him anymore?" Cam's softer voice broke through the tension, and Kate turned to look at her son. His eyes were filled with unshed tears, but while Meg was radiating anger, he had a look of quiet contemplation on his face. She could sense the upset and hurt in his face, but he had clearly been thinking about what Kate had said rather than steamrolling in like Meg.

"Honey." Kate leant over, resting her hands over his where they lay on the counter. She studied them for a moment, no longer the tiny little hands she had held so tightly when he was an upset little boy. Her and Cam had always been closer. His nature had always been gentler than Meg's, his emotions so much more freely expressed. She had always been worried that wearing his heart so openly on his sleeve would leave him vulnerable, but she never anticipated the pain would come from her actions. "I know this is...huge for both of you. Me and your dad have been together for so long; we've always been there in every part of your life, together, but things haven't been good for a while. We've—I've—been carrying on ignoring the signs for so long." *Until Seph came along*, she thought to herself, but that wasn't a necessary piece of this conversation. "But people change. Feelings change."

"And yours have?"

Kate took a breath. "Yes. They have."

Kate heard Meg scoff from where she had taken to pacing across the room. "Does Dad know?"

"Yes. I told him last night, then I came and stayed here."

"So you essentially just walked out on him? After dropping this bomb?" Meg practically screeched from across the room.

"I left because nothing was going to happen last night. Your dad was angry, rightfully so, but we needed space to process what was happening before we could talk again."

"Says who? You again, no doubt."

"Yes, me Meg. You seem to forget that your short temper comes from your father. Just like we can't talk rationally when you're upset, neither can me and your father. Trust me, I've dealt with him for long enough to know that it was the right thing to do at the time."

"Bullshit. I'm not listening to any more of this." Meg snatched her handbag from where she had left it when she arrived.

"Where are you going?" Kate asked, not that she really needed to.

"Going to see Dad. Since he's the one who's had his heart ripped out and no-one is there with him." And with that, Meg's heels clicked furiously across the wooden floor, followed by a deafening slam of the front door.

Kate pulled her hands back from where they still cradled Cam's, instead letting her head drop into them. Her headache was only getting worse, ever-present since last night when she finally managed to lay down in bed in her parents' spare room and start to process everything going on.

"She'll calm down Mum."

Kate let out a half-hearted laugh. "I appreciate what you're trying to do Cam, but you and I both know she won't. Not anytime soon." She looked up at Cam. "I'm sorry, sweetheart. I never wanted to hurt you or your sister."

"I—"

"Don't say it doesn't hurt. I know you, Cameron Bailey. You'll always deny your own pain for the benefit of others. But not this time."

Cam moved around the kitchen island, taking a seat next to Kate. "Yeah, it hurts, Mum. And it's going to take a while to get used to. Have...have things really been that bad? Have you really been that unhappy?"

Oh, if only you knew, Kate thought to herself.

"Yes. I mean, don't get me wrong. There was nothing wrong between me and your dad. Not really. There were no arguments; it's not like we were fighting. But we just drifted apart. And if Meg was to hear that, I know she'd just argue that's not an excuse to end things. That it just means we should try harder. But I think we want different things in life now. And this isn't a decision I've taken lightly, Cam. I didn't just wake up yesterday and decide to leave your dad."

No, you woke up sick with worry about Seph.

"I know you wouldn't, Mum."

"I was just so unhappy, Cam. And it hurts so much to know that I've hurt you and Meg. But I had to do this Cam. I had to walk away."

Cam nodded, clearly contemplating Kate's words. And then she felt the warm comforting arm slide around her shoulders and pull her close. The touch was all it took to give Kate the permission she needed to crumble.

Burying her face into her son's shoulders, she shook with sobs overtaking her body, taking the comfort he so readily offered. Trust Cam to be the one who saw her, saw what she needed in this moment. Meg would rarely see Kate like this, rarely give her a chance to show her vulnerability. It wasn't that she tried to hide it around the children; she'd always tried to raise them to be open with their emotions and that meant being open with her own. But while Meg usually reacted as she had done today, storming out before she could even show her cracks, Cam was the one who she could seek mutual comfort in. But usually never to this extent. Never so openly had she cried into her son's shoulder, let her emotions so freely take control of her. But today, right now, as she focussed on the feel of Cam's warm arms wrapped around her and the steady thrumming of his heart, she afforded herself this luxury. Because if Cam could still offer her this love, then maybe there was hope after all.

CHAPTER NINE

I t had been three days since she sent Kate away. Three days and she'd not heard a thing. It's not like she had expected to wake up on Monday morning and find Kate standing on her doorstep, but she had thought she might have heard something by now. Especially considering what they had said to each other—what Kate had said to her—on Saturday. Maybe she was even more cowardly than she was the first time. Maybe she had thought things over again, seen the mess Seph was, and reconsidered. But then she thought of her parting words, the longing in her voice, the kindness she had shown her from the second she had seen her. Something within her couldn't help but think those weren't the words and actions of someone who was going to walk away and leave.

The toaster popping jolted her out of her spiralling thought pattern for a moment, and she grabbed the hot bread, dropping it when it stung her fingertips. She'd look like a slice of toast soon, she thought to herself, as it was the only food she had been able to stomach over the past few days. Her rational brain was telling her that she needed to eat something more nutritious; fruit or vegetables wouldn't be a bad thing, but she couldn't bring herself to do it. Even though picking up an apple was technically less labour-intensive than buttering bread, it just wasn't a viable option to her brain at this moment in time.

She dropped down onto the sofa, curling her feet underneath her and pulling a blanket over her. The television was playing something inane she'd found on Netflix, but she wasn't concentrating on it. She hadn't concentrated on anything the past three days apart from her encounter with Kate; everything she had said and done playing on repeat in her head.

Monday morning, she had attempted to get up and go to work, but the thought of walking into the office and seeing Tim made her feel sick, and she spent twenty minutes on the bathroom floor, talking herself through avoiding an anxiety attack. It was enough, along with everything else life had thrown at her the past five months, to finally give in and call in sick. Although even then, she mentally chastised herself for being a coward. This was a mess she could only blame herself for; why should she hide and avoid the consequences of her actions?

She closed her eyes and felt the blood pulse through her eyelids, letting the rhythm ground her. This was more than just Kate. This was the fact that she had been struggling for months. And whatever the reason, she needed, she deserved, to take the time to recover.

The sound of her phone vibrating across the coffee table startled her. The sensation was far too intrusive for her delicate head, and she flinched. It would either be Fiona or her sister. Neither of which was entirely welcome right now. She still wasn't ready to explain everything which had been going on, if only because she didn't have the energy reserves to deal with such an intense conversation right now. Her brow creased as she took in the name on the screen, not believing what she was seeing.

Kate: Hey...sorry I've been quiet. Can I come over now? I need to see you xx

Kate: I've missed you xx

Her hands shook as she slowly tapped out a reply, deleting and rewriting as her clumsy thumbs mis-spelt the words, even though the message was short.

Seph: Yes, come over whenever.

Kate: Be there in 30 min sweetheart xx

Thirty minutes simultaneously flew by and dragged, and when there was finally a knock at the door, Seph's head snapped round. There was a part of her that had thought she had imagined the message, even though she had read it more than once to make sure she wasn't being fooled. But as she opened the door, Kate was standing there, under the soft glow of the porch light, proving to her that it wasn't all in her head.

"C-come in," she stuttered, noticing how Kate stood hunched over, shielding herself from the cold.

She watched as Kate was again in her house, unfurling the layers of scarves and coats until she could see her face clearly. She ran her fingers through her hair, shaking out the droplets of rain, pausing when she lifted her head up and saw Seph. Kate reached out and brushed her fingers down her cheek, the touch timid, almost transient. Seph held her breath, probably not the wisest thing since she was already breathing quicker than she should, as Kate leant in. Kate paused, hovering millimetres from her lips, before she seemingly changed her mind, ducked her head to one side and placed a whisper-soft kiss on her cheek.

"Hey," Kate said as she pulled back.

"H-hi." The stammer in her voice made her sound nervous at Kate's presence, but the fact she was here alone was enough to knock her off guard.

"It's *so* good to see you," Kate said, with a level of sincerity and honesty that touched every part of her heart. She grasped her chin gently in between her fingers and angled Seph's face up towards her to look into her eyes. "How are you feeling?"

Seph thought the answer must be pretty obvious. Kate's own face was full of sympathy and concern, frowning as she tracked her gaze across her features. Seph felt the pressure of her scrutiny, but then Kate's expression softened as she sighed, her hand drifting around to cup her cheek. Seph curled into the touch, her body relaxing at the gentle feel of Kate's fingertips tracing her skin, her eyes fluttering shut. Kate's touch had always soothed her and now was no different.

"I'm okay," she mumbled, her tone giving away her true level of exhaustion.

The reprieve from her dread was short-lived, however, when she opened her eyes and realised she was still standing in the hallway with the woman who she had given an ultimatum and sent away three days ago. Kate's gaze suddenly became overwhelming. Turning and pulling out of the stare and the hold, Seph shuffled back into her house and out of Kate's space, distancing herself from the woman who was once her sanctuary.

Kate could see Seph's anxiety flooding through as she walked away from her. Her shoulders were stooped, her complexion pale and drawn, and when she looked into her eyes, she could see the deepest, blackest despair swim within them. She had to summon every last ounce of energy just to drag her body across the kitchen, her fingers pulling at her jumper sleeves, and there was a small but noticeable shake as Kate watched her try to spoon coffee into a mug. It was like there was a spark of light missing from behind her eyes. She longed for it to be temporary, longed to be able to restore it. She stepped closer, placing her hand over Seph's to still it.

"Stop," she said softly, waiting until Seph dropped the spoon before she curled her fingers around her hand and brought it up to her chest. She held it tight, resting it against her breastbone, as she studied Seph some more. She was close enough that she could see Seph's breathing was rapid and shallow, clearly still fighting against her body's reflexes. "Follow my breathing."

Kate waited until she could see Seph try and follow her instructions, deliberately slowing her breathing to the rhythm of her own. But she still hadn't looked up, eyes focussing on the counter below her. She knew what she was waiting to hear. "I've done it. I've left Tim."

"Y-you..." Seph stuttered as her eyes shot up to look at her.

Kate saw the moment when it happened; Seph's eyes glazed, and her chest constricted as she silently choked on the air around her. She stumbled, trying and failing to brace herself on the counter, knocking over one of the mugs. Kate quickly let go of her hand, instead wrapping an arm around her shoulders and pulling her into her body to take her weight.

"Okay, okay, sweetheart. I've got you. Let's go sit down, yeah."

Any remaining colour in Seph's face had drained, which was an achievement in itself considering the grey pallor she already displayed. Guiding her slowly back through into the living room, Kate managed to make it to the sofa, trying and failing to gently sit Seph down. Instead, she slanted with an ungraceful bump, but at least she'd made it to a seat and not collapsed on the floor.

"Seph, look at me." She hooked her finger under her chin and lifted her head up. "I need you to breathe with me, okay? One, two, three, four..."

Seph choked again, panic shadowing her face as she struggled to get enough oxygen in her lungs. Once, when they were talking about Seph's previous struggles with her anxiety, Seph had described what an attack felt like to her. It was clinical and second-hand, but Kate could only imagine the fear she must be feeling right now as her vision started to swim, the heat crept up her neck, and a suffocating feeling like someone was gripping her windpipe overwhelmed her. Pushing the images from her mind, Kate also focussed on counting in a slow, rhythmic manner, knowing it was the only thing Seph had to cling onto.

Long minutes passed as Kate counted out loud, Seph following the pattern. Every time she stuttered, Kate would reassure her, start again. Choke, sob, count. Choke, sob, count, until eventually, the choke became less frequent, and the count became longer. After a while, Kate eased on repeating herself, confident that Seph was now settling and able to regulate her own breathing pattern, although ready on standby to start again if necessary.

Kate watched as the come-down started, Seph's head hanging heavy on her shoulders, her eyes falling shut with long, heavy blinks. Seph shivered against where Kate was sitting beside her, and she felt her fall into her a little as if trying to share her body heat. Kate could feel how cold she was against her, but she wasn't surprised. All her warmth had drained as her energy was sapped by the effort to just carry on functioning.

"You're exhausted. When was the last time you got a good night's sleep?" Kate asked as she pulled the blanket from behind them and wrapped it around Seph's shoulders, tucking it over her legs.

"D-don't know," Seph stammered through her haze.

Kate had seen the effects of Seph's insomnia when they were together before. She always wondered how she managed to function on so little rest when it reared its head. She remembered seeing her near exhaustion once, shocked when Seph admitted she'd not slept for nearly a week. Kate had never seen her this tired, though, and the fact she could sense a subtle slurring to her words worried her even further.

"Have you slept since I saw you on Saturday?"

"Not really. Been trying, but my stupid brain wouldn't stop."

Kate let her hand rub up and down Seph's back, hopefully soothing her further, while the fingers which were resting on her knee were still tapping out her breathing rhythm, keeping her grounded.

"You're not stupid, baby. Just keep concentrating on your breathing for me."

After a few more minutes, Seph forced her eyes open, her eyelids heavy with that elusive sleep. She turned to Kate, and Kate had to hold down the sob which she could feel struggling to get out at the sight.

"I'm sorry," Seph slurred.

"What are you apologising for?" Kate asked, confused.

"This. I'm such a mess."

"You never have to apologise for this. This is not your fault. If anyone should be apologising it's me—"

"You didn't do this—"

"Yes, I did. Or at least, I was partly responsible. Not only wasn't I there when you needed me, but I had already put you in a terrible place when..." Kate's voice drifted off. She'd spent hours and hours thinking about Seph, about the overwhelming grief she must have felt, the loneliness and isolation she must have suffered when trying so desperately to hold it all together for her family. Her heart broke at the shell of a woman in front of her. She wasn't sure how she could ever make up for the months of hurt Seph had been going through. All she could do was try and take care of her now and hope that soothed some of the pain.

"You were telling me about Tim." Seph's words snapped her out of her self-pitying musings, and she mentally did a double take as she realised what Seph was talking about.

"We can talk about it later," she dismissed, not wanting Seph to worry herself with anything more tonight.

"Has he been trying to convince you to stay?" Seph continued to push.

"No, not really." Kate sighed. She really wanted Seph to rest, not talk, but she could see she needed to know what happened. "Or at least, not for the right reasons."

"What do you mean?"

"I don't know whether he genuinely thinks things within our marriage were okay, but the truth is, we've been living a marriage of convenience for years now. It works for him, even if he doesn't want to admit it." She clocked Seph's confused look. "When I set up Earnshaw and Harper with Sarah, he wasn't particularly supportive. He thought I was taking an unnecessary risk. But then we became more successful than any of us anticipated. Even though we are a smaller firm, and deal with more domestic matters than his firm, I quickly started earning more than him. And that was when his opinion changed. Suddenly it became beneficial to him to have me beside him at social events. He thrives on the idea of being a power couple."

"I had no idea, Kate."

"I know. And I think I kept quiet about it for a reason. My parents aren't Tim's biggest fans, and even though apparently everyone else could see it around me, I just didn't want to admit it to myself." Kate took a moment, the gravity of the past three days and the realisation of just how much of a sham her marriage really was taking their toll. "I'm not proud that I've hurt him, Seph, but the fact is I don't love him anymore, and I haven't for years. That wouldn't change even if you weren't in the equation. I'd have just stayed unhappy in my marriage even longer."

Kate clasped her hand over Seph's, rubbing her thumb over her knuckles in a comforting repetition, her other hand coming to tuck her hair behind her ear. She smiled softly as Seph allowed herself to curl into the touch.

"You've really left him?"

Kate nodded, her thumb stroking across Seph's cheek.

"I'm sorry I've been away so long. I spoke to Tim on Saturday straight after I left here, but it was a long night. And I had to talk to the kids, tell them what's happening. I didn't want you panicking, but I also wanted to try and sort some stuff out so I could come back and give you my full attention."

Kate smiled and watched Seph do the same. It was tired and small, but it warmed Kate's heart to see it. The fingers she had resting next to her ear gently stroked against her cheek again, and Seph's eyes fluttered closed, heavy with exhaustion. Kate leant forward, resting her lips against her forehead.

"I'm sorry I haven't been there when you needed me. But I'm here now, and I'm not going anywhere, I promise," she whispered against her skin.

Minutes passed, and they stayed like that, Kate leaning against Seph, not putting any weight on her, but taking in the sensation of just being next to her, with her, touching her. She let herself bathe in all that Seph was right now, her scent, her warmth, her breathing. She closed her eyes as she just savoured the sheer honour of being allowed in Seph's aura at this moment. The silence between them was broken when suddenly Seph winced, her forehead screwing up in pain and a quiet but audible groan escaping from her lips.

"Seph?" Kate pulled back, holding her face in her hands as she tilted it to see it clearly.

"It's nothing. Just a headache." Seph tried to dismiss.

"I'll get you some painkillers." Kate dropped her hands and went to stand, halting as she felt Seph's cold grip around her wrist. Her hold was weak, but it was enough to get Kate's attention.

"No, it's fine." She winced again. "I took some a couple of hours ago. I can't have any more for a while."

"O-kay." Kate thought quickly for anything else she could provide which may offer some form of relief. "Then let me make you something to eat. Have you eaten anything today?" She went to stand again.

"Please, Kate." Seph caught the end of her fingertips and rubbed her thumb across them lazily. "Please, just sit down. You don't need to fuss."

"I just want to make sure you're alright," Kate admitted as she made herself comfortable next to Seph again.

"I know. And I appreciate it, but can we just sit for a bit longer?"

"How long ago did you make that toast?" Kate gestured to the plate on the coffee table.

"Not long before you messaged. Maybe an hour or so." Seph shrugged.

"And before that? When did you eat something?" Seph went to answer before Kate cut her off with a raised finger. "And I mean something other than toast."

"I don't know," Seph answered, and Kate could tell she was being honest from the way she slumped as she answered.

"Okay." Kate thought for a moment. She wanted to make sure that Seph had eaten well, and she suspected she hadn't showered today, maybe even longer. If she could just get her to do one act of self-care, then she would count today as a win. "How about we get you in the bath? It'll warm you up, make you feel a little more human at least. And there's no effort required. I'll go run it. All you have to do is sit and soak."

Seph nodded her agreement, and Kate got to her feet. She knew a bath wasn't going to solve everything, but Seph was cold to the touch, shivering slightly, and weary on her feet. The perfect thing to do right now was to sink into a steaming hot bath to help wash away some of that tension.

"You want to come up with me now, or want me to come get you when it's ready?"

"I'll come now," Seph said, standing up. She swayed and stumbled slightly as she did so, but Kate was quick to steady her with a hand to her arm.

"Take it slowly. There's no rush."

Slowly is exactly how they took it, Kate letting Seph set the pace, grateful that she seemed to have dropped the facade of being okay, and instead showing just how exhausted she really was. Once they'd got to the top of the stairs, Kate led Seph through to her bedroom, guiding her to sit down on the bed. A sudden wave of emotion hit her, remembering the last time she was here.

CHAPTER TEN

September, the previous year

Kate watched Seph sleep, her chest gently rising and falling with each breath, cheeks still a little flushed from their recent activity. Right now, she looked so calm and peaceful. So happy. But she knew that within an hour, her body would slump slightly, her eyes would glisten over, and she would swallow back the tears as she put on a brave face when Kate kissed her goodbye and left. Again.

Seph started to stir, shifting under the covers and rolling over towards the warmth of Kate next to her. Kate rolled onto her back, allowing the slumbering body to snuggle further into her side. She tore her eyes away, unable to look at Seph without the threat of crying, instead staring up at the ceiling.

Why the hell could she just not make the leap? She knew where she was happiest. Even in these fleeting stolen moments with Seph, she was happier than she could ever remember with Tim. So why couldn't she just follow her heart? She held back the tears she could feel coming despite her best attempts to repress them, hoping that the tell-tale tremble didn't give her away to Seph.

"I can hear you thinking from here," Seph mumbled after another minute or so of silence, panicking Kate into thinking she had been caught.

"I thought you were asleep." Kate still didn't turn to look at her, her voice barely a whisper.

"I couldn't over the sound of your cogs turning. What's wrong?"

"Nothing." The shake in her voice was becoming more noticeable, and she knew that her protestations weren't going to wash with Seph.

"You're a terrible liar."

"Can't be that terrible. I'm lying all the time these days."

Kate felt Seph moving, still not bringing herself to look at her, only sensing the way she was propped up on her elbow beside her.

"Kate?" Kate still didn't say anything, just continued to stare upwards. "Kate?" Seph repeated, this time placing her hand on the bare skin of Kate's breastbone. The warmth of her body felt too much, almost as if it scalded where her palm was laid. She inhaled a shaky breath, knowing that suppressing her emotions anymore was futile.

"I don't know how much longer I can keep doing this," she breathed into the silence of the room.

"W-what do you mean?" Seph asked as she sat up, but it was clear that she knew what Kate was talking about from the look of agonising realisation on her face when Kate finally looked at her.

Kate shifted up the bed to sit next to Seph, bringing the duvet with her to cover them both.

"I mean, this is killing me. I love you so much, and I can't keep seeing you hurting like this."

"I'm fine." The argument was feeble, and Kate knew it was only spoken out of habit rather than an actual belief she was fine.

"You're not. You know it, and I know it, and it gets worse every time I leave." Seph shook her head, her eyes filling with tears. Kate leant forward, cupping her cheek in her hand and brushing her thumb gently across her skin, catching the first one as it traitorously slid down her cheek. "You wear your heart on your sleeve. You've got so much love to give, and you're so open to giving it. It's one of the things I love most about you. But it also means you're so much more vulnerable to hurt. I can see it breaking you. And I can't do that to you."

"Kate..."

"No, I can't be the reason you close yourself off to the world. I won't let that happen."

"S-so, what are you saying?"

"I-I think I need to..." Kate couldn't even bring herself to finish her sentence. Tears started to roll down her face at the thought of being without Seph.

"No. Don't do this." Seph pleaded, clearly knowing exactly where Kate was heading.

"I don't want to—"

"Then don't!" Seph exclaimed, cutting her off.

"But it's destroying you. It's destroying me! Every time I walk out of here and leave you—"

"Then stop leaving me." Seph's solution hung in the air between them. They'd never seriously broached this topic before, the unavoidable truth of what was going to happen someday. There were only two options, and neither seemed an easier choice to Kate. On one hand, she had to hurt Seph, the woman she had undeniably, irrevocably fallen in love with. On the other, she had to destroy the family she had spent twenty years building and protecting. "If walking out that door hurts so much, then stop doing it. Be with me."

"Seph, it's not that easy," Kate said, her voice softening with the weariness which had just hit her. She pulled her knees up to her chest, resting her elbows on them and running her hands down her face.

"Why not?" Seph asked. That was the one question she knew Seph was going to ask. And the one she knew she didn't have an answer for. "Kate? Why isn't it that easy?"

"Because..."

"Because what? I thought you loved me. You say you love me. And that you want to be here, with me. But then you leave. You walk out that door, out of my house, and for days all I get are messages telling me how much you can't wait to see me and that you miss me. Is all of that a lie?"

"No, of course not. I do love you. I hate leaving you; every moment I'm away from you, I'm thinking about the next time I can see you." She grasped Seph's face in a desperate attempt to convey just how much she meant what she was saying. "God, I've never felt like this about anyone. But I have a family to think of. The kids..."

"Oh, for fuck's sake..." Seph pulled herself out of Kate's grip, sliding out from under the duvet. Kate watched as she searched for her clothes, pulling them on angrily. "The kids are adults."

"They're still my children," Kate protested, although she knew what Seph meant. She wasn't trying to be heartless, but when both children had already moved out of the family home and started their own lives, the separation of the parents seemed a little less damaging than if they were young children, without the added complications of custody and splitting homes. Cam would be the more level-headed of the two, disappointed but definitely more willing to listen to reason. Meg, on the other hand, was a daddy's girl. Always had been, always will be. It could be Tim who'd been cheating, and she would still take his side.

"And Tim's still your husband, but that doesn't stop you coming round here every other day and sleeping with me," Seph continued, breaking her out of her thoughts.

"Seph, please," Kate begged as she moved to the edge of the bed.

"Please, what? Please stop getting upset? Getting angry? I've just asked the woman I love to be with me. Properly, not sneaking around behind everyone's back. Because apparently she loves me so much, she can't bear to see me hurting. But instead of saying yes, she gives me some bullshit answer about her kids."

"Seph, it's just not that easy for me to leave my family—"

"But it's easy enough to leave me."

"Seph, you know it's not like that," Kate said, reaching out for her, only to be denied when Seph ignored her hand and continued to get dressed.

"Do I? Because right now, you're not giving me any reason to think otherwise." Kate had no response. She didn't know what to say as Seph stood there, expecting an answer that never came. She shook her head. "Jesus Christ, I was a fucking idiot. I mean, you're a straight, married mother. This has literally got mid-life crisis written all over it. And I fell for it! I fell for you," she spat, moving away to retrieve her hoodie from the chair in the corner of the room, pulling it roughly over her head.

"Seph, please..." Kate pleaded, tears now falling freely.

"Don't." Seph threw out her hand, keeping Kate at a distance. "Don't come anywhere near me. Here." She threw Kate her clothes before storming out of the bedroom.

Ten

Kate made her way downstairs and found Seph in the kitchen, her back to her and her head down, leaning against the counter. Her body was rigid with tension, and Kate hated being the reason for it. Wiping her face of more tears which had fallen while she got dressed, she tentatively walked up behind her and placed a hand on her back. Seph angrily shrugged it off. The action hurt more than Kate ever realised it could.

"Please, Seph, you have to understand. This isn't easy for me, but I can't keep doing this. You mean too much to me for me to keep putting you through this."

"If I meant that much to you, then you would want to be with me." Seph's voice was quiet and tinged with the unmistakable sound of her own tears.

"I do want to be with you." That much Kate knew. She knew it didn't look like it, she knew she wasn't proving herself to be true right now, but she did want to be with Seph. There were just so many other things to consider when reality came into play. Seph spun around to face Kate.

"But not enough to do it properly! Not enough to be with me outside these four walls!" Seph's tone had changed again to one of anger, and Kate could sympathise. If she was hearing the same things back to her, wouldn't she think the same?

"I can't..."

Seph gave a sad smile at Kate's response, slumping against the counter.

"You can. You just won't. There's a difference. And it's got nothing to do with your children or your husband. But it has got everything to do with the fact that going back to being in an unhappy marriage with your husband is an easier option than being happy with me."

"Seph..."

"Just go, Kate. If you can't...if you can't make the commitment to me, then just go."

"Please, Seph. Not like this..."

Seph scoffed. "How did you think it was going to go? This is you." She pointed at Kate. "You wanted this."

"I didn't—"

"Just go, Kate. Unless you're going to tell me that you'll leave Tim, there's nothing else you've got to say that I want to hear."

Kate paused for a second, regarding the look on Seph's face. Her eyes were red, ready to cry again, her face pale, and she was slumped in silent resignation. Kate's stomach twisted with the knowledge that it was her who had caused Seph to be this way; her words and actions, which usually acted as such a soothing remedy, were now causing her indescribable pain. But she knew she couldn't give her the answers she wanted. Something was still holding her back. And for every moment she stood there, she was only torturing herself and Seph. After all, it was she who set this ball rolling.

Silently, she collected her things, shrugging her coat over her shoulders. When she turned around, those tears which previously sat in Seph's eyes were now rolling down her face, staining her cheeks. Something unexplainable took over, and she gravitated towards Seph, walking over and standing in her space. She brushed away a tear with the back of her fingers, tracing across her cheekbone before cupping her face in her palm. Leaning in, she kissed her, a desperate, messy kiss mixed with tears and pain, and she could feel Seph fist her hand into her shirt to hold her close. Pulling away, she kissed her again, a feather-light touch on her cheek, her lips next to her ear, holding her there, feeling her body shake with her sobbing.

"I love you," she whispered, before pulling away out of Seph's grasp and heading towards the door, her own tears falling uncontrollably.

CHAPTER ELEVEN

January, present year

Seph curled up against herself, pulling the blanket around her tighter. She closed her eyes; the thudding behind them was still there, just incessantly pounding away, not getting any better, but not getting any worse. She was taking that as a win. Despite the scratchy feeling behind her eyelids, she was still a distance from sleep, and she could tell it would be that way for a while. Her mind was busy, whirring away, processing, stumbling over the facts and thoughts that filled her head. Kate was here, in her house, for the second time in days, and this time apparently having left her husband. No, she must have imagined it. None of this could be real.

The sound of a plate being pulled out of a cupboard and placed on the counter brought Seph back into the space she was physically inhabiting, confirming her memories. If Kate was just a figment of her imagination, then she couldn't be in her kitchen making her something to eat. She couldn't have held her while she felt like she was drowning, talked her through her anxiety attack, ran her a bath, and set out clean clothes while she waited for her to finish. But she'd done all of these things, so the evidence pointed to her being real.

As if answering her doubts, Kate appeared from the kitchen, carrying a tray and placing it down on the coffee table.

"You don't have loads in, but I found you some soup, so this should hopefully warm you up a bit as well," she said as she lifted a steaming mug of tea off the tray and onto the table.

Seph sat up, smiling shyly, as Kate lowered the tray onto her lap, making sure it was steady before letting go.

"Thank you."

"No problem." Kate sat beside her. "I know your appetite's probably not great, but try and eat a little of it."

Silence descended over the room as Seph began to eat, lifting up the spoon with a slightly shaky hand and blowing on the soup to cool it. Seph sighed as the warmth slid down her throat, feeling the hot soup heat her from the inside out. She had to admit, it was doing its job and tasted good, even though she would never have made the effort to make it herself. She hummed after another mouthful, and Kate chuckled.

"Good?"

"Mmm, thank you. I think I needed this more than I realised."

"I'm just glad you're eating something, baby," Kate replied, tucking a loose strand of hair behind Seph's ear.

Seph stirred the soup around in the bowl with a chunk of bread, contemplating what she wanted to say. She still had so many questions, and she wasn't sure when, if at all, there was a right time to ask them. But there was an overwhelming sense of foreboding, an unresolved tension which Seph felt, and she also felt that the only way to answer it was to ask what she needed to know.

"Kate?" Seph asked, breaking her attention away from the television, which was on but playing quietly. Seph had a feeling Kate wasn't really paying attention anyway, more likely only having it on to avoid it being too quiet.

"Yes, baby?" Seph knew she had turned back to face her, but she still focused on the thick ripples where she was still stirring her now soggy piece of bread into her soup.

"Is...is it really over? Between you and Tim?" Seph asked timidly.

"Yes," Kate answered just as quietly.

"Why?" She had to ask. Because honestly, she was struggling to believe that it was because she was the preferred choice. Strong, reliable Tim, or anxious, sobbing, depressed Seph. She knew which was the better option.

"Because I love you. And I choose you. You were right the other night and all those months ago. I was a coward who stayed where I was because it was the easier option. I thought I was doing the right thing when in reality, I was hiding and lying to myself."

"And you really want this? To be here with me when I'm..."

"When you're what?" Kate asked, frowning.

"Like this. I'm not the same as I was. I'm not that person anymore. I lost her, and I don't know whether I'll ever find her again." Seph honestly thought she couldn't cry anymore, but her body seemed to disagree as she started sobbing at her biggest fear being revealed.

"Oh, baby." Kate swiftly moved the tray off Seph's lap, tucked her arm around her shoulders, and pulled her into her chest. "Come here."

Seph sobbed into Kate's chest. Long, wracking, heaving sobs which shook her whole body. For so long, she had tried to stay strong, ignoring all her own warning signs about the direction her mental health was heading. Sooner or later, that dam was going to break, and right here, right now, hearing someone had given up so much, hearing someone had dedicated so much to her, was that final crack in the foundations. Emotions she had hidden away for months, not told anyone about, not even Fiona, came cascading out in one huge torrent of tears.

"I don't care," she heard Kate say. "I don't care if you are struggling or a mess or however you see yourself right now. Because I see something different. I see a woman who has had the hardest time these past few months and coped on her own for far too long, and now, she's just showing the toll it has all taken on her. That's nothing to be ashamed of. Because all that pain and suffering, all that selflessness, comes from a place of love. It comes from that big heart you own, Seph. And it's that big heart and generous soul I fell in love with. And the fact that you are hurting so much still is a sign it is still there, hidden deep underneath all this. So you may not think you'll ever find that person again, but I know she's there. And I'll be here, holding your hand, being your friend, being whoever you need me to be as we search for her together."

Seph settled her breathing, taken aback by Kate's words. They didn't completely convince her that she was fixable, that she would return to how things were before, but she also knew that self-doubt was just a symptom of her illness.

She breathed deeply, inhaling Kate's perfume, letting it wash over her senses and ground her.

"I know," Kate continued after a minute, "That you have loads of questions, and you're worried still. And I get that—I do. And I'm not holding anything back from you. You can know it all; there's no secrets. But right now, I don't think you need to know all the tiny details. Right now, I think you need to rest. So please, can you do that for me? And then later, we'll talk."

"Yeah," Seph croaked. Kate was right. As much as she wanted to know more, she was struggling to comprehend the information she already had, let alone anything new.

At her answer, Kate leant back, pulling Seph gently with her, resting her head on her shoulder. Seph relaxed into the embrace, pulling herself even closer and revelling in the warmth of Kate's body pressed against her. She felt Kate run her fingers through her still-damp hair, scratching slightly at her scalp in the way she knew soothed her. A feather-light kiss was pressed against her forehead, and her eyes fluttered closed. They were both less tense than earlier in the evening, but still, there was so much left unsaid.

"Are you going to eat any more?" Kate asked after a while.

"No, I'm not hungry." Her appetite may have been fleeting, but it was probably still the most nutritious and fulfilling meal she'd had in days.

"You need to eat, baby. I don't like how thin you're looking."

"I'll try again later," Seph half-promised, although she wasn't sure if she'd have much more success then. She yawned, suddenly feeling like she could actually sleep if she stayed here like this. "Can you stay a while?" she asked sleepily.

"I can stay all night if you want."

Seph snapped her head up to look at Kate. The prospect of having Kate with her throughout the night was something she'd only been able to dream about before. Now the prospect of it being a reality was literally being dangled in front of her. Surely she couldn't be serious.

"You don't need to go home?" It seemed odd, and she hated saying it after everything she had previously said to Kate, but she wasn't näive enough to think that she could just leave her marriage and be with Seph wholly and completely.

"I've moved out, and I'm staying with a friend. So, would you like me to stay?"

Seph managed a tired smile before letting her eyes close again and laying her head back down. "Yeah, I'd like that."

"Then try and get some rest, baby. I'm not going anywhere."

Seph shuffled around, winding a hand around Kate's waist, finally accepting that maybe she was living in a world where this was a possibility. Where she could hold Kate without the constant threat and knowledge of her leaving hanging over them. She smiled as she felt Kate resume stroking her hair, closing her eyes and letting it soothe her into a tentative slumber. Maybe, just maybe, she could get through this and let herself be happy.

Chapter Twelve

The shrill sound of an alarm brought her around quicker and sharper than Seph was prepared for. Her hand flailed around aimlessly from under the duvet, trying to find the offending noise. She grunted as she struggled to find the source before it stopped as rudely as it started. A rustling movement from behind her caught her slowly-functioning attention; she felt an arm snake around her waist and tug her backwards, her back coming into contact with a warm body, bare legs tangling with her own, and a soft kiss pressed to the skin at the base of her neck. Her mouth quirked into a small involuntary smile as the memory of the night before came back, and she turned onto her back to confirm it was true through half-opened eyes.

"Morning," Kate whispered into the quiet, her eyes still closed but with a matching smile gracing her face.

"Morning." Seph's eyes slid closed again, the lids feeling too heavy to keep open any longer. "You're still here."

"Of course. Where else would I be?" Kate questioned as she shuffled closer, her front pushed into Seph's side with her arm draped across her stomach, a leg across her legs, effectively pinning her into place in a warm cocoon.

"Don't know. Didn't know if you'd have sneaked out early."

"It's six-thirty; I don't do much earlier. Besides, not going to pass up the chance to see this sleepy mess first thing." Seph pulled a face of mock outrage towards the ceiling, earning a soft chuckle from Kate. "Just when I thought you couldn't get any cuter." Kate rose up, pressing a soft kiss to Seph's lips.

Seph savoured the moment, still not believing that she was in this situation. The feeling of waking up beside Kate was something she had imagined many times, but she never let herself fully believe it could actually happen. To have her here was a little overwhelming, but she took a deep breath, trying not to let it drag her under. Kate must have sensed her thoughts turning heavy, and she was suddenly aware of a ticklish sensation as Kate started tracing nonsensical patterns across her arm.

"You okay?" Kate asked.

"Yeah. Just...processing. Trying to steady all the thoughts." Seph tried to wave her arm to signal what she meant, but it was still heavy, and she let it drop to the bed.

"Need to talk anything through?"

"No. I don't think so. Not at the minute." Seph turned to look at Kate, smiling gratefully. "Thank you, though."

"Any time," Kate whispered.

Seph yawned, stretching her body out, feeling the muscles and bones pulling taut and cracking.

"Did you sleep okay?" Kate asked when Seph coiled back inwards and into her embrace again.

"I think so. Feel like I slept better last night than I have in a while."

"Really?" Kate sounded surprised, and Seph looked up from where she had snuggled into her chest.

"Yeah. Why?"

"You just didn't seem very settled, that's all. You were tossing and turning a lot, and there were a couple of times when you were talking in your sleep..."

"Oh," Seph said sheepishly, pulling back slightly. "Sorry."

"No, no, it's fine," Kate reassured, pulling Seph back into her. "It's not a problem, I just..." Kate sighed. "I guess I just didn't realise how badly you were sleeping. If last night was a good night..."

"It was a good night because I actually slept. More often than not, I just lie awake," Seph admitted. She could see an emotion flick over Kate's face as she cast her eyes downwards.

"I'm sorry, baby. I had no idea how bad it was."

"I should have warned you. Maybe you should have gone home and got a proper night's sleep." Seph shrugged, assuming that Kate was regretting her offer to stay. She could only imagine how much of a disturbed night's sleep she had gotten if she was really as unsettled as Kate said she was.

"That's not…I'm not bothered about that." Kate pulled back and tried to catch Seph's gaze. "Right now, I couldn't care less about how much I did or didn't sleep. I'd have probably worried more *not* being here." Seph's eyes fluttered shut as Kate brushed her fingers over her face, tracing the contours of her cheekbones and around her mouth, down her jawline. Her mouth twitched as she stroked over a ticklish spot before her thumb dragged across her lips. "I hated being away from you for so long, knowing you were like this."

"I'm fine," Seph responded, almost robotically.

"Really? That's why you've been in a constant state of anxiety since I saw you on Friday night, is it?" Seph cringed at the painfully accurate description of her state over the past week, eyes darting down to the space between them. "Sorry, that was harsh," Kate added quickly, clearly mistaking Seph's embarrassment for hurt.

"No, it wasn't. You're right. I've been fighting against it for days. I've been hiding how bad things have been getting for even longer. It's just strange to see someone's noticed."

"Of course I noticed. When I came here on Saturday night…" Seph looked up as Kate's wavering voice drifted off, close to breaking, and she swallowed back the tears. "When I saw you, it hurt so much. I was so scared. I'd never seen you looking so ill."

Seph found the hand which rested on her hip, intertwining their fingers together and giving them a squeeze. While she knew she was struggling, she couldn't ignore how hard it must be for Kate to see her like this. She recognised how much she had changed, the difference from the person she first met, and if the roles were reversed, she would be crushed. But here, in her bed, laying in the arms of the woman she loved but never thought she would have, she felt for the first time in months like she could finally start to climb back out of the hole she had found herself in.

She looked up and placed a feather-light kiss on Kate's lips, and Kate responded with a sharp breath. It was the first time that Seph had initiated a kiss between them; Seph hadn't felt able before now to show any of that emotion.

Kate leant forward, resting her forehead on Seph's, keeping the two of them close but not pushing for anything further, an act which Seph appreciated greatly. It was a silent thank you; *thank you for taking the chance, for letting me be here, for letting me help you.*

Minutes passed as they lay there, not moving, not saying anything, just being in each other's presence, before Seph broke the silence.

"Don't you need to get up?"

"Don't want to," mumbled Kate, sounding like she wasn't far away from slumber again.

Seph huffed a laugh. "Well, your alarm went off for a reason. And I need coffee." Seph reluctantly pulled herself out of Kate's warm embrace, her body still aching with weariness.

"Fine," Kate relented, sounding remarkably like a stroppy teenager to Seph's amusement. It was small, barely present in fact, inconsequential to many, but for the first time in well over a week, she felt like smiling. A joyous, freeing feeling she couldn't contain. It had been so long that it felt foreign, but the respite from the darker thoughts which usually plagued her mind was welcome. Seph pushed up off the bed, swinging her sock-clad feet out of the covers and placing them down on the plush carpet. The moment she stood, though, her head swam before beginning to throb. She fell back down onto the bed with a grunt.

"Nope." She paused, exhaling deeply and screwing her eyes shut, waiting for the nauseating feeling to pass. A warm hand appeared on her back, rubbing gently.

"Baby?"

"I'm fine. Just a little dehydrated on top of everything after all the ugly crying yesterday. I'll be good in a minute."

"Please tell me you're not planning on trying to go into work like this?"

"Actually, I haven't been at work all week." Seph looked up sheepishly. She never mentioned anything last night; the sheer level of exhaustion and information which she had to process pushed that detail to the bottom of the list.

"You've taken some time off?"

"More like the doctor recommended it." Seph looked down at her feet, avoiding Kate's gaze. A familiar feeling of unwarranted shame started to grow inside her chest, and she steeled herself for a judgement that never came. Instead, she felt Kate shifting to sit beside her fully, wrapping a hand around the back of her neck and pulling her close.

"I'm so proud of you, baby. I know it's not easy for you to admit you're struggling, that you need time and help to recover, but this is the best thing you could do for yourself." She spoke low and directly into her ear, and the words flowed through her like a soothing comfort blanket wrapping around her shoulders.

"It doesn't feel like it. I feel like I'm just hiding." She'd never admit that to anyone else. But for some reason, and it had always been this way, talking to Kate was easy.

"No. No, baby, you're not. You needed this a long time ago."

"Part of me knows this. But it was seeing Tim and..." She stuttered over the words, unable to finish the sentence. "The thought of going into the office just... It made me..."

"Did you have an attack?" Kate asked, worry filling her words. "Seph?"

"A small one. It wasn't as bad as Friday's, but afterwards, I—"

"What do you mean it wasn't as bad as Fridays?" Seph kept quiet, closing her eyes. Suddenly, the small amount of energy she had recuperated dissipated, that familiar ache settling in her bones. It wasn't that she was angry with Kate for asking—she should have known the question was coming, really—and she knew that her questions were only coming out of a place of concern. It was more that she had lowered her guard enough to let the information slip and open her up to these questions. Kate must have misread her silence as discomfort, switching her tone to something altogether softer and empathetic. "I'm sorry, baby. I'm not angry or upset. It's just...I knew that something must have happened on Friday, but with how you were on Saturday, I was just so concerned with that moment. And the same last night. I should have asked sooner."

"It's okay," Seph offered, placing a hand on Kate's thigh and squeezing gently. It was all she could offer in reassurance right now. She knew Kate would beat herself up for this, but she didn't have the energy to talk about it in any great detail at this moment. "I guess there's loads we still have to talk about."

"Yeah, I know," Kate answered with a sigh, her annoyance at herself still evident in her tone, but Seph was grateful for her not pushing it any further. "When you're ready, we can talk about it all, but *only* when you feel up to it."

Seph gave Kate a small smile of thanks before Kate leant over and placed a gentle kiss on her cheek, then finally stood and stretched. Seph watched as she dragged her blonde hair up into a messy bun on the top of her head, exposing her long slender neck. She was wearing a pair of Seph's shorts and one of her oversized t-shirts and for the first time ever, a sense of possessiveness twisted in her gut.

Here was Kate, having stayed over in her bed and slept next to her all night, wearing her clothes in the morning. It was a life she could never have imagined when she first met this woman. Her wandering thoughts must have shown on her face because when Kate turned back to her, she gave her a curious smile.

"What are you grinning at?"

"Am I grinning?" responded Seph with surprise. It had been a long time since her mind had given her anything to grin at, and she hadn't realised she was doing it.

"Yeah, you look miles away, and you have this little smile on your face." Kate leant down, bracing her arms on the bed at either side of Seph, dropping a gentle kiss to her lips. "It's nice. I haven't seen it for so long."

"Me neither." Seph cleared her throat, not wanting to unpack anything she wasn't sure about just yet. She changed the subject to something she was sure was fairly neutral. "So, busy day?"

Kate pulled out of her space, flashing her another small smile as Seph shuffled back up the bed, leaning back against the headboard and watching Kate get dressed.

"A few clients, nothing too difficult today." She paused and Seph saw her shoulders rise up and down with a deep exhale. "Then I'm seeing the kids."

"Oh." Seph wasn't sure what more to say. She'd been so consumed with trying to figure out the situation she hadn't given anyone else much consideration. "H-how are they?" Seph cringed at her own question. It seemed foolish considering their lives had been turned upside down.

"They're...confused. Angry. Upset. I've basically torn apart everything they thought was a constant and they don't understand why."

"What do you mean?"

Kate turned, coming to sit on the bed beside Seph. "I haven't told Tim or the kids about you. And it's not because I don't want them to know about you. It's because if I can deal with all this separation stuff without having to get you involved, then I will."

"But—"

"No. This is my mess to deal with. You need to focus on getting better." Seph watched as Kate took a breath. "I know that everything is happening really fast. Trust me, I do. And the last thing I want is to put any more pressure on you. The divorce, everything to do with Tim and the kids—you don't have to be involved with any of that. But please don't think that it's because I don't want us to be open. I'd just rather try and protect you from anything that's going to come from the mess I've created at home. I don't expect it to be easy, and I don't want you stressing over it or being in the firing line. If I can try and get through this bit without having to put you through anything else, then I will."

There was a part of Seph that wanted to argue, to tell Kate that she wanted to be there and stand by her throughout it all. But there was a bigger part of her, a more selfish part that appreciated the respite from being involved in someone's issues, even if that person was Kate. "I appreciate what you're doing. But when the time comes, can we please talk about it? I don't want you to think that I don't care or that I'm not interested in what's going on because I am."

"I know you are. And I promise we'll talk it all through when you're feeling a bit stronger." Kate leant forward, kissing Seph on the forehead before shuffling off the bed. She continued to get dressed, buttoning up her shirt as she carried on speaking. "Besides, I'm fairly sure that most of today will be Meg yelling at me while Cam tries to calm her down again."

"She's pissed?"

Kate chuckled. "I think that's an understatement. She's always been Tim's daughter, and when she's angry, everyone knows about it. She can argue until she's blue in the face and is like a dog with a bone if she feels she's been wronged. I guess that's what happens when you have two lawyers for parents."

"Yeah, I guess." Seph closed her eyes. She wanted to ask more, but part of her knew Kate probably didn't have any more answers right now and the early morning conversation had tired her out enough that she actually felt like she could sleep again.

"Why don't you get some more sleep?" Seph felt the mattress dip as Kate sat back down before the gentle sensation of her fingertips brushing the hair off her face tickled her.

"Mmm, I might do when you've gone. I actually feel like I could sleep rather than just lay here."

"That's good. Do you want me to come by after work tonight? I can bring something for dinner."

"I..." Seph started before realising what day it was. "Shit, what day is it?"

"Wednesday. Why?"

"I said I'd go to dinner at Helena's. I try to go more since Dad..." Seph choked on her words as a lump crept up her throat.

"Hey, it's okay. Go see your sister. It's important that you keep doing that. Just let me know if you want me to pop round afterwards; it doesn't matter what time it is. But also, if you just need some time to yourself, that's okay as well, yeah? Whatever you need."

"Thank you," Seph muttered quietly, weary but grateful for Kate's consideration.

"Anytime," Kate answered with the softest of kisses to her cheek.

Chapter Thirteen

"What the fuck are you thinking?"

"Meg, just calm down."

"Oh fuck off Cam, stop trying to play the fucking peacemaker for once in your fucking life!"

"Well, yelling isn't getting us anywhere!"

Kate pinched the bridge of her nose, inhaling deeply before counting to ten and releasing it. It had been following the same pattern for the past forty minutes; Meg would yell, Cam could try and calm her down, Kate getting a chance to say something before Meg would once again take offence and start on another tirade. Kate's head had started pounding before she had even met with Cam and Meg, and the throb had only gotten more insistent. For the past ten minutes, Kate had even barely got a word in, instead the argument devolving to a shouting match between her two children.

"Can you two just stop!" Kate snapped, her patience finally giving out.

Meg turned, giving her an incredulous look which could wither a weaker person from across the room. "I don't think you have any room to speak. This is all your fault!"

"That..." Kate took a breath, trying to rein in her anger. Of course her children had every right to be angry, but she hated seeing it being directed at each other. If anyone should be the target of Meg's vitriol, it should be her, not Cam. "That's not what I'm implying. I absolutely take full responsibility for this situation, but it doesn't mean you can just yell at your brother. Not when all he is trying to do is diffuse the situation."

"I just don't get it Mum. You can't just wake up one day and decide you don't want to be married. Dad's devastated." Kate tried hard to suppress the eye roll she felt rising at that comment. "And you're just sitting here like nothing's happened."

Meg really was blinded by her love for her father if she thought that Tim was really so distraught, and if she really thought that Kate was unaffected by it all. But that was nothing new; when she was like this, Meg could be blinkered to everything by her indignation.

"Trust me, Meg, that's not what I'm feeling at all. I hate that I've hurt you, that you're angry with me, and I understand why. But until you calm down, I don't think you will ever understand what I'm trying to say."

Meg stared her down, clearly contemplating something before striding over to the chair opposite Kate and dropping down onto it. Leaning back, she crossed her arms on her chest. "Go on then."

Kate had to hold back the snicker of mirth she felt rising in her chest. There was no way that Meg was ready to listen, and her whole demeanor screamed that she was anything but. But taking the opportunity when it presented itself, Kate ignored the retort she wanted to scold her child with and instead took a deep breath.

"When I married your dad, we were only a little older as you and Cam are now. We've been through so much together, but also separately. We've never had the type of relationship where we were dependent on each other. We've always been independent even as a couple.

"But as you get older, your priorities change. The things you want change. When I was in my twenties, I wanted everything. I wanted a career and a family. And I was lucky enough to have both. It was hard, and I had to make a lot of sacrifices to have it. But not once did I regret the decisions I made. Even though my career was important, it was you two who made me happiest. I would give it all up if you two had asked me to. And I still would. I would do anything for either of you. But you're both older now, you have lives of your own. And while my love for you two will never diminish, I'm now in a place where I can be a little more selfish about what makes me happy."

An image of Seph, half asleep in bed before she left this morning flashed across her mind, but Kate suppressed the smile which tried to creep out at the memory. "I don't expect you to be happy about this. Be angry, be upset—they're all valid and fair ways to feel. But all I ask of you is to take the time to listen to me when I try to explain and believe me when I say that I never wanted to hurt you."

Kate noted that Meg's shoulders had sagged slightly, her posture minutely more relaxed than when she first sat down. Kate was surprised; she honestly hadn't expected to say so much without being interrupted, and she certainly hadn't expected her words to have so much of an impact that Meg might be opening up to her. It was barely there, but it was enough to allow a tiny glimmer of hope bloom in her chest that Meg might be willing to understand.

"Imagine being fifty and still wanting that dickhead you dated last year Meg," Cam piped up from behind her.

"Shut up, shitbird."

Kate couldn't help the bubble of laughter which burst from her at the sibling bickering which broke the atmosphere. As infuriating as it could be at times, she cherished these moments. It reminded her of when they were younger, constantly butting heads and winding each other up in a way that only a brother and sister could do.

Meg's eyes met hers and for the first time in two days, Kate saw a softening in her gaze. Her laughter died down and tears rose, threatening to break through and cascade down her face. She held them back, not quite ready to be so emotionally raw in front of her children again just yet.

"I'm still angry, Mum."

"I know. And you have every right to be. I'm not telling you that what you're feeling isn't valid, you need to process this in whatever way works for you. But I just wanted a chance to try and explain this as best as I could to you."

"There's really no chance—"

"No." Kate cut Meg off, knowing what she was asking. "I'm sorry sweetheart, but no. I don't care for your dad the way I used to. And he has every right to be angry as well."

And trust me he is, Kate thought. Her phone was still going off with angry text messages and voicemails, although they had become slightly less frequent over the past twenty-four hours.

"This isn't going to be easy for any of us, least of you two. We're all going to be feeling a lot of things over the upcoming months, and I'm not expecting you to just stop being upset at me. Tomorrow you might wake up and feel angry again, and that's okay. I just want you to know that no matter what, you two are the most important thing in my life and I will always love you."

Seph slid out of the back seat of the taxi, which Kate had insisted she book and insisted she let Kate pay for. She had to admit, it probably wasn't a great idea that she be driving, not with her lack of sleep, poor focus, and the headache which was still lingering after nearly five days. So when Kate argued that she would book her a lift, she hadn't resisted too much.

She trudged up the front path, lifting her shoulders up to keep the winter chill from nipping down the back of her scarf as she made the short journey to the front door. She'd spent all day trying to get warm; the last thing she wanted now was to catch a chill. She opened the door, grateful when she was hit with a wall of almost suffocating heat from inside. There would be no chance of being cold in this house, not considering Helena would have been in all day with Millie, her youngest niece, and then once the two older kids got home from school, would have had the oven on to cook dinner.

Despite having three children inhabiting it, the house was oddly quieter than she expected. The muted sounds of music drifted down the stairs, and since it was Ed Sheeran she could hear, she assumed it was coming from Cassie's room. She walked through until she found her sister in the kitchen, apron on, and busy preparing whatever they were having for dinner. Her arrival garnered a gargle and squeal of delight from Millie, who was sitting in her highchair, face smeared with what Seph assumed, and hoped, was yoghurt.

"Sep!" Millie exclaimed, overjoyed at seeing her aunt, instantly reaching up with sticky fingers. Her tiny, chubby face, with or without yoghurt, never failed to make Seph smile, and although recently, and especially today, it was forced, it didn't mean it hadn't had some sort of effect.

"Hey there, kiddo!" she grinned back, avoiding the grabby hands which lunged for her and instead placing a kiss on her head. She took a second to breathe in her scent, always amazed at how it calmed her. "How's my favourite niece?"

"You can't say that," Helena scolded gently.

"Why not? I tell the other one the same," Seph retorted.

"Yeah, well, funny Aunt Seph." Helena turned and crouched beside Millie. "Is Auntie Seph funny? No, I don't think so either," she added when Millie blew a raspberry, splattering the table with flying yoghurt.

Helena looked at her sister, and Seph suddenly wilted under her gaze. There was something about how her older sister looked at her, like she was scrutinising her, formulating an opinion, that made her uncomfortable. She had always had it, this ability to make Seph squirm. And it wasn't Helena's fault, she didn't do it intentionally, or at least not all the time, but even now, in her thirties, she couldn't stand to be looked at that way. Avoiding her gaze, she instead focused on Millie, trying to ignore what Helena was doing.

"Seph?"

"Mmhmm," she said, trying to be blasé about whatever Helena was trying to do. She knew it was coming from a good place, but she also knew she wasn't ready for whatever conversation she wanted to have.

"You look tired. Is everything okay?"

"Mmhmm." Seph could already hear her voice betray her. Helena had asked this before, and up until now, she had managed to hide how she was really feeling. But once again, she had reached a breaking point. Something about opening up to Kate, maybe. Or maybe just the dam breaking meant that she couldn't hide any longer.

"Seph? Talk to me."

Seph slumped down in a dining chair, legs once again feeling unsteady. She wondered when she would be able to stand for longer than ten minutes without feeling like she was about to collapse.

"Seph, you're scaring me now. What's wrong?" Helena said, the noise of a chair scraping across the wooden floor signalling she had also sat down.

"Nothing."

"It's not nothing. You look awful, like you've not slept. And don't think I haven't noticed that you've lost weight. Are you...is it back?"

"I've...things have just been..." Seph played with one of Millie's toys which sat on the table, a toy car which she wheeled back and forth in a repetitive motion, matching the breathing with the action. Back and forth. In and out.

"I know it's been hard recently. With Dad. And I know I've been so focused on making sure the kids are okay with it all that you've taken a lot of the other stuff. And I love you for that. But Seph, if you're struggling, why didn't you say anything?"

"Because I started to sort everything out so Mum didn't have to worry, and so you could focus on the kids, and I didn't have anything else which needed my attention." *I wanted the distraction*, she felt like saying, but she wasn't ready to reveal that part just yet. "I felt like I was the right one to take on that burden. And at the beginning, it was fine, but by the time I realised it was too much, I felt like I was in too deep. I couldn't just stop and drop everything on you months down the line."

"Are you kidding? Seph, that's exactly what you can do! I never expected you to have to carry the burden of Dad's death on your own. Jesus, how many times do we have to go through this?"

"Please," Seph lifted her hands to her head, the sound of Helena's voice going through her head like nails down a blackboard. "Please, don't shout."

"Sorry, I just can't believe we're here again. For God's sake Seph, after everything we went through last time—"

"You're angry with me? This is one of the reasons I dread telling you things sometimes."

"Really?" Helena looked taken aback. Seph thought that she and Helena had had this conversation before, but maybe she hadn't told her just how much pressure Helena's instinct to be annoyed put her under.

"Yeah. Sometimes you think having a conversation is all it takes. One talk, and it's all done with. But it's not like that, H. Sometimes it takes more than one talk. And sometimes it's just really hard to talk in the first place."

Seph sighed, another wave of exhaustion rolling through her. She needed to explain herself better, or this would spiral. Seph and her sister didn't argue often, but when they did, it could go on forever.

"You think because we've been here before, that it makes every other time easier? It doesn't. Because while we can sit down and talk about how much more open I need to be when I'm in a good place, that doesn't always translate when the bad place is the reality. Let alone when it's the norm. Knowing I should talk about it and *actually* doing it are two very different things. That's the thing with this, this..." She waved her hands limply around her head, before letting them drop with a sigh. " When I'm depressed, my mind takes all the rational things I know I should do and skews everything."

Helena looked down at her hands, fiddling with the towel she held. Seph recognised her own nervous habit mirrored in her sister.

"Sorry, Seph. I'm not angry at you, not really. I just...I kept asking if you were okay, and you told me you were, so I thought that was the truth. I'd noticed some changes, but not enough to make me think it had gotten this far. I just thought that they were normal, you know, with Dad passing. I should have been more aware of what was going on."

"No, that's the thing, H. Sometimes you can ask if someone is okay until you're blue in the face, but if they're determined to hide it and appear fine, then they will. You only noticed today because I'm not here in my work clothes with my makeup on, and I'm not keeping up appearances."

"Why aren't you in your work gear?" Helena asked, suddenly leaning back and taking another look at Seph. She imagined she looked rough, hair scraped up into a messy bun, face pale, eyes dark and sunken, wearing her joggers and a baggy hoodie. But she had managed to shower before she left the house this afternoon, so she was counting that as a small win.

"Because I've taken some time off. I rang the doctor, and he's signed me off for a while."

"Good. That's good." Seph could see the gears turning in Helena's head as she started to formulate a plan. This was how Helena dealt with things, putting a plan in place. Formulating a response. And Seph had a feeling she knew what this one would be. "So you can move in here for a bit. I can move Millie in with Cassie for a while, and you can take her room. It's not perfect, but—"

"H," Seph interrupted her. "I'm not moving in."

"It'll be fine," Helena continued, either not hearing Seph or choosing to ignore her. "It'll be a bit cramped, but we'll manage. At least that way, you don't have to worry about cooking for yourself or anything."

"H," Seph said again, this time a little firmer, placing her hand on the top of Helena's arm, "I'm not moving in. You've got a busy enough house without me getting under your feet."

"But—"

"No. I know you want to keep an eye on me, but you can do that without me being here. I've told you what's going on." *Well, almost*, Seph thought. "Now I need to focus on getting better. And I can't do that with the kids around. It's too chaotic here."

"Yeah, I guess you're right." Helena conceded, "But you're still coming for dinner every week. And come at the weekend. And we'll go out for lunch. Oooh, you could come on my buggy walk with me on Fridays with the nursery mums."

"Yeah, that's not happening, H," Seph said with a tired smile.

"Okay. Coffee and cake afterwards? Here, if you don't feel like going out."

"Sounds good."

CHAPTER FOURTEEN

The door swung open before she had even managed to knock, a tired but smiling Seph greeting her from the warmth inside.

"Hey." Kate smiled back, walking past Seph and into the house so she could close the door.

"Hi."

"How was dinner?" she asked, unbuttoning her coat and slipping it off her shoulders.

"Chaotic, as usual. But good." Kate studied Seph as she stood in front of her. She looked tired still, but she was certain that there was a little more colour in her cheeks, and she definitely didn't seem as heavy in her stance as she had when Kate showed up last night. The change was minuscule, practically impossible to notice to the casual observer, but to Kate, who had watched her every movement and action since she laid eyes on her last night, who still had the image of a broken and sobbing Seph burned into her mind from Saturday, she could see the difference.

She leant forward, chancing a gentle kiss as a greeting. She smiled as Seph reciprocated, relishing the little hum of appreciation from the other woman. They lingered, and feeling buoyed by Seph's reaction, she ran the tip of her tongue across Seph's bottom lip. The action garnered a soft, throaty chuckle from Seph, a sound which fired up the smoldering embers which always sat within Kate when she was around Seph. Reluctantly she pulled back, ever conscious not to push too quickly or too hard. She wanted this relationship to be built with a happy, healthy Seph, and her main priority was helping her reach that state. She couldn't, however, bring herself to move entirely out of

Seph's aura, instead resting her forehead against hers, just savouring having her so close.

"It wasn't too much?" she asked quietly, not wanting to break the peace between them but still concerned that the evening was too overwhelming for Seph.

"The dinner or the kiss?" Seph asked with a hint of mirth in her voice.

"The dinner," Kate replied with a small chuckle.

"A bit loud, but I told Helena that I was off work and why."

"How did she take it?" Kate looked up, cupping Seph's cheek and running a thumb across her cheekbones, which were more pronounced with weight loss than she remembered.

"She was worried. I think she felt guilty more than anything. And annoyed that I didn't say anything."

"I get that." Kate really did. They were the exact same gamut of emotions Kate had gone through when she first discovered how much Seph was suffering. She still felt them now, in varying degrees and at different times. "Just keep talking to her. It doesn't have to be long, meaningful conversations, but just try to keep her in the loop, yeah? I'm sure now she knows she'll check in on you as well."

"Oh, without a doubt. I practically had to break my way out of the house for fear of her locking me in."

"She wanted you to stay?"

"Yeah. And while I appreciate the offer and the meaning behind it, she's got three kids to take care of as well. She doesn't need me there. Besides, it's not like I'm on my own. Is it?"

Kate noticed the change in her tone as she ended the question, genuine concern and fear creeping in that she was, in fact, on her own and she had got it all wrong.

"No, baby. You're not on your own." Seph leaned into her touch, and Kate pressed a firm, reassuring kiss to her forehead. "Why don't we go sit down, and you can tell me all about dinner if you want."

Kate linked her fingers into Seph's and led her through to the living room, gently urging her to sit back down, where she had been before Kate arrived, clearly marked by the mound of cushions and blankets which were piled up on one end of the sofa. She sat down next to her, kicked her heels off, brought her legs up, and tucked herself in as close as she could get to Seph. She sighed when Seph sank into her side, slipping an arm around her waist as she wrapped one around her shoulders.

"How are the kids?" Seph asked once she was settled.

"They're okay," Kate replied. "I think they're calming down a bit. I actually managed to have a conversation with Meg, which is a miracle within itself. But I'm not foolish enough to believe the worst is over. Tim will no doubt have his side of the story, and while I know that Cam will have an open mind, Meg has always been more swayed by her father's words."

"Hmm. I'm glad you got to talk to Meg. I know it hurts when she's angry at you."

"She deserves to be angry." Kate sighed, and suddenly, she felt exhaustion roll over her. "Can we talk about something else? Something less heavy, maybe? I think both our heads could do with a break."

"Sure." Seph sounded grateful for the respite and shuffled further into Kate's body, resting her head on her chest. Instinctively, Kate leant down and dropped a kiss to Seph's hair, fingers scratching along her scalp to a soothing hum. "Talk to me about something else then."

"Like what?" Kate said with a smile, not expecting to be put on the spot so suddenly.

"Don't know. Anything. Everything. I've got five months to catch up on."

"There's not a lot to tell. To be honest, I think I've been a bit of a nightmare to live with." Kate punctuated her statement with another kiss to Seph's hairline, holding her face there and breathing the scent of her shampoo. It smelt fresh, and Kate realised that meant Seph had showered today. She smiled at the fact that Seph had managed to do the simple yet often monumental self-care task under her own steam.

"How come?"

"I've just been miserable. I haven't wanted to do much, and when I have bothered, I've not been very interested in it. Tim called me out on it a couple of times, asked what was wrong with me, but I just brushed him off. I just didn't want to be out or around people at all. But being at home reminded me of why I wasn't with you. I hardly spent any time there if I could help it, so I just worked as much as I could, just trying to keep myself busy. But it never worked. I always found myself thinking about you. I would find myself imagining what it would have been like if I'd made a different decision that day. If I had chosen you the first time."

Kate suddenly felt a distance between her and Seph as she thought about those months apart, like she was physically drifting away. In an attempt to close the gap, she wrapped a hand around Seph's thigh and encouraged her to swing her legs over her own. Seph was almost sitting on her lap, but Kate was now able to fully wrap her arms around her waist. Kate pulled impossibly closer, needing her as close as she could get. Even now, wrapped around each other, it didn't feel enough.

"Like what?" Seph asked although Kate could hear the impending slumber start to slip into her voice.

"Oh, everything. We went on holiday; Tim picked some God-awful golf resort, and I spent all my time by the pool, taking advantage of the all-inclusive bar and thinking about that conversation we had when we planned our perfect break. Do you remember? We were going to find that little private beach on the Portuguese coast."

"Hmm, I remember." Seph let out a long yawn.

"Come on you. Let's go curl up in bed," Kate said softly.

"But it's still early."

"Who cares? You're tired. I'm tired. And I want to snuggle you while you fall asleep."

Kate urged Seph off her lap, standing before her and holding out her arms to pull her into a standing position, quickly wrapping her arms around her waist.

"Well, that's two nights in a row I've fallen asleep on you. Is this as exciting as you imagined?" Seph half-heartedly joked, self-doubt still seeping through her words.

"That's two nights in a row I've got to go to bed with you. That's all the excitement I'll ever need."

CHAPTER FIFTEEN

S eph woke, her head feeling like someone had buried an axe right through the centre of her skull. There was hardly any light in the room, so it must have still been the middle of the night, but when she turned to look at the time, her surroundings swam, and the luminous red numbers of the clock hurt her eyes.

From nowhere, rising through her body, a wave of nausea hit her. She threw herself out of bed and down the short hallway towards the bathroom, hoping to God she made it in time. Her knees hit the floor with a thud, the pressure vibrating through her bones as she started to retch. The force of her vomiting only served to make her headache even worse, her brain feeling as though it was bouncing against her skull with each heave. Her eyes ached and stung, and she could feel warm tears slide down her cheeks. She stopped bringing up anything quickly, a consequence of not having eaten much in the first place, eventually just dry retching as her stomach contracted and attempted to expel something which wasn't there.

Once she'd finally finished, she slumped back down against the wall, and only then did she register she wasn't alone. She could hear something next to her, but the sound was muffled as if it was being made underwater. After a second, the sound came into focus; a cool hand on her forehead and a soft whisper, bringing her back into the room.

"It's okay, baby. I'm here."

She tried to open her eyes, but the harsh light seemed to burn, and she screwed them shut again with a hiss. All her senses were being attacked by her surroundings; even the sensation of the wall behind her back was uncomfortable against her skin. She tried to move, to push herself up, but her body ached with exhaustion.

"Tell me what's wrong, baby. What can I do?" Kate's voice swum onto her consciousness.

"M-migraine," she managed to mumble.

"I'll get you some painkillers," Kate answered.

"M-my...my bag."

"Okay, try not to move. I'll be back in a second."

She sensed Kate leaving her side but feared it was too late for her medication to have too great an effect. Usually, vomiting relieved some of the pressure, but she felt no different this time. She should have known this would happen; she'd been fighting exhaustion for so long, something had to give sooner or later.

Suddenly another wave of pain crashed through her head, a white-hot heat that seemed to sear through her mind. Her hands came up to her temples, gripping into nothing, and her body slid to the floor, finding a small volume of relief in the coolness of the tiles beneath her. She curled her legs and head inwards, squeezing tight against her own arms in an attempt to counter the pain in her head. She must have started to drift off or black out—she wasn't sure which.

"Oh, shit," she heard Kate exclaim to herself as she returned to find Seph curled into the foetal position on the floor. "Seph. Seph, sweetheart. Can you hear me?"

Seph groaned from behind her hands. Kate stroked her arm gently, although to Seph, it was like flames licking her skin.

"Can you try and sit up for me to take your tablets? They'll make you feel better."

She slowly braced her hands against the floor and tried to push herself up, her arms shaking and elbows threatening to buckle at any moment. She was grateful when she felt Kate sweep her arms underneath her, contributing most of the effort into pulling her upright and propping her against the wall. Hesitating for a second to make sure she wouldn't collapse again, Kate handed her the tablets, keeping hold of the glass of water for when she was ready. Seph forced the tablets and a sip of water down her throat, nearly gagging at the harshness of swallowing.

Kate took the glass off her so she didn't drop it and then moved to sit beside her against the wall. She felt herself slump, sliding down the wall again, until a warm arm hooked around her shoulder and guided her. The safe haven of Kate's lap greeted her cheek, and she let go of her final shred of control, letting herself drift away again. Kate ran her fingers through her hair, brushing strands from her face where they had stuck, and Seph tried to focus on the feeling rather than the nausea she could feel churning in her stomach.

After a minute or so, another sharp stab of pain pierced through her head, and her body tensed. Kate quickly looped her hand in Seph's and held it tight.

"It's okay. I'm here," she murmured quietly.

Seph's hand gripped tighter around Kate's, her knees drawing up again as she curled into a tight ball against Kate's body, tensing until the wave passed. Once it started to subside, her grip loosened, and her body started to relax as she exhaled the breath she had been holding.

After a while, Seph felt the reassuring, medically-induced, tug of sleep start to draw her under, and Kate must have felt the change in her body as well.

"Do you think you can get up?" Kate asked, stroking her arm softly to get her attention. Seph gave a shaky nod, bracing to push herself up. "Hold on. Let me help you."

Kate's hands wrapped around her shoulders, steadying her and guiding her upwards, but the small movement was still too much, and she frantically scrambled towards the toilet, vomiting any remains of what was in her stomach. Kate sat behind her, hand rubbing up and down her back until she was finished, slumping back into Kate's body. She felt her arms wrap around her, legs braced around her hips, her chin resting on her shoulder, cocooning her in a blanket of warmth and support.

"Take your time. You let me know when you're ready," Kate reassured her.

"Juuuusllpppherre," Seph mumbled, words slurring completely unintelligibly this time.

"What was that, sweetheart?" Kate asked, leaning forward so her ear was right next to Seph's mouth.

"Jusssh schleep here," she slurred again, trying harder to make herself clear.

"Nope. You'll be much more comfortable in bed. But there's no rush. Whenever you feel able to move, we will."

Another ten minutes passed before Seph felt stable enough to even attempt to move again, Kate standing in front of her, holding out her hands to pull her up. As she stood, her legs felt weak, and for a moment, she wasn't sure she could make it back to the bedroom. But then she felt an arm wrap around her waist, the other remaining clasped around her hand. If she was on her own, she probably would have resigned herself to staying on the bathroom floor, but Kate was there, taking small, timid steps with her. She sat her down on the bed, urging her to lie back and swing her legs round, covering her back over with the duvet. She stroked her hair away from her face, disappearing from Seph's space for a minute before Seph felt the coolness of a damp cloth being wiped over her clammy face.

"Try and go back to sleep, baby," Kate whispered, the last thing she heard before she welcomed the familiar pull of sleep with open arms.

Kate couldn't sleep. *Wouldn't* sleep. Instead, she sat up against the headboard, Seph's head in her lap as she slept, watching her every move, every flicker of her eyelids, every twitch of her forehead, every wince of pain.

It had taken Seph a while to fully fall into a deep sleep. The pain of her migraine must have lessened but not subsided entirely, as she cried out a few times, her face twisting and contorting as a fresh wave of pain shot through her head, her hands scrabbling for Kate's touch. Blindly she found Kate's top and grasped onto the fabric, while all Kate could do was try and soothe her with gentle words and timid touches until she drifted off again.

Seph's grip loosened again, but her fingers still curled into the cloth, twitching every time another dagger of pain threatened to shoot through her, and that's where it stayed for the rest of the night, tethered to Kate like a boat moored in a storm.

How had it gotten this bad? How had *she* let it get this bad? It was a futile question, and she knew it, but that didn't mean she wasn't still asking and blaming herself. She couldn't predict the future any more than the next person, but if she'd been stronger, if she'd stuck by what she knew to be right and true to her heart, then she would have been there for Seph. She would have been able to support her while she supported her family. Held her when she needed to break down, comfort her when she needed to cry, stood by her side when she buried her father.

God, she really hoped this was the last thing. The crest before the wave finally calmed. Although she had seen some improvement in Seph's demeanour, she still had a long way to go before she was anywhere near the woman she'd first met. And she knew this wasn't going to be an easy or straight road. She was preparing herself for the ups and downs, the days of self-doubt and hatred which were, without doubt, to come as Seph recovered.

They had had conversations and discussions when they were together before about their own personal struggles. Kate had listened carefully as Seph told her about her past, her depression and anxiety, honoured and privileged at being let into that painful part of Seph's life. She had seen her have an anxiety attack before, triggered by something small but clearly not insignificant. But that was an isolated incident, a one-time thing which, despite the come-down, was over quickly. She had even learnt how to coach and talk Seph through it, her techniques for coming round and grounding her. But this was on another level. She could see that when she knelt in front of a pale and shaking Seph on Saturday night, the fear and panic in her own body rising with each excruciating second as Seph remained within her own mind. And now, five days later, the final straw had broken. Her body, which had been holding on for so long by such a tenuous link, was giving in.

Now all she could think was how determined she was to get the old Seph back. It was going to be a long road, one she had no doubts would have its pitfalls and obstacles, but one she was adamant Seph wouldn't be travelling alone. She wasn't even sure if it was possible to get the same woman back, and if she thought about it, she wasn't bothered by that. The past five months would undoubtedly have shaped Seph, and the mark made by the loss of her father would remain forever, as it should. But if she could get anywhere near, if she could make any positive difference, make any step, however small, towards Seph being in a happier place, she would count it as a success. This was going to be a tough journey for both of them, but one she was determined to see through to the end.

Kate felt Seph stir and looked up from the laptop perched on her knee before glancing at the clock behind her. Seph had slept for nearly eight hours, and it was now coming up to eleven in the morning. It hadn't been solid, it hadn't been peaceful, but it was better than the night before and, Kate suspected, better than she had slept for quite a number of weeks. She could probably do with more, but rather than waking with a strangled cry or a broken sob as she had done the previous night, her eyes fluttered open, and her body shuffled under the covers, signalling she was coming around naturally and ready to wake.

One eye cracked open, and a weary Seph looked up at her, squinting at the light coming through the curtains. Kate had kept them closed, instead choosing to work under the soft light of the bedside lamp, in both an effort to not disturb Seph but also so it wasn't too harsh if she did wake with her migraine persisting.

"Morning, sleepyhead," she said quietly, again so as not to be too blunt on Seph's senses.

"Morning," Seph replied, her voice croaky. Kate watched carefully as Seph rolled over, pushing herself upright, ready to support her at the drop of a hat if she looked like she was about to collapse. She didn't, though, and although shaky, she seemed a lot stronger than in the early hours. "What time is it?"

"Just before eleven."

"Hmm." Seph tipped her head back and closed her eyes as she let herself come round. Suddenly her eyes shot open, and she turned to face Kate. "Wait. It's Thursday."

"Yeah?" Kate asked, unsure what the day had to do with things. Maybe Seph had somewhere to be that she had forgotten about.

"Why aren't you at work?"

Kate couldn't help but smile at the question. It was typical of Seph to think about others, even when she should be thinking about herself. Even the smallest thing, like the fact it was eleven on a Thursday and Kate wasn't at the office, made her concerned.

"I called in and rearranged my appointments. I didn't have many booked anyway," she quickly added before Seph could argue, "but today's weren't urgent, so I took some time off and said I would catch up with anything I needed to from home."

"Hmm." Kate suspected that the only reason Seph wasn't arguing back was her residual tiredness. Instead, she shifted closer to her, laying her head on Kate's shoulder. Kate tried hard to hide the gasp she wanted to let escape at the gesture, her heart racing at the fact that Seph was being so open and affectionate with her. It wasn't that she wasn't used to it; Seph was always open with her emotions and displaying them previously, but it was the fact that she was doing it now. Apart from the kiss in bed the previous morning, it had been Kate who had initiated any affection between them, and even then, it had been with some hesitation. Coming to her senses, she rested her head on top of Seph's, placing a gentle kiss on her hair. "How do you feel?"

"Oh. Not too bad considering. Sorry," Seph looked up at her without moving her head. "Not really very attractive."

"It's alright. You just scared me a little."

"Sorry." Seph looked down, guilt painting her features.

"No, you don't need to say sorry, baby. I just meant I was worried about you. But I'd rather be here with you than let you go through that alone. Do you get them often?"

"No, not really. A couple of times in the past few months. I should have known that it might happen with everything going on. Something was bound to break sooner or later."

"They're stress related?"

"Yeah, more often than not."

Seph's stomach rumbling interrupted the conversation, eliciting a chuckle from Kate.

"Hungry?"

"Yeah."

"Well, I'm not surprised. You probably didn't have a lot in your stomach to begin with, and that was before you were sick. Want me to get you something?"

"Hmm, in a bit. Might have a bath as well."

"That sounds like a perfect plan. I'll start running it while I go make you some tea and toast if you want? Nothing too heavy, just enough to get something in you."

Kate leaned over, lifting her laptop from her legs and placing it on the bedside table, and dislodged Seph's head with a grumble of protestation from the younger woman. Sliding out of bed, she leant down and placed a kiss on Seph's lips. Seph grimaced in response.

"Ew, I wouldn't. I need to brush my teeth," she complained, screwing her nose up.

"I don't care," Kate insisted as she picked up the dressing gown she had borrowed from the back of Seph's bedroom door. She smiled coyly as she pulled it on, the faint scent of Seph's perfume wafting across her nose. It was like she was wrapping herself in a cocoon of all that Seph was, warm and comforting and filled with love. She cleared her throat of the emotion which was in danger of lodging there. "I'll pop to the shops when you have freshened up and eaten, maybe grab us something for dinner?"

"Oh, I'd not thought of that. Good idea," Seph said, screwing up her face in concentration. Kate chuckled at the sight.

"It's not a problem. Anything we need?"

"Don't think so, but rummage through the fridge to check. I think there's some cash in my wallet," Seph replied, eyes still closed and voice quiet. Kate suspected that although she felt a little better, her senses were still feeling particularly sensitive.

"Don't worry about it. Anything *you* need?" she emphasised, implying the question was less about necessities and more about luxuries.

"No. Oh, yeah, actually!" Seph exclaimed with a little more vigour, wincing at the volume of her own voice. "Can you get me something salty? Crisps. Popcorn. Anything like that. I always crave salt after a migraine." Her voice slowly drifted off towards the end of her sentence, energy rapidly depleting from her earlier outburst.

Kate smiled softly at the new, small snippet of knowledge she had just learned about Seph, softening even further when she realised that Seph was on the verge of sleep again. She leant over, pulling the duvet up and making sure she was fully covered and comfortable, dropping a soft kiss to her forehead.

"Get some more sleep, baby. Everything else can wait."

CHAPTER SIXTEEN

K ate had reluctantly gone to work on Friday, Seph reassuring her that she did not need someone to look after her a second day but promising to call her immediately if she needed anything. Despite the fact that she didn't want or need her to be fussing over her all day, she had to admit it was lonely in the house without her. It had only been two days, but it already felt like Kate had been in her house and life properly for much longer. It felt like she belonged. She smiled as she remembered Kate kissing her softly in the kitchen before she left, hand delicately cupping her cheek, noses nudging. It was reassuringly domestic, and she found herself relishing in the feel of it.

The past few days had been exhausting, and she had appreciated the peace and isolation. Apart from one evening when she had dinner at Helena's, Seph hadn't seen anyone since the party a week previously. One person she couldn't avoid for much longer was Fiona; apart from a few vague messages to throw her off the scent of anything being wrong, Seph hadn't texted her. She couldn't bring herself to tell her the truth, and she couldn't flat-out lie, so she had just kept fobbing her off, saying she was fine, delaying the inevitable. Now though, home alone with nothing else to keep her mind busy, she couldn't bring herself to avoid her friend any longer. Once she had built up the courage to text Fiona and told her that she was at home with the after-effects of a migraine, she had invited herself round for lunch, with the excuse to bring Seph what she assumed were some much-needed supplies.

But once she had arrived, Fiona was surprised to find the fridge stocked with fresh orange juice and bacon, a big bag of salted popcorn on the counter, and a box of Seph's favourite chocolates sitting on the coffee table. Seph studied her carefully as she took in what was in the kitchen, then followed it up with a look around the rest of the house. There was a definite pause as she clocked the pair of heels which Kate had left at the bottom of her stairs this morning.

"Has Helena been over?" Fiona asked, her raised eyebrows making it clear she knew the answer already.

"No," Seph answered too quickly. Her reflex action to tell the truth was annoying at best and right now wasn't serving her particularly well. Her eyes dropped closed as she realised that she had opened herself up to more questioning.

"Then who's stocked your fridge?"

Yeah. There it was. Fi had never been one to hold back. If she wanted to know something, she would just ask. They were different in that way, Seph being much more considered, while Fi was much more forthright. At times, the balance treated them well. Right now, though, Seph was cursing her friend's bluntness.

"Umm..." Seph mentally cursed herself for walking into that trap and without a plan for what to answer.

"Must be someone special. She knows your favourite chocolates," Fi continued. Seph couldn't help the grin which crept across her face at the fact that Kate *had* remembered her favourite chocolates, let alone bought them. Strategically she hid her happiness, grateful her back was turned to her friend. Fi wasn't done with her observations yet, though. "She's also got good taste in shoes, judging by the ones at the end of the sofa. Expensive, mind you..."

Seph continued to stir the drinks she was making, kicking herself for not clearing up the traces of Kate which had quickly become scattered across her home. She felt Fi come up behind her and look over her shoulder.

"It's fun watching you squirm." Fi chuckled, taking her coffee from Seph and leaning back on the counter, blowing the steam from the cup, her eyes not leaving Seph. "So..."

"So what?" Seph asked, trying to act as nonchalant as possible. It was hard enough in front of her best friend, let alone when she had limited energy reserves and had spent the past few days being uncharacteristically open with her emotions. Suddenly, going back to trying to put on a front after days of being honest with Kate seemed like a mountain she wasn't sure she had the drive to climb.

"So who is she? And more importantly, why haven't I met her?"

"It's nothing." Seph shrugged, trying and failing to downplay things.

"Nothing? She's clearly been taking care of you these past couple of days. No one who's nothing would do that."

"Maybe she's just a nice person. Apparently, they do exist."

"Ha! Not in my world, they don't. So come on, I want details!"

Seph grabbed her mug and spun around to walk past Fi into the living room, putting a little too much force behind her actions and spilling her hot coffee over the side of her mug. She swore as the scalding liquid ran in between her fingers, much to the amusement of her best friend.

"What is wrong with you?" Fi chuckled again, watching as Seph hastily mopped up the spilled drink with a disgruntled look on her face.

"Nothing."

"Yeah, right. You're acting weird."

"Am not." Seph was suddenly aware she had somehow reverted back to being a grumpy, petulant teenager.

"You absolutely are! You're all jumpy and odd. And you won't tell me about the woman you're so obviously seeing."

"Fine. What do you want to know?" Seph conceded, brushing past Fi as she made her way into the living room. While she really enjoyed just having Kate to herself, wasn't this what she wanted? To be able to tell people they were in a relationship? So why was she hesitating so much now? *Because Fi is not going to like what you have to tell her.*

"Well, a name would be a good start," Fi countered, sitting down on the opposite end of the sofa. She brought her mug up to her lips and took a cautious sip.

"Kate."

"And what does Kate do?"

"She's a lawyer."

"Oh, so you met each other through work?"

It was a valid and not entirely untruthful assumption. But the way Fi flippantly concluded that it was "through work" made Seph's stomach turn.

"Yeah, kind of. We met at a conference."

"Oh, God, you hate those things. She must be something if she managed to get you to talk at an event full of strangers."

A flashback of that first meeting popped into Seph's mind, and she couldn't stop the smile which crept across her face. For months, those memories of their first days together, the hidden smiles and illicit touches, only served to drive a dagger further into Seph's already wounded heart, ripping at the muscle and making the bleeding more profuse. Now though, there was a tentative first sign of healing, the pain reduced to an ache, as Seph thought back to those early days and how special and seen Kate had made her feel.

"Oh my God, look at you. You're like a fucking teenager, grinning like a loon! You're really smitten!"

"Fuck off." Seph really wasn't in the mood for Fi's teasing today. Although she meant no harm by it, her brain was still lagging, and she wasn't in the right place for the back and forth Fi so readily relished in.

"I'm sorry," Fi relented. "I'm just stoked that you've met someone. And she seems to be good for you, judging by your fridge. And that smile on your face."

"Yeah, she is." Seph softened. She couldn't deny that Kate did have a positive effect on her. Even though it hadn't been that way recently. But now things were changing. Things were good. And for the first time in months, Seph was feeling tentatively positive about the future. It was a feeling which was alien to her, but she was trying to remember what Kate had been telling her. She *wasn't* alone anymore.

"So come on. I want details! How long has this been going on?"

"Oh, umm…" Her joy was short-lived. She could lie, omit the past five months of heartache, but what would be the alternative? If she were to tell the truth, say it had begun over a year ago, then Fi would begin to ask questions about where Kate had been. Why hadn't she been around through easily the most difficult thing she had ever had to live through? Where was she when she stood at her father's funeral, holding together her family with barely capable hands? "Well, it's kind of complicated. It's not really been that straightforward."

"How come?" Fi asked, sympathy lacing her words. That wasn't going to last.

"Well…"

"She isn't married, is she? Oh God, can you imagine!" Fi laughed, but a cold, icy feeling crept up Seph's spine. Of all the things she had to say, all the jokes she had to make…

Her silence lingered, and she was suddenly aware of the fact that Fiona's laughter had also died off, a strange tension settling over the room.

"Seph, she isn't married, is she?" Seph could still offer no words; she couldn't even bring herself to look at her friend. "Tell me she isn't married, Seph."

"I…"

"Oh, for fuck's sake!" Fi suddenly shot up from the sofa, slamming her cup down on the table and sloshing coffee everywhere.

"Please, Fi, it's not what you think." Seph also stood up, a little less vigorously, still weak on her legs.

"So far, I think you're seeing a married woman. Is that right?"

"Yes, but—"

"But nothing! She's married. Jesus, I thought you knew better than to get involved with someone like that!"

"Someone like what? Fi, you don't know what's happened. Please, let me explain."

"Fine. Go on then."

Fi stopped in her tracks, crossing her arms. She turned and looked at Seph with a glare that said anything *but* readiness to listen. Seph, however, took the opportunity, knowing that although Fi was only listening to find something she could use in her argument against her, she couldn't let her chance pass by.

"Her marriage was…things weren't…it just wasn't working. I know this is difficult for you—"

"Difficult for me? I think that's the most understated thing you've ever said."

"Please, Fi." The headache, which had finally subsided after nearly a week of being ever-present, was starting to make a reappearance, and suddenly, Seph didn't feel very stable on her feet. She braced herself on the back of the sofa, willing her legs to hold out.

"Please what, Seph? Please don't be mad? Please don't take it personally? Please don't compare it to what happened to me? Of course I'm going to do all of those things, Seph! How could I not?"

"I know, I just... Please hear me out."

"Go on then." Fi bent a leg, hip cocked out with a look that Seph knew was the one she used to intimidate people. It wouldn't entirely work with Seph, but it also meant this was going to be a hard fight to get Fi to hear what she had to say.

"Kate was married when we met. But she has left her husband—"

"Husband? So she's straight as well?"

"No." Seph took a breath, trying to maintain her composure. It was getting harder and harder, and she could feel her energy ebbing away with every failed argument and ignored word. If she had the stamina and inclination, she would bring up the fact that just because a woman is married to a man doesn't make them automatically straight, but that was a discussion for another time. "She's left her husband and is getting divorced."

"But that didn't happen before you met. I mean, you two started sleeping with each other while she was still with her husband, right?"

"Yeah."

"So she's still a cheat. Whatever she's done recently, she's still a cheat, and you're"—Fi jabbed a finger in Seph's direction—"complicit in that cheating."

"Fi, it's not the same as—" Seph tried to argue as Fi walked away.

"It's absolutely the same!" she screamed, spinning on her heel and pointing a finger in Seph's face. "It's exactly the same. Except you're *her*, and this-this Kate woman is Rob. Jesus, of all the things I thought you would do, I never thought you would do this."

"Fi, I didn't do it to you. I didn't do anything to you..." A wave of lightheadedness washed over Seph, and she braced herself back against the sofa once more, breathing through it. "I know this is difficult for you—"

"You have no idea! For fuck's sake, after everything I went through with Rob, I thought you might have had enough consideration to not get into something like this. Have you any idea what that poor man is going through? He will be crushed, his whole life ripped apart because you couldn't keep it in your pants."

"It's not like that. He doesn't know; he just thinks—"

"He doesn't know? So she can't even be truthful when she's tearing the guy's heart out?"

"It's not like that. She's doing it for me."

"Sure she is." Fi scowled while pulling her coat on. "Fuck, no wonder you were so shifty about telling me. You knew I'd go fucking crazy at you for this. Wait, is this why you've not texted me in a week? I've barely heard from you since last weekend. Is this why?"

"No, I've not been—"

"Don't fucking talk to me," Fi spat as she flung open the front door and stalked out into the cool winter air. Seph flinched as the door slammed behind her, letting her suddenly heavy eyelids close with exhaustion.

Kate tapped her fingers against the table, watching Tim intently. He was putting on an extremely good show of the broken man, but Kate had seen how he worked over the years, knew his traits and tells, and she could see right through it. He'd let his stubble grow, no doubt to look unkempt, but had trimmed it slightly. His top button was undone, and his tie hung loose in an attempt to portray untidy and ruffled. But the tie was a new addition, clearly only there so it could be undone, and his shirt was still pressed. And the look he kept flashing her across the table was steely and cold, not the look of someone heartbroken but of someone who was out to get her. But she had faced far worse and more intimidating clients in her line of work, and so she cleared her throat and drew her attention back to what her lawyer was saying.

"Mrs Bailey is offering the following conditions in return for a swift and amicable divorce. Sale of their joint home, with the proceeds being split evenly. Mr Bailey will be in receipt of the Landrover and the Jaguar as well as the holiday home in Spain. Mrs Bailey asks for full ownership of the apartment in the city, which is currently rented to your son. Any bills or costs relating to either of the children, including university fees, will be shared equally between both parties."

Kate watched as Tim leant over towards his lawyer, who sat next to him, and whispered something in his ear. It was a power play, and she was surprised that Tim thought it would work on her. Although, maybe he had spent so much of their marriage together uninterested in her work aside from the money she brought in that he'd forgotten just how good a lawyer she was.

"No." Tim's lawyer broke the stagnant silence with the bluntness of the word. "Mr Bailey wants the house to be transferred fully into his name—"

Kate scoffed, stopping him in his tracks. "No chance."

"Mr Bailey has spent the past fifteen years putting into the property; he would like to retain it, considering you are the one who has left the family home."

"Family home? I would like to remind him that neither children reside at the property anymore, both having moved out to attend university and start their own lives. To imply that it is a family home in the sense of something which acts as a source of stability for the children is a huge misconception," Sam, her lawyer, fired back, also clearly seeing where Tim was trying to take this.

"You still left it," Tim countered across the table.

"Yes, I did, Tim. And until recently, we were both discussing downsizing now that Cam and Meg have moved out. But if it really means so much to you, since we made *so* many happy memories there, you can have it."

"Kate..." Sam whispered through gritted teeth.

"For the market value."

"What?" Tim cried incredulously.

"You want the house? Buy me out. Otherwise, it's going on the market." Kate kept a steely look on her face, not allowing herself to be intimidated by him and his cheap mind tricks.

"No chance."

"Then we're done here." Kate and Sam stood, neither of them looking across the table again while gathering their things.

As they left the room, Kate could hear Tim already ranting and raving at his lawyer. She suppressed her smile until they were safely in the lift and the doors had closed.

"I must admit," Sam spoke first, "I wondered what you were doing for a second back there. But then, you did tell me that you were the better lawyer out of the two of you."

"Tim used to be a better lawyer than he is now," Kate sighed, staring ahead at the distorted reflection in the lift doors. "I knew he was going to try and pull the wounded husband card. And his attempt at getting the house is his way of trying to show that he can get one over on me. But I've given him enough over the years; I'm not prepared to give him anymore. Even if it was me who ended the marriage."

The lift doors opened as they reached the ground floor, and Kate stepped out, Sam a step behind her. Before she could go further, though, Sam caught her wrist.

"Are you being completely honest with me?"

Kate regarded Sam, wondering if she had said something to indicate anything about the other reason she had left Tim.

"Kate, I know you're claiming irreconcilable differences and a breakdown of the relationship, but I also know when there's something else. *I'm* the best at what I do for a reason."

Kate sighed. She should have known that she couldn't fool Sam. Sarah was right, she was the best at what she did, and Kate had been impressed with her from the first moment they met. She knew Tim couldn't match her legal representation, even with his bullish attitude and boys club connections. It was another reason why she felt so confident standing up to him just now.

"Let's talk back at the office."

"Oh, sweetheart. I'm sorry."

Seph curled into Kate's side, her head resting on her chest. Kate ran her fingers through her hair, listening as Seph told her about her lunch with Fi. Kate had come straight to Seph's house after meeting with her divorce lawyer, and even with her own head pounding from her argument with Fiona, she could see that Kate was mentally and physically exhausted. She immediately met her with a hug, both relishing in the contact and comfort it brought, although Seph was aware of the residual tension in Kate's shoulders as she refused to let herself relax fully. Both too tired to do anything, they had ordered takeout and crashed on the sofa for the rest of the evening.

"It's okay. I kind of deserved it."

"Do you? You're not the one who is married."

"Yeah, but I didn't exactly say no, did I? And she's right, it takes two. And while we're trying to do the right thing now, we didn't before." Seph sighed, picking at a spot on Kate's joggers. "She's been on the other end of it; she was never going to just accept it without remembering that."

"What happened?" Kate asked. Seph relaxed further as she felt Kate card her fingers through her hair.

"Her husband, Rob, came home one evening and told her that he'd been having an affair with a woman from the gym. They'd only been married for eighteen months, and the affair had been going on for nearly a year. She was devastated. She'd been making plans about moving house and starting a family, and all the while, he'd been cheating."

"That's awful. I can see why our situation would upset her."

"I know," Seph sighed. "It makes me wonder if we're doing the right thing."

She felt Kate stiffen beneath her. "You're not having second thoughts, are you?"

"No." Seph knew that she would show more conviction if she looked at Kate, but she was afraid that if she did, her emotion would overwhelm her yet again. Instead, she continued to look down, focusing on Kate's hand, which rested on her lap. For the first time, she noticed the pale, white mark which ran along her finger, marking where her wedding ring used to sit. She wondered how long it had been gone, shocked by the show of commitment. Yes, she knew Kate had hired a lawyer, and Kate kept telling Seph that she was here for her, but something about the absence of her wedding ring, the symbol of her marriage, was like a bulldozer smashing through her last few doubts. Running her own fingertip across the mark, she spoke quietly. "You've taken your wedding ring off."

"Yeah. The night I left Tim."

"How did I not notice?" Seph did look up at Kate then, instantly getting lost in the mossy green depths of her eyes. "I'm sorry I didn't notice."

"It's okay, sweetheart. You've had other things to concentrate on."

Seph darted her gaze back down to Kate's slender fingers, focusing on the band of untouched skin.

"How did your meeting go?" Seph felt the need to change topics, the threat of being overwhelmed imminent once again.

Kate blew out a deep, long breath. "It wasn't exactly easy, but then I didn't think it would be. He tried his best devastated husband act, and I get that that may be the case, but I honestly believe it was all for show. It would have been more believable if he wasn't trying to get me for all he could."

"He wants a lot?"

"He wants the house signed over to him."

"Just like that?" Seph asked, looking up to see Kate's face.

"Yeah. Claimed he had invested into it over the time we had it, and since it's the family home, wants it for the kids." Kate explained, rolling her eyes as she thought of the sob story which his lawyer had tried to pull. "I told him he could have it, but he would have to buy me out."

"Oh." Seph thought about it for a moment. "And you're happy with that?"

"Yeah. I mean, yes, it's the home the kids have grown up in most of their lives, but they're not there anymore. Cam moved in with his friends from uni a couple of years ago, and Meg likes to come back now and then, but even she has her own place now. It's not like they're young kids who need a stable home. Now it's just a shell. The house we both live—*lived*—in while we drifted further apart. I have the memories; I don't need the house to keep them."

Seph listened intently as Kate spoke, noting how her emotions changed throughout from glassy-eyed and regretful but with a sense of pride when she spoke about Cam and Meg to resignation as she described her home as a shell. As if the actions she hadn't taken recently to show Seph she was serious and committed to building their relationship weren't enough, then the dead tone behind her voice when she spoke about her life with Tim was enough to prove it to her. Unsure what to say in response, she just laid her head back down on Kate's shoulder, taking her hand in hers and stroking the blank skin on her finger.

"Guess we're hurting a lot of people," she muttered quietly after a few minutes.

"Is that what you meant by wondering if we're doing the right thing?" Kate asked her.

"Yeah. And it's not that I'm näive enough to think no one would get hurt. But it just seems everywhere I look, there's someone getting hurt, and we're to blame."

There was a pause as both women digested what Seph had said and the day they'd each had, Kate going back to rhythmically running her fingers through Seph's hair. She wondered if it provided Kate a comfort as well as herself. She wondered what Kate was thinking, whether her words just now were the thing she needed to hear to finally decide that this was a mistake.

"When I told Mum about you," Kate broke the silence, "she told me that there was nothing wrong with doing what made me happy. That I'd worked hard for so many years to make sure everyone was happy and had what they wanted, and maybe now it was time to put myself first. And I think she's right. I know we're hurting people with our actions, and especially with the kids, it's going to take a long time to mend that, but don't I deserve to be happy? Don't we?"

"Believing I should be deserving of happiness is a big issue for me."

"I know it is. I know you struggle with putting yourself first, and that's why I'm here. To remind you of that. And I think you'd remind me of the same thing, wouldn't you?"

"Of course. You deserve everything," Seph mumbled, suddenly feeling very coy and shy.

"I have to tell you, though...I spoke to Sam about you."

"You did?" Seph was surprised. As far as she was knew, Kate was trying to keep Seph out of the divorce proceedings as much as she could. Telling her lawyer about her seemed at odds with that decision and everything else she had done.

"Yes." Kate sighed. "It wasn't exactly my intention, but Sarah was right when she said Sam was good at what she does. She basically called me out on the fact there was something else."

"And does she think it's going to make a difference?"

"She still thinks that the relationship was irreconcilable. But she has said that it would be better if I was honest."

"You mean admitting adultery?" Seph's chest tightened at the thought. If Kate filed for divorced and admitted she was unfaithful, Seph could be named in the court papers.

"Yes. But I also told her why I'm reluctant to do that. I know that wasn't exactly my place, and I didn't tell her all the details, but I was an idiot to think even for a second I could do this without her knowing everything. Baby, look at me..." Seph felt Kate's warm palm come and cup her cheek, pulling her face around to meet her eyes. "I will still do everything I can to keep this away from you. I promise."

"I know. It's just—"

"I know you're worried. But I trust Sam. If you can trust me?"

Seph nodded. "I do."

"Good. Because whatever they have to throw at us, we will deal with it together. Right?"

Seph was hesitant and didn't fully share Kate's apparently unwavering belief that it was going to be that straightforward, but for a second, sudden unexpected and unfamiliar feeling of strength and support rose in her chest at Kate's declaration. "Yes. Absolutely."

Chapter Seventeen

Kate poured the boiled water into two mugs before glancing at the clock, which read nearly a quarter to nine. She frowned and looked towards the stairs. She'd come down nearly twenty minutes earlier, made herself breakfast, and already had one cup of coffee, and Seph hadn't made an appearance yet.

While it was too early to call it a routine, there was a definite pattern emerging through the past week. Kate would be dressed and downstairs first, having breakfast while making coffee for them both, while Seph would follow a few minutes later. Even though she had nowhere to go, Seph still insisted on getting up when Kate did and seeing her off to work. And although Kate wished Seph would stay in bed and get some more sleep, she knew she could rest during the day and loved the sweet, gentle goodbye kiss she left with every morning.

Kate walked to the bottom of the stairs, listening out for any movement. Today was Saturday; they had risen a little later in agreement that the past week had been a lot for both of them, and since neither had anywhere to go or anything to do, they could move at a more glacial pace. But Kate had left Seph in the shower while she went downstairs, and she knew that she was nearly finished and so was expecting her only a few minutes later. She couldn't think of a reason she would be this long.

"Seph?"

When no reply came, her worry grew even greater, and she started up the stairs and into the bedroom. Walking into the bedroom, she found Seph sitting on the floor, leaning back against the wall.

"Seph?" she softly asked again.

There was no shaking, no crying, no panicked, hiccuped breaths which signalled another anxiety attack, but she stepped gently, not wanting to startle her just in case. Seph looked up at the mention of her name, and Kate crumbled under the sight of the tears which flowed freely down her face. With a sigh, she lowered herself down the wall and settled next to Seph, gently running her hand across her shoulders when she dropped her head to her knees again. Seph visibly relaxed a little at the contact, but Kate waited patiently, sitting silently beside her for the next few minutes.

"Sorry," Seph apologised, lifting her face and wiping away the tears with her hands. "I thought I was done with the crying."

"It's okay. It's not a straight road."

"For once, it's not actually because of that," Seph said with a watery chuckle. "Although I'm fairly sure you must be sick of me by now."

"No, never, baby." Kate noted the minuscule trace of a smile that appeared at the mention of the term of endearment. She'd always called Seph that, but at first, she felt wary every time it slipped past her lips. Now though, it came out as easily as the air in her lungs. "I told you I'm here for the long run. Now, what's going on?"

Seph shuffled, looking at something beside her, out of Kate's view, before picking it up and handing it over with shaky hands.

"I knocked it off the bookcase on my way past. I'm always doing it—surprised it didn't smash before, to be honest." She sniffed, wiping her face again. "But this time, when I looked at it, I just…"

Kate looked closer at the frame sitting in Seph's hand. Behind the large spider-web crack across the glass, she could make out the smiling faces of Seph and Helena, standing behind her parents at what appeared to be a family occasion.

"I'll go into town and get you a new frame this afternoon."

Seph finally looked up at her, eyes glistening with the tears which were pooling in the corners of her eyes. Kate's hand pushed some hair behind Seph's ear, fingers tracing across her cheekbone.

"I know. It can be easily fixed. It's just, I…I think it just reminded me that I haven't…I haven't been to see him yet."

Suddenly, the tears made sense. Although Kate had never lost a parent, she still remembered the feeling of residing in the grey space between having some-one there and the closure that they were never coming back from when she had lost her grandmother. It was a stormy sea awash with memories of times gone by and possibilities for the future. Except there was no future, no possibilities, and the swirling clouds of grief confused everything until you remembered that that person was gone.

"Would you come with me?" Seph asked shyly.

Kate slipped her fingers behind Seph's neck, pulling her gently towards her. She brushed her lips across her forehead in the softest of kisses.

"Of course I will, baby."

"I think I've been avoiding it because it was just too much to deal with, you know? But these past few days, I've been wondering if avoiding it is adding to that pressure. Maybe if I go and get it over with, it'll free some headspace up to really focus on getting better."

"Grief is really funny. It's not like one day you just stop grieving. There will still be moments when you go to say something to him or wish he was here to see something, and you'll be sad because you suddenly remember that's not possible. I still think of my gran all the time." Kate took another look at the photo in her hand, smiling when she saw the happy, almost carefree expression Seph was displaying. "How about we go into town, pick up a new frame for this, and then I'll drive you over to the cemetery? If you're ready to go today, that is?"

"Yeah. I think I just need to do it. Putting it off is not going to make it any easier."

"And I'll be there as much or as little as you want or need me to be. If you want me to wait in the car, that's fine, but if you need me to be right beside you, that's okay too."

"Thank you," Seph said softly as she buried her head further into the crook of Kate's neck.

"Anytime, baby," Kate replied, smiling as she placed another kiss on Seph's hair.

Ten

"I never know what to do at a cemetery. I think, from what Mum's said, she talks to him like he's still here. But I always found that a bit strange, having a conversation with no one."

Seph and Kate sat on the bench opposite where Seph's father's grave stood. The stone was still fresh and stark amongst its more weathered neighbours. The wind was unseasonably warm, and Seph inhaled deeply. Her breakdown and realisation that she was yet to fully mourn her father that morning had released the chains she had been carrying around, and although she was still tired and had a long road ahead of her, there was an undeniable lightness in her bones.

"You don't have to do anything if you don't want to. For some people, just sitting here is enough."

"That also seems weird. Plus, let's face it, I'm not great at being in my own head for too long."

"Hmm." There was a silence, punctuated only by the sound of Seph rustling her hand in the bag of wine gums they had bought in town. They were her father's favourite, and Kate suggested getting something that reminded Seph of him for the cemetery. She was slowly chewing when Kate spoke up again. "If he was here, what would you say to him?"

Seph inhaled deeply before letting out a loud breath, pulling back her shoulders at the question. She shuffled on the seat slightly, the hard wooden bench not particularly comfortable when sat in one place for too long.

"I guess," Seph said with a smile, "I'd tell him about you."

"Really?" Kate seemed surprised, turning to face Seph.

"Yeah," Seph replied, her grin growing wider. She laughed when she noticed how Kate smiled at the sound. She guessed it had been a while since she had laughed out loud and certainly not since Kate had returned. She understood the glimmer of joy in Kate's eyes. She felt it in herself, somewhere deep, like a light being switched on in a dark room.

"And what do you think he'd say about us?"

"You mean our situation? How we met, and where we are now?"

"Yeah, I guess. I mean, not everyone is going to be happy about it."

Seph hesitated before answering. She couldn't help but think about Fiona. After talking to Kate last night, she decided she would leave it a few days before taking the first steps in contacting her friend. She knew her situation was triggering for her, but she didn't want to lose her friendship over it. She hoped after a few days to cool off, she would be willing to talk.

"I think he would be angry. But through worry, you know. But I think after his initial concern, he would come round to it and ask about you."

"He would worry?"

"Yeah. I mean, just because he always overreacted. Sometimes, if it's wasn't the path he would choose for us, he would get annoyed. He worked hard to give us everything we could ask for, you know. It's not that he was a snob, just that he didn't always understand why someone would take the harder path if they didn't have to. But that's where he and Mum worked so well together. He would be impassioned and emotional, and she would bring him back down to earth. But once he got over it, he would like you, I think."

"You think?" Kate raised her eyebrows, an almost comical look on her face. "Well, that is high praise."

"No, he would." Seph shoulder bumped Kate, causing them to sway on the bench, another laugh passing her lips. "He had time for everyone; he was just that kind of person that he needed to see you were serious and dedicated to whatever it was you wanted. You needed to prove your worth, but it wasn't some arduous rite of passage. Just a conversation, get a feel for you, and you'd soon win him over. And I think he was more wary once Helena and Jonathan split. They were perfect for each other, and Dad saw him as a son, so when they split, it was a shock. And even though no one was at fault, he still went through a period when he thought he'd been fooled by him. It took months before Helena convinced him otherwise. And after that, he was a little more protective of us both."

"I get that," Kate said, sliding her hand into Seph's.

"What's your Dad like?" Seph asked. They had had conversations about Kate's family before, but nothing too deep into their relationships with each other. Now she wanted to know more, her brain finally feeling like it had more space to add more details.

"Dad is," Kate paused to think, "Dad is like a big child. He's sixty-nine and going through some regression where he insists on spending his money on all these new things which he's seen and has no purpose for. But he's always had that childish streak, you know. Never really took himself too seriously. But both Mum and Dad are like that. They've been through enough in their lives to not take it for granted. If they'd listened to everyone around them, they wouldn't be together."

"What do you mean?"

"Oh, both Dad and Mum were engaged to other people when they met. People who their families were very happy with, apparently. But then Mum got a job at Dad's law firm as a secretary, and as they tell it, it was love at first sight. Neither was particularly unhappy in their relationships; it was just that they found something which was more real for them. When they told people, it upset quite a lot of the family. It was still a time when they were expected to act a certain way, there were reputations to think of and status within the environment they existed. But they ignored it all to be together."

"That's beautiful. And I'm glad they didn't listen to everyone and followed what they wanted. I mean, if they hadn't, there wouldn't be you." Seph wrapped her arm around Kate's and gave it a squeeze.

"I see them, and it makes me happy. That's what I want. A relationship to grow old together in, you know. Through the thick and thin of it. I see them, and it gives me hope for us when the shit hits the fan, and we have people no doubt passing comment on us."

Seph swallowed back a lump in her throat at the revelation that Kate saw their relationship as something akin to her parents' relationship. To know she held her—them—in such high esteem, had such grand plans and saw such longevity in their union, made her heart sing.

"I think that's a beautiful thing to aim for."

CHAPTER EIGHTEEN

Kate watched the steady rise and fall of Seph's chest as she lay sleeping beside her. This had become something of a habit of late, Kate always waking before Seph, who, much to her relief, had experienced a much-needed improvement in her own sleep pattern. So as Seph slept that final hour or so, Kate would stay in bed, lying beside the woman she loved and so very nearly lost, cherishing the time with her. Something about the peace and solitude of first thing in the morning, the fact that the weather was slowly starting to inch its way into springtime, and the relaxed expression on Seph's face, made her own stresses and worries ebb into nothing.

The past month had been difficult for both of them. Tim was making life as hard as possible for Kate, refusing to sell the house and move forward with the divorce. It was the only way he had any power over the situation, and while Kate understood his reasoning to some degree, she wished that he would just give in and stop being so proud. Meg, after a very short period of tentative understanding, had reverted back to practically hating her, begging her on a daily basis to return home, something Tim wasn't afraid to throw into every discussion they had. She suspected the change in Meg's attitude towards her was more to do with Tim laying on the blame thick and playing the hurt party. Cam was more understanding but was still hurt and confused by the changes in his life. She understood that, and for every angry message she got from Meg, she got a supportive one from Cam. She suspected that Meg was venting at Cam as well and could only imagine the rows they would be having. They had always been polar opposites in that respect; Meg was hot, fiery and emotional, and Cam was cool, logical and more considerate. Just like their parents.

Just three evenings ago, Meg and Cam had both come round for another dinner at Sarah's house Kate had considered telling them that she was seeing someone, sparing them some of the details but hoping that the information would help them move past the impasse they seemed to have found themselves at. But as Kate had listened as Meg threw hurtful words her way, clearly delivered from Tim via their daughter, she changed her mind. Cam had tried his hardest to defend Kate, but Meg was adamant that Kate was tearing their family apart and not giving her father the chance he deserved. She was right on one count, Kate would admit, but as long as Tim was playing the devastated husband to their youngest child, she wasn't going to be able to win that fight. And Meg clearly wasn't in the right frame of mind to hear that her mother had begun to move on. So she had quickly retracted the idea, instead shielding herself from more vitriol from her daughter.

Her respite from all the arguments and stress, however, was lying right in front of her now. She was finally seeing a return of the Seph she knew before. It started that day she finally went to see her father's grave, finally dealing with and accepting her grief head-on. Once they returned home, there were more tears as Kate encouraged her to remember her father, but the sadness at losing him was balanced by the stories she told and memories she had of him when he was alive.

Slowly, over the past month, mentions of him were becoming more frequent and with less grief attached. It wasn't a linear process; some days, she could see the sadness in Seph's eyes when she spoke about him, or something triggered a memory of him, but overall, she was finally on the path to accepting his death.

With that came an improvement in her mental health. Her body didn't seem so wound up, her shoulders not as tense. The way she spoke was more free-flowing, and her eyes were starting to brighten a little bit. And now, the signs of affection Kate had so easily fallen for when they first met—the soft touches, the chaste kisses, the gentle looks, and tiny knowing smiles—were more the rule than the exception. Kate relished the feel of Seph coming up behind her and wrapping her arms around her when she was busy in the kitchen. Or how she lay in between her legs while they watched television, hands stroking up and down her thighs. Just yesterday morning, when Kate walked into the bathroom while Seph was brushing her teeth, she had surprised her with a kiss, mouth still full of toothpaste, and chuckled mischievously when Kate screwed her face up at the sensation. And then, last night before she went to sleep, she kissed her, long and slow and lingering, before burying herself in Kate's embrace. Seph had always treated her as if she was something precious, and Kate never truly felt deserving of the love she gave. Maybe she wasn't. Someone worthy of that love wouldn't have hurt Seph as Kate had. But Kate had been given another chance to prove herself, and she wasn't going to waste it.

Seph's eyes flickered behind her eyelids before they opened wearily, blinking a few times to bring the room into focus. A smile spread across her face as she registered Kate beside her.

"Morning," Seph said, her voice still croaky from sleep, hair mussed in an adorable fashion. It had grown longer in the past few weeks, as Seph focused on getting her mental health back in a good place, but Kate had come in from work one evening last week to be told Seph had booked a hair appointment for this weekend. It may have been a small, simple piece of information, but to Kate, it was another sign that Seph was returning to a better place.

"Morning baby," Kate replied as she leant in and pressed a soft kiss to her lips. Seph hummed in response, lingering slightly before she pulled away. "Did you sleep well?"

"Like a baby," Seph mumbled, and Kate had to agree. The nights of constant tossing and turning, of bad dreams and crying out, were, for the most part, gone. Instead, Seph now slept soundly and was looking all the better for it. "How long have you been awake?"

"Don't know. Not long, though."

"Why didn't you wake me?"

"You looked too peaceful."

Seph smiled again, her eyes full of love and adoration as she looked at Kate. She shuffled closer, burying her hands underneath her pillow to raise her head slightly. Instinctively, Kate's hand wrapped around her hip, pulling her into her.

"What were you thinking about?" Seph asked as Kate stroked her fingers across the sliver of bare skin she found between her t-shirt and her pyjama bottoms.

"Nothing," Kate replied, grinning when she felt the goosebumps erupt across Seph's skin as she brushed over a sensitive spot.

"Nothing at all?"

"Well, not nothing. But nothing important. Not really."

"You're really making sense, you know that?" Seph retorted as she let her eyes flutter shut. "I can see why you're such a highly sought-after lawyer with those skills."

"Funny." Kate tickled her in retaliation, and Seph let out a squeak. "Okay, if you want to know, I was thinking about you. About how much better you are looking, how well you're doing," Kate leant in close, pressing a kiss to Seph's lips. "How proud I am of you."

Seph dipped her head, but not quickly enough for Kate not to notice the subtle blush which swept across her cheeks. She'd forgotten how cute she was when she got embarrassed.

"I wouldn't have been able to do it without you, you know."

"Oh, I don't know," Kate said, a wave of guilt rolling through her and ruining her elation. She really wasn't prepared to take any of the credit for this. Realising her smile had dropped, she quickly fixed it back in place so as to not give Seph any idea that something was bothering her.

"Kate, what is it?"

Kate cursed inwardly at the fact she obviously hadn't done a good enough job of hiding her true emotions.

"Nothing. I'm fine." Her voice wavered. Seph's face creased at the sound of tears in Kate's voice, her eyes immediately dropping and becoming full of concern. Her hand came up, wrapping around Kate's fingers, which rested against her face.

"Kate..."

Kate shook her head slightly and swallowed back her tears, angry that now was the time they decided to make themselves so blatantly apparent.

"Kate, what is it? Tell me, maybe I can help..."

Kate let out a laugh between her tears at the offer, but not because she didn't want Seph's help. But because she really couldn't accept it in this case.

"God, I don't deserve you."

"What do you mean?" Seph asked as she ducked her head, trying to catch Kate's eyes. If Kate looked into those beautiful blue eyes now, she would fall apart.

"After everything, *you're* the one asking me what's wrong? How *you* can help?"

"It's what we do, right? You'd do the same for me. You *do* do the same for me."

"It's hardly the same when it's my fault in the first place, though, is it?" Kate pulled away from Seph, no longer feeling worthy of being able to touch her, to be so close to her.

"Your fault? What's your fault..." Seph's question petered out as she clearly realised what Kate was referring to.

Kate watched as Seph pushed herself up, shoving her pillow behind her and punching it gently a couple of times to make it comfortable before settling back down onto it. She let out a long sigh before speaking. "Okay, let's talk about this."

"There's nothing to talk about. It's fine."

"That's my line, and you can't use it back on me," Seph joked as she gave Kate a soft smile. "Tell me what's wrong."

"I don't want to—"

"If you say you don't want to burden me, I swear to God... Kate, this is a partnership. You cannot be the one to listen all the time. We need to be equal in this, and that means you being open and honest with me too."

"I am," Kate exclaimed with a slight hint of panic in her voice. She didn't want Seph to think she would lie to her or keep things from her. But this? Was knowing this really going to make anything better? Wasn't this something she just had to keep to herself? She couldn't lay her own guilt on Seph's shoulders, especially not now when she was just starting to get back on her feet.

"No, you're not." Kate felt Seph take hold of her hands where they lay on top of the duvet, running her thumb over her knuckles. "Not about this anyway. I know you're worried and you're blaming yourself, but please, don't. This is not your fault."

"But if it wasn't for me—"

"No. No, you're not doing this."

"But—"

"No buts. This is not your fault. This, my depression, was here a long time before you and will remain for a long time yet. You are not to blame."

"But it wouldn't have been so bad if I hadn't—" Kate tried to argue back.

"You don't know that. Even if things had been different with us, things would still have happened. Dad would still have died, and I would still have grieved for him."

"But I could have been there. I *should* have been there. I hate the thought that you struggled and I wasn't here for you," Kate blurted, the tears finally falling down her face. Her chest ached at the release of what she had been feeling for the past month, ever since that night when Seph had uttered those words which shattered her heart. She pulled back from Seph's hold, uncomfortable in the loving touch of her girlfriend.

Something on Seph's face changed. Her expression dropped into something even softer, if that was at all possible.

"Kate, it wasn't your fault, babe."

"You were on your own because of me. Because I was weak." Kate was raising her voice. But it wasn't in anger at Seph. It was in anger at herself and her cowardly actions.

"Kate." Seph reached out to take her hand again, but Kate couldn't bear to receive her sympathy. She pulled back and climbed out of bed.

"You don't understand, Seph! I was there, at the end of your street, every day for nearly a month afterwards. Arguing with myself about what was the right thing to do. Every single fibre of my being wanted to come back here, to you, but I was too much of a coward to do it. And now I know that you were dealing with all that grief alone, and I was literally at the end of your street, and I did nothing!"

The veracity and meaning behind her words stunned Seph into momentary silence.

"You came back..." Seph uttered with wide eyes.

"Every day. But I would convince myself I was being selfish. That you were still better off without me. When the truth was, I was still too weak to admit this was the life I wanted. I was too scared of the possibility of a few disapproving looks and instead chose a life of privilege and ease over being with the person I loved more than anything. *You* deserve so much more than me."

"No, Kate—"

"I promised you I'd be there, and I broke that promise. It kills me to think you struggled. That I let you down when you needed me the most." Her voice wavered again, but she swallowed it down. The anger she had been feeling at herself and her actions were finally starting to seep through, and she wasn't sure how much longer she could keep it contained.

"Hey, hey, it's okay." Seph crawled across the bed, stopping in front of where Kate stood.

"No, it's not! I'm a coward, and I hurt you. How can you trust me again?"

Seph brought her hand to her face, gently rubbing her thumb across her cheekbone, before resting her forehead against Kate's.

"Because you *did* come back. Because you're here now, and you took that risk. And because I love you. Was it hard without you? Yes. But I got through it, and now I have you to help me through the rest." Seph leant forward, kissing Kate. "And you have me. And we'll get through this together. But I don't want this hanging over us, Kate. I don't want to think you are here out of some obligation to me and my health. I want you to be here because you want to be."

"I do! I want to be here more than anywhere. I just feel so guilty about leaving you."

"Then for it to be a fresh start for us, we *both* need to move on from what happened before. Otherwise, this will never work."

"I *need* this to work," Kate pleaded, honesty seeping through every word, "Because I feel so lost without you. I never knew I had anything missing before. I thought I had what I wanted from life, that I was happy. But you, you showed me what it felt like to be truly loved, and I can't live without that now. I've had this huge hole in my life, in my heart, for the past few months, and that's because I didn't have you, Seph. You make me feel complete."

"Then this, this moment right here, is where it starts again. Everything out in the open, no secrets. Just me and you against the shitty world and everything it's got to throw at us, right?"

"Yeah." Kate let out a chuckle at Seph's comment, looking up to see eyes glistening with tears but shining with love and happiness. "Yeah, this is it, baby."

Chapter Nineteen

S eph spotted her sister and waved her over to the table, smiling as she sat down opposite her.

"Hey. Your hair looks great!" Helena greeted her.

"Thanks. I thought it was about time I got it sorted," Seph replied, running her fingers through her freshly styled waves. She'd kept it a little longer than usual, a fresh scarlet red dye popping against the dark brown of her undercut. For the first time in forever, she felt like she could honestly say she was feeling herself.

"Yeah. In fact, you're looking really well. Have you put some weight back on?"

"A little, I think. But you only saw me on Wednesday," she said, chuckling. "I've not changed that much since then."

"I know, but you look better just for making an effort." Helena grimaced at how that sounded. "I mean—"

"I know what you mean. It's fine," Seph chuckled, although Helena had a point. Despite moving on from wearing pyjamas all day, she hadn't exactly made much of an effort the past few weeks. She was surprised Kate hadn't gotten sick of the sight of her dressing gown and burnt it.

"So what's the plan for the rest of the day? You're not going to spend all that time and money on your hair to go back home and change into your sweats, are you? Oh!" Helena exclaimed, looking up from the menu. "Why don't you come over tonight? We could get a takeaway and watch a movie or something. The kids are at Jonathan's, so I'm on my own."

"Oh, umm..." Helena looked so excited at the prospect of a night in with her sister, but Seph had something else planned. It wasn't even a thing earlier in the day, but after their heart-to-heart in bed this morning, Seph had had an idea and was excited to see it through. "I can't. I've kind of already got something on. Sorry."

"Oh, no worries. What are you doing? Seeing Fi?"

Seph swallowed down the anger at the mention of her supposed best friend's name. After radio silence for nearly a week after their argument, Seph had built up the nerve to text her. In fact, Seph had texted her more than once, each one ignored. After another week, she decided that if Fi didn't want to talk to her, Seph couldn't do anything about that. And if she was honest, thinking about her best friend and how she was ghosting her wasn't going to help her state of mind.

"No," Seph said, looking down intently at her own menu and hoping that Helena would drop this soon. But why would she? It wasn't like she'd given her an answer.

"Seph..."

"Yep."

"Have you got a date?"

Seph laughed. "When have I had time to date? Like you said, I've barely been out of my sweats for a month."

"Yeah." Helena didn't sound convinced. "It's just that you've had your hair done, and you've got secret plans tonight..."

"They're not secret plans. And I got my hair done because it needed doing, and it makes me feel good."

"Right, so if they're not secret plans, then why not tell me about them?" Seph ignored the pointed tone in Helena's voice. "Seph?"

"I'm kind of seeing someone." *There*, thought Seph, *it's out in the open.* It wasn't her plan to tell Helena today, but then she wasn't sure when she was planning on telling her. Or how. Maybe it was the universe giving her a helping hand.

"How..." Helena looked confused, and in fairness, rightly so. "Hang on, so is this a new thing? If that's the case, I have a lot of concerns. Or an older thing?"

"Kind of an older thing. I knew her before, so you don't need to worry about them taking advantage. They know the non-depressed anxiety riddled me."

"Good. That's good," Helena said cautiously, "but I'm still confused. When did this happen?"

"We met over a year ago. You remember that conference I went to in Manchester? I met her there."

"Okay, so, you were friends first?"

"No, not really. We were together for a bit last year, but things were complicated, and we split up. But then we met again, and things... Well, things had changed."

"Why do I feel like you're not telling me something? You're being very cagey about it all, and that's not you. Usually, you can't wait to tell me about whoever you're seeing. Was she seeing someone else?" Helena scrutinised Seph, and she wilted under her gaze. Helena obviously got her answer from the expression on Seph's face. "Seph...really? Why can't you find a nice unattached, uncomplicated woman? You'll be telling me she's straight next." Seph scrunched her face up. "Of course she's straight. Because anything else would be too easy."

"She's not straight. Just so happens that the last relationship she was in was with a man. And that it was for a while, so people just assume she's straight."

Seph was oddly proud of her use of semantics, but she knew it wasn't going to last. She also felt for Kate's frustration that people assumed Kate was straight because she had been married to Tim for so long.

"How long?"

"Huh?"

"How long has she been with this bloke?"

"Erm, twenty years-ish," Seph mumbled quietly.

"Twenty years?" Helena exclaimed. Her face dropped, and Seph saw the exact moment that Helena realised what was going on. "Oh, God. She's married, isn't she? For fuck's sake, Seph, what are you thinking?"

"Shh, keep your voice down," Seph urged her sister, not particularly wanting the world to know her business.

"Oh, I don't believe this." Helena sat back in her chair, staring Seph down. "This is not what you need to be getting yourself involved in right now, Seph."

"It's not what you think."

Helena leant forward and hissed in an angry whisper, "I think you're seeing a married woman. Is she married?"

"Yes, but—"

"Then it's exactly what I think."

"She's left her husband."

Helena was stunned into a momentary silence. "For you?"

"Yes. And you don't have to sound so shocked by the idea," Seph retorted.

"Sorry. Sorry, it's not that. It's just...these things rarely work out, do they? I wasn't expecting you to say it, that's all." She shook her head as if to shake herself back into the right state of mind. "Sorry. I just assumed the worst. Surely you can't blame me with everything recently?"

Seph sighed and conceded. "Yeah, I know. But honestly, if it wasn't for her, I'm not sure where I'd be right now."

"What do you mean?"

"She was at that work party I went to about a month ago. Turns out, in a really shitty turn of events, her husband is one of the partners at my new firm." Seph held up a hand, stopping Helena's comment before it left her mouth. "I know, but I didn't know at the time. Anyway, she saw right through me. Knew there was something wrong straight away. I could never hide anything from her. Right from the beginning, she got me and saw through everything I put up to face the world. The day after the party, she turned up on my doorstep."

"To ask for another chance?"

"Yeah."

"And you gave it to her?"

"Not straight away. I didn't just roll over and let her walk back in. I told her she needed to make a choice. That if she was really serious about giving us another shot, she needed to show it." The information about Seph's ultimatum seemed to release some of the tension she could see in Helena's shoulders. "But honestly, she's not pressured me into anything. Once she saw just how bad I was, she pushed it to the side. She just wanted to make sure I was okay. She...she took me to see Dad."

"You'd not been?" Helena asked, seeming surprised.

"No. I'd been avoiding it, not knowing how I'd be, what I would do. I'd been so focused on making sure that Mum didn't have anything to worry about, about sorting out all the legal stuff, I'd avoided grieving for him properly." Seph picked awkwardly at the napkin on the table, not looking at Helena.

Helena shifted her chair around so she was sitting next to Seph, picking up her hand and holding it in her own. The last time Helena had held her hand was at their father's funeral, but at that time, it had been a desperate tether to a sister for support, whereas this time, it was soft and gentle, an understanding embrace as she opened herself up to listening to Seph.

"How do you feel since going?"

"Better. I think it's what I needed. I hadn't realised how much I had been holding on to by not going."

"I'm glad you went. And I'm glad you went with someone."

"Yeah," Seph took a deep breath. "Kate's been great, and I know that this relationship isn't what everyone would want for me, but she's good for me. I know I should have said something before, but honestly, I just needed some time. To get used to her being there, to get my head straight. And to be honest, I was scared about telling you."

"Scared?" Helena asked.

"Yeah." Seph sighed. "I told Fi, and she went completely crazy. I guess I was just worried you'd do the same."

Helena nodded slowly, taking a moment before she spoke again; Seph guessed she was trying to take everything in and think about what she wanted to say next.

"You want my opinion?"

"Depends what it is..."

"This Kate, from what you've said, saw that something was wrong before any of us who see you more often. She's stuck around, been there for the last four weeks while you've been trying to get better. She's left her husband of twenty years, a life which is probably pretty comfortable and safe, to most likely be the subject of someone's gossip. And she's done all of that for you. Sounds like she's serious about doing this right. That being said...I reserve the right as your big sister to be wary."

"Wouldn't expect anything else from you."

CHAPTER TWENTY

S eph lit the last candle, placing it down on the mantelpiece, before taking a final glance around the room. After their heart to heart this morning, Seph felt they really had started a fresh page in their relationship. There was something about Kate's admission and her own strength at the situation, coupled with a general, overwhelming feeling of lightness she hadn't experienced in months, which made her feel more settled than she had done in a long time. And to officially mark the beginning of their fresh start, Seph had decided to do something for Kate.

After meeting Helena for lunch, she picked up a few things to make dinner, determined to do more of the things a couple would normally do in the first few weeks. Yes, they'd been here before; Seph would often make romantic dinners at her house for Kate when they were seeing each other the first time, especially considering they couldn't exactly go out anywhere, but this time was different. Besides, Seph had enjoyed cooking something other than pasta and toast, which was all she had really managed to do the past few weeks. She was fairly certain that Kate would appreciate and enjoy it, the meal being one she had cooked before.

It was fairly simple—garlic and rosemary roasted spatchcock chicken with glazed root vegetables, followed by a rich chocolate mousse—but last time she'd made it... Well, Kate thanked her in ways that left her aching for days. Her skin flushed at the memory, a familiar but long-forgotten heat pulsing through her body. It surprised her a little. It was the first time in months she had even considered anything remotely sexual, her mind killing any desire dead five months ago. The last time she and Kate slept together, it hadn't exactly ended with a happy memory. But determined to stick to her side of the pledge the two women had made this morning and not wanting to cast a dark cloud over her evening, Seph shook it off, reminding herself that tonight, Kate wasn't going to leave. Instead, she was going to climb into bed next to her, and they would fall asleep in each other's arms again.

She wandered into the kitchen, making sure everything was ready for when Kate arrived so she didn't have to spend too long apart from her when she did. Asking Alexa to play a romantic playlist, the dulcet tones of Alicia Keys filled the house, finishing the perfect setting. Well, almost perfect. She just needed Kate here, and then she would be fully content.

It was only a couple of minutes later when her wish was answered, Kate's arrival announced by warm arms which wrapped around her waist from behind, along with a gentle kiss to her neck. Seph smiled, the sensation of it only fanning those flames which had ignited earlier.

"Welcome back."

"What's going on? It looks very romantic here. And something smells amazing."

"I thought it was about time we had a proper date night. So I cooked dinner, and I thought we could spend the evening together."

"We spend nearly every evening together," Kate countered.

Seph spun in her arms, finding herself pinned between Kate's body and the counter. The feel of her in such close proximity, looking almost ethereal in the soft light of the candles, made her heart race.

"I thought it was about time we did things properly. A little romantic dinner never hurt anybody, right?"

"Absolutely not. And definitely not with you looking like this." Kate ran her fingers over Seph's freshly shaved undercut. "I love your hair. You look amazing."

"Thank you." She had to admit she felt good as well. Something about having her hair cut and the idea of making dinner for Kate had made her want to dress for her as well. It had been a long time since she had spent so much time and effort on her appearance, but Seph felt almost reformed by it.

"I feel very underdressed, though," Kate admitted, her eyes shining.

"You look gorgeous," Seph reassured her. She may have only been wearing skinny jeans and a loose v-necked t-shirt under a military-style jacket, but Seph thought Kate looked beautiful all the time. Casual Kate was one of her favourites. "But if you want to freshen up, dinner won't be ready for another twenty minutes."

"Perfect." Kate stroked her thumb over Seph's cheek and down, catching on her bottom lip in a move that was beyond sensual. Seph swallowed, feeling her pulse thunder. She kissed Kate's thumb, bringing herself back under control.

"Go on then. I'll see you in a minute," she said, her voice husky as she sent Kate away.

"Mmm, that was delicious. Thank you, baby," Kate said as she licked her lips and put down her knife and fork.

"You're welcome. I'm glad you enjoyed it," Seph replied, smiling at her from across the table.

"I did. Although I'm stuffed, I can't remember the last time I ate so well."

"Aw, that's a shame. Guess you won't be wanting the chocolate mousse I made as well then?" Seph teased, her eyes turning from soft to playful in a matter of seconds.

"Well, if you've taken the time and effort to make it, it would be rude not to. Although, how about we have dessert on the sofa? So we can relax together?"

"Sounds perfect. Go make yourself comfortable. I'll go get it."

Kate wandered into the living room, taking their wine glasses with her and leaving them on the coffee table, before collapsing onto the sofa, swinging her legs around so she could watch Seph in the kitchen. Within seconds Seph joined her, carrying the half-empty bottle of wine they were sharing in one hand and balancing two small glass bowls in the other. She reached out to relieve Seph of one of the bowls, waiting until Seph had sat down before settling back.

Spooning a mouthful of chocolate mousse into her mouth, she hummed when the flavour hit her taste buds, eyes fluttering closed at the richness which coated her tongue.

"Oh, wow," she said, almost moaning, "that's amazing."

"Glad you like it," Seph replied.

Kate opened her eyes and saw Seph watching her, a mischievous, almost sexy smirk on her face. Taking a mouthful of her own dessert, she licked the back of the spoon clean, the action igniting a desire deep within. She smiled back, trying not to focus on the arousal which had started pulsing through her body, instead appreciating the cheeky glint which was in Seph's eye, realising it was something else she had missed recently. She was grateful to see it return. Any other time she would say that Seph had planned this evening, right down to the chocolate mousse, with a particular end in mind, but despite the re-emergence of the affection in their relationship, she still wasn't going to assume anything further. Seph was still healing, and any advance to the next level of their relationship would have to be on her terms. Still, she couldn't help but remember when Seph had made this chocolate mousse for her last time. Or how she had licked it off her gorgeous body... A heat flashed through her at the memory. Before she could get carried away, she tried to force the image from her head.

"What are you thinking about?" Seph asked, a knowing look on her face.

"Nothing," Kate replied hastily, clearly having failed in her attempts at hiding her thoughts.

"Mmhmm, sure. Then why are you blushing?" Seph retorted, licking her lips in an altogether too-alluring manner.

"Just...reminiscing." Kate shrugged, focusing on her dessert again.

"About anything in particular?"

"Oh...I reminisce about lots of things. All the happy memories I have of us, and how I can't wait to make more of them."

"Yeah?" Seph seemed surprised. Why, Kate didn't know. The memories of their time together, however fleeting, got her through the lonely nights when she was apart from Seph. "Like what?"

"Like, the first night we met and had drinks in the hotel bar. The time you surprised me with a candlelit dinner when I'd had that horrific day with that total arsehole of an opponent in court. The afternoons we spent in the garden in the summer, just lounging about in the sun. The first time we slept together—"

"Oh yeah?" Seph quirked an eyebrow, another smirk gracing her features. "What about it?"

"Not like that! Well, not completely." Kate smirked in return. She couldn't deny the effect the memory had on her. "Just how you made me feel so special. Apart from the truly amazing sex, it was the first time in a long time anyone had made me feel wanted."

"I was so fucking nervous, I'm surprised you felt anything past my raging anxiety," Seph said, taking another spoonful of dessert.

"Why were you so nervous? You were never really nervous around me up to that point. But that day, I do remember. You were so hesitant..."

Nerves fluttered in Kate's stomach as they stumbled into Seph's bedroom. This was the furthest they had reached so far, and although she wasn't doubting where this was going, she couldn't help the anxious excitement which coursed through her. She focused on the soft feel of Seph's lips against hers, their kisses passionate and slow, but within them, she also sensed Seph's hesitation.

"Are you okay?" she asked, reluctantly breaking their kiss.

"Yes. I just...are you okay?"

As if to reassure her, she gently placed her hands on top of Seph's, where they rested on her hips, and guided them up slightly, pushing up the hem of her top to brush across warm skin. Seph's breath hitched at the first touch. Kate could feel the tremble in her fingers against her, and she moved her own hand across to her waist, teasing the fabric of her own t-shirt, tracing her fingers across her stomach. The act must have buoyed Seph's confidence as she pushed her shirt further up, urging it over her head. As Kate discarded it to the floor, Seph's hands stroked their way over her shoulders and down her chest down to her breasts, catching the top of her bra. Kate watched as Seph's hands moved across her body, her touch gentle and delicate, mapping every curve of her. Seph brought her eyes back up to Kate's, bringing her in for another slow kiss, her fingers tracing around her sides and down her spine as their tongues danced against each other. She felt Seph's hands on her hips, urging her gently to sit back on the bed behind them.

The temporary distance between them was too much, and Kate pulled on Seph's waist, moving her to stand in between her legs, pushing up her t-shirt to expose her stomach. She leant forward, placing gentle, soft kisses across it, smiling as goosebumps peppered her skin. Seph's fingers wound into her hair, holding her close, a soft moan falling from her, and Kate lost herself in the taste and feel of her skin against her mouth. God, she was overwhelming every one of her senses, and she couldn't get enough, each kiss only serving to make her want more. She needed to see her, kiss and explore every inch of her. Urging her to remove her t-shirt, Kate took in her body, her hands running over the soft skin which was exposed. Scattered across her sides, moving towards her hips, were the raised scars of slash marks. None looked fresh, but they were still standing out against her skin as if her body hadn't fully accepted them yet. Looking up, she found Seph staring up at the ceiling, her eyes closed and her breath held as she felt Kate's thumb run over the one which marked her left hip bone.

"You're so beautiful," she whispered.

A silent tear escaped Seph's eyes, rolling down her cheek. Kate could understand, for the most part. They must remind her constantly of a part of her life she would rather forget. For Kate's part, the need to show Seph how much she cared had only been heightened by this unspoken revelation that, at some point, she had been so desperate, so lonely, that she had felt there was no other option than to make the marks which now permanently adorned her body. She pushed back on the bed, gently tugging on Seph's hand.

"Come here."

Seph climbed onto the bed, laying down alongside Kate. She ran her fingers down her neck, across her chest, and down her stomach, smiling slightly at the gasp it caused. She traced them back up, watching as Seph's eyes fluttered shut with the delicacy against her skin, coming round to stroke her cheek. Her fingertips noted the damp tear track from seconds earlier, and as she looked again, she could see more resting on her eyelids.

"Are you okay? Do you want to stop?" she asked, brushing away the tear which was threatening to fall with the pad of her thumb.

"No," Seph whispered, the emotion in her voice overwhelming, even in that one word.

Kate leaned forward, taking her lips in a soft kiss. As their lips moved together, Kate slid her hips forward, her leg coming to rest in between Seph's, her fingers tracing from her face down across her chest. Seph's hands wound around Kate's waist, pulling her closer, confirming silently that she did indeed want this. Kate pushed her back gently, coming to lay on top of her, her thigh pushing in between Seph's legs a little firmer than before as she peppered her body with gentle, butterfly kisses. Seph's breathing rapidly increased with each soft touch of her lips against her skin., and when she pulled her bra down and enveloped her nipple in her mouth, Seph gasped and arched into her.

She felt Seph's hands roam down her spine before sliding into the back of her trousers, cupping her backside and pulling her closer, the friction between them causing her to moan. Her arousal spiked again, and the clothes between them suddenly felt like a brick barrier between her and truly being with Seph. Pushing off Seph, she pulled at her trousers, sliding them off her legs, never taking her eyes off her while she unbuttoned and let her own trousers drop to the floor. Climbing back onto the bed over Seph, Kate cupped her cheek, taking her lips in another gentle kiss.

The feel of Seph's hand cupping her over her underwear startled Kate, and she had to pull away from her lips, her mouth dropping open as Seph's fingers stroked her through the lace, knowing that they were soaked with her arousal. Her breath came out as shallow, open-mouthed pants, desperately needing more than the teasing strokes Seph was giving her. She rocked her hips into Seph's hand, chasing the more solid feel of Seph's touch.

"Seph, please..." she begged.

In one fluid movement, Seph had rolled them both over, Kate now staring up into her eyes, their colour darker and stormier than usual. She watched as they tracked over her face, down her body, taking her in with a look of hunger that stole her breath away.

"You are so gorgeous," Seph murmured, still taking in her features.

Grasping her face in her hands, Kate brought Seph towards her for a searing kiss, full of desperation and want for the woman braced above her. Seph, seemingly understanding the silent plea, returned her hand to where it was before they rolled over, only this time Kate gasped as she felt her touch slip through her arousal, shivering as fingers teased around her clit.

"Okay?" Seph asked, dropping a gentle kiss on her cheek.

"Yes. Don't stop."

Seph carried on, her fingers moving with long, slow strokes against Kate. With each moan of pleasure, Seph seemed to get a little braver, pushing a little harder, a little faster.

"Oh God, Seph."

Kate's hips chased the movement of her fingers, her own fingers curling into the sheets below her. She felt Seph shift, sliding her leg in between her own, and the pressure in between her legs increased, serving to intensify her arousal. Seph dipped her head, kissing the pulse point in her neck, Kate fully aware of just how fast it was beating. Kate could feel the extent of Seph's arousal, her wetness against her thigh, the sensation turning her on even more. She slid her hand round Seph's thigh and in between her legs, trying to feel her more intimately, before warm fingers curled round it and pulled it away, pinning it to the mattress.

"Seph..." she whined, desperate to touch the woman above her and missing the fingers where they were before.

"Soon," Seph breathed in her ear, quickly replacing her hand between Kate's legs.

Kate's eyes fluttered shut at the return of her touch, unable to argue any further. After a few more exploratory strokes, Seph found a spot which caused Kate's body to tense underneath her.

"Shit, Seph. Oh, that feels..." Kate didn't know how to describe what it felt like, only knowing that she needed more of it. Seph responded by rocking her hips into her, the action giving her more of the pressure she desperately craved.

"Seph, more, please..." Kate begged.

Seph groaned at the request, quickly obliging by sliding two fingers inside Kate, causing Kate to curl her fingers into the flesh of her shoulders and release a deep moan. The introduction of her fingers combined with the sensation of her thumb rubbing against her was the perfect combination, and Kate could feel herself tighten around her, her groans becoming louder and faster with each thrust.

Kate's climax was intense, and through her own haze, she could feel Seph's arousal against her thigh. Kate arched into her as she ground her hips again, Seph urging every drop of pleasure from within her. Kate fell back against the bed, her chest rising and falling rapidly, as Seph kissed her gently, bringing her through her comedown. Her hand stroked across her forehead, tucking a stray hair behind her ears, her fingers lingering on her cheek as Kate opened her eyes.

"Hey," Seph said quietly, her fingertips dancing across Kate's jaw. "You okay?"

A smile crept across Kate's face as she opened her eyes, her look so intense it took Seph's breath away.

"That was...amazing. You," Kate rose up and dropped a kiss on her lips, "are amazing."

Seph laughed gently, her eyes fluttering closed as Kate brought her own hand up to cup her cheek, kissing her again. What started off slow quickly deepened, Kate clearly eager to repay the favour and do what Seph stopped her from doing earlier. Kate rolled them both over, gently sliding her leg in between Seph's. Seph moaned softly into her mouth.

"Oh my god, you're so wet. Can I take these off?" Kate's fingers brushed across the waistband of her briefs. "I need to feel all of you."

Kate's boldness caused another groan to escape Seph, and her hips lifted from the bed in a silent answer to her question. "Please..." she said breathlessly.

She felt the fabric being pulled slowly down her legs before Kate's fingers brushed back up, her hands mapping the curve of her calves, around past her knee and up her thigh. She felt a light kiss pressed against the skin of her thigh, where she knew *there was a scar, and her whole body tensed, rigid under Kate. Kate pushed herself up, Seph instantly missing her grounding weight on top of her as she screwed her eyes shut, cursing herself internally at her reflex.*

"Sorry, I didn't mean to..."

"No, no, it's okay. I just..." Seph struggled to form a sentence, to articulate what it was she had recoiled at. A warm palm on her cheek silenced her.

"Look at me."

She opened her eyes to find Kate staring down at her, her eyes soft with concern and apologies, contrasting with the blush which still coloured her cheeks from moments before.

"You are beautiful. And I want you, this, but only if you want it too. Do you want me to stop?"

"No. God, no. Just...not there. Please?" Seph asked, not willing to break the moment with the conversation they needed to have at some point.

"Anything. You just tell me what you want."

"Kiss me?"

Kate shifted so she was pinning her down with her hips, her body spanning the length of Seph's. The feel of so much skin touching Kate's skin made her gasp unexpectedly as a jolt of arousal went through her. Soft lips came to capture Seph's nipple, and she let out a whimper at the touch, making her forget any of the insecurities which had clouded her mind just a moment before. Kate's hand slid from where it was resting against Seph's hips, pushing gently in between their bodies. As Kate's fingers finally touched Seph, she momentarily held her breath before letting out a deep sigh, her face creased with pleasure. Kate rocked her hips, grinding herself into Seph's core, teasing out a soft moan, her fingers undoubtedly feeling the extent of Seph's arousal.

"God, you feel incredible..."

Kate's words sent a rush of arousal through Seph's body, a shaky exhale ghosting across her skin. Kate's fingers stroked again, measured in their movements, as her eyes studied her face. Another stroke and Seph's hips jumped of their own accord, fighting against the weight of Kate's body. Kate rolled her hips again, and Seph let out a sinfully deep moan. Kate dropped her head, her lips coming to rest on Seph's shoulder, trailing their way up her neck, each kiss timed perfectly with another stroke of her fingers. Seph could feel herself tremble beneath her, becoming wetter with each flick of Kate's fingers, and after another guttural moan, her fingers slid deeper into Seph with ease.

"Oh, fuck." Kate breathed into the warm skin of Seph's chest. Seph opened her eyes at Kate's exclamation, seeing her completely entranced in the pleasure she was delivering to Seph, and as she moved, Seph could feel Kate's own arousal building again against her. One particularly skillful flick of her fingers had Seph's fingers curling into her hair, her hips chasing her touch.

"Oh God, Kate...I'm..."

Suddenly, after a final well-positioned thrust of her fingers, Seph's grip in her hair pulled tighter, her free hand bunching into the sheets below them as her body tensed, this time with undeniable passion and pleasure, arching into Kate, and she could feel herself release wave after wave of pleasure, as she screamed out Kate's name. Seph slumped, exhaling a long-held breath. Her body went limp in Kate's gentle hold, Kate's hand smoothing over Seph's cheek and grounding her with its soft pressure.

"Because," Kate waited patiently as Seph took a deep breath, gathering her thoughts, "It changed everything. Up until that point, I think we both had an out. It would hurt, and it would have been hard because we were both already emotionally in deep, but it seemed like it was cementing something between us. And after that, there was no going back for either of us. Well, not for me, anyway."

Kate leant forward, pressing a kiss to Seph's lips.

"It was absolutely the same for me, baby," she whispered before kissing her again. It was slow and lingering, unhurried as each savoured the sensation of their lips coming together. Kate's fingers moved from Seph's hips, coming up to brush the hair back from her face and tucking it behind her ear in such a gentle gesture, almost as if Seph was made of glass. A familiar burn was stoked deep inside her, the kiss only encouraging the arousal she felt from reminiscing earlier, but she tried desperately to ignore it, not wanting to push too hard too soon. But as she went to pull back, Seph leaned in further, deepening the kiss, this time firmer and more sure than any of the kisses they had shared in the past few weeks. She felt the familiar, sensual touch of Seph's tongue running across her lips, and she couldn't contain the soft moan that fell from her.

The moment was broken, however, when Seph let out a yawn.

"Oh shit, sorry," she offered, covering her mouth sheepishly.

"No need to apologise, baby. You've had a busy day. And I've loved tonight. But maybe now, I can take you upstairs, undress you, and fall asleep with you in my arms?"

"Sounds perfect, babe."

Chapter Twenty-One

Seph brushed the tip of her nose along the bare skin of Kate's back which showed from under her vest, kissing it before bringing it back down. Kate's skin became peppered with goosebumps at her breath ghosting over her, and she reached for the hand around her waist, interlacing their fingers and squeezing them.

"Hmm, I could get used to being woken up like this."

"It can be arranged," Seph replied with a small smile against the skin of her shoulder.

They lay there in silence for a minute, Seph's face still against Kate's back. As she breathed in, she could smell the scent of Kate's shampoo mixed with her own body wash she had started to use while staying. She closed her eyes, relishing the feel of just having Kate close to her, her arm subconsciously squeezing a little tighter around her waist. Kate, apparently feeling the subtle change in pressure, rolled over, releasing their hands as she came to face Seph, leaning in to give her a soft, lingering kiss.

"You okay?"

"Hmm, I just still can't quite believe you're here some days."

"I know. I used to imagine this, you know?" She spoke softly, fingers gently toying with the hair around Seph's ear.

"Hmm?" hummed Seph, enjoying the feeling of Kate's fingers brushing down to the nape of her neck and the way it ignited her senses.

"I hated leaving in the evenings. All I wanted to do was to go to bed with you, so I could wake up with you."

Seph opened her eyes again, surprised and overwhelmed by the adoration in Kate's gaze.

"Me too."

Seph kissed Kate again, long and slow, Kate's lips soft under hers, before pulling back, but not far, her breath still ghosting over Kate's face. She brushed her fingertips across her cheek, tucking her hair behind her ear, letting them trace their way down her neck and across her collarbone. Kate's breathing hitched at the lightness of her touch, barely even making contact yet enough to send goosebumps across her skin. Seph's mouth quirked into a quiet smile at the reaction. Her fingers moved back up and wound their way round Kate's neck, tangling through her hair, as she kissed her again, this time with more force and urgency. Kate moaned into the kiss, pulling Seph further into it from where her hands were resting on her hips. Her moan only encouraged Seph to kiss her deeper, this time the tip of her tongue darting across her lips in the smallest of teases.

"Seph..."

Something about the way Kate uttered her name when they were aroused and in bed together had always felt different, the want and desire behind it clear as day, the heat which it caused to rise through her body unparalleled by anyone before her. In response, she pulled her even closer and kissed her again, her tongue this time leaving no room for hesitation as it slipped past Kate's lips. While Kate was disarmed by the action, Seph rolled them over, Kate now pressed underneath her. Her kisses travelled from her mouth and across her neck, rendering Kate helpless to the onslaught, her tongue shooting out soft, small licks to tease her further. She let her fingers trail down Kate's body, stopping and reversing their direction when they reached the hem of her vest. They brushed gently up her side, sending more goosebumps shooting across Kate's skin, dragging the shirt with them in an attempt to reveal the soft, luscious skin she knew was underneath.

Kate released her grip from around Seph's hips, lifting herself up and allowing Seph to pull her vest over her head, exposing herself fully. As she did, Seph's hungry stare raked over her body, her lip between her teeth, as she took in the delectable slight curves. Not wanting to waste any more time, she dipped her head back down and returned her attention to Kate's neck, nipping at the skin over her pulse with her teeth while her hands explored Kate's naked chest. As her fingers brushed over an already sensitive nipple, Kate moaned, arching further into her touch.

"Seph..." Kate's voice was breathy and barely a whisper, and it sent shivers down Seph's neck where it landed.

In response, Seph sucked harder against Kate's collarbone. Kate involuntarily let out another low moan, her hand finding Seph's free one and linking their fingers together. Seph moved their joined hands above Kate's head, bracing herself on them as she shifted, kissing further down Kate's body and taking her hard nipple into her mouth. Sliding her leg in between Kate's, Seph's fingers continued to graze across her stomach as she rocked into Kate's body. Releasing her nipple from in between her lips, Seph pushed up to place a kiss on the soft flesh where her jaw met under her ear, a spot which she knew was particularly sensitive, followed by a slow lap of her tongue, and was rewarded with a low groan of appreciation.

"I've missed doing that," she whispered in Kate's ear.

She could feel Kate's breathing becoming faster beneath her. Her fingers continued their slow and torturous journey across her body, trailing circles round her now hard nipples.

"Oh, God," Kate said, her voice raspy as Seph's fingers teased her nipple, and her teeth nipped at her neck simultaneously.

Seph felt Kate pull at her t-shirt, breaking the attention she was lavishing on her neck to bring it over her head before Kate dragged her fingernails down her back in a move Seph suspected was meant to disarm her. She groaned at the sensation, even more so when she started to feel Kate rock her hips, clearly desperate to ease the ache she was feeling. Holding her in place by her hips as she ground her body into her, she started to give Kate what she needed. Kate's breathing was getting faster as she quickly spiralled towards her climax with the smallest and softest of touches. Seph's fingers slipped inside her underwear, slowly sliding up and feeling her, Kate grasping against her skin as she pulled at

Seph's hips even harder. Seph groaned, her own hips involuntarily bucking at the sudden change in pressure.

"Oh..." Kate breathed as Seph's fingers slowly started tracing circles with the same tenderness as across the rest of her body. Kate started to move her hips with more force, pushing into the motion of Seph's fingers, and Seph couldn't help her own moans as she rocked against her. Seph let her head drop by Kate's ear, her breath tickling across her shoulder as her fingers worked between Kate's legs.

"Seph, I..." Kate shakily whispered against her cheek, unable to finish her sentence.

Seph already knew what she needed. For all the heartache and pain, she had also missed feeling Kate in the most intimate way possible. She had spent hours mapping her body with her hands and mouth in their stolen moments together, learning where she was most sensitive, how her body reacted to her touch, what she needed and when. She knew that she had reached as far as she was going with her fingers where they were and that she needed something more. She slid her fingers further down, gently sinking into her, the action winning her a deep moan of satisfaction in her ear. Kate dug her fingers deeper into the soft flesh of Seph's hips as Seph built up a rhythm, her body coiling tighter and tighter at her touch. Suddenly Seph could feel her clench against her fingers, tight around her as she continued to thrust into her.

"Oh, Seph. I'm...I'm..."

Kate slammed her eyes shut and threw her head back, and the sight of her coming apart beneath her was enough to send waves of arousal through Seph. Kate grasped Seph's hair in her hand, pulling her in for another kiss. Seph swallowed her moans, thrusting her hand against her harder. She worked Kate through her orgasm, slowing as she felt her movements shift from jolts of pleasure to twitches of over-stimulation. Kate went limp underneath her, her body relaxing back into the bed beneath her. Her chest was heaving, and Seph could feel the sheen of sweat across her skin. Gently she pulled her fingers out from her underwear and laid down beside her, watching as Kate's body relaxed, her eyes still closed. After a moment, Kate rolled over, their faces barely apart from each other as she opened her eyes and kissed Seph, her fingers running through her hair, down her neck, and coming to rest on her chest. They lay there for a couple of minutes, their foreheads resting together, Seph's fingers tracing tiny circles across Kate's stomach, breathing each other's air.

"That's definitely better than I remember," Kate said with a sigh, her breathing still adjusting.

Seph chuckled softly. "Glad I lived up to expectations."

"Oh, you certainly did that." Kate kissed her with a mix of softness and passion, "but then again, you always did know how to drive me crazy," she muttered against her lips, her tongue darting out to lick Seph's lips.

Seph exhaled a shaky breath, heat pooling deep inside her at Kate's kiss. Kate traced her fingers up Seph's side and across her stomach, sending a wave of goosebumps across her skin.

Kate pushed them both over, so she was now on top of Seph, moving so her thigh was in between her legs. It had the added advantage of increasing the friction against Seph's core, making her moan even louder, her fingers sliding in between them to tease at her aching clit.

"Oh…" Kate wasted no time, swiftly dropping her leg, which allowed her to push her fingers inside Seph, her thumb still rubbing against her clit. "Oh, fuck."

"Do you know how much I thought about you? Thought about this?" Kate murmured in her ear as her fingers started to move inside her. She could already feel she was on the edge, and it wouldn't take much, Kate's fingers working her perfectly to a climax she wasn't sure she would come back from. "I missed you so much…"

"Kate…"

She couldn't hold out any longer. The combination of already seeing Kate through her own climax, the words she was whispering in her ear, and the movement of Kate's fingers were rapidly sending her over the edge. Kate braced herself on her elbow, letting her hand curl round her neck, rubbing her thumb across her jaw with the most gentle touch Seph had ever felt.

"Look at me," Kate whispered into Seph's ear as her pleasure began to build.

The atmosphere had shifted. Now the air was thick with adoration and love, of lost time and missed opportunities. As Seph looked up, Kate stared deep into her eyes, her gaze so intense that Seph found herself unable to break away from it. It was enough to send another pulse from deep within, her body trembling with intensity.

"Oh God," she panted, tangling her fingers through Kate's hair, pulling her close with desperation as the waves threatened to take over her body.

"It's okay. Let go, baby."

Seph tightened her grip, Kate pushing into her body, holding her tight against her as Seph's body was wracked with wave after wave of blissful pleasure. Seph let out one final long moan of pleasure, her body shaking and twitching as Kate eased her through it. Eventually, she settled, the pulses becoming fewer and further apart as she let her head fall against the pillow, one final shiver as Kate slid her fingers from her briefs. Kate shushed her, running her thumb across one cheek to soothe her as she caught her breath, dropping soft kisses across the other.

Suddenly, emotion overwhelmed her, and she felt unmistakable hot tears rolling down her face. Kate pushed herself from where she was lying by Seph so she could see her face, concern painting her beautiful features.

"Hey. Hey, what's wrong?" Seph tried to turn and bury her face into the pillow, hiding her tears, but Kate wrapped her fingers around her chin and gently pulled it back round to her. "What is it? Sweetheart, what's wrong?"

"Nothing." Seph sniffed quietly, feeling foolish for crying straight after they'd just had sex.

"Then why the tears? Did I hurt you?"

"No, no. It doesn't matter. It's nothing, really. It's stupid."

"It matters if it made you cry. Tell me, baby."

"It's just...I just felt a bit overwhelmed, that's all."

"Oh, sweetheart." Kate wiped her thumb across her cheek, brushing away a tear. "I'm sorry."

"No. No, I didn't mean..." She looked up, Kate's stare threatening to be too much again. "You have this look, like I'm the only thing in the world to focus on. It used to make me forget that you would be leaving. And now you're not, so when you gave me that look this time, I...it's just too much sometimes, that's all."

Kate broke into a soft smile, her fingers brushing under her ear before skimming under her chin and pulling her face back round to give her a soft, lingering kiss.

"I love you," she whispered against Seph's lips. "Sometimes I struggle to comprehend just how much I love you. There's just too much I'm feeling, and I can't adequately express it. It scared me at first because I'd never felt anything like it before. But now I know I just want to spend every day making sure you know how much I love you." She wiped another tear from Seph's cheek, which had slowly rolled down her face during her heartfelt confession. "I'm sorry if that overwhelms you."

Seph smiled slightly, turning her face into Kate's touch. "I can think of worse things."

From nowhere, a yawn broke across Seph's face, and she quickly masked it with her hand. She sighed and realised her eyelids also felt heavy. "Think you've worn me out."

"Maybe it was a little too much, too soon. You're still recovering."

"No such thing as too much, too soon, when it comes to that," Seph mumbled through another yawn, sleep taking its hold even against her best efforts.

"Hmm, if you say so, but your sleepy eyes are telling a different story. Come here."

Kate pulled her in close again, Seph nuzzling into her chest with a contented hum.

"Go back to sleep, sweetheart. Then when we get up, I'll make us some breakfast."

CHAPTER TWENTY-TWO

Kate sat at the table, the remains of dinner still sitting on their plates as she watched Cam and Meg bicker amongst themselves about something mundane and inconsequential. It was moments like these that she cherished the most; sure, when they were younger, their endless arguing about pointless subjects and the ensuing temper tantrums were tiring, but now they were older, and both knew that the other wasn't serious in their jibes, there was something oddly comforting about witnessing it. Especially now, of all times. Things had been so tense between them all that the mindless to-ing and fro-ing which so uniquely symbolised a sibling relationship was a welcome sight.

As she chuckled at something Meg said to Cam, she wondered about what Seph was doing tonight. Whether her evening was proving to be equally as restorative to her. Whenever Kate had dinners with the kids, Seph would go to spend the evening at Helena's, usually Wednesdays, just like it had been at the beginning. It was a comfortable routine they had easily fallen into, both allowing each other the respite and space which they needed from each other as they tentatively rediscovered their connection with each other. But as the weeks passed, their relationship becoming stronger with each passing moment, Seph becoming stronger alongside it, they were afforded the space to leave their little bubble, both painfully aware that spending each moment they could with each other was painfully too much like the stolen time they had granted themselves the first time around.

Kate thought back to the conversation she and Seph had last week. How Seph told her, somewhat nervously as they lay in bed together after their candlelit dinner, that she had told Helena about their relationship. While Seph was anxious about revealing the information, and she could understand why, all Kate could feel was an overwhelming sense of happiness at the fact that Seph felt so comfortable and safe with their current situation, she felt it solid enough to tell her sister. And Kate...well, Kate was beginning to finally see what life with Seph could really be like.

She had always imagined it, imagined how they would so perfectly fit around each other, complement each other in the best possible ways. But to experience it was something entirely different. She loved coming back to Seph every evening, finding her cooking dinner for the both of them before asking about Kate's day. She loved slipping under the covers each night, curling up behind the warm body of Seph, feeling her fall asleep in her arms. And she loved starting their day together, Kate making them coffee before she went to work, leaving Seph with a soft kiss and promise to return later. It was everything she had desired in life, everything she had been missing with Tim for so many years, and everything she had hoped for with Seph.

The sound of Meg's laugh broke through her inner thoughts, and she looked back at her children. The only thing which hung over her now was the fact that Seph was still a secret to those most important in her life. Yes, her parents knew, and Sarah, but to Kate's children, Seph didn't exist. An ache formed in her chest at the fact she was still hiding her relationship with her, even though she had justified it to herself and Seph so many times. Seph's new-found calm was welcome but still so tentative, and Kate was worried that any more curveballs thrown at her would only serve to knock her back while she was still on shaky ground. Seph, to her credit, seemed to understand and appreciate Kate's reasoning, but with each passing day of their relationship blossoming, the need to shout it from the rooftops that she was with such an amazing person was becoming more and more tempting.

"I'm seeing someone," Kate blurted out, surprising herself with the sudden announcement. That was most definitely not how she had planned on telling her children. In fact, she had not planned on telling them at all this evening. But apparently, it seemed her happiness had other ideas. That happiness was unsurprisingly short-lived.

"I'm sorry? You're what?" Meg asked, her eyes having suddenly switched from being light and carefree to something altogether more stony and hard.

"I...I'm seeing someone," Kate repeated, this time the words tripping over her own tongue.

"How?"

Kate opened her mouth to reply before realising she didn't actually know what to say. Her forehead crumpled in confusion at Meg's question.

"What do you mean?"

"I mean, how are you seeing someone? You've barely been apart from Dad for more than five minutes."

Oh. It was a fair point and one she had previously thought of when her mind had been more rational, on those nights when she had spent long hours playing over a million different scenarios as to how to break this news to her children. Not once did any of those scenarios look like this, though.

"Well...things are...we're taking things slowly." Not a complete lie, and Kate was simultaneously proud and ashamed of herself at how she managed to seemingly dodge the obvious answer.

"That doesn't answer my question," Meg stated simply.

"We just...met." *Oh, good answer, Kate.* "Look, they are fully aware of my situation. And they also have things going on that need their attention. It's not like we're rushing headfirst into marriage."

"Well, I'm so pleased you can be open and honest with this person at least."

Kate had to admit that one stung. But she knew it was true, and she knew why Meg felt the need to say it. Kate brought her hand up to her forehead, rubbing it firmly. This was a nightmare, and she only had herself to blame.

"Meg, ease off a little bit, yeah?" Cam's gentle voice filtered through the tense silence which had engulfed the room for a moment.

"Why should I?"

"Because I'm fairly sure this wasn't the way Mum wanted to tell us."

Oh, trust her Cam to see the situation in front of them. Her sweet boy and his innate ability to see the truth of a situation in front of him was both a blessing and a curse.

"Cam's right. I wasn't planning on telling you. Not tonight at least."

"Then why just blurt it out like it was nothing?"

"I don't know, Meg! I honestly don't know." Kate took a deep breath. "Look, I know and understand that everything has been confusing for you recently. I've thrown your lives upside down, and I will continue to apologise for the hurt that I caused you by doing that until my last breath. But while you are still processing these changes, for me, I have been on my own for years. Not literally, obviously. But in my head, my heart, I haven't had that connection to your dad in a long time. I guess actually leaving him... It just made me actually feel free for the first time in a long time. And I'm not saying this to be more hurtful, but you deserve all the information about how I felt to have any chance of really understanding this."

Kate looked at Cam, finding empathy on his face, before turning her attention to Meg. There was no such look on her, although instead of the angry glare she was expecting, there was something more akin to resignation at her words. Maybe she was starting to understand. Or at least letting herself be open to it.

"This thing, it's tentative and delicate. And I'm not prepared to tell you anything else at this time because of that. I really hope you respect that."

"Of course, Mum," Cam answered immediately.

"Fine." Meg slumped back in her chair, arms crossed over her chest in a move which reminded Kate of when she didn't get her own way as a child. "I mean, I'm not wild about it. But I respect that things between you and Dad are over. And that at some point that will mean both of you moving on. But I can still be upset about my parents' marriage being over, can't I?"

Kate pushed back her chair and went round to where Meg was sitting. She crouched in front of her, placing a hand on her knee. "Of course you can, sweetheart. I would never expect you to just get over something this big happening in your life quickly. I'm really proud of you for taking this in the way that you have."

"Yeah, well, no promises I won't wake up tomorrow furious with you."

Kate chuckled. "And if you do, feel free to let me know. I don't ever want you to bottle things up and keep them from me. I love you both, you know. Nothing will ever change that."

"Love you too," Meg muttered back begrudgingly.

"Really feeling it sweetheart." Kate smirked, the look mirrored by her daughter.

Chapter Twenty-Three

Seph climbed out of the car and stretched. It had been a long couple of hours sitting in the car, but the cool coastal breeze on her face made it worth it. She took a deep breath in, filling her lungs with the salty sea air, smiling at the happiness it evoked.

"You okay?" Kate asked from behind, and she turned to see her standing on the other side of the car.

"You have the best ideas," Seph replied with a beaming smile.

Kate had surprised her last night, coming home from work and announcing she had taken the day off and that she thought they could take a trip to the coast together. The idea instantly appealed to Seph. She had been trying to get out and take a walk every day so she didn't get stagnant in the house, but some time away with Kate was perfect. She watched as Kate made her way around the car, coming to stand in front of her, hands settling on her hips.

"I thought we deserved a day away. Some time somewhere completely different, with no reminders of what we have going on. I thought *you* deserved it. And I know it's not exactly the height of summer, but we can still go for a walk down the beach, find somewhere to stop and get some lunch—"

Seph stopped Kate in her tracks, wrapping her palms around her cheeks and bringing her in for a soft, gentle kiss.

"I love it. I love you," she whispered, sincerity lacing every word.

"I love you too," Kate replied. "Shall we go for a walk?"

"Yeah, come on. I might even treat you to an ice cream later," Seph laughed playfully as she leant back into the car to grab their jackets.

"You know how to spoil a girl," Kate retorted.

Ten

"I love it here," Seph said into the emptiness of the beach. They'd walked for an hour or so, hand in hand, chatting about nothing in particular until they reached the main town. There, they found a little fish and chip shop and bought some lunch, eating it while sitting on the seawall. Kate looked around as Seph spoke, studying her as she looked out across the sea, a wistful look on her face.

"You look like you do."

"What's that meant to mean?" Seph laughed, turning to Kate.

"I don't know. You just look like you belong. Like you're at peace. I noticed it while we were walking. It was like as soon as you stepped out of the car, there was a weight lifted from you. You just seem so content here."

"I guess..." Kate watched as Seph composed her thoughts. "Being by the coast always makes me feel like there's nothing to worry about. Maybe it's the vast openness, maybe it's the sea or the fresh air. I don't know, but the coast has always kind of been my happy place. I know it's not glamorous or white sands on a tropical island, but there's just something beautiful about this place. Every time you come, there's something different to see, something has changed. Nothing stands still at the coast, yet time seems to move slower. Does that make sense?"

"Yeah, it does." Kate smiled softly at Seph and her description. "Didn't know you could be so poetic, though," she added with a gentle nudge to her arm.

"Hey!" Seph spoke with a chip in her mouth. "I can be quite eloquent when I want to be!"

"Mmm, sure." Kate laughed. "Do you ever think about moving somewhere like this? Maybe it could be good for you?" Kate asked after a second.

"How do you mean?" Seph asked with a quizzical look on her face.

"Well, finding a place where you feel at peace is important. I just didn't know, with your depression and anxiety, if you'd ever considered living anywhere different. Somewhere less hectic, with less pressure."

"Not really. I mean, not that I wouldn't consider it. I never really thought of it as an option, you know." Seph shrugged, clearly ruminating on Kate's comment. "Maybe that's because I always thought that where I called home, or at least where I lived, was a constant. Like it wasn't ever directly where I was that was causing the problem. But I do always feel more relaxed out here."

"I just wondered, that's all," Kate said, staring down at her food. An image of her and Seph walking along the beach in the early morning sunlight flashed into her mind, and there was something strangely familiar and welcoming about it.

"What about you? Have you ever considered living somewhere else?" Seph threw her question back at her.

"I couldn't really, not with the kids in school and work."

"Yeah, I know. Logistically, before, it wasn't an option. Everyone has dreams. Their ideal place where they want to live or to grow old."

Kate thought about it. It wasn't something she had considered, at least not for many years. Between raising her family and building up her business, she had always expected to live in or around the city. But she also couldn't deny the freedom and relief she felt when she was out in the open. Something about not being surrounded by people, the lack of noise calming her mind. But she figured it was like that for most people when they took themselves out of the hustle and bustle of daily life.

"I guess I never really thought about it. Not for a long time, anyway. Life was always so busy. First getting started in my career, then marriage and the kids, then more work alongside it all. I've never really taken the time to think about where I wanted to end up, physically." She took a deep breath. "But then, maybe that was part of the problem. Mum did say that it was time to put myself first, and I know she was talking about being with you, but maybe I need to think long-term. I mean, I'm in a position where I don't have to stay where I am anymore. It's not like I have the kids to tie me to any one place; realistically, I could cut back at work or even retire early in a few years. But it's never really been something that's crossed my mind." She paused again, turning to face Seph, "Until now."

"And now? What do you want your future to look like?" Seph asked timidly, and Kate could sense the uneasiness in her voice as if her own question had created doubts in her mind.

"Things are very different now. I guess it's hard in some respects to imagine what my future will look like, especially with things so up in the air." Since she had revealed to Cam and Meg that she was seeing someone, the delicate truce which had once settled was well and truly broken. For Meg, it was another reminder that her mother and father were never going to reconcile. Kate suspected that it was being fuelled by Tim and his attitude towards the news. The idea that Kate was moving on with her life had been met with another wave of hostility, and it was constantly laying heavily on Kate's shoulders. "But now, whenever I imagine my future, all I see is you. And honestly, I don't care where that future is lived, whether it's back home or somewhere completely different. As long as I wake up next to you every day, I don't care where I wake up."

A smile split Seph's face at her words, a beaming grin that made Kate's heart sing every time she bore witness to it. Suddenly she jumped to her feet, holding out a hand to Kate.

"Come on. I owe you an ice cream. And maybe a quick fumble under the pier," she said mischievously.

"In this weather? You must be joking!" Kate chuckled as she let herself be pulled up by Seph. As she made her way to her feet, Seph pulled her tight into her body, finding a sliver of skin where her scarf didn't meet her face and pressing a lingering kiss on her pulse.

"I would keep you warm," she said, with a hint of desire in her voice that made Kate's clit throb with anticipation for when she did get her on her own later.

Chapter Twenty-Four

K ate awoke, her eyes blinking into focus too quickly for her liking. She knew instantly she was wide awake and wouldn't be able to go back to sleep, partly due to how alert she was but also because the dream she had awoken from was still fresh in her mind. She rolled over; Seph was still soundly asleep next to her. It had just started to get light outside, and the room was bright enough that she could make out the angles of her bare shoulder blades peeking out from under the duvet, the curve of her spine disappearing under it. It was still a surprise, waking up next to Seph. For nearly a year, she had only dreamed of it; to begin with, a sense of anticipation for when she would next see her, later with a sense of regret at how she would never see her again. In those later moments when she did wake, aching and longing for Seph after her imagination played cruel tricks on her during her sleep, she would slide out of bed silently, lock herself in the bathroom and see to her need, imagining it was Seph who was touching her before sobbing silently on the floor, feeling more alone than ever.

Now, as she woke, the sense of disbelief at the woman asleep beside her only abated as her fingers reached out and touched her solid form. As her finger traced a line from the nape of her neck down the inside of that tantalising shoulder blade, her body tingled with the residual arousal her dream had filled her body with. She was intoxicating, Kate had always struggled to resist her, and for a while, she wondered if having her freely would diminish the desire she felt towards her. However, it had done the opposite, only resulting in fueling the fire which burned deep within Kate.

She drew her finger back up, her touch so light on the return journey that Seph's body became peppered with goosebumps. She pushed herself forward so she was pushed against her body, breast to back, legs slotting into place behind Seph's, feet entwining, her hand sliding across her waist to lay against her stomach. She brushed her nose into her neck, inhaling her scent, her already shaky breath ghosting down her back. Her fingers traced across her stomach back and forth, causing Seph to involuntarily twitch as she caught the ticklish spot along her side. Seph began to stir, her body being roused in the most pleasant way imaginable. Kate moved her face slightly, grazing Seph's neck with her lips, leaving a trail of feather-light kisses where she had been. Seph shuffled, a small smile creasing at the edge of her mouth as she realised what had disturbed her sleep. She hummed a soft sound of approval.

"What time is it?"

"Don't know. Sorry. I had a dream, and it woke me up."

"Was it a bad one, babe?" Seph muttered, her voice still laced with sleep.

"No. In fact, it was a very good dream." Kate nipped her neck as if to make her point before soothing it with a long press of her lips.

"Oh. I see." Kate could sense the smug tone in her voice.

"Mmhmm. I woke up, and all I could think about was touching you," Kate admitted.

"That good of a dream, huh?"

"Definitely." Kate pulled and held her closer, the need to feel Seph's skin against her own too tempting to ignore. Seph's breathing hitched at the contact as her naked breasts brushed against her back.

"Tell me about it," Seph said breathlessly.

"We were downstairs; I had you up against the kitchen counter. You were wearing nothing but this black lace bra, and I could feel your nipples through it against my mouth. Your legs were wrapped tight around my waist, and I was deep inside you." Seph let out a soft sigh, her breathing becoming heavier. "I remember, when I used to dream about you, I would wake up so turned on, I would touch myself and imagine it was you." Another sigh, this time gently melting into a soft groan. "So when I woke up this time, and you were here, I needed to feel you so badly."

Seph pushed back further into Kate's body. "Tell me more."

Kate caressed Seph's side, and even that small action caused her breath to stutter again, her thumbs tracing just under the swell of her breasts.

"I remembered and thought about every little thing. I used to think about them when I was alone. Like how you get goosebumps when I kiss you here." She kissed where Seph's neck met her shoulder at a point she knew to be particularly sensitive. Seph sighed at the feel of it, her body reacting just as Kate predicted. "The little noise you make when I would do this..." Her fingers deftly brushed around the curve of her breast, dangerously close yet frustratingly far from where she knew Seph wanted them. "And how it would change to something altogether different when I did this..." In one fluid motion, Kate pushed up and rolled Seph onto her back before her lips came around her nipple, tongue quickly flicking over it as her mouth closed completely. Seph whimpered, her body reaching up into the sensation.

"Kate..."

Kate lifted herself further again, allowing Seph to lay fully on her back as she moved to kneel in between her legs. Her fingers stroked down her body, in between her breasts, down her stomach, and across her hips. Kate loved the feel of Seph's skin under her fingertips, mapping it out and committing every piece to memory. She watched as Seph's body reacted, how her chest heaved with each laboured breath, the way her eyelids fluttered shut, every small twitch of her already over-stimulated muscles. Seph's head pushed back into the pillow, her back arching impossibly at the feather-light touch.

"You are so beautiful," she muttered, her eyes never once leaving the curves and contours of Seph's body.

Kate leaned down, knowing that the smallest slither of contact between them was sending sparks through Seph's body, her lips tantalisingly near to her ear. "Can I tell you a secret?" she whispered, her fingers ghosting up Seph's thigh. "That dream? With you wrapped around me? That's my favourite way to have you. I love feeling you so close, pressed up against me, every part of you touching me."

She sat back up, watching as Seph reacted to her confession, her body bucking upwards into thin air and a pressure that wasn't there.

"Kate, please..."

Kate stroked her hands back up her thighs, her thumbs tracing towards her core as she got higher.

"What, baby? What do you need?" she asked, fingers playing idly on her hip bones.

"You. That. I need you."

Kate swiftly pulled Seph up by her arms, and Seph almost threw herself forward into Kate. Kate's arms wrapped tightly round her, one hand around her backside, pulling her closer, as Seph slid across her lap, their mouths meeting in a heated, much-anticipated kiss. Seph instantly rocked against Kate, desperate for friction to ease her ache, her arousal at Kate's words blatantly obvious against Kate's thighs. Kate's free hand found its way into Seph's hair, pulling her head back so she could break their kiss and move her lips down Seph's neck.

"God, I love you so much," Kate mumbled, barely lifting her mouth from Seph's skin, "I've never wanted someone as much as I want you."

Her hand left its grip in Seph's hair, trailing down to come to rest on her breast, cupping it and rolling the nipple between her fingers. The action caused a shaky, strangled moan to escape Seph, the pitch of which heightened as Kate's nipped at the skin above her pulse. With each touch, stroke, and lick, she could feel Seph becoming desperate for more, grinding closer into Kate in a futile attempt to relieve the tension which was unbearably coiling inside her.

"Lift up," Kate almost growled, herself just as desperate to touch Seph as Seph was to be touched.

Seph trembled as she slid her fingers between her legs, and she moaned as her wetness coated them. Kate felt her quiver above her, almost overwhelmed by the smallest of touches where she needed them the most. She neither had the patience nor the cruelty to tease her any further. Seph needed her now, and she wanted Seph with even more urgency. With ease, her fingers slid inside Seph, and they both gasped. Seph began to grind into her hand, and Kate reciprocated the action, her arm around the small of her back, pulling her as close to her own body as possible, her mouth hot against her chest. It took mere seconds before she felt Seph clench around her, the build-up so intense it took very little to actually bring it to its peak.

Seph hadn't even touched Kate, but her dream and the way that Seph had reacted so extremely to her had left Kate balancing on the precipice herself. She knew that all she needed was to feel Seph release around her, and her own need, which had been ignited by her dream, would be seen to.

She rocked hard into her again, curling her fingers inside her until she felt Seph's fingers dig into her back. Her back stiffened and arched, pushing her breasts further into her own chest and exposing her neck with a strangled moan. With that, Kate's own body reacted, her legs trembling underneath Seph's body. Their bodies shook together, their hands frantically grasping for a hold to keep them grounded.

Kate dropped her head, resting it on Seph's sweat-slicked skin above her heart, feeling it beat through her chest as fast as her own. She felt Seph start to come down, her head resting on top of her own and her fingers stroking through her hair, down her neck and spine. She repeated the action over and over, calming both herself and Seph. Kate didn't loosen her grip for what felt like forever, holding Seph close like she was holding onto a raft in a stormy sea. Her lifeline. The woman she loved with all her heart. Finally, she let her hands slip down and around Seph's waist, guiding her down so she was laying on the bed again, following her down and draping herself half over Seph's body, still not ready to sever their contact. She sighed as she felt Seph's arms come up and enclose her, wrapping her tightly in her embrace. They stayed there for what seemed like an age until Seph shivered as their bodies cooled.

"You okay?" she whispered, not wanting to speak too loudly and break the silent atmosphere which had settled over the room, as she leant over and wrapped the duvet back across their bodies.

"I...I...uhh." Kate chuckled softly at the incoherent response, pressing a soft kiss to the skin of her chest. Seph took a deep breath before trying again. "Where did that come from?"

"Are you complaining?"

"God, no. Just was...unexpected. Very much appreciated, just...wow."

"Yeah, well. Like I said, I woke up and was a little turned on."

"A little?" Seph shifted beneath her, and Kate looked up from where her head was resting on her chest to see impossibly deep eyes looking back at her.

"Okay," she said, chuckling. "A lot."

Seph softly laughed, closing her eyes, and Kate watched as she relaxed, a small smile on her face. Suddenly her eyes snapped open, startling Kate. "Did you come?"

Kate blushed, something she thought wasn't possible considering how much blood was still pumping around her body. Her reaction was apparently enough to answer Seph's question. "But I didn't even—"

"You didn't need to."

Seph shuffled herself up, propping herself on her elbow as she looked at Kate. "I'm that good, huh?"

"Don't be so smug." Kate tucked a piece of hair behind Seph's ear, her fingers resting against her cheek. "There was just a big build-up. And you reacted so..." Her fingers trailed down Seph's neck and across her collarbone, her skin now cool. Seph's eyes fluttered closed, and she took a sharp intake of breath and shivered, her body still sensitive. Her hips twitched involuntarily as an aftershock rippled through her body. A sly grin spread across Kate's face.

"Who's smug now?" Seph mumbled.

"You're not even looking at me."

"I can sense your smugness." Seph suddenly rolled over, pinning Kate to the bed. "But I missed out on touching you. So now it's my turn."

Chapter Twenty-Five

"Are you sure I look alright?" Seph asked for the hundredth time as she smoothed her clammy palms down the thighs of her jeans.

"You look gorgeous," Kate reassured her, honesty filling her words despite having to tell her a hundred times in return.

"I don't want to look gorgeous when I'm meeting your parents, though!"

"Why not?" Kate chuckled.

"Because that's not exactly what I aim for when meeting the parents of my girlfriend for the first time! I'm not hoping that when I leave, your dad will comment with *'oh, well, she's gorgeous!'*"

Kate laughed at Seph's little rant, leaning over towards her and pressing a kiss to her cheek.

"Okay, *I* think you look gorgeous, but I'm sure my dad and my mum will just think you look nice." Her voice dropped as she leaned in closer to her ear. "But when we get home, I'm looking forward to peeling those skinny jeans off your beautiful body and making love to you all night long."

"Oh, great!" Seph exclaimed, suddenly feeling very hot in the confines of the car. "Now I'm nervous and turned on!"

"Come on," Kate said with a mirth-filled chuckle as she opened the car door. "Otherwise, they will wonder why we're sitting out here and not in there. And I'm fairly sure you don't want to explain the problem to them."

Seph begrudgingly climbed out of the car and followed Kate to the front door, grateful when she felt Kate's hand slip into hers and give it a reassuring squeeze. When Kate had suggested this dinner with her parents during their day at the beach, Seph panicked. Kate, being the ever-insightful and attentive person she was, noticed immediately and tried to backtrack, clearly worried that it was too much too soon. But on the drive home, Seph had time to think about it and knew that she was going to have to do this sometime.

Their conversation that day over lunch had only confirmed Seph's thoughts about their relationship, that Kate really was in this for the long haul. And she couldn't continue forever as the absent girlfriend. If she was going to do this, she needed to make the first step. And that first step was meeting Kate's parents.

She did question if it was right to do this before she met Cam and Meg, but she also knew the kids being ready to meet her was a long way off—and the same was true in the other direction. While she undoubtedly wanted to be a part of Kate's life in every way, she could be patient in that respect. Plus, Kate said that she wanted it to happen since her parents already knew about Seph and their history. But that didn't mean she was any less nervous about the dinner tonight.

"I hope they don't hate me too much," she mumbled as they walked into the house.

"They won't hate you at all." Kate smiled. It was meant to be reassuring, and usually, it probably would be. But right now, Seph was feeling sick with nerves.

"Really? I find that hard to believe. I'm the woman who broke up your marriage."

Kate stopped in her tracks and turned to face Seph. "You are the woman who made me realise my marriage was over. And the woman I love and want to spend my life with. And that is all that matters."

"We'll see when they kick me out."

"They're not going to kick you out," Kate laughed. She may have thought Seph was joking, but for Seph, it was a very real fear.

She followed Kate into the kitchen as Kate called out and announced their arrival. They were instantly greeted by a friendly-looking older woman, who undeniably was Kate's mother. They shared the same mossy green eyes and defined cheekbones, and there was a warmth to her which did calm Seph's nerves a small amount.

"Kate! Hello, my darling." The older woman leant in and gave Kate a kiss on the cheek. Seph held back, not wanting to intrude on the greeting, despite Kate not letting go of her hand. "And you must be Seph. I'm Maggie. It's so nice to finally meet you."

"Hi. Nice to meet you too," Seph greeted with an awkward handshake.

"Where's Dad?" Kate asked, looking around the room.

"Where do you think he is? In his office. He bought some new smart speaker and is trying to set it up, but as per usual, it's outsmarted him. Go give him a shout and let him know you're here while I get some drinks."

Kate looked at Seph with a silent question.

"I'll be fine," Seph tried to tell her, her voice quiet and betraying her nerves slightly.

"I'll be two minutes," Kate promised before leaving a soft kiss on her cheek. Seph felt herself blush at the sign of affection Kate had so openly offered in front of her mother, considering it had barely been two minutes since they'd walked in the door.

"Can I get you a drink, Seph? "

"Oh yes, thanks," Seph replied.

"Kate will be back in a minute. David's always buying some new toy or gadget, and he can never get them to work. God only knows what he's going to be like when he does retire and he has even more free time on his hands. I'm going to have a glass of white wine. Would you like one? Or I have red, or a G&T, or I can put the kettle on?"

"Oh, white's fine, thank you." Seph looked around the large open-plan room, desperately trying to think of something more insightful to say. "You have a lovely home."

"Oh, thank you. It's still a bit of a mess, I'm afraid. We haven't long moved in, and well, I never knew how much stuff we'd accumulated until I had to box it all up and move."

"How long ago did you move?" Seph asked, taking the glass which Maggie offered her, grateful she was able to make some level of small talk, however menial it seemed.

"Around six months ago. We downsized from a bigger property. Didn't need all the space now Cam and Meg are all grown up. While they were younger, they used to stay over a lot, with Kate's job keeping her busy. But well, these days, it's just David and myself, and neither of us is getting any younger, so somewhere smaller and easier to manage seemed like the right idea."

"Well, I like this space. It's nice how it's so open. Your kitchen looks amazing."

"Ah. The kitchen was a dealbreaker for me. And having the living area next to it seemed like a good idea, so we could all spend time together when Kate and the children came for dinner. The old house had a separate dining room, and it felt so isolated when we had guests over." Seph could sense that Maggie was a natural conversationalist. The way she was talking so freely, even about something as trivial as a kitchen, put her at ease. "Kate tells me you enjoy cooking, Seph."

"Oh." Seph was slightly taken aback by the fact that Kate had talked about her in such a way. "Yes. When I get the opportunity. Sometimes it's hard, though. When I was working..." She cleared her throat at her slip-up. "I am working, but I try to cook most evenings, really. Even if it's just something small, you know. It kind of gives me time to decompress."

"I understand completely," Maggie said, guiding Seph to the sofa in the living area. "Are you due to go back to work soon? I hope you don't mind, but Kate mentioned that you had taken some time off after your father's passing. I'm so sorry to hear about it."

"Oh." This time Seph really was at a loss for words. Kate had told her mother about her father's death and the fact she was off work. It wasn't that she was angry or that her father dying had been a secret, but she hadn't expected Kate to talk so openly about her.

"I'm sorry, my darling. I've made you uncomfortable. I didn't mean to," Maggie said sympathetically, placing a gentle hand on Seph's forearm.

"No. No, it's not that. I'm just surprised that you knew. I didn't realise Kate had told you so much."

"Oh, my darling," Maggie said with a warm chuckle, "Kate talks about you endlessly. Every time she's here, she has something to tell me about you. And I love hearing it. Because when she talks about you, she lights up."

"Really?" Seph asked, somewhat shocked. She knew how Kate was around her, in the sanctuary of their own space, but to hear that her love was so openly on display and clear to see around people as close to her as her parents was a little overwhelming.

"Yes." Maggie's smile softened. "You know, that first day she came round here and told me about you...well, I'd never seen her so broken. It broke my heart to see my little girl in so much pain. But I could also see through it all, all the love she had for you, and regret at what she had done. I knew then you must be special to make her feel the way she so obviously felt for you."

"I'm sorry," Seph said, suddenly feeling the need to apologise.

"What are you apologising for?"

"For...I never intended to fall for a married woman. I never wanted to break up her family. That's not who I am."

"Oh, my darling, you have nothing to say sorry for. The heart wants what it wants, and sometimes, even if it causes pain and upset to those around us, taking the chance is the only option we have if we want to be happy. God, I remember my mother's face when I told her I wasn't going to marry Brian. You know, David and I were engaged to different people when we met?" Seph nodded. "Well, my mother went crazy. Told me I would regret it if I followed through with it. What would people say if they knew I had left my fiance, a steady man like Brian, who had a secure job and good prospects, to be with David, who was, even back then, even with his law degree and his fancy job, a little eccentric. I remember he had a little moped back then, to beat the traffic when he went into the city. Oh, you should have seen her face when he turned up one Sunday morning to take me out. She told me it was a death trap, and he was a rebellious troublemaker, and if I wanted any chance at a steady life with some security, I should leave him straight away and go back to Brian. Obviously, I told her there was no way in hell that was happening." Maggie chuckled with the memory she was clearly replaying in her mind.

"What are you two talking about?" Kate asked as she reappeared in the room. "Oh, I see you got started without me?" She gestured towards their wine glasses.

"I think Seph needed a little bit of Dutch courage. Besides, once your father gets going about whatever he decides this evening, we'll all need it. You sit down with Seph; I'll get you a glass." Maggie stood, giving Seph a soft, reassuring smile before leaving the two of them.

"Everything okay?" Kate asked quietly as she sat beside her, her arm instantly looping around her shoulders in an act of support.

"Yeah, everything's fine. Your mum's lovely," Seph said honestly. She leant into Kate's embrace, still grateful for the gesture even though it wasn't necessary.

"I knew you'd get along," Kate replied with a smile.

"Yeah. I see a lot of her in you now I've met her."

"You do? I think that's the best compliment I've ever been paid," Kate claimed humbly.

"You're both fantastic. I really must thank her for having made such an awesome human."

Chapter Twenty-Six

K ate sat at the table, scrolling through her phone. She looked up when the waiter came over to take her drink order before returning her attention to the screen. She skimmed through the list of properties that fitted her search criteria, not really paying attention to the finer details. This was proving harder than she first thought.

Over the past six weeks, Kate had watched as the Seph she had known before had slowly returned. Her sleep pattern was more or less back to normal, she was eating properly, and the return of their sex life was...well, more than welcome. And satisfying. She cleared her mind, shifting the image of Seph coming undone underneath her this morning before they ventured out of bed. Yes, there were still some bad days, but on the whole, Seph was doing much better.

A large part of the disappearance of that final weight she was carrying was Seph's decision to hand in her notice, a decision that Kate agreed with on every level. Her position at Bailey, Bradshaw and Haynes was untenable, and even the thought of her going back for the shortest period while she found another job concerned her. But Seph decided, on her own, that she could use some leave and take some more time doing the things she enjoyed while looking for another job. She'd started searching almost immediately, with no great urgency to find something, but this week was the first week of her temporary unemployment, and she already had an interview today. Kate was unbelievably proud of her. Both for this and for the way she recovered.

Despite technically living at Sarah's, Kate had spent most of her time at Seph's house, to the point where she was now regularly contributing to the grocery spend, and most of her clothes were at Seph's. Anything non-essential, or what she didn't wear often was packed up in boxes and stored in her parents' spare room. Neither was complaining, though; Kate loved coming back from work to find Seph cooking them dinner before they curled up together to talk about work and life in between lazy long kisses. Even on those nights when Kate had to bring work home, Seph would lay against her, keeping her near-silent company while she rediscovered her love of reading, one of her favourite things to do, which had fallen by the wayside in the past six months. They had found themselves their own little paradise of a routine, and Kate wasn't in a rush to end it.

She was broken from her train of thought by a hand stroking across the back of her neck and a breath against her cheek before a soft kiss followed it.

"Hey, you," a voice whispered in her ear.

Kate twisted her head up to find Seph smiling down at her, her eyes shining with a love she never got tired of witnessing. Suddenly, though, it morphed into something more nervous, and Seph shifted, her hand falling from her shoulder as she sat down next to her.

"Sorry, was that too much? I kind of forgot we were in public."

"Never." Kate leant forward and gave her another kiss to reassure her. "How did the interview go?"

"Yeah, really good. I think I did okay."

"I'm sure you did better than okay. Your CV is impressive, and the firms you've worked for in the past are some of the best in the area. You'll have a new job in no time," Kate tried to reassure her. And it wasn't just for reassurance. Seph really did have an impressive background, and her skills were ones any firm would be lucky to have.

"Yeah, well, we'll see," Seph answered, looking at the menu. "How did the viewing go?"

Kate had taken a long lunch in order to fit in a house viewing before she met Seph. "Okay," she shrugged, looking at the menu as well.

"You don't sound so sure."

"No, it was fine..."

"Just fine? Well, that sounds like a winner."

Kate looked up to see Seph giving her a knowing look. Seph could always see right through her when she had something on her mind. It was one of the things that she loved so much about their connection, but sometimes it could be more of a curse than a blessing.

"There was nothing wrong with the house," she said matter of factly. "It was lovely. It just didn't feel right."

"This is like the sixth house you've looked at in the past two weeks that hasn't been right. What is it that you're looking for?"

Kate dropped her menu and ran her hands over her face. "I don't know," she mumbled into her hands. Except she did know. She knew exactly what was missing from every house she had looked at.

"Babe." Seph took her hand from her face, and something in her voice urged Kate to look at her once again. "I'm going to suggest something, and I want you to hear me out before you say anything. Maybe the reason you can't find the right house is because you don't want to."

Kate sat, staring at Seph for a second as she processed what she was saying. Or at least what she thought she was saying. She thought her talk of looking for houses and the fact she was actually viewing some was enough to hide her dejection at the idea of no longer living with Seph. But maybe it wasn't. Maybe her despondency had seeped through more than she had realised.

"Seph, I—"

"Kate. It's been six weeks, and you've barely left. I can probably count on one hand the number of times you've slept at Sarah's. Everytime you've gone to pick up more stuff, it stays at mine. Your shoes live by the bottom of my stairs, my bathroom is full of your makeup, and on the weekends, you do the grocery shopping."

"I thought you didn't mind. I know I've been there a lot, but—"

"I don't mind. I love having you there. But maybe you can't find a place you like because you like where you are."

"But we said, *you* said, it was too soon. Especially since Tim and the kids don't know about us." They had had this conversation, in a roundabout way, a few weeks ago when Kate had to go back to Sarah's one evening to meet the kids for dinner. They'd had a phone call that night before they went to bed separately for the first time in days, where Seph had expressed how much she disliked Kate being away. Kate agreed, but they both agreed that living separately was the right thing to do until things were more settled with Kate's separation, and Tim and the kids knew exactly who Kate was seeing.

"I know. But you don't seem to be going anywhere."

Kate looked down at the table, fiddling with the knife which lay there, not wanting to say anything in case she had the wrong idea. Right now, she wasn't sure if Seph was telling her she wanted to live with her or that she had outstayed her welcome.

"Do you actually want to find somewhere else?" Seph asked quietly, dipping her head to try and catch Kate's gaze. She looked up at her, Seph waiting patiently for an answer.

"Can I be honest?" she asked with a sigh.

"Of course."

"It doesn't feel like I'm staying with you. It feels like I'm living with you. It's always felt like I'm living with you. When I come to yours in the evening after work and find you cooking, or when we fall asleep together and wake up together, it feels like I'm home. I feel at home *with you*. And I love that feeling. But I didn't want to say it because I didn't want you to feel pressured or awkward if you weren't ready for it."

"I love it too."

"Yeah?" Kate couldn't help the tentative smile which crept across her face at Seph's admission.

"Yeah. I know it means we have to tell the kids and Tim, but maybe that's a good thing. Maybe we need something to force our hand into having that conversation." Seph leant forward in her chair, so she was almost touching Kate, the tiniest of space in between them. "I love you, and I want us to start doing the things we want to do together. I want to take you out; I want to go away with you. I want us to do the stupid little things that every couple does, like go for coffee on a Saturday morning or shopping together or sit in a restaurant that isn't thirty minutes away from the office so we can have lunch without the fear of being seen." Kate chuckled at Seph's summary of why they were here of all places. "And I want to call the place where we are together all the time our home. So, yeah, maybe it is time to get this out in the open with everyone else. And maybe it's time we make this living situation official."

Kate leant forward, closing the gap between them, and kissed Seph softly, lingering slightly as they reluctantly broke apart.

"I love you so fucking much. I wish I could show you right now just how much," Kate said, her voice low and sultry in a way she knew did things to Seph.

"Maybe you can show me when you get *home* tonight." Seph pulled back, clearing her throat. "But it also means we need to go furniture shopping this weekend. You already have half of my wardrobe, but I know you've got a tonne more stuff at your mum's. Plus, you have far too many shoes."

"I don't have that many shoes! Just because you only have three pairs." Kate laughed, glad of the light relief. In an effort to wind Seph up, she'd also managed to stoke her own desire.

"Four. And I still don't understand why you need any more than that."

Kate took a moment to regard Seph as she went back to looking at her menu. The grin on her face was wide and beaming, happiness shining through, but she needed to make sure one final time that this was happening. That this really was what Seph wanted.

"Are you really sure about this?"

"Yes, babe. I'm absolutely sure."

"But it could put a lot of pressure on us. On you." Once again, Kate was conscious of Seph's well-being, worried this was too much too soon with all the other changes she was making.

"I'll be okay. I've got you, right?" Seph asked with a smile, already knowing the answer.

Kate leant forward again, capturing Seph's lips in another passionate kiss.

"Always."

She sat across the restaurant at the bar, carefully watching the interaction across the room. When she'd first seen Kate walk in, she did wonder why she was there, the restaurant seeming an odd choice since it was so far away from her office. But then she recognised another familiar face walk in. Her interest was most definitely piqued when she watched Seph lean down and greet Kate with a kiss to the cheek. It was nothing too openly affectionate, but it definitely aroused her suspicions.

From this distance, she couldn't hear what was being said, but the body language between the pair was unmistakable, the two women closer and more tactile than just two friends should be. As if she needed any more convincing, she watched as the pair leant in and kissed, a long, lingering passionate exchange that could only mean one thing.

Oh, wait until he hears about this, she thought with a sly grin.

CHAPTER TWENTY-SEVEN

"Hey honey, I'm home!"

Seph laughed out loud at the greeting as she heard Kate kick off her shoes and come walking into the kitchen.

"How long have you been waiting to say that?" she asked, turning as Kate came up next to her.

"All afternoon." Kate wrapped her arms around Seph's waist and immediately captured her lips in a searing kiss, taking Seph's breath away. Seph couldn't help the soft moan which escaped her as Kate's tongue slipped into her mouth, desire pulsing through her veins and settling between her legs. A familiar ache had already started, and she knew where this evening was heading. "And I've been waiting just as long to do that as well."

"Shit. If that's what living with you is going to entail, babe, I'm all in."

"You mean you weren't before?" Kate asked, pulling back with a mischievous look in her eye.

"Oh no, I was."

"Good, because all I've been able to think about all afternoon is how much I want to make you come in *our* house."

Seph stumbled as Kate pushed her back against the counter, pinning her there with a hand on either side of her before crushing her lips to her own once again. Seph loved when Kate was like this, raw and uninhibited like she wanted to devour her. She loved the softer, gentle side of her as well, but right now, she could feel her clit throb with how much Kate was turning her on, and she knew she couldn't wait until later this evening. She needed Kate to touch her and soon.

"Kate..." she breathed, as Kate broke the kiss only to trail her mouth down her neck.

"How long will dinner be?" Kate asked, not lifting her face from where it was pressed into Seph's skin, licking and nipping with her teeth at the skin over her pulse.

"I-it'll keep," Seph managed to stutter as cool hands pushed up her t-shirt and grabbed her breasts, thumbs instantly finding her nipples which were hard through the soft cotton of her bra.

"Fuck, I've wanted you all day," Kate spoke against her ear, goosebumps erupting over her sensitive skin, "Ever since you kissed me in that restaurant. I wanted to have you there and then."

"I-I know." Seph really did. She could see it in Kate's eyes as they pulled away, the way her voice was just a little lower when she spoke, the way her hand stayed resting on her thigh throughout lunch, leisurely but teasingly stroking up and down.

"And you looked so hot in that suit. It was driving me crazy."

"Really?" Seph was a little surprised. She had no idea that Kate found her work suits so attractive. And judging by her reaction right now, they really did have an effect on her.

"God, I love you when you're wearing a suit. You're gorgeous all the time, but in a suit? Fuck, I struggle to keep my hands to myself."

Seph knew that Kate must be desperately turned on, as if her actions weren't enough to show it, by the way she was swearing so freely. She only ever swore this much when they were having sex. Seph loved it—the way she let herself go and said whatever she was feeling in the moment. She felt Kate's hands creep back down her t-shirt and find the button of her jeans, making quick work of it and the zip before sliding her hand inside them. Seph moaned again as Kate's hand cupped her through her boxers, knowing her arousal was already very evident. Kate teased Seph, rubbing her clit through her pants as she captured her mouth once again, tongue pushing against her own as they both fought for dominance. Before she could get too submerged in the moment, though, Kate's hand and mouth disappeared, leaving Seph aching for more.

"You know, the first time I saw you, you were in a suit," Kate spoke as her hands reappeared to greedily push down the waistband of Seph's trousers, sinking down on her knees. "I remember it like it was yesterday." Kate started to trail sloppy, hot kisses up her legs, and Seph could feel them tremble beneath her. "It was this dark grey check, and you had this waistcoat on which showed off all your curves so perfectly. God, I'd never seen anything so sexy."

"Kate...please," Seph practically begged, burning with the need to feel Kate do something, *anything* more than what she was doing right now.

"Please what, baby?" Kate asked, and as Seph looked down at the woman she loved on her knees in front of her, pressing her against her kitchen counter, she could feel herself getting wetter, her arousal slipping down her legs.

"Please, I need you."

"Not as much as I need you, baby," Kate replied before pulling her boxers down to join her jeans. Seph's head fell back, a loud, unfiltered moan coming from deep within her as Kate's exquisite tongue took its first lap in between her lips. Her hips jerked uncontrollably, Kate's hands quickly coming to pin them in place.

"You taste amazing," Kate said before repeating the action, swirling around Seph's clit with the tip of her tongue.

Seph gripped the counter, her knuckles turning white with the force as Kate continued to lick and tease at her, the sounds of Kate's own moans of pleasure coming from between her legs only serving to stoke the fire in her to unimaginable levels. For all their encounters, all the passionate and forbidden moments they had snatched together, the lust and desire they had given in to so many times, nothing was as all-consuming as this moment right now. Seph lost herself in the feel of Kate, sucking her into her mouth and teasing her with her tongue until suddenly, the sensation was gone.

"What—" Seph exclaimed, hips bucking again as the cool air hit her clit where Kate's warm mouth had been seconds before. But then Kate appeared in her vision again, kissing her hungrily. She moaned as she tasted herself on Kate's tongue before nimble fingers stroked through her arousal.

"You're soaked, baby. Fuck..." Kate mumbled against her mouth. "God, I can't wait to make you come."

"Babe..."

"Is this what you need?" Kate asked, pressing her forehead to Seph's as she slipped two fingers inside Seph with ease. The feel of her inside Seph almost made her knees buckle, but she locked them, determined not to collapse just yet.

"Yes..." Seph answered, breathy and already on the edge. "Shit, I'm close already."

"I know you are. I can feel you, baby. You're so tight when you're ready to come," Kate continued as she pumped her fingers in a steady motion. "God, you feel so good around me. I could do this forever."

"Shit! Kate!" Seph screamed as Kate added her thumb to the sensations she was feeling, circling it around her clit in a double onslaught that had Seph careering towards the precipice. "Babe, I'm c-coming."

Seph let out a long, unadulterated moan as Kate carried on regardless, determined to seek out every bit of pleasure from Seph's body and claim it as her own. She could take it all as far as Seph was concerned; this woman could have everything for the way she made her feel. Suddenly the rope which was wound tight within her snapped, and she came, shaking and trembling with every pulse through her body. The strength she had within her to keep her standing dissipated, and she felt her legs waver beneath her, but before she could fall, Kate slipped out of her and wrapped her arms around her, holding her close.

"Babe...fuck..." she managed to say, barely more than an exhale of shaky breath.

They stood there for a second, Seph coming down from the high Kate had just delivered, the solid weight of her body pressed against Seph's comforting and exciting all at once. She licked her lips, mouth dry from the inability to keep it closed and her moans contained as Kate took her to her edge and over it, the feel of her arousal between her legs cool against her burning skin. After a moment, she opened her eyes and leant her head back, Kate lifting her own from where it had rested against Seph's forehead throughout it all.

"So, my suits, huh?" Seph asked with a glint in her eye.

Kate chuckled. "What can I say? You look gorgeous in whatever you wear, but yeah. You in a suit really is something special."

"Well, I'll remember that. But in the meantime..." She pushed Kate back, kicking off her jeans and boxers which had pooled around her feet, before walking her backwards towards the sofa, sitting her on it with a gentle shove, and standing over her. "It's my turn."

Tim heard the knock at the door, grumbling as he stood to answer it. He had no idea who it could be; his children both had keys, and he wasn't due any visits or meetings with his lawyers. Stumbling slightly from another evening spent with a bottle of the finest whiskey for company, he threw it open, surprised when he saw his assistant, Natalie, standing there.

"What are you doing here?" he asked gruffly.

"Jesus, Tim. How much have you had to drink?" she asked, waving her hand in front of her face.

"A bit. Why?" he asked, still confused.

"You stink of booze," she explained bluntly as she walked past him into the house. Tim watched as she made her way towards his den, following the sound of the television. "Have you been in here all day?" she asked, gesturing to the empty takeaway containers on the table.

"No. I had a meeting this morning," he replied, slightly disgruntled that his assistant was calling him out on his behaviour. The meeting with his lawyers this morning had not gone his way, with them suggesting that he take Kate's offer of putting the house on the market. To him, it was a sign of defeat. He wanted to prove that he didn't need Kate's money, and to begin with, he saw Kate's offer of buying her out of the house as a way to prove her wrong and show his independence. But as Kate had the house valued and his lawyer looked over his financial details, and with their joint bank account frozen, he realised just how screwed he was. It wasn't so much the fact that he couldn't buy her out, but his lawyers knew that more than anything this was just Tim being stubborn rather than for any actual financial advantage. He just wasn't entirely prepared to admit defeat and wanted to make Kate's life as difficult as possible. He just didn't like being called out on that fact.

And so, with another hit to his pride, and another win to Kate in his mind, he'd sloped off home to drink away his frustrations. He slumped back down on the sofa, grabbing his glass from the table as he did so. "Did you want something?"

"Actually, I found something out today which might be of interest to you," Natalie said, perching on the end of the sofa and crossing her legs. Tim could see her already short skirt ride up her thighs as she did so, granting him a teasing glance of what was underneath. Maybe he could go there...

However, he wasn't drunk enough to forget the fact that Natalie probably only saw him as a free ride, and she would be sorely disappointed once she found out the truth. Kate really had fucked everything up for him. Still, if Natalie was going to flash him her legs, who was he to ignore them? He looked back up at her face.

"Yeah, what?" he asked, not really caring.

"I was at lunch today at this new place just outside the city centre, and just as I was about to leave, I saw your wife arrive."

If it was meant to pique Tim's attention, it really didn't. All he felt was annoyance at the fact Kate was getting on with her life. *It's alright for some*, he thought to himself.

"Yeah?" he said dismissively, then took a long swig of his drink.

"Yeah. And I thought it was a bit odd, being so far from her office and everything, so I watched her for a bit before I left." Natalie paused, though for what, Tim didn't know, but he wished she just got to the point so she would leave him alone. "She was joined by someone. They looked very...well acquainted with each other."

Tim turned slowly at Natalie's words, understanding the implication perfectly.

"She was with him?" he asked, his voice cold and stony. "Who is he?" he growled?

"Oh, no," Natalie corrected him, "It wasn't a him. And in fact, it was some-one you and I both know..."

Chapter Twenty-Eight

"Hey, baby," Kate greeted Seph as she walked into the kitchen, presenting her with a huge bouquet of flowers. "Congratulations, gorgeous."

Seph's face broke into a huge beaming smile, taking the flowers from her and getting lost in their beauty.

"Oh. They're beautiful, thank you. And lilies—my favourite."

"Beautiful flowers for my beautiful girlfriend." Kate leant in, placing a soft kiss to Seph's lips. "I'm so proud of you."

Seph had called her excitedly this afternoon to tell her that the job she had interviewed for earlier in the week had called back and offered her the position. Kate was beyond proud. For Seph to go from the lost, scared woman she was only a couple of months ago to the happy, successful woman she saw in front of her now was an achievement she thought would take much longer.

"Thank you," Seph replied shyly.

"You're going to be amazing."

"We'll see. Their HR department called me back after I spoke to you; they've given me a start date of two weeks' time," Seph continued as she wandered over to the sink, finding a vase and filling it with water ready for her flowers.

"That's great." Kate followed, wrapping her arms loosely around her waist and resting her chin on Seph's shoulder as the other woman set about arranging the flowers in the vase.

"I know, I'm just nervous," Seph admitted.

"I know, baby, but you're going to smash it. I just know it." Kate pressed another delicate kiss to her cheek. "I thought, since we have something to celebrate, we could open a bottle of wine, and I'd order us a takeaway so we didn't have to cook."

"Sounds perfect."

Kate nuzzled her face into Seph's neck as she finished arranging the flowers. Her eyeline dropped, and she became distracted by the expanse of skin on show where Seph's dressing gown had parted, exposing her chest and teasing her where she couldn't see. She let one of her hands slide under the robe, instantly finding soft skin.

"Are you wearing anything under this?" she said into the skin of Seph's neck, punctuating the end of her question with a teasing brush of her lips, her breath ghosting across her skin.

"I've just had a shower."

"So that's a no?"

"That's a *maybe you could find out*," Seph replied, tipping her head back to find Kate's lips.

She swept her hand upwards slowly, finding nothing but bare skin until her hand came to cup Seph's bare breast. Seph sighed at the touch, mirrored by the soft groan from Kate. But no sooner than it had begun than the moment was broken by a sharp, heavy knock on the door.

"Who the fuck is that?" Kate moaned, disappointed her exploration of Seph's body had been interrupted. Another impatient thud sounded over and over.

"I don't know, but if they don't calm down, they're going to take the door off its hinges," Seph replied, equally as frustrated and now annoyed at the persistent hammering. Pulling out of Kate's hold, she wrapped her gown shut, tying it tighter as she headed towards the door.

Kate exhaled a long, deep, calming breath as she started to get two wine glasses, filling them from the bottle in the fridge. She jumped when the unmistakable sound of the front door slamming into the wall reverberated around the house.

"Where the fuck is she?"

A cold sense of fear ran through her at the familiar voice. Almost dropping the bottle, she ran out of the kitchen to find Tim walking into the living room, backing Seph into her own house.

"I-I don—" Seph stuttered.

"Don't fucking lie to me!" Tim shouted, pushing further into Seph's space. "I know you've been fucking my wife, so where is she?"

"Tim!" Kate shouted, her stomach churning at the sight of him screaming at Seph and how Seph was recoiling. He turned at the sound of his name, a look of horror and disbelief flickering across his face as he saw his wife standing in front of him.

"What the *fuck*?" he asked no one in particular, confusion painting his features as he tried to comprehend the situation unfolding in front of him.

But Kate's priority wasn't Tim. She was more concerned with Seph, her face pale and hands clearly shaking as she wrapped them around herself. With a quick stride, she placed herself in between Seph and Tim, taking hold of Seph's upper arms and urging her to look at her.

"Are you okay?" she asked quietly. Seph gave a small, shaky nod in return.

"I'm fine." Her voice was shaking slightly, but she was unhurt, more startled at the sudden intrusion than physically harmed. She noted how Seph only quickly made eye contact before shifting her gaze back over her shoulder where she knew Tim stood. Kate, a little more confident that Seph was okay for the time being, turned her attention to Tim.

"What are you doing here?"

Her words were measured and slow. She could already feel the fury at Tim barreling into Seph's home, unannounced and unwelcome, bubbling up within her, but she didn't want to raise her voice in front of Seph. She was acutely aware that Tim's intrusion could have already set off a snowball of anxiety within her and she wasn't prepared to do anything to make it worse.

"What am *I* doing here? What the fuck are you doing here? Why the fuck is my wife in your house?" He leaned towards Seph, jabbing his finger in her direction.

"Don't speak to her like that," Kate said with a hard stony tone, instinctively stepping further across to shield Seph from Tim.

"I'll speak to her how I want since she's the one going around sleeping with my wife!"

"We've separated, Tim. What I do with my life is none of your concern."

"Yeah, you made that very clear when you filed for divorce. But when I heard you were on a date, and with *her*...I didn't believe it. But then I followed you here, and she opened the door wearing that—"

"You followed me?" Kate repeated, incensed even further that her and Seph's privacy had been intruded upon. "How dare you?"

"How dare I?" Tim's voice raised again, his face red with rage. "You've been fucking around with my staff, and you ask me that? How long has it been going on?"

"You need to leave," Seph said from behind Kate, her voice quiet but firm. A sense of pride rose within Kate's chest.

"I'm not going anywhere until I get some answers. So tell me, when did you start fucking her? Before or after you started working for me?"

"You don't have to say anything, Seph."

Tim paused, a look of horrific realisation spreading across his face. Kate wasn't sure what it was that caused the revelation to sink in, whether it was her defence of Seph, or the way she had subtly held her hand as she spoke up a moment ago.But clearly the reality of the situation had dawned on him. His eyes flitted from Kate to Seph and back again.

"It's true," he said, his voice dropping but his emotion still clear. Something about his tone now was more terrifying than when he was shouting earlier, the quiet rage behind his words striking a sickening sense of fear within her.

"Seph asked you to leave," Kate repeated, her own voice starting to waver with the emotion crashing within her.

The silence in the room was deafening; the only sound which Kate could make out was the rapidly increasing rate of Seph's breathing behind her. Giving Tim a final warning glare, she turned to Seph. "Seph, baby. Are you okay?" she asked quietly, wishing that it was only her and Seph here if only so she could give her all her attention. She heard Tim scoff behind her.

"Oh, for fuck's sake."

It was the final straw. Kate spun back around to look at Tim, getting into his face. "Fuck off, Tim. If she's on the verge of an anxiety attack, all my focus will be on her and only her. I don't give a fuck what you think. Now get the fuck out before I call the police."

"Fine," he spat back, almost nose-to-nose with Kate. "But this isn't over. And if you think I'm putting the house on the market now, you've got another thing coming. I'm going to take you for everything I can after this."

Kate watched as Tim stalked out of the house, slamming the door behind him, the windows rattling with the force of it. The moment that she was confident he had gone, she turned back to Seph. She cupped her face gently in her hands, bringing her gaze up to meet her own.

"Baby..." She could hear the fear in her voice, too shaken to try and hide it any further.

"I'm fine," Seph replied, her own shock and panic reflected back at her in Seph's eyes. "Really, I'm fine. I'll just..." She broke out of her hold and headed back into the kitchen.

Seph stood in the archway which separated the kitchen from the living room, watching Kate. She was sitting on the sofa, head down and in her hands, her shoulders shaking with tears. Closing her eyes and steeling herself, she took a step closer and another until she was beside Kate. With shaky hands, she placed down the two cups of tea she had made as a front for her sudden departure, although she was fairly sure Kate could probably do with something stronger. She knew she did. She pushed away the voice in her head that chastised herself for walking away, but she knew she needed a few minutes to control her own emotions. Kate needed her right now, and having an anxiety attack wasn't going to be any good for either of them. Now was her time to be strong for Kate. She dropped down beside Kate, wrapping an arm around her shoulder and pulling her tight into her.

"Hey, come on, it's okay," she murmured into Kate's ear as the torrent of tears grew stronger.

"I'm sorry," she managed to choke out between her sobs. "I'm so sorry."

"Hey, you've got nothing to be sorry for," she tried to convince her, knowing it would take more than a few words.

"I never thought he'd find out this way. I never thought he would come here..."

"I know, neither of us did. Hey, come on, babe, try and calm down for me." Kate's sobs were getting more uncontrolled, and she was struggling to catch her breath.

Seph released Kate from her embrace, instead wrapping her hands around her face and pulling it up to look at her. Kate's eyes were red and swollen, cheeks wet with the cascade of tears rolling down them. Her thumbs wiped across her cheeks in a futile attempt to try and dry them, fresh tears replacing them just as quick. She forced her to make eye contact, and something in the action caused Kate's breathing to start to slow. She encouraged her to continue, to control her rhythm.

"That's it, nice and slow," she coaxed as Kate's breaths continued to calm. "You know the pattern. Just usually this is the other way around," she joked half-heartedly with a weak smile.

She swiped her thumb across her cheek one final time before leaning under the coffee table and reappearing with a box of tissues. She pulled one out, wiping delicately at Kate's face before Kate took another from her hand.

"A-are you okay?" Kate asked, her voice still unsteady.

"I'm fine. I'm sorry, I just had to..." She didn't know what to say. How was she meant to finish that sentence?

"Did you have an attack?" Kate asked, still overwhelmingly concerned with Seph's well-being. It made her heart ache that even now, Kate was worried about her.

"No. I just needed a moment, you know? And I made us tea. I don't know why..." Seph looked at the mugs on the table with a frown. "I don't think tea's going to cut it."

She gave a weak smile, in no way convinced that Kate was convinced. Kate dropped her gaze, focusing on the tissue in her fingers, pulling it apart with her anxious fiddling. She could see the guilt on her face; it was radiating off her in waves that threatened to drown Seph.

"I wouldn't blame you if you changed your mind."

"What are you talking about?" Seph asked.

"I know that wasn't what you signed on for. And I wouldn't ever force you to stay through what is going to happen now. If you wanted to walk away, I would understand. If I-I've lost you..." Kate's voice broke again, and fresh tears fell.

Seph's heart broke. Kate thought that this was too much for Seph, that she wasn't going to stick around and that this meant the end for them.

"Hey, I'm not going anywhere." She slid to her knees on the floor in front of Kate, trying to catch her gaze again. Resting her hands on Kate's, she ran her thumb across her knuckles. "Kate, babe, please look at me."

She felt her own tears start to fall when Kate looked up, her face conveying just how broken and devastated she was at tonight's turn of events. God, she never wanted to see Kate like this, and she wished she'd had the guts to tell Tim where to go when he first arrived. But she was so shocked, so terrified when he pushed her backwards into her own house, that she had been rendered completely speechless. Maybe if she'd had more courage and foresight, she could have prevented Kate from feeling this shattered.

"I'm not going anywhere, babe. I love you so fucking much, and he will not change that. We have not come this far to just walk away now, okay?"

"Really?" Kate asked, still not convinced.

"Really. You got me through, and I'm going to do the same for you, okay? We will get through this together."

"I love you, I'm sorry he came here and—"

"Doesn't matter. We'll work it out."

"I know he's just going to go straight to the kids and tell them. Twist it into something horrid and sordid."

"Do you want to call them? You could go see them tonight?"

"No, he's probably already spoken to them anyway. I'll know soon enough. I imagine Meg will call if that's the case."

"Okay, what about calling Sam? Or Sarah? Letting them know what's happened?" Seph was just trying to think about the next logical step. Giving something which Kate could control might be the key to helping her calm down and think more rationally.

"I might call Sam. Let her know what he said. That he knows."

"That sounds like a good idea," Seph encouraged, rubbing her hand up and down Kate's thighs in a comforting pattern. "Why don't you give her a call? I'll go run you a bath. Maybe a nice soak will help you come down a little."

Kate gave a smile that tore at Seph's heart. It was small and sad, and as she lifted a hand to Seph's cheek, Seph leant into the touch, reassuring her she was still there.

"I'm so sorry that you were involved in that. I never wanted you to get caught up in this," Kate whispered.

Seph turned her head, pressing a kiss to the palm of Kate's hand. "Ring Sam, and I'll have that bath ready for you when you're done, babe."

CHAPTER TWENTY-NINE

Seph could hear the shower start running upstairs, signalling that Kate had finally risen from bed. Neither of them had gotten much sleep the previous night, both of them no doubt replaying the events that had happened. Kate had finally fallen asleep in the early hours, so when Seph woke at seven and Kate was still asleep, she left her, making her way quietly downstairs. She'd spent the past couple of hours watching television, trying hard to ignore the thundering beat of her heart and the nauseating feeling in her stomach. She was *not* going to have another anxiety attack.

While Kate was on the phone with her lawyer last night, Seph started running her bath as planned. But within minutes of being alone in the bathroom, her resolve finally crumbled, legs buckling as she managed to find her way to the toilet seat and sit down, her chest suddenly tight and her vision swimming. The sound of Kate's voice drifting from downstairs kept her from drowning too quickly, and she started to tap out the steady *one, two, three, four* beat on her leg, attempting to match her breathing along with it. It was slow, stuttering, restart after restart needed, but eventually, she managed to get her breathing back under control before Kate made an appearance. Standing on shaky legs, she washed her face, cleaning away more tears she hadn't even realised she had shed, before turning the tap off and calling Kate.

Realising her cup of coffee was empty, Seph stood from the sofa, wandering into the kitchen to make herself another and one for Kate. While she was waiting for the kettle to boil, she popped two tablets out of their blister pack and swallowed them down in an attempt to stop the headache blossoming behind her eyes. While she was at it, she also took her regular antidepressant, noting she needed to refill her prescription soon.

A knock at the door made her jump, her nerves on edge from last night and the last time someone had turned up unannounced. But rather than the angry banging of Tim, this knock was quieter, and she breathed a sigh at the fact it wasn't likely to be him this time. Still, she was cautious as she opened the door; no one she knew was likely to be turning up at this time on a Saturday morning.

She was greeted by a young man standing on her doorstep. He couldn't have been any older than his early twenties, his mousy brown hair styled into a messy fringe that covered his forehead. He had the start of a beard, although Seph couldn't make out if it was intentional or just from lack of shaving today. The man looked uncomfortable, hands shoved deep in his pockets in a nervous habit Seph knew well. But there was something about him, his eyes in particular, which had a soothing effect on her.

"Oh, hello. I'm looking for Kate Earnshaw," he said sheepishly.

"Who's asking?" Seph asked in return. There were only a couple of people who knew to find Kate here, and she wasn't about to reveal her location to someone she didn't know.

"I'm her son, Cameron."

"Oh." Seph was taken aback. She'd never considered the possibility of Kate's children turning up at her house. But now he'd introduced himself, she realised why his eyes felt so comforting. They were exactly the same soft, mossy green as Kate's. Realising she hadn't said anything further, she shook her head. "Sorry, yes. Come in. I'll just get her."

Seph walked into the house, looking over her shoulder awkwardly, watching as Cam followed her. "I'll just…" she started, gesturing up the stairs before making her way up, meeting Kate as she came out of the bedroom.

"There's someone here to see you."

"Sam?"

"No. Cameron."

"Cam?" Kate squeezed past Seph in the hallway, sprinting down the stairs, Seph following a couple of steps behind her. She arrived to mother and son standing awkwardly on opposite sides of the living room.

"Cam?" Kate said, disbelief painting her words.

"Hi, Mum," Cam replied quietly, uncertainty in his voice.

An uneasy silence settled over the three of them for a few moments before Seph broke it.

"If you give me five minutes, I can get out of here and leave you two to talk," Seph offered, starting back towards the stairs.

"No, Seph. It's fine. We can go—" Kate tried to argue.

"No, really, it's fine. I'll just go get dressed, and then I'll be gone." Seph ran up the stairs, faster than her legs could or should probably have carried her, and into the bedroom quickly getting changed. By the time she returned downstairs, Kate was in the kitchen, leaning against the counter, head hung low.

"Kate?" Seph announced softly so as not to startle her. "I'll just go shopping or something, and you can just let me know when you're done."

Kate turned, her face still pale and tired from the previous night's lack of sleep. "I don't want you to feel you can't be in your own house," she said quietly.

"I know. It's not that. I just think this is a conversation you and Cam need privacy for, and you won't get that if you're at a coffee shop or somewhere. It's fine. I'll just do the grocery shop or something to kill time."

"I'm sorry he just showed up," Kate said, taking a step towards Seph, her hand coming to cup her cheek. Seph, for the first time ever, felt uncomfortable with the action and stepped back. Kate looked at her with pain and confusion on her face.

"I'm sorry, babe, it's just..." Seph looked towards where Cam stood in her living room. "It doesn't feel right. Not with Cam here, not how things are at the moment. I know he knows you're seeing someone, but you have no idea what Tim's said to him." Kate sighed, the worry at what her husband had said to her children evident on her face. "Look, just talk to him. He hasn't come in here with all guns blazing, which can only be a good thing." She inconspicuously took Kate's hand where it hung between them, clasping her fingers tight within her own. "And when you're done, I'll be back. Just remember I'm not going anywhere, okay?"

"I love you," Kate whispered, and Seph wasn't sure if it was for Cam's benefit or because she was so tired she couldn't find the energy to speak any louder. Either way, she wouldn't leave before letting Kate know she felt the same.

"I love you, too."

Ten

Kate leant against the wall of the archway, watching Cam as he looked at a photograph on the mantelpiece. She knew what photo it was; she could tell from the frame that it was the selfie she and Seph had taken when they visited the coast a few weeks ago. Windswept and cold, hair blowing across her face, she'd never been happier. Now the inevitable reality had come crashing down around her, her life suddenly spiralling out of control. The only thing she knew for certain right now was that Seph was standing by her, and her son was here to talk. She just didn't know how that talk would go.

Cam must have sensed her presence, turning around with the frame still in his hand.

"Is it true?" he asked. His question reminded Kate of hearing something similar from Tim last night, but while his father was full of quiet rage, Cam was full of resigned disbelief.

"What exactly did your dad tell you?"

"He said that he'd found out you've been having an affair with a woman who worked for him."

Kate couldn't argue with the description. It was concise and blunt and missed a lot of crucial details, but in terms of what the basics were, it summed up the scenario perfectly.

"It's not exactly that simple, Cam," she tried to counter.

"Isn't it? I mean, have you had an affair with a woman who worked for Dad?"

"Yes, but she was not the sole reason I left your father, and we didn't know she worked for him." Kate sighed as she saw that Cam didn't care for the details. "Please, Cam, can we just sit down and talk?"

Cam hesitated before placing the photo back down where it belonged and walking towards the sofa. Kate sat on the opposite end, desperately missing the hug she usually got in greeting from her son, but understanding that today, she didn't necessarily deserve that right.

"I just...I'm just so confused, Mum. I mean, I was still kind of coming to terms with you and Dad separating, then you told us you were seeing someone. But to find out that you've been having an affair... I mean, how long has it been going on?"

"Seph and I met just over a year ago, but we've not been together all that time."

"But you have been together while you and Dad were together?"

"Yes." There was no point in keeping anything back now. "But I ended things because I had reached a point where I had to make a decision."

"But I don't understand. If you ended it, then how come you left Dad? And you're living here with her now?"

"Because, Cam..." She let out a long breath. "Sometimes doing what makes you happy and what is right aren't necessarily the same thing. I did what I thought was right at the time, but the truth is it made me miserable."

"Is this why you were so down when we were back for Christmas?"

The question shocked Kate, and she looked up at her son with a puzzled expression. Tim, despite his protestations at everything being good between them, had noticed her constant bad mood over the past few months before she left, but with Cam and Meg out of the house and living their own lives for most of the time, she thought she had managed to hide it from them. She was clearly wrong.

"What..."

"Oh, come on, Mum. You were miserable at Christmas. You hardly spoke to Dad, you started drinking champagne at breakfast, and after dinner, you disappeared for an hour into your office. I think Dad thought you were going to sleep off the champagne, but I saw you come out when I went to the bathroom, and it looked...well, it looked like you'd been crying. I didn't say anything at the time, since you hadn't seen me, and whatever it was, I figured it was private; otherwise, you wouldn't have locked yourself away. But now I'm wondering...was it because of her?"

"I'm sorry, Cam, you were never meant to see that. I thought I'd managed to hide it from you and Meg."

"Well, I'm not saying Meg noticed. You know what she's like. Doesn't notice a thing unless it's about her or hits her in the face. But was that why you were upset? Because of this woman?"

"I missed her so much, Cam. And while I still loved spending Christmas with you and your sister, there was a part of me that wanted to be sharing it with Seph and not your dad. I'm sorry if that's hard for you to hear."

Cam sat silently for a while, Kate letting him sift through his thoughts and feelings without interrupting him. They'd managed to speak calmly, but Kate wasn't surprised; Cam, throughout all this, had managed to maintain his level head and composure. Her chest swelled with an insurmountable feeling of pride for her son. "I saw you two earlier," Cam started out of nowhere, "in the kitchen. I don't know what you were talking about, but you were really close, and...I don't know, you looked different. Something about how you looked at her...I've never seen you look at Dad like that."

"I thought I loved your dad, and I did once. But people change, Cam, and both me and your father have. I never set out to hurt him or anyone else, but life doesn't always go the way you expect it. I'll never regret the time we had together; to start with, it gave me you and Meg, but I love Seph. She makes me really happy. And maybe, when you're ready, you can spend some time with her and see that for yourself. But I won't rush you into anything. This is all on your own time, okay?"

"She...she seems nice. I mean, she wasn't angry at me for just turning up here and was polite when I asked about you."

"She was probably a little surprised," Kate smiled softly, "but then again, so was I. But she'll be more worried about me and you talking than anything else.

She knows how much I love you and your sister and how worried I've been about telling you everything."

"And she's good to you? Like, she makes you happy and treats you well?"

Kate couldn't help but be touched by Cam's concern. She was proud of the young man he had grown into, his compassionate nature, something which she had ensured she had nurtured when he was younger and which had led him to medical school. She shuffled closer to him, cupping his face in her hands. "You are the sweetest boy I've ever known."

"Mum!" he exclaimed, pulling out of her grip. "I'm twenty-two."

"You'll always be my little boy. Yes, she treats me well, sweetheart. She's a bit like you. She puts everyone else first. Including me. When, if, the time comes, I think you'll get along with each other."

Cam leant forward, enveloping his mum in the hug she had so desperately been craving. "Then I'm happy for you, Mum. And I can try to speak to Meg—"

"Don't worry about your sister," Kate stopped him as she pulled back. "I'll speak to her. I don't want you two fighting, and you need to be focusing on your exams, not trying to fix my problems."

"I don't know if Dad's told her yet..."

"Oh, I'm sure he will sooner or later. But that's my issue. Now, have you got time to come to brunch with me? We'll go to that bistro you like and can carry on talking if you want?"

"I'd really like that, Mum."

Kate exhaled a deep breath as she knocked on the door. After her lunch with Cam, she had built up the courage to go and see Tim, as she had promised she would. She knew her promises probably didn't hold much weight with him anymore, but she also knew this conversation, however it was going to go, was not going to get any easier with time. So she had phoned Seph, telling her she was going to speak to Tim, hopefully reassuring her not to worry too much, even though she could still sense the concern in her voice as they hung up. Hearing someone moving behind the closed door, she steeled herself for the reaction she was about to receive, surprised when she was met with her daughter and not her husband.

"Meg..."

"What are you doing here?" Meg spat, anger lacing every one of her words.

"I came to see your Dad. Is he here?"

"Of course. He's not the one who left."

"Meg..."

"What do you want?"

"I came to speak to your Dad."

"Why? So you can spit out a load more lies?"

"Meg—"

"No!" Meg cut her off, stepping out onto the doorstep. "Haven't you done enough? I could just about understand you two separating because you didn't love him anymore, but to find out you've been lying all this time?"

"Meg, please. Let me explain—" Kate wasn't above begging at this point.

"Explain what? You ripped this family apart, and for what? Jesus, Mum, of all the people I never thought would do this..." The look on Meg's face was one of utter betrayal, and she could understand it, but she never thought that Meg would be so vicious in her delivery of what she had to say. "How could you do this?"

"I'm sorry, I really am. Please, if we can just talk—"

"No! I don't want to be anywhere near you right now, let alone talk to you. Just fuck off!"

"Meg! That's enough!" Kate hadn't noticed the door opening again behind Meg; she had been too engulfed in the look of disappointment her daughter was bestowing upon her in the moment. "Go inside," Tim ordered.

"But Dad—"

"No. Whatever she has done, however you are feeling, she is still your mother. You do not speak to her like that."

Meg stared at Tim for a moment, a look of disbelief flickering across her face at his reprimand, before being replaced with the rage which had been there previously. Turning on her heel, she stormed back into the house, and Kate closed her eyes, feeling more tears slowly slip down her face.

"Come inside," Tim said, his voice stony. "I think we need a drink and to talk."

CHAPTER THIRTY

S eph sat on the floor, the tiles cool against her calves where her joggers had shifted up. Her eyes dropped closed in a long, laborious blink, stinging and dry behind the lids. She once again had lost all track of time, but she was slowly becoming aware that she had been sitting on the hard floor long enough that her backside was uncomfortably numb. She shifted, pulling herself up the wall, bending to scoop up her glasses from where they had been thrown, before straightening herself up completely.

She washed her face, trying to wake herself up, but her body was depleted and screaming to collapse in its post-attack haze. *Shit*, she thought. *Twice in two days*. She really hoped that it was just the residual emotion from the night before, her mind still processing events, coupled with the fact that Kate was seeing Tim. She had received a phone call a couple of hours earlier, letting her know that Kate had finished lunch with Cam but was going to go see Tim, but nothing since then. The knot in her stomach grew again with each passing moment, and it was making her nauseous.

She realised that somewhere along that train of thought, she had made her way downstairs and into the kitchen. She took a glass from beside the sink and filled it with a generous helping of wine from the fridge before making her way over to another cupboard and popping two capsules from a blister pack. It probably wasn't best to try and quell the raging headache with paracetamol washed down with pinot, but she didn't really care at this moment.

She picked up the packet of cigarettes that sat on the counter and headed towards the back door. Settling down on the cold wooden bench, she opened the pack, cursing at the fact there were only two left. Her smoking habit had also notched up a gear over the past day. She lit up and took a sip of her wine, exhaling a plume of smoke into the dusky air. Kate *would* be home soon. She wasn't exactly going to be able to text while with Tim. And who knew what was being said and how long it would take. But she expected to have heard something by now. She expected her to be home by now. She *wanted* her home now. Lost in another train of thought, she didn't hear the click of heels on the kitchen floor or sense the body behind her.

"Hey, beautiful."

The voice was tired and quiet but unmistakably Kate. Seph spun round, the relief on her face visible.

"You're back," she breathed, as she jumped out of her chair and quickly made her way over to where Kate was standing in the doorway. She captured her lips in a soft kiss. Her fingers wound into her hair, tugging slightly, as if she was testing that she was really there, before deepening the kiss. As she pulled away, she grazed her bottom lip with her teeth, and Kate hummed with pleasure.

"Mmm, what was that for?"

"Just missed you, that's all." Seph left it there. Kate didn't need to know right now just how much she had been worrying this evening. She didn't need to know the panic she had felt at not knowing where she was. She pulled Kate closer, their foreheads touching, her grip loosening as she brought her fingers around to stroke her cheek.

"I missed you, too," Kate said quietly into the cool air.

"How did it go?"

Kate sighed. "Meg was there." Something about the way Kate uttered her daughter's name told Seph everything she needed to know. "She wouldn't even let me in the house to begin with. But once Tim knew I was there he managed to get her to leave us for a while so we could speak."

"And?" Seph wasn't entirely sure she really wanted to know what was said. But the fact that Kate was here, and she could focus on the feel of the skin of her cheek underneath her fingertips, kept Seph grounded that whatever was said, Kate had come back to her.

"It was okay." Kate sighed. "He was upset but strangely not that angry at me. I think he and I were both too concerned about Meg to be mad at each other at the time. Obviously, he's hurt about the fact I lied to him, as he should be. But I also think some part of him is just getting tired of all the shouting and arguing as well. That's not to say it's all over because I'm sure there will be more. But for today, we both agreed that however angry we are at each other, we need to just try and be civil for the kids." Kate's hands rested in a reassuring hold on her hips, although Seph wasn't sure who it was reassuring more. They stood there for a moment, neither of them speaking, Seph rubbing her thumb over Kate's cheek, the repetition soothing both their nerves. Seph reveled in the feel of Kate next to her, the touch of her skin under her fingers, the sound of her breathing into the silent night air, using all of her presence to ground her. The past couple of days had been unexpected, to say the least, but here, in this moment, she was trying to draw all the strength she could from being in Kate's space. After a while, she felt Kate shiver, the late evening air suddenly dropping. She pulled back, reluctantly separating from Kate.

"Come in. I'll get you a drink, and we can sit down and relax."

Seph walked back into the house, letting her hand drag lightly against Kate's stomach as she walked away, catching her fingers loosely and pulling her inside. She busied herself moving around the kitchen, pausing for a second at the fridge while her face was hidden to take another deep intake of air, silently counting to four, before breathing out. She didn't want Kate to see her struggling. She had to be strong for Kate; she had to support her now.

Once again, time skipped, and she was back at the counter, pouring wine into the glass in front of her. Warm arms wrapped around her middle and squeezed her close, grounding her. Kate pushed her chin into the crook of her neck, trying to get as close as possible to Seph, trying to get as much contact as possible. Seph placed her hands over Kate's, holding her there in an act of soft, comforting support, suppressing her own anxious, racing heartbeat.

"I might go get a bath, see if it helps me relax. If that's okay?"

"Of course it is. This is your home now. I-if you still want it to be?" Her voice drifted into a nervous silence at the suggestion, and she felt Kate lift her head. Her stomach dropped as her mind raced with what was about to be said next.

"Of course I do."

Seph stared down at her hands, still resting over Kate's, afraid to look up in case her face betrayed her real fears.

"Seph, look at me." She heard the plea by her ear, soft and desperate, as she closed her eyes and steeled her nerves before turning her face. "Of course I still want to live with you. This doesn't change that. It was always going to be difficult, this part, telling him and the kids. But I absolutely still want to be here, with you. I told Tim that I'm living here."

"You did?"

"Yes. Cam knows anyway, so it was only a matter of time."

"So you told him because you had to?" Seph's voice wavered, something like annoyance starting to swirl in her gut.

"No. I told him because it was the right thing to do. I'm tired of the lies and secrets."

"You never had to lie to anyone about me. I never asked you to do that," Seph responded sharply. Was Kate regretting the decision she'd made? She'd just said that she still wanted to be here, but did she? Now things were getting real, maybe she was starting to realise the weight of their situation. She pulled out of Kate's hold a little, angry that her own emotions were insistent on being so volatile this evening.

"Hey." Kate grabbed hold of her wrist gently, stopping her from moving further away. "I know you didn't, and that's not what I'm saying. I made that decision, and I stand by it. But it's still tiring, not telling the whole truth to people so close to me. As much as I love our little bubble and the way we are inside of it, I want to get to a point where we don't have to be like that anymore. Don't you?"

Seph sighed, regret washing over her. *Great, another emotion to add to the list.* "Of course I do. I'm...I'm sorry, I'm trying to not let this affect me, just to support you, but it's still hard. I'm just a bit all over the place today."

"Are you okay?" Kate regarded Seph with that soft look that spoke volumes more than those three words.

"I'm fine. Just a stressful day, that's all." Seph gave a small smile, as she opened her arms. "Come here."

Kate fell into her embrace, exhaling a tired breath as she lay her head on Seph's shoulder. She let her stay there, quiet for an indeterminate amount of minutes, trying to ground herself in the feel of Kate in her arms.

Kate broke the silence. "You cooked dinner?" Her voice was tinged with even more sadness for some reason, and Seph couldn't determine why.

"Yeah, but it's fine. It'll reheat if you don't want it tonight."

It had taken Seph all the energy she could muster to even contemplate cooking, but not only did she want Kate to come back to dinner, she also knew it would be a good way to hide her plummeting enthusiasm levels. Putting a normal front on things seemed the only thing to do at the moment.

"I've not eaten since lunch with Cam, and I didn't have a lot." Kate looked into the pan, smiling when she saw Seph's bolognese sauce she had made. Seph had picked it especially, knowing it was one of Kate's favourites.

"Are you hungry now?"

"Maybe a little."

Seph hung her arms loosely around Kate's waist. "How about you go get that bath and get changed, and I'll have it ready for when you get out? Then we'll have an early night, try and get some sleep."

Kate hummed at the idea, and a small smile graced her lips as she leant into Seph's space again, placing a gentle kiss on her mouth. Seph felt her emotions spike again, this time with uncertainty about where they were at. Kate suddenly felt like she was in very real reach of slipping out of her grasp again.

"I love you." Seph's voice wavered, her front slipping slightly. Kate must have sensed the change.

"I love you, too. It'll be alright, I promise."

"I should be telling you that."

"As long as I've got you, I know I'll be okay. I know the past couple of days have been horrible, but it'll get better, I promise."

"I know," Seph replied, plastering on a fake smile in an attempt to misdirect Kate. "Go on, go get a bath. Dinner will be ready in twenty minutes."

Kate kissed her again, whispering a soft *thank you* against her lips before pulling away and disappearing upstairs. Seph watched her, taking tired step after tired step, before turning, her hands gripping the counter to steady herself.

Chapter Thirty-One

K ate sat at the table, tapping her fingers impatiently against the side of her glass. Meg's time-keeping was bad enough as it was, her attitude that the world would wait for her the cause of many an argument over the years, but this was now just ridiculous. She turned her wrist, glancing at her watch. Forty minutes late. She was doing this on purpose.

"I'm sure she'll be here in a minute, Mum," Cam offered.

"Cameron, stop trying to smooth the path with your sister. It's about time she started to take responsibility for her own actions. Including being on time."

Between Tim treating her like she was made of gold and Cam's overwhelming need to try and keep the boat from rocking, Meg had always got away with far too much. It was only ever Kate who stood up to her daughter's churlish attitude, and even then, she was usually shot down by her husband—*ex-husband*—she corrected herself, using the excuse that Meg was the youngest. Like it gave her some free pass to being inconsiderate. Today, Kate wasn't in the mood to put up with Meg's venomous attitude, which she had been subjected to over the past few days, the line between hurt daughter and entitled brat being crossed a long time ago.

The sound of heels clicking furiously across the tiled floor of the restaurant gave Kate an inkling that her daughter had decided to make an appearance. Kate would have usually stood up to greet her, politeness always over-taking anything else, but today Meg did not deserve that platitude. As Meg rounded the table, she made no attempt to look at Kate or greet her brother, let alone offer an apology for keeping them both waiting for over half an hour, instead pulling the chair out at the opposite side of the table with such force it screeched across the floor. Kate grimaced at the sound.

"Nice of you to join us, Megan," Kate said, barely concealed irritation seeping out from every word.

"Sorry, I was busy," Meg offered poorly as she shrugged.

"Well, so am I, and so is your brother, and we managed to get here on time and then had to wait for you for the past forty minutes, so an apology wouldn't go amiss."

"Whatever. I'm here, aren't I?"

"You didn't have to come if you didn't want to."

"And miss the opportunity to hear you try and explain yourself out of this? No thanks," Meg scoffed.

Kate closed her eyes, taking a deep breath in before continuing. If Meg was planning on being like this the whole lunch, it would grow very tiring very quickly.

"There's no explaining my way out of anything, Meg. I just wanted to talk to you both, calmly, about what's been going on."

"What's been going on," Meg hissed, leaning forward across the table. Kate had strategically chosen somewhere public to have this talk in the hopes it would put a curb on Meg vitriol. "Is you've been shagging some absolute bitch from Dad's office while he's been busy at work."

Kate had to hold a snigger in at that. Meg was so far into her idolisation of her father, she didn't even know what the truth was anymore. "Meg, I can honestly say your father hasn't had a busy day at work for at least five years. Where do you think the money comes from? To pay for your apartment, your car? It's not solely your dad's wage."

"Dad got me my car—"

"Yes, with money from our joint account, which we both pay into for things you kids need. It's always been that way. But I put more into that account each month, so if you want to argue semantics, go ahead. But just remember what I do for a living."

"Do *you* still actually do any work? Or are you too busy going around sleeping with Dad's employees?"

"Okay, that's enough," Kate hissed. "I get that you are angry, I really do, but how do you expect us to have a conversation when you won't even speak civilly to me?"

"What's the point? You'll only try to lie your way out of it."

"Meg, give her a chance," Cam intervened.

"Why should I? She's took everything and just ruined it for some cheap tart—"

"Enough!" Kate shouted before realising she had drawn attention. She glanced around, aware that other diners were looking over at their table. Lowering her voice but keeping her stern tone, she leant closer to Meg. "You can say whatever you want about me, be as angry as you want, but you do not *ever* speak about Seph that way."

"Seph? So she has a name."

"Yes. And if you'd taken more than two seconds out of your self-righteous tirade to ask, you would know that." Kate took a breath, sitting back in her chair. "Everyone is hurting in this, and that's all down to me. I'm not trying to deny that. But I am asking for you to just give me five minutes to explain things from my side. If you still hate me after that, then fair enough, but first, I want you to have all the information."

Meg fell back into her chair, crossing her arms defensively across her chest. "Go on then."

"I met Seph over a year ago at a work event. Nothing happened straight away; I had told her I was married. But I couldn't help the feelings I had for her, and they only got stronger as time went on. I fought for a long time over what was best to do, and at one point, I put you two and your father first." Kate sighed. "But sometimes, sweetheart, and you'll realise this as you get older, your feelings can't be controlled. Even though I was apart from Seph, I didn't stop loving her. And the pain at leaving her only got worse. I was miserable, Meg, and it got to the point where the only option was for me to be selfish and do something I wanted for once. It wasn't a decision I took lightly; I knew the consequences. But it was something I had to do for *me*."

"Don't you love Dad anymore?" Meg asked, her tone slightly softer but still judgemental.

Kate sighed. She'd lost count of the times Meg had asked her that over the past few weeks. She understood why; it must be difficult to comprehend that your parents no longer loved each other. But before the revelation about who Kate was seeing, she was starting to feel that maybe Meg was coming to terms with it. "Sweetheart, I know this is difficult to understand, but no, I don't. Not the way I used to. And not the way I should. I'll always love your dad in some way, sweetie; he's your dad, and without him, I wouldn't have you two and the memories we've made. But like I've said before, no-one is the same person they were when they were twenty-five. We've both changed."

An uneasy silence settled over the table, Kate watching as Meg looked down at her lap, clearly processing everything she'd just said. She wasn't accepting, but at least she wasn't shouting anymore, and Kate would take that victory.

"You should give her a chance, Meg. She seems nice," Cam offered.

Meg's head shot up, that fire back in her eyes. "You've met her?" she sneered.

Well, that was short-lived, thought Kate.

"Yes, I have. I went round the other day when Dad told me... I had to talk to Mum, and Dad told me where Seph lived. That was all," Cam clarified as Meg's glare hardened, clearly thinking she'd been kept out of the loop even further.

"Might have known you'd side with her."

"I'm not siding with anyone, Meg. But come on, you have to admit Mum has been miserable these past few months. And since she left Dad, even though it's been really stressful, she seems...I don't know, lighter. Like something has lifted from her."

"Yeah, well, if she was that unhappy, maybe she should have tried talking to Dad rather than jumping into bed with the first person who showed her some attention."

"For fuck's sake, Meg!" Cam exclaimed, startling both Kate and Meg, the outburst uncharacteristic for him. "Stop being such a spoiled brat and pay attention to what's going on around you. No-one's saying that Mum did the right thing, and she's apologised to us all, but you can't keep being so blinded by this perfect relationship you thought they had. All she wants is a chance to explain, and you won't even answer her calls. You're not a child anymore; you don't get to throw a tantrum and expect everyone to bow to your demands." Cam took a breath. "Seph makes Mum happy, and we might not be happy about how things happened, but all Mum wants is for us to stop fighting."

Meg sat stunned, staring at her big brother. "Well, shit, Cam. I didn't know you had that in you."

"Yeah, well, maybe I'm tired of trying to deflect your attitude to try and keep the peace."

Kate leant over and took Cam's hand where it was resting against the table, giving him a small smile of thanks. She knew she could rely on his support on some level, and his visit the other day had only served to prove that, but to see him so passionate and emotional was rare. Just like Kate, he was notorious for putting everyone else before himself for the sake of an easy life. To see him stand up for himself, and for her, made her proud.

"Cam's right, sweetie. I'm not expecting anyone to be okay with this at the moment. I'm not expecting you to come over and have dinner with us or have family days out. All I'm asking is for you to listen and try to think about what I've said."

"I don't know, Mum. It's a big change."

"I know. And I'm not saying you have to accept it straight away. I appreciate this is going to take some time for all of us to get used to. I also don't expect you to take sides between me and your dad. Although I appreciate that right now, you will side with him."

"Dad doesn't want that either. In fact, he told me I should come and see you today."

That did surprise Kate. While she and Tim had tentatively agreed to try and remain amicable for the sake of the kids, behind closed doors it was an entirely different matter. Tim was still very much angry at finding out about Seph and her involvement in the end of their marriage. But to find out he was actively encouraging Meg to speak to Kate; maybe he wasn't as stubborn as Kate had him down for.

"Really?"

"Yeah. He's still pissed. I mean mega pissed. But he's trying hard not to be angry in front of me. It doesn't stop me being angry though, Mum."

"I know, sweetheart. I'm sorry you're feeling this way, I really am. And I know there's nothing I can do to stop it. This is all my fault."

"You could stop lying to begin with."

Kate bit her tongue. Although her nerves were on edge and she was at the end of her temper, it wouldn't help anyone if she snapped at Meg again. And wasn't what Meg saying grounded in some element of truth?

"There are no more lies. I promise. And I'll do anything to try and make this right between us again."

"Would you leave her?"

Kate wasn't expecting that. Maybe she should have been, but she didn't really think twice about the promise which had just come from her mouth. All she was thinking was trying to start on rebuilding the relationship with her daughter. Her silence must have been enough to answer her question, but before either of them said anything, Cam spoke again.

"That's unfair, Megs. You can't ask that of Mum."

"Why not? She just said she would do anything."

"Because you're essentially asking her the same as if you were asking her to give Dad another chance. It would involve Mum not being with Seph, and that would make her unhappy. You're asking her to be unhappy."

Meg seemed to think about what Cam was saying. "Fine. But I'm not meeting her. Not yet."

"That's okay." It was small and imperfect, but the most she had got from Meg in days, and she was willing to take any small morsel she was giving. "Would you like to stay and have lunch with me and your brother? Don't worry, I'll pay," Kate said with a small smile, desperate not to ruin the moment but aching to spend some time with both her children in a relatively normal fashion. Every time they met recently, it had ended with raised voices or tears.

"You know I love the Caesar salad here. That's a low blow, Mum," Meg replied.

"I'll use anything I can, sweetheart."

CHAPTER THIRTY-TWO

Seph sat at her desk, quietly concentrating on the notes she had in front of her. It was a Friday, and she was coming to the end of her second week at her new job. So far, so good, she thought to herself. She'd instantly got a good vibe from Lister and Windsor when she interviewed; they had a good reputation and weren't afraid to take on the harder cases, doing a lot of work for clients who otherwise wouldn't be able to afford decent legal cover. It was a firm that had a worthy heart. It wasn't that Bailey, Bradshaw and Haynes didn't, but she couldn't imagine being allowed to take on some of those cases there. This firm had a much more civil client base, while Bailey, Bradshaw and Haynes were very corporate. On top of that, she felt like she fitted in. Or at least that she could, after a while. The staff were friendly and down to earth, no one seeming too flashy or showy, and for once in her life, she didn't feel like so much of the ugly duckling. *This is good*, she reminded herself. *Life is good.*

And truthfully, things were good. Kate and her had settled into a more than enjoyable routine since Kate moved in officially, and this weekend they were due to go pick up the last of her stuff from Sarah's. There wasn't much, most of it had already found its way to Seph's house, but there were some bits which Kate had taken with her in the first few days which were still there. Everything else had been packed up and was stored in Kate's parent's spare room, while the bigger stuff was still at the house where Tim was living. He was still being stubborn about selling it, but Kate wasn't backing down, and despite the flurry of activity from his lawyer when he discovered Kate and Seph's relationship, he had otherwise quietened down.

Things were also going better between Kate and the kids. Cam was polite enough that if he came to the house to see Kate, he would engage in conversation with Seph, but still, both felt a little awkward around each other. But at least he would speak to her. Meg, while no longer quite as angry at Kate, still wouldn't agree to meet Seph, and Seph could understand why. These things took as long as they took, but at least Meg was speaking to Kate now, and Seph couldn't be happier with that. She knew how much having her daughter not talk to her was hurting Kate, despite Kate's words that Meg was showing her spoilt and childish side.

Seph thought about their plans for this evening. Fridays were the time that Kate really could wind down for good, and after being back at work for two weeks, Seph was remembering why. Kate was cooking tonight, she had insisted on doing more of it now Seph was back at work, so all Seph needed to do was drive home, maybe take a nice hot bath, and then snuggle up on the sofa. Yeah, life was pretty good at the moment.

Then why do you feel like this?

She tried to push back the voice which just popped into her head, fanning the flames of her own quietly smoldering self-doubt. But it had been there a lot recently, just quietly murmuring in the background, tainting everything she was doing. *Life is good*, she told herself again.

"Bye, Seph. Have a good weekend, yeah?"

Seph looked up at the voice, having gotten lost a little further in her own head than she realised. Standing beside her desk was Anna, one of the other lawyers who worked in the same department. Anna was lovely, probably the same age as Seph, but had made an effort to take her under her wing and show her the ropes while she was still finding her feet.

"Oh, is it that time already?" Seph asked, glancing at her watch.

"Having that much fun you're losing track of time?"

"Oh no, I am so ready for home," Seph said, standing and powering down her laptop.

"Are we working you too hard?" Anna asked with a smile.

Seph chuckled. "No, it's just I'm still getting into the swing of things. Everyone assumes you're fresh-faced and relaxed when you've had some time off, but it takes it out of you when you have to start the daily grind again." Seph had confided in Anna that she had taken some leave before starting this new job but hadn't revealed any real details. It wasn't needed, Seph felt, and Anna seemed to take it as a given when she just said she had had an extended holiday.

"Any plans for the weekend?" Anna asked as Seph continued to pack up, leaning back on the edge of her desk.

"Furniture shopping. My girlfriend has twice as many clothes as I do wardrobe space." Even though the idea of walking around a load of furniture shops sounded boring and exhausting to Seph, she was excited by the idea that it was to buy *their* furniture. For *their* home. Seph was worried that her house might be a bit small for the both of them to begin with, but Kate soon put her mind at ease, saying that even though she was moving from a drastically bigger house, she also now no longer lived with two grown-up children. And that most of the stuff within her old house she could do without, having bought on a whim or because it was something Tim wanted. But Seph had suggested that if they were planning on staying at her, no *their*, house much longer, they should use the opportunity of Kate moving in to redecorate. She hadn't done much to the house since she first moved in, spending a lot of her savings on knocking the kitchen and living room walls through to make it one room, and after that, casually decorating just to freshen up the rest of the rooms. Her bedroom had been seriously neglected.

"You sound like my boyfriend. He always complains about how many shoes I have."

"Don't even get me started on her shoes." Seph laughed, holding her hands up. "I have no idea how many pairs of heels a woman needs, but Kate's got to be above her quota."

"Sounds like me and Kate could get along. Maybe we should all get together sometime, maybe go for a drink or something?"

"Oh." Seph was taken aback. She wasn't used to being someone who got asked out for drinks with colleagues. Her shock at the situation, partnered with her normally occurring social anxiety, must have made her look horrified by the thought.

"You don't have to if you don't want. It was just a—"

"No! No, sorry. I just...we'd love to."

"You sure?"

"Yes, sorry. Long week—just zoned out a little. I'll speak to Kate. Maybe we can do something in a few weeks when I'm over this starting period?" Seph scrabbled, hoping to claw the conversation back.

"Sure thing. Okay, well, I'm going to get off. See you Monday?"

"Yeah, see you Monday."

Seph watched as Anna walked out of the office, the door swinging behind her as she left, exhaling slowly as she disappeared from sight. Suddenly her legs felt weak, as though all the energy had just drained from her feet and into the floor, and she slumped back down into her chair. Why did the offer of a drink with a work colleague blindside her so much? *Because you're slipping again.*

Chapter Thirty-Three

S eph shut her front door behind her, kicking off her boots and dropping her satchel on the floor. It was Friday, she was exhausted and all she wanted to do was crawl under a blanket and snuggle with Kate while binge-watching the next few episodes of *Motherland: Fort Salem* and eating a takeaway. She smiled as she thought about how much Kate would probably want to do the same. She'd become obsessed with the show since Seph introduced it to her a few weeks ago, and they were flying through her box sets. And even though the weather was becoming brighter, the evenings a little light as April took hold, her favourite place was still snuggled with Kate on the sofa. But tonight, they had some function to attend. Some fancy dinner and drinks thing an associate of Kate's was holding. Kate had asked her a month ago if she could attend with her, and to say Seph had been hesitant would be an understatement. It would be their first public outing within Kate's inner circle since their relationship became common knowledge, and Seph was unsure how her showing up would go down. But Kate had assured her that it would be okay, not forcing her to go, but making it very clear that if she was to agree, Kate would be extremely proud and honoured to take Seph. Still, her nerves at being introduced as Kate's partner were adding to the ever-present feeling of anxiousness she'd been experiencing the past few weeks. These people were used to seeing Kate with Tim, and although no doubt they were aware of their marriage ending, it didn't mean they were ready to open their arms to Seph. Still, Kate wanted her to attend with her, and Seph wasn't about to let Kate down.

"Hey, Kate?" Seph called when she found the living room and kitchen empty. Jogging up the stairs, she found the hairdryer blasting from the bedroom and understood the lack of answer when she called.

"Hey, I'm back," she shouted as she walked into the bedroom. "Woah."

She swallowed thickly at the sight that greeted her. Kate stood, hair thrown to one side as she tussled it while drying it, wearing nothing but a matching black lace bra and pants. She suddenly felt her breathing quicken, and heat rushed up her body. She'd never get tired of seeing that body. For a forty-nine-year-old mother of two, she had the body of someone half her age. Kate didn't work out, she was too busy to go to the gym, but her busy lifestyle kept her on the move enough she didn't need to, and Seph could only imagine she had been blessed with a metabolism most women would die for. Having met Maggie and seen that she too shared Kate's build, she could only presume it was a genetic blessing passed down on her mother's side. The sound of the hairdryer stopping broke Seph's daydreaming.

"Hello. You okay there?" she asked with a knowing smirk.

"Yep. Yep, fine. You look...umm. Fuck, you look hot."

There was something about when Seph got flustered, which really got to Kate, and Kate had told Seph just as much. Judging by the widening grin on her face, she knew exactly the reaction she was causing in Seph right now. But Seph didn't care. She wasn't about to hide how gorgeous she thought her girlfriend was in fear of being embarrassed. It had been a while since Seph had felt anywhere near this ready and willing. After initially reintroducing their sex life, it had taken a back seat over recent weeks with divorce proceedings, fighting families, and work pressures all doing an excellent job of sapping her sex drive and energy. Not to mention the increasing knot of anxiety that sat low in her stomach every day. Kate walked up to her, slowly running her fingers down the buttons of Seph's waistcoat before leaning up and kissing her, slow and long and lingering, her tongue darting across her bottom lip. Seph felt the blood pounding through her body, her anxieties washing away, and an overwhelming desire flooding her.

"I'm just going to finish getting ready..." Kate turned and headed back towards the bathroom, leaving Seph stunned. She blinked a couple of times, shaking herself back into focus, just in time to see Kate saunter down the hallway, disappearing into the bathroom with a wink. A switch flicked in her, and without hesitation, she headed towards Kate. When her girlfriend looked at her like that, all other thoughts disappeared from her brain. As she walked through the bathroom door, Kate was standing there, waiting, that sly grin on her mouth and eyes almost black with desire. Kate hooked her arms around her neck as Seph pushed herself close, kissing her with pent-up frustration. Seph walked her back until they hit the sink behind them, her mouth hungrily taking Kate's before moving down her neck.

"I know you've been worried about tonight, baby, so I thought a little stress relief beforehand might help."

"You planned this?" Seph muttered as her kisses dragged across Kate's skin. Planned or not, it was having the desired effect.

"Well, personally, I think it was your fault for leaving for work in *this* this morning," Kate whispered in her ear, running her hands across the buttons of Seph's waistcoat. "I've wanted you all day."

Seph's hands reached for her hips, smoothing around Kate's backside and gripping tightly before lifting her up and resting her on the edge of the cabinet. Kate took a sharp breath at the sudden movement before wrapping her legs around Seph's waist to pull her closer. As she continued kissing every inch of smooth, beautiful, exposed skin, Seph's fingers went to undo her own waistcoat and shirt, desperate to be closer to Kate.

"No. That stays on," Kate whispered, stopping Seph's hands. Seph pulled back to look at Kate. Her eyes were dark and full of lust, the skin on her neck pink where she had been kissing. She'd never found her so breath-taking before. "These..." Kate's hands moved to the buckle of her belt, "these only."

Kate swiftly undid the buckle, followed by the button of her trousers, pushing them down over Seph's hips. She pulled her back closer by the waistband of her black girl boxers, but not before she took a look full of appreciation. She found them equally as sexy as Seph found her lacy lingerie, and she frequently told her, either through words or the look of desire she had right now. Seph surged forward for another hungry kiss before trailing her mouth down Kate's neck, kissing over the swell of her breasts, finally taking her nipple in her mouth through the lace of her bra. Kate let out a deeply sinful moan at the feel of her but didn't let her linger for long, gently tugging at her hair to bring her back up.

"I need you, baby..." Kate panted, her desperation for Seph's touch clear in her voice.

Seph didn't need any more encouragement when her girlfriend was that desperate for her that she was practically begging for her. Who was she to deny her? She took a second to look at Kate, eyes closed and head thrown back, as she ghosted her fingers over the lace of her panties, ready and waiting to feel her fingers push past the thin fabric and take her. However, she dropped to her knees, pushing her mouth to them and pressing a hot kiss to where she needed her.

"Oh, fuck!" Kate exclaimed, hips jerking into the sensation.

"These," Seph tugged on her waistband, "need to be off for me to do what I want to do." Kate quickly pushed herself up, allowing Seph to slip her pants off and down her legs before kissing up the inside of her thigh.

The moan of pure pleasure which escaped Kate the moment Seph's mouth touched her was intoxicating. Seph groaned as she felt Kate's hand grip her hair, pulling her tighter against her. With every jerk of Kate's hips, Seph chased her body, letting out her own sounds of enjoyment against Kate's throbbing clit, knowing that she could feel every vibration. Her tongue traced meaningless patterns across her, teasing Kate before focusing solely on that one tiny area she knew would have Kate coming within seconds. As predicted, Kate writhed against her mouth as she placed all her attention on that sweet spot, savouring the taste of Kate as she got wetter with each flick of her tongue. Suddenly, Kate's thighs clamped around her head, involuntarily holding her in place, Seph unable to escape, even if she wanted to. With a final, deep, everlasting moan, Kate came against her mouth, Seph continuing to seek out every last ounce of pleasure from her shaking, writhing body before pulling away, placing one last wet kiss against her thigh. As Kate's body relaxed, boneless and spent from her orgasm,

Seph quickly got to her feet, wrapping an arm around her waist and guiding her to the cool tiled floor before her legs buckled. For a few long, quiet seconds, all Seph could hear were Kate's and her own harsh breaths as she watched her girlfriend come down from her high.

"Okay?" Seph asked, though the blissed-out look on Kate's face was answer enough.

"More than okay," Kate rasped, her voice hoarse, as she wrapped her still shaking legs around Seph's waist, urging her closer. "Got to admit, didn't *quite* expect that reaction when I bought this underwear…"

"What can I say? It looks good on you," Seph muttered as she leant forward, taking Kate's mouth in another kiss.

Kate met her in another languid kiss, her hand slipping down and fingers brushing gently across the skin of Seph's neck. Seph gasped, the soft touch enough to fire her sensitive nerves once again, her body twitching of its own accord, desperate for more contact. She saw Kate smirk, knowing what her body was craving, her hand trailing lower until it rested in between Seph's thighs, her arousal desperately obvious through her pants. Kate hummed against her lips at the feeling, another jolt of arousal shooting throughout Seph's body.

"Oh, well, it certainly did have an effect on you…"

She stroked her hand up inside Seph's thighs, more deliberate and slow than before. Seph groaned, her need still unseen to and in no way helped by the slow, teasing manner with which Kate was touching her. Kate got to her knees and crawled forward and, in doing so, pushed Seph down to the floor.

"Let me take care of you," she whispered over Seph's mouth before running her tongue slowly over her lips.

"I-I don't think it's going to take a lot," Seph stuttered, her breathing already rapid. "I was pretty close with just feeling you…oh."

Kate's hand slid past the elastic of Seph's boxers, her fingers taking a long, slow swipe of her arousal. Seph's hips instinctively bucked, desperate for more friction, embarrassed and surprised at just how soaked and needy she was. While she would willingly give her girlfriend everything she asked for, she wasn't expecting to feel quite so turned on.

"God, I can't wait to see you dressed up tonight. To show the world you're mine," Kate muttered in her ear as her fingers continued to move against her.

As if someone somewhere had just shut the faucet off on her arousal, Seph felt the euphoria drain from her body. Screwing her eyes shut, she tried to focus on the feel of Kate, the way her fingers stroked against her clit, the weight of her body on top of her, the soft huff of breath by her ear. She could smell her shampoo and the subtle scent of the shower gel she had used, the feel of her wet arousal against her own leg. Everything she was surrounded by right now should be taking her to unimaginable heights, but something somewhere was stopping it. A dam holding back the connection she wanted to feel. The connection she *was* feeling until just moments ago. She tried to clear her mind, push away those negative thoughts which were growing, like a fog, coming in thicker and faster with each second. She felt Kate kiss her neck, pulling up until she was hovering over her again and Seph's vision was filled with her beautiful face. *What is wrong with me?* Seph thought, as she stared into those deep green eyes which were filled with so much love, they made her heart clench. Guilt washed over her, the thought of not being fully in the moment as Kate tried to bring her to orgasm too painful to contemplate. For a split second, she thought about faking it, maybe even if she carried on, the feeling would come back. But the feel of Kate's fingers were no longer soft and sensual, and the physical signs of her arousal also starting to subside. She wrapped her hand around Kate's wrist, stilling it.

"What's wrong?" Kate asked, a small wrinkle of confusion on her forehead. Her breath was still ragged from her own orgasm, and Seph really wished she could be there with her.

"N-nothing. Just...I don't think...I..."

Kate withdrew her hand, placing it on the tiled floor by Seph's head as she understood what Seph was trying to say. Pushing herself up so she was no longer bearing all her weight on her but still remained bracketed around Seph's body, she studied her face.

"Did I...did I do something wrong?"

"God, no! You were doing everything right, trust me. It's just...I don't know." Seph could feel tears starting to collect behind her eyelids and willed them to go away. The last thing she needed to make this situation even more humiliating was for her to start crying. "I'm sorry."

"Hey, hey, no, it's okay. It's fine, baby." Kate shifted so she was on her side, brushing the hair from Seph's face and tucking it behind her ear.

"Sorry, I was...I was there, I swear, but then I just...something in my brain just switched, and I lost it. I'm so embarrassed," Seph said, hiding her face behind her hands.

She felt more than embarrassed. She was mortified. The woman of her dreams, the woman she loved, who had given her the most incredible life, even if it was only over these past few weeks, was about to make her come, and her brain put the brakes on it. And not just slowly. A full-on emergency stop situation.

A warm hand wrapped itself around her fingers and gently tugged her hand away. "There's nothing to be embarrassed about," Kate tried to reassure her with a soft smile.

"Easy for you to say," Seph mumbled.

Kate leant down, her hair falling in front of their faces like a curtain to protect them from the world. She pressed her lips firmly to Seph's, the gesture going some way to settling the churning mixture of humiliation and anxiety in her gut. "Don't worry about it. You've had a busy few weeks; it's stressful starting a new job. And while you're doing really well, it doesn't mean that something like this, a moment where your mind works against you, isn't going to happen." Kate pressed another gentle kiss to her lips. "Is it tonight? Are you worried about it?"

"Just..." Seph took a deep breath, trying to organise her thoughts. "It's just that everyone there knows you as Tim's wife. Not *only* as Tim's wife, I mean. They're used to seeing you and Tim together. And I hate big groups and social-ising..."

"I know. I still remember how totally out of place and uncomfortable you looked, sitting at that bar at the conference." Seph groaned, again going to cover her face. Kate's hands wrapped around her fingers, stopping her before they could reach. "I get you don't really fancy going out tonight. Trust me, I would much rather be snuggled at home with you than going out to some fancy party."

"You don't have to say that to make me feel better."

"I'm not, baby."

"But you were excited to go."

"I was looking forward to going out with you, and getting to spend the evening with you. And seeing you all dressed up in that gorgeous shirt I bought you last weekend. You look so sexy in it, and it makes your tits look amazing." Seph couldn't help the laugh which escaped her at the comment. In response, Kate's grin widened. "I was excited to be with you, and I am, wherever we are."

Seph exhaled a long slow breath, trying to let the words wash over her and soothe her racing heart. They dulled it, like placing your fingers in your ears at a loud sound, but she could still make out the noise seeping through.

"Baby, if you really don't want to go—"

"No. No, let's go. We can't avoid it forever, so let's just get it over with."

"Wow, I've never felt more wanted."

Seph shoved Kate playfully on the shoulder. "That's not what I meant."

"I know, baby. I'm only messing." Kate placed another lingering kiss on Seph's lips. "I love you. And I promise I will not leave your side."

"I love you, too. You really do look amazing."

"Hmm, well, unfortunately, I don't think anyone else will appreciate it if I turn up in just this. So I better get some clothes on."

CHAPTER THIRTY-FOUR

S eph leant against the bar and waited for the barman to come over to serve her. The evening had been pleasant enough, all things considered, even though there were some definite looks of surprise when Kate introduced Seph to some of the guests. But Kate had kept her promise and barely left her side all evening. Seph wasn't sure if it was protectiveness or just the need to be close, but either way, she wasn't complaining. She would always calm down with the feel of Kate's hand in her own, and although the feeling wasn't as all-encompassing as it usually was, she couldn't deny that it had tempered the anxiety a little.

She looked around the room, finding Kate in the sea of people instantly. She was deep in conversation with someone who she had been introduced to earlier but couldn't remember the name of. She'd been introduced to so many people tonight, she was never going to remember everyone's names. Luckily, Sarah was also at the party and had spent the evening laughing and joking with them both. Seph liked Sarah; she could see why she was Kate's best friend, her easy-going nature making Seph feel at ease quickly. She couldn't help but think about when she had that with Fiona, but it had been months now, and she still hadn't heard anything from her. Seph watched as Kate conversed with ease, in awe of how well she could talk to just anyone. She really wished she could have even half of Kate's confidence. But she guessed that's why they made such a good pair. Kate instilled a sense of capability and self-esteem in Seph, and Seph gave her...something in return. There must be something, but Seph would be damned if she knew what it was.

Suddenly, the sound of Kate's name being uttered in the crowd caused her ears to prick and automatically tune into the conversation behind her.

"...oh you don't know what happened? She left him. Apparently just walked out on him one night and shacked up with some woman she'd been having an affair with."

"No! Poor Tim."

"Yep. I mean, I can't imagine how the poor bloke's feeling."

"So the woman she's with tonight..."

"Her *girlfriend*." Seph almost winced at the tone she was being referred to in.

"I never knew Kate was...well, you know."

"Maybe she is. Maybe she's not. All I know is that woman who she's here with must be riding a high."

"What do you mean?"

"Rumour has it, she, this *what-ever-her-name-is*, was a junior associate at BBH."

"She worked for Tim?"

"Yep. And we all know that Kate earns a pretty penny through Earnshaw and Harper, so she's found herself a nice little cash pot with Kate."

"Yeah, but would you really go for someone married?"

"Well, some people just like to cause trouble. If you ask me..."

Seph couldn't bear to hear anymore. She knew what they were insinuating. Suddenly, bile burnt the back of her throat, and she swallowed it down, struggling to remain grounded. As she moved away from the bar on autopilot, the sounds of the room dulled through the blood rushing in her ears.

"Seph? Haven't you forgotten something?" The sound of Kate's voice broke through the haze, and she realised she had somehow made it to her. She looked up at her, watching as the smile quickly slipped from her face. "Seph?"

"Sorry...I...I don't feel...I might just get a taxi home..."

Kate slipped a hand around her wrist, turning them away from the small group of people they were standing next to, concern painting her features. "Baby, what's wrong?"

"I just don't feel..."

"Are you having an attack?" Kate asked quietly.

"I'll be fine once I get home. You...you stay." Seph really wanted Kate with her, but she also wasn't going to drag her away. People already thought she was playing her, and if she demanded that they leave now...

"No. I'm coming with you." Kate started to move them both, walking out of the main room and into the quieter area outside. The cool evening air felt like a wave of relief across Seph's flushed cheeks, but she knew she wasn't going to be able to hold this off for much longer.

"No. No, I don't want...I don't want people to think I'm making you leave."

"You're not. Why would people think... Has someone said something to you?"

"N-no." Seph couldn't even say that convincingly, hearing the waver in her own voice.

"Seph, tell me—"

"Kate." The voice from earlier sent a shiver of dread through Seph's body, and she could feel her breath stuttering. "It's lovely to see you tonight. Are you and your guest coming back inside?" She could feel the other woman's eyes boring into her, and Seph couldn't do anything but stare at her shoes and focus on her breathing.

"Lynne, hi. Maybe in a bit. I'll come find you."

"Okay, see you in a bit."

Seph didn't see her walk away. The next thing she was aware of was Kate gently tipping her face upwards and her warm green eyes regarding her with the utmost empathy.

"Baby, what happened? Tell me, please. Did someone say something to you?"

"Not...not to me. I heard someone talking, that's all." Seph desperately tried to downplay it in the hopes that Kate would let it go.

"About us? Seph, I can't imagine anything else being said which would have you reacting this way unless it was about us. So was it?"

Seph paused before giving a small nod. She was losing the energy to be able to argue differently anymore.

"Who was it?" Kate's voice had changed. Gone was her soft, comforting tone, replaced with a steely hardness. Seph really didn't want to cause any trouble.

"I don't—"

"Kate! Kate, come and have a glass of champagne. Bring your guest!"

Seph tensed at the sound of the woman's voice again, and she went rigid under the soft hand which was cupping her cheek. She hoped Kate hadn't noticed her reaction…

"Was it *her*?"

Seph knew it was a slim chance that she would get away with hiding it, and she opened her eyes where they had closed moments earlier to see Kate giving her a look she had only ever seen once before—when Tim barged into her house, demanding answers. That look terrified her; it was so removed from the Kate she knew with her warm gaze and loving words. She knew it wasn't directed at her, but she still hated the fall-out which would come with it.

"Kate, please…" Seph tried to plead.

"What did she say? Tell me, Seph. I'm either going to find out from you, or I'm going to ask her."

"She…" Seph swallowed down the lump in her throat, struggling to speak. "She said that…or she made it sound like…like I was only with you for your money. And that's why I have…that's why I'm interested in you. To cause trouble and to get your money."

"She said that?"

"Please, Kate—"

Before Seph's protestations could even reach her, Kate had spun on her heel and was marching back into the room.

"Ah, Kate, there you are!" Lynne greeted her, holding up a glass of champagne.

"Don't you fucking dare!" Kate hissed.

Lynne's arm dropped, and she regarded Kate with feigned confusion. "What's wrong?"

"Don't you ever fucking utter Seph's name again, do you understand?"

"Kate, please." Seph had tentatively come up behind Kate, wrapping her hand around her arm and trying to tug her away inconspicuously. Suddenly Lynne's eyes shot up to hers, a smirk playing at the edge of her mouth.

"I don't know what she's told you, but I didn't say anything."

"Bullshit."

"Look, Kate, we all have midlife crises, but maybe just buy a convertible rather than switch teams and have a dabble, yeah?"

"Are you serious? This isn't just some fucking experiment."

"That's what she's told you, is it?" Lynne asked, nodding her head in Seph's direction. "Come on, Kate. You can't honestly tell me this is what you want from life. I mean, look at her. I've had clients who look more reputable than her."

"You fucking cow! You're nothing but a nasty gossip."

"And good luck to you, love," Lynne continued, addressing Seph herself over Kate's shoulder. "Once she sees you for what you really are, you'll be left high and dry. No one in the legal profession is going to want to touch you after this."

"Back off, Lynne." Sarah appeared from nowhere, sliding in between Kate and Lynne. "You're out of order, so I suggest you take your little champagne harem and fuck off somewhere else." Keeping her body protectively in front of Kate and Seph, she turned her head. "Take Seph home, Kate. Go look after her."

"Kate, please..." Seph was close to tears, and she could hear it in her voice. She wasn't sure how much longer she could survive in this room, feeling the stares of people on her, feeling their judgement. She needed to get out. Something in her voice must have gotten through, and Kate turned, her face instantly crumbling when she saw Seph. Kate took a step towards her, wiping a tear that had rolled down her face.

"It's okay, baby, we're going."

Chapter Thirty-Five

K ate slammed the door behind her, the taxi ride home doing nothing but stoking her burning rage at Lynne Williams. Seph had sat, quiet and pale, but with no other symptoms on the journey home, Kate didn't want to potentially set her off on a spiral until they were in the safety of their home. So she sat, instead repeating all she had said and heard over and over in her head. How could anyone think that of Seph? Kind, caring, compassionate Seph, who had done nothing but been caught up in all of this? She was to blame for this, not Seph, and the insinuation that she was using Kate had hurt. Not for Kate and the possibility it could be true, but for the little faith it put in Seph and her nature. Those people knew no better; they didn't know Seph, but what gave them the right to use their lack of knowledge to assume the worst of her?

She heard a soft thud and looked around. Seph slumped on the floor by the door, the tears she had been holding coming like they were never going to stop. In three long strides, Kate was beside her, kneeling next to her shaking body.

"Oh, sweetheart, come here. I'm sorry, I'm so sorry." She wrapped an arm around her shoulders, pulling her in close. "Just ignore her, baby. She's a horrible excuse for a human."

"I-is that what e-everyone thinks? T-that I broke up your marriage for fun?"

"No, baby, no. Not the people who matter. They know the truth."

"M-maybe I am a bad person—"

"No, don't you ever believe that. You are one of the most generous, kind, and loving people I have ever known."

"If t-that were true, I wouldn't h-have…"

Kate watched as Seph started to choke on her words, breaths coming out sharp and stuttered. She started to panic as Seph spiralled faster than she had ever seen before until she realised her inaction was only making things worse. She swung round to kneel in front of Seph, placing her hands on top of hers, trying to snap her focus back to her.

"Seph? Seph, baby, you need to breathe for me. Just follow me. One, two..."

Seph knew that the words were meant to reassure her, but she felt the knot of self-hatred and anxiety tighten even further. Her fists had balled tight into themselves, every muscle clenched like a coiled spring. She swallowed down some air, but it hit her like a wave, and her body started to heave. She felt as though she was drowning. She grasped at her chest, at the collar around her neck, trying desperately to breathe. She could hear something by her side, but it was fuzzy, and she couldn't make out what it was saying. Something touched her near her neck, and she tried to push it away, but the feeling returned, and she continued to feebly fight it. The tight constriction around her neck eased slightly as she realised her shirt was being undone around her still panicked hands. She squeezed her eyes shut, then opened them, hoping to clear her senses, but her vision was peppered by floating black spots. She could still hear the indistinguishable words being uttered in her ear, and a hand came to her cheek, pulling her face around.

"Seph..." Her name drifted into her consciousness. "Seph...listen to my voice. I need you to follow the pattern. Breathe with me. In for four and out for eight. Ready? One, two..."

Seph couldn't do it. Every breath filled her lungs with tar, breathing becoming impossible as she sunk deeper and deeper. The voice was still there, calling her to the surface with a dull, muffled *one, two* count, starting again with each failed attempt. She clung onto it like a life buoy, letting it pull her towards the surface, letting it take her weight so all she had to do was think about counting. *One, two, three...*

Slowly things started to come back into focus. Her hearing became less muffled, and her sight became clearer. She blinked, Kate becoming distinguishable in front of her. Only then did she notice that Kate's voice was ragged with worry, her eyes red and mascara running from where she had been sobbing. She tried to say something, but her throat was hoarse, and her word's slurred with the exhaustion which had taken her over completely.

"Shh, don't try to speak. Take a minute, then we'll try and move, okay?"

Seph closed her eyes again, and her head rolled back, unable to answer. She distantly felt someone tugging at her legs as Kate took off her boots, the heavy clunk as they hit the floor reverberating around her head. She wondered how long she had been sitting on the floor, time no longer seeming to run in the correct way.

"Do you think you can get upstairs? Then we can lie down in bed," Kate said, Seph grateful for the way she whispered softly.

Seph nodded, only a tiny movement, too drained and in too much pain to do much more. With Kate's help, her hands found the solid wood of the door behind her, pushing against it with what little strength she had in order to lift herself up, feeling the solid supporting weight of Kate beside her helping. She wobbled once upright, but before she could fall, Kate wrapped her arm around her waist, pulling her into her body.

"Okay, we're going to take it really slow," Kate reassured her.

Slow, heavy steps took her up the stairs, one at a time, her fingers gripping the wall. Once in their bedroom, energy she didn't even know she still possessed dissipated as she eyed their bed, and she collapsed onto it as soon as she was close enough. She lay there, unable to do anything as she felt Kate slowly and carefully undress her, urging her up to take off her shirt and replacing it with a warm fleece, the fabric instantly doing something to soothe her nerves. Once she was done, she rolled back over, staring at the wall in front of her, unable to say or do anything, a vast void slowly growing from the very centre of her chest. She registered the heavy weight as Kate wrapped her weighted blanket around her, a gift that Kate had bought her when she had first returned a few months ago, and she pulled it close, bringing her knees up to her chest. She sensed the bed dip beside her before an arm snaked its way around her waist and a body pressed close against her back.

"It's okay, sweetheart. I've got you," Seph heard Kate whisper into her ear.

The warmth of Kate's embrace seeped into her bones, and she willed it to do more to fight off the tremble which ran through her body. The adrenaline was long gone, the comedown in full swing as she shook.

"I'm s-sorry," she mumbled, guilt settling in the pit of her stomach at her own failure.

"You've got nothing to be sorry for."

"Shh-ould have been ss-tronger," she slurred as exhaustion dragged her under.

The last thing she registered before her heavy eyelids blinked for a final time was the soft stroke of fingers through her hair and a watery, tearful reassurance from Kate.

"It's okay, baby. I'm here."

Chapter Thirty-Six

Kate stormed into the coffee shop with a sense of indignation on Sunday morning. She threw her handbag on the table, startling Sarah, who was pouring herself a cup of tea. Her initial fury had subsided over the weekend, her focus mainly on Seph, but now she was out of her space, her rage had come back tenfold.

"We are not doing business with Lynne Williams again."

"I think that's a given after Friday night. I can't believe the entitled bitch was walking around saying what she was."

"I can. She was always a nasty little gossip." Kate dropped down into her chair, massaging her forehead. She'd been secretly medicating the headache she'd had since the early hours of Saturday morning, not wanting Seph to see that she had been so drastically affected by what had been said.

"Still. That was a low blow. How anyone could think Seph is that type of person is beyond me."

"Yeah, well, she doesn't know her, does she? She didn't take the time to, just fucking jumped to her own sordid conclusions and then decided to spread it around like it was gospel."

Sarah placed a cup of tea in front of Kate, resting back in her chair. "How is Seph? She looked pretty freaked before you left."

"She's..." Kate took a moment to compose herself. To be honest, she wasn't sure how Seph was. Saturday had passed in a blur, Seph sleeping a lot as she recovered from one of the most severe anxiety attacks Kate had ever seen. Kate hardly left her side, to the point where she was sure she must have been an irritation. But Seph was gracious about it, probably too exhausted to argue otherwise. However, as Seph fell asleep against her last night, both curled up on the sofa under a blanket, Kate finally let some of the tears and emotion she had been feeling come out. This morning, she had insisted that Kate take some time, suggesting that she go see the kids, but knowing that they were both busy, she had instead reluctantly texted Sarah to see if she was free. "I don't know. She broke down when we got home, and I can understand why. She still holds so much guilt. She was already nervous about going in the first place. I should have just insisted that we stayed home." Kate looked up at Sarah. "I've never seen her have an attack that severe before. It was like her whole body was giving up."

"Where is she now?"

"At home. She's still pretty wiped out from it, and I think she just wanted some space."

"I'm sorry, Kate. It must be awful. I know you've told me about this, but seeing it first hand…"

"That was nothing. She held it in until she got home and then just…collapsed." Kate took a breath. "I hate seeing her like that. And I know she can't help it, I know it's just an illness, just like anything else, but God, it makes me feel so helpless."

Sarah leant across the table, resting her hand over Kate's and giving it a squeeze. "She has you, though. And that means everything to her. You know what else I saw on Friday night? Someone who knew she was safe enough with you that she could break down, even behind closed doors. Someone who wanted to just protect you and herself from hurtful words. And you, who literally got in a woman's face to the point I thought you were going to knock her lights out because they had said something which hurt the woman you loved. You are not helpless, and she knows that. You mean more to her than anything."

"I just wish she didn't have to go through this. She'd been through enough already."

"She'll be fine. Because she has you. Why don't you take an hour to clear your head? Go buy her something nice, then go back and spend the rest of the day with her."

"Yeah. Yeah, you're right."

Seph

The house was quiet, eerily so. Kate had made her promise that she would rest. Seph knew that Kate was reluctant to leave, but she practically pushed her out the door, the condition being she would rest. Not that she felt up to doing anything. The last thing she wanted was for Kate to feel as though she was a babysitter. Besides, she wanted the space and the quiet. Or she thought she did. Now she was on her own, and it was suffocating.

Seph dragged herself upstairs and into the bathroom, switching on the shower and turning it up high until steam started to billow out. She shed her clothes and stepped under the near-scalding cascade of water, hoping to wash away the past few days. Instead, her mind decided to start shouting at her, hurling a repeat track of everything which had been thrown at her over the past few weeks.

I know you've been fucking my wife.

When did you start fucking her?

Some people just like to cause trouble.

Once she sees you for what you really are, you'll be left high and dry. No one's going to want to touch you after this.

She felt her chest tighten and her breathing become rapid, the air becoming thin, her head spinning with the heat of the shower and the struggle to inhale enough oxygen. She tasted salt as her tears mixed with the water, her chest heaving as the tears came thick and fast, quicker than she could breathe. Beneath her, she felt her legs start to buckle, and she let herself slide down the tiles, coming to a stop as she reached the bottom of the bath. She sat there sobbing uncontrollably, her breath hitching as she fought back the crushing force which pushed down on her chest. Through the fog of her tears, she reached out, almost on autopilot, like she was detached from her body, and her hand found its way to the razor which sat on the edge of the bath. She rolled it round in her hand a couple of times; it felt light, too light compared to what it was capable of.

Suddenly, that lightness took over her body, as if she was looking at the answer to all her prayers. An epiphany that could solve all her problems. Her hand shook as she placed it against her skin, the metal of the twin blades cool against the flesh of her thigh. She swore she would never get to this point again. She swore before that she would cope better, find a way without turning to this.

But in this moment, she felt so much pain and hurt and chaos it was physically aching within her, and she needed it released. She screwed her eyes shut as she pushed hard against her leg and dragged her hand to the right. She sucked in the air through her teeth as the sting started to follow the path of the blade, followed by the comforting warmth as blood started to trickle. She looked at it, the blood washing away with the water, before pushing the blade in again. A dizziness overtook her, like she was drifting, floating away on a calm sea after a storm. She let her head fall back, and her hand unclenched, dropping the razor in the bath.

CHAPTER THIRTY-SEVEN

Kate walked into the house and instantly felt something was wrong. She didn't know what, but there was an atmosphere that unsettled her. It was too quiet.

"Seph?"

She looked around the living room, making her way into the kitchen, finding it empty and the back door locked. She started up the stairs, hearing the shower running. It should have settled her, giving her a reason why Seph hadn't heard her and answered, but something still didn't feel right. A shiver ran up her spine as she got closer.

"Hey, sweetheart, I'm back," she called through the door, pushing it slightly further ajar.

On her first glance, nothing seemed amiss, but then she spotted the bent leg peeking out from behind the shower curtain. She could immediately tell from the angle and height that the person it belonged to was not standing up but more likely lying the length of the bath. Her heart shot into her throat as she pushed the door further and flung back the curtain.

"Oh, shit."

She leant over and turned off the shower, not caring that the icy cold water soaked her sleeves, before kneeling at the side of the bath.

"Seph? Seph, can you hear me?"

Kate cupped her face in her hands and pulled it round to face her. The combination of the water stopping, her voice, and her touch started to stir Seph, and she mumbled something incoherent, trying pathetically to pull her head out of Kate's grip.

"Seph, what happened?"

She shook her head, only slightly but enough for Kate to see, before screwing her eyes tighter and rolling her face away again. Kate scanned the bathroom, looking for anything which may give her answers. On her first glance, she was none the wiser, nothing immediately jumping out. The only other thing which could have possibly drained her this much was an attack, and after Friday, one so severe she could end up slumped in the bath wasn't out of the question. She internally chastised herself for leaving. She knew she should have stayed in case something like this happened.

"Did you have an anxiety attack?" she asked, still searching for answers so she knew what to do next.

Seph nodded, her throat making a soft grunt as she tried and failed to speak.

"Listen, sweetheart, I need to get you out of this bath before you freeze."

She was worried the cold had already started to take effect. She had no idea how long Seph had been lying there, she'd been gone for a few hours, but her skin was grey and covered in goosebumps, her lips a slight shade of blue.

Kate took hold of Seph's shoulders and started to roll her towards her in an attempt to get her close enough to hoist out. There was a sound of something falling, and it was then that she noticed the razor at the bottom of the bath. Taking another look at Seph, she finally saw the angry slashes striking across her thigh. It wasn't bleeding much, but the flesh was swollen and bruised, the cuts from the two slashes so close to each other making it seem even more inflamed.

"Oh, God." She swallowed the lump in her throat as tears filled her eyes. She stared at it for a second, morbidly mesmerised, before taking a deep breath and bringing herself back into the situation. She had to get Seph out of the bath and quickly.

"Okay, sweetheart, you have to listen to me." She hoped that by talking through everything she was going to do, it would revive Seph enough to quell some of the all-consuming fear which was rapidly rising in her chest. "On the count of three, I need you to push up while I lift you, okay?" Seph nodded, a small movement but enough to reassure Kate that she had heard her. "Okay. One. Two. Three."

Kate hooked her arms under Seph's and heaved with all her strength, aware that although Seph had moved her arms, she really wasn't in a fit state to muster any real effort of her own. It was clumsy and ungraceful, and Kate winced as she heard Seph's legs thud against the side of the bath. Once her top half was over the edge, gravity assisted, and Kate fell to the floor as she tried to break Seph's fall.

"Okay, okay. I've got you," she whispered as they landed in a tangled heap on the floor.

She pulled Seph's shrunken, shivering form into her, grabbing a towel and wrapping it round her. Her clothes were wet, sticking to her where Seph's damp body was pressed into her, but she gave it no thought, only trying to imbue some warmth into the woman in her arms. She cradled her face, stroking the sodden hair from it as she shushed and rocked Seph.

"I'm sorry," Seph said, still sleepy but clearer than before, the movement rousing her slightly, much to Kate's relief.

Kate rubbed her hand more firmly against Seph's body through the towel, but her efforts to keep her warm were futile, her shaking getting worse and her teeth chattering. "It's okay, but we need to get you up and dried off. Do you think you can stand?"

"I-I don't know."

Kate thought for a moment before shifting from where she was wrapped behind Seph. Gently, she lifted her and propped her against the side of the bath, making sure she wasn't about to fall over, before crouching in front of her. Wrapping the towel around her shoulders, she grabbed another, gently drying her skin, taking extra care when she got to her thigh. The action of getting out of the bath had pulled open the scab which had started to form, and thick, scarlet blood started to seep out again. The sight made her stomach turn, and she fought back against the wave of nausea that washed over her. Throwing the towel to the floor, she braced herself on her feet in front of Seph, holding out her hands.

"Hold onto my hands. I'm going to pull you off the floor, and then we can take it slowly to the bedroom."

Wrapping her hands tightly around Seph's, she counted to three again, pushing down on her own legs and pulling Seph into a standing position. As soon as she was on her feet, Seph began to wobble, and Kate quickly looped an arm around her waist to keep her upright. She felt Seph lean into her, her weight against her a small comfort in the midst of the overwhelming situation. Tentatively, and letting Seph set the pace, she led them out of the bathroom and to the bedroom. Once there, and once Seph was safely sitting on the bed, Kate quickly grabbed her dressing gown and wrapped it around Seph's shoulders, feeling a little more secure in the knowledge that now she at least had something on to try and keep her warm. She knelt down in front of Seph, finally taking the time and courage to look at the wound on her leg properly. Another shot of nausea hit her, and this time she honestly thought she was going to be sick. Her beautiful Seph, who she had only seen hours ago, had become so desperate and lost *right in front of her eyes* that she felt that this was the only thing left for her to do. She tamped down her self-hatred and scolding, keeping her focus on what Seph needed.

"This needs dressing," she said gently, running her fingers around the red, inflamed skin, "I'm going to get the first aid kit. I'll be right back."

Kate didn't allow herself any time to stop and dwell on what had happened in the past few minutes. She had no idea how long it had taken to get Seph into the bedroom from when she first walked into the scene in the bathroom; in one respect, it felt like it could only be a few minutes, but at the same time, it was like the minutes and seconds had slowed to a long, dragging pace. She didn't remember much of the journey downstairs or back again, apart from tripping on her own feet in her haste, but before she knew it, she was back in front of Seph.

"This might sting, but I need to make sure it's clean, okay baby?"

Seph winced at the first touch of the antiseptic to her broken skin, and Kate apologised quietly. Satisfied it was clean and all the blood, dried and fresh, had been cleaned away, she pulled the cuts closed as best she could with a dressing, smoothing the corners down gently. As she did, Seph's hand covered her own, and she looked up. Dark, empty glassy eyes stared back at her, and the sight sent a physical dart of pain through her heart. Tears she could no longer hold back welled in her eyes at the look of shame that painted Seph's features. It was a look that said so much; *I'm sorry, I've failed, I've let you down,* even though none of those things were true.

"Come on, lay down," she whispered softly, pulling back the duvet and urging Seph down gently.

"You seem to end up doing this a lot," Seph whispered into the silence of the room.

Kate knew what she meant, memories of when she first returned flashing through her mind. She knelt down by the side of the bed, stroking her fingers through Seph's damp hair.

"And I'll keep doing it. Every time you need me to."

She quickly rose, shedding her own damp clothes and kicking her shoes off, leaving them on a pile on the floor, before pulling on her own joggers and hoodie and climbing into bed next to Seph. She wrapped her arms around Seph, pulling them as close together as possible in a dual attempt to both comfort and warm her up. She could feel Seph's uneasiness, her body still tight like a coiled spring.

"I'm going to stay right here with you, okay?" she reassured Seph.

After a moment of hesitation, Kate felt a soft nod against her shoulder before Seph buried into her neck and the unmistakable feel of warm tears soaked into her skin. Safe in the small piece of knowledge that Seph was alive, beside her and resting, Kate finally let her own tears fall as well.

CHAPTER THIRTY-EIGHT

May, the previous year

It was a Tuesday. Tuesdays were precious to both of them, Tim would go to the golf club straight after work and be gone until the bar shut. Kate had always cherished Tuesdays, but now with Seph in her life, she worshipped them even more. It meant they had the whole evening to themselves, the time when they had to say goodbye to each other pushed further and further out until they literally ran out of seconds. Today had been even more precious, no afternoon meetings meant that Kate had escaped the office at lunchtime, and with some prior notice, Seph had managed to take the afternoon off work so they could spend even more time together.

The thought of seeing Seph sooner than usual had set a fire in Kate, desperate to touch her again. Their time together, arranged or spontaneous, was becoming more and more, any excuse they could find to see each other being used, but it only served to make the yearning in those times they were apart greater. No sooner had Seph opened the door to her, did Kate capture her lips in a searing kiss, something more akin to being away for months rather than a few days.

Three hours later, and they had managed to drag themselves out of the bedroom, only due to their growing hunger. Now, they lay on the sofa, Seph laid back in Kate's arms, Kate's legs wrapped around her hips. Kate's fingers idly traced across Seph's stomach, dipping down where her t-shirt had ridden up slightly. She felt the raised skin of her scars, brushing back over them again. Over the past couple of months, Seph had become more relaxed about Kate touching her scars, her body no longer tensing as it had done that first time she saw and felt them. She tilted her head, brushing her lips against the supple skin of

Seph's neck as she shifted slightly to look at where her fingers were stroking. She knew Seph felt it, both her gentle kiss and her touch, as she hummed and leant back further into her embrace. She studied the marks across her skin, tracing her fingers over each short, sharp scar. It wasn't the first time she had done so, although possibly the first time she had done so so openly. Often, she gazed at them while Seph was sleeping, wondering what had plagued her so much she felt so desperate.

"What made you do it?" she asked quietly, as her thumb drew over a particularly prominent scar across her hip bone. She felt Seph shuffle, clearly uncomfortable at her slightly bold question. While she may have felt more comfortable at Kate knowing they were there, she feared her question was still too much, too soon. "Sorry, you don't have to answer that." Kate quickly pulled back her query and her fingers, cautious about upsetting Seph.

"No, it's okay. I've wanted to tell you, it's just...it's hard."

There was a pause while both contemplated how best to move forward. Kate's fingers returned to her stomach in a gentle act of reassurance, confident that she hadn't overstepped. She could feel Seph shift, a deep sigh as she contemplated what and how to say whatever she was thinking.

"When did it start?" Kate asked, wondering if asking questions was easier than Seph trying to form the conversation wholly in her mind.

"Umm, I guess about six or seven years ago. I'd always had periods when I used to kind of retreat. I wouldn't want to see anyone or do anything, even when I was a teenager. I always used to come out of them though. Then one time I didn't."

"What happened?"

"Nothing. Not really. I didn't really have anything in my life then, and I think that helped me to hide. I just used to go to work, then come home and sit on my own, eat dinner, watch TV, go to bed, before starting it all over again. Slowly it started to get worse. I wouldn't go see friends, or go out, I would make excuses to spend less time at Helena's or my parents'. I lost my appetite, and I'd just spend evenings drinking and smoking before going to bed. Except that became pointless because I wouldn't sleep. I'd just sit up, thinking. When

I did manage to sleep, it would be because I'd end up just falling asleep on the sofa. My mind wouldn't shut off, I'd just go over and over the same thoughts, dissecting everything I'd done or said, building it up in my mind that something was wrong, or I'd upset someone. Everything would be my fault, even though there was no fault to logically place. And once the thoughts started, then they'd just spiral." Seph exhaled and Kate got the feeling that now she had started talking, she was finding it easier than she had anticipated.

"Is that when you started..." Kate swallowed, unable to finish her sentence. Saying the words seemed to make it too real. Instead she traced over the same scar as before, committing to memory what it felt like underneath her fingertip.

"Yeah."

"Why though?"

"It feels like there's a weight crushing me. There's a physical pressure I can feel, on my chest, and nothing shifts it. I think, if I can just have an outlet, a way to relieve that pressure, then I'll feel better. And because I can feel the pain, because it's physical and real in front of me, that it will help. I don't know, this probably isn't making any sense."

"No. I think I understand what you mean. I don't understand how awful you must have felt, or how desperate you must have been, but I get how you were thinking, then." Kate cupped Seph's face, pulling it around so she could see it. Seph's eyes glistened with unshed tears which were mirrored by her own. "I'm sorry you felt that way, that you felt so alone."

"After a couple of months, Fiona had had enough of me giving her shit and came over, found the house in a right state. I'd been managing to make myself presentable for work, but outside of that I was a mess." She dropped her head again, pulling out of Kate's timid grasp. "She didn't know how bad it had gotten though. I never told her about the—"

"Why not?"

"I don't know. She dragged me to the doctor, and then started driving me to my counselling appointments so I didn't back out, but I never really spoke much about what had actually gone on with her. Then over time, it just became harder and harder to bring it up."

"Do you still see them?"

"Who?"

"Your counsellor"

"Not anymore."

"And, have you felt…I mean, has it come back?"

"Yes." Seph paused, and Kate let her have a moment, feeling there was something more. "I've just come to realise that I'm one of those people for whom it's always there. It's not going away, it's not one thing I can blame for it. And I'm still trying to learn that, if I do slip, it's not my fault, it's nothing which I've done or haven't done. It's just one of those things. I get anxious about little things, and I just have to try and remember not to let it consume me."

"And how do you do that?"

"My meds help. They keep me steady, stop the distance between my highs and lows too great. But if I do have an attack, I have breathing techniques which my counsellor taught me."

"What are they? Will you tell me?"

"Why?" Seph seemed genuinely confused at the request, and Kate wondered if anyone had ever taken the time to find out how to help her if she needed it.

"So I know." Kate pulled herself up fully, dislodging Seph from where she lay against her. Kate took her hands in her own, running her thumb over her knuckles. "I don't ever want you to feel like that again. And I know I can't necessarily make that stop or go away, it's part of who you are, but I can try and help when it does happen." She reached out, brushing a tear away which had started to roll down Seph's face. "It breaks my heart to think that you ever felt so alone."

Seph looked down, clearly uncomfortable under Kate's scrutiny. Kate placed a finger under her chin, lifting her face up, as her thumb gently ran across her bottom lip.

"Promise me, you'll tell me if you ever feel like that again. It doesn't matter how little, or how small you think it is, you are not to try and deal with it on your own. I'll do anything for you." Her voice dropped slightly. "Because I love you."

CHAPTER THIRTY-NINE

Seph screamed into the room, her body shaking, covered in a thin layer of sweat. Whatever it was which had plagued her dreams, it had more or less instantly dissipated to nothing more than a residual feeling, an emotion lingering without the details. Her chest heaved, as she struggled to comprehend where she was and what was going on. Until a warm hand wrapped around her own, and gentle words were whispered into her ear.

"Shh. It's okay, baby. I'm here."

"Kate?" At some point she had started crying, tears clouding her eyes, and along with the fog remaining from being asleep, she struggled to focus. It sounded like Kate, it felt like Kate, but hadn't Kate left? There was a feeling of emptiness, of loneliness which lingered. But maybe that was from her dream? Oh God, everything was such a mess.

"Seph? Seph I need you to breathe with me, okay? Listen to me and copy me. In for four. One, two..."

Her breathing started to falter, catching in her throat, her eyes filled with panic at not being able to breathe yet again.

"Okay, sweetheart, sit up for me, that's it. Look at me, now breathe with me. One, two..." Seph choked and inhaled sharply. "Okay, start again. One, two, three..."

They sat there for ten minutes, Kate patiently repeating the count over and over, her hands gripping Seph's tightly, her thumb running over her knuckles in a grounding action. Once her breathing had calmed, she stopped the count, but kept her grip on her hands. Seph's eyes blinked heavily, every bone in her body aching and screaming with the pain which came with just being empty.

"Are you still cold?" Seph looked at Kate, hearing her speak but not register-ing what she was saying. She frowned, trying and failing to pluck a word from her memory so she could figure out what Kate was saying. "I said, are you still cold? You're shivering."

She didn't realise she was shaking, but now her senses were starting to clear, she was aware of the coldness seeping through her body. She nodded, barely, but noticeably, as Kate pulled the weighted blanket from behind her back over her shoulders, cocooning her. Seph sunk into the soft fabric, barely able to keep herself upright.

"I'll go make you a cup of tea, that might help," Kate said softly, standing and leaving Seph to go into the kitchen.

Seph spun round, curling up into herself and laying back down. Closing her eyes, she focused on the sounds she could hear around her, using them to try and ground herself and keep her in the present. Everything felt like too much, too loud, too bright, too heavy, but at the same time, she felt like she wasn't there at all, like she was just looking in from above. The sensation of the sofa dipping beside her signalled Kate's return, and she dragged open her eyes to see Kate sitting in the curve of her body.

"Hey," she whispered softly, tucking a strand of hair behind her ear. "How are you feeling?"

Seph exhaled deeply, not knowing how to answer. She knew Kate wasn't expecting a deep and meaningful deconstruction of events, she was just asking for her immediate, on-the-surface feelings, just like she would any other day. But even those were difficult to determine, too much clouding her head to distinguish one thing from the other. Kate didn't say anything, giving her the space to form her thoughts into what she wanted to say, just sitting there, soothing her with soft strokes through her hair.

"I thought you would have slept longer."

"I had a bad dream. And it hurt."

"Your leg?"

Seph gave a small nod. "Think I rolled onto it when I was sleeping. Then when I woke up I panicked that you were gone."

"Oh, I'm sorry, sweetheart. I'd not gone far." Kate brushed the hair from where it had stuck with sweat to her forehead and pressed a kiss to it. "I'd never go far," she muttered against her skin.

Suddenly, her gentleness became too much to bear, and Seph let out a strangled sob. Tears rolled down her face uncontrollably, her body shaking with the force. Kate knelt down on the floor and pressed her forehead to Seph's, closing her eyes as her own tears started to fall.

"Shh, it's okay, sweetheart. It's okay, I'm here."

"Why? I'm such a mess."

"Oh, baby. You're not. You're not a mess."

"Yes. I am."

"No. And I'm still here because this is where I want to be. With you. And I don't care that right now things aren't good. Because they will get better. You will get better. And until then, I'll be here, every step of the way." Seph tried to let Kate's words sink in, tried her hardest to believe them, but it was like pushing through quicksand, and instead she closed her eyes again, not knowing what to do or say next. "Has your anxiety been getting worse again?"

Seph nodded.

"And your depression?"

She nodded again. It was all she could muster right now, but it was all Kate needed.

"How long?"

"Maybe...six weeks," Seph muttered. She watched as Kate did the maths in her head, thinking back to what happened six weeks ago, until a look of realisation passed across her face. A range of emotions flickered across her face, as she took a deep breath and steadied herself.

"How often?"

"Maybe every few days. I haven't had one as bad as yesterday for years." Her eyes drifted down to her leg. "Haven't done that for years..." Her voice was barely a whisper. She looked up at the admission but couldn't bear to be under Kate's view and quickly shifted her eyes back down.

"Why didn't you say anything?" Kate's voice, if at all possible, had gotten even softer. But still, as much as Seph searched, there wasn't a hint of disappointment or anger in it. Seph was convinced it was there though, well hidden behind the sympathy.

"You had so much on that I didn't want to give you anything else to worry about. I'm sorry I let you down." She choked out the final sentence, tears threatening to fall again.

"Oh no, baby, no. You've not let me down. You could never let me down."

"I just...everyone seemed to hate me. They blamed me for this, us. And everytime someone said something, everytime...it just added to the voice in my head which was telling me I was to blame. That I was causing all this. That I wasn't worth all this trouble, all the arguments and stress..."

Kate cupped Seph's face, in the way she did when she wanted to make a point, when she had something important she wanted to say and make sure that Seph was listening.

"The *only* person who gets to decide if you're worth it, is me. And everyone who has had something to say, everyone who has had an opinion on us, can shove it up their arse as far as I'm concerned. Because the only thing I need you to listen to, the only thing I need you to believe, is that I love you, and I am here. And that's where I'm staying."

"You're not mad at me?"

"Why would I be mad?"

"Because I lied to you. Because I told you I would talk to you and I didn't." Seph could hear her voice waver. She wasn't sure she had any more tears left in her, but somehow they were balancing on the cliff, ready to fall at any moment.

"Oh, sweetheart. I'm not mad. I wish you'd told me sooner, so you weren't struggling on your own, but you've told me now, and I'm not mad." She leaned forward again, pressing her forehead against Seph's. "We'll get through this, okay?"

Seph nodded, grateful that Kate seemed to be leaving the conversation where it was and not pushing it any further. Even that small disclosure, as brief and vague as it was in the grand scheme of things, had drained her of any residual energy she had remaining.

"You said your leg hurt?" Kate asked.

Seph nodded. "Yeah, I think I laid on it."

"Can I take a look? I just want to make sure it's not bleeding."

Seph nodded again. She felt like she had used up all her available words in the brief conversation they had just had. Instead, she directed all her strength at pushing herself upright, Kate helping her to shuffle her pyjama bottoms down her legs without her standing up fully. Kate started to peel the dressing off and Seph winced at the pull at her raw skin.

"Sorry, sweetheart."

Seph dared to look down at her thigh. The sight made her queasy. Four cuts, each about three inches long, stretched from the centre to the outside of her thigh. They were paired up from the twin blades of the razor. Each one was an angry red, inflamed and swollen, almost throbbing out from the rest of her skin. Her whole thigh felt like it was on fire, burning and aching. Kate gently soaked around it, trying to remove the dried blood. The pressure on it, however soft, only added to Seph's nausea. "I think I'm going to be sick."

She pushed herself up and towards the kitchen, moving as fast as she could, tripping on her unsteady feet. She reached the sink and heaved, but there was nothing in her stomach to bring up, collapsing to the floor as her legs gave way. Kate reached her as she landed, a cool hand on her face; despite the cold she still felt from earlier, her skin was flush with her nausea. "I don't think I can move."

"That's okay, sweetheart. We can stay here for as long as you need. I'm sorry though, I'm going to have to finish your leg."

Kate handed her a glass of water, before settling again on the floor next to her. She resumed cleaning the cuts, Seph's dash across the kitchen having opened them up once more.

"I'm worried these might need stitches, sweetheart."

"No. I don't want to go."

"But I don't want them to scar—"

"They're going to anyway. Please," she turned to look at Kate, her eyes pleading, "Please, I just want to stay at home."

"Okay." Kate reached up and held her face. "Okay, I won't do anything you don't want to do."

Kate let her hand drop, and started to turn, but before she could, Seph caught her fingers, letting them rest loosely in hers. Kate looked back up at her.

"Thank you," she whispered, her voice hoarse.

Kate held her face again and brought their foreheads together, stroking Seph's cheek with her thumb. For the first time in six weeks, she actually let herself believe that Kate was there, and not going anywhere. And that maybe, she could find a way out of the darkness.

CHAPTER FORTY

S eph was still asleep when Kate left. She didn't want to; the last thing she
wanted to do was leave her alone but she needed to do this. She left a note
by her bed, along with some water, some painkillers and her antidepressants, in
case she woke up while she was out, hoping it was enough not to panic her after
her breakdown the day before about Kate leaving.

She rubbed her eyes. She was tired, she hadn't slept much, not wanting to
close her eyes in case something happened overnight, instead watching Seph
for any signs of discomfort or fear which may have arisen during her sleep. She
looked at the front door which she was parked outside of and took a deep breath.
She wasn't sure this was the right thing to do, but she was feeling lost as to how
to help Seph. Steeling herself for a conversation she didn't know how to have,
she got out of the car and walked up to the house, knocking at the door. The
door opened, revealing a tired and somewhat frazzled looking Helena. A pang
of guilt shot through Kate at turning up like this. She remembered what it was
like raising young children.

"Kate, hi." The surprise at seeing her sister's girlfriend at her door was evident
on her face.

"Hey, Helena. I'm sorry to just drop in uninvited like this..."

Helena took a step forward, her head tilted as she studied Kate. Kate knew
she must have looked a mess, she'd seen it in the mirror this morning when
she was getting ready. Her face was pale and drawn, the circles under her eyes
from the lack of sleep and worry even more evident due to her naturally pale
complexion. A look of fear shadowed Helena's face as she made a conclusion

as to why Kate was here, quickly replaced by an understanding softness which Kate appreciated.

"Come in, you look like you could do with a brew."

Ren

Kate sat in the kitchen, hands wrapped round the hot mug of tea, staring into it. Helena had disappeared to put a DVD on for Millie, saying something about making sure they weren't interrupted. She had come back, and Kate was aware of her sitting in front of her, but she still didn't know how to say what she came to say.

"How bad is it?" She looked up at Helena. "I know it's not easy to talk about it. Must be even harder trying to tell me." Kate nodded slightly before looking back down, grateful that Helena was able to read the situation enough to start the conversation. "What's happened?"

"She's been hiding the fact that she's been struggling again. For six weeks she's been having anxiety attacks and sinking lower and lower, right in front of me...and I didn't see it."

"I thought she was doing better. She seemed happier. Did something happen to trigger it again?"

"She didn't say, but my guess is judging from when she said it started, it was Tim finding out about us."

"When he came round to the house?" Helena knew about Tim showing up at Seph's house, Kate had been there when Seph had told her. She thought back to that day; were the signs there for her to see? Seph had seemed quieter, more nervous than usual, but she had just taken it as her processing everything. No one would have been okay after that confrontation, especially when it had happened in their own home.

"Everything's just been so crazy, with the kids, and Tim, and trying to sort the divorce. And then Seph got her new job, and I honestly thought it was going to be the last piece of the puzzle for her to move on, you know? But maybe it was just one more thing to deal with. And then there was that fucking party on Friday..."

"Yeah, Seph mentioned something about going out."

"I knew she was hesitant about it. I should have just insisted we stayed at home when she told me her worries. But she said she would be alright. And then Lynne Williams opened her mouth."

"Who's Lynne Williams?"

"She's this lawyer who works for another firm. Loud. Brash. The kind of woman who gives independent women a bad name because of her attitude. She," God, even now the rage was bubbling up inside Kate, threatening to spew over once again. "Seph overheard her. She was basically telling people that Seph and I were a mistake. A mid-life crisis on my part, and a free ride on Seph's. God, Seph's face when she came to find me... I knew something had happened straight away, I could see it in her eyes. I should have just taken her away right then, but I saw red and gave Lynne a piece of my mind." She closed her eyes and took a deep breath, trying to steady her emotions. "When we got home, Seph collapsed with the worst anxiety attack I've ever seen. It was like she wasn't even in the room anymore."

"Oh, God. Is she okay?" Kate heard the fear in Helena's voice, and she hated the fact she had to utter the next part of this story to her sister.

"No. I came home yesterday to find her—" Kate couldn't say it, a huge gasping sob breaking her sentence.

"Kate? H-how bad is it?"

"S-she'd had another attack. I found her in the shower. She...she'd..."

Kate couldn't finish, more tears overpowering her. They came, thick and loud and free instead of the silent, hidden ones of the past few hours. She felt Helena wrap her arms around her, letting her cry into her for what felt like an age, not saying anything just letting her sob until there was nothing left inside. She could feel Helena shake against her, her own tears soaking into the shoulder of her hoodie, strangely grateful that she could cry with someone, release with someone who knew the enormity of it all. After a few more minutes, she pulled back, wiping her hand across her cheeks in a futile attempt to clear the tears.

"F-for a second, I thought, when I saw her lying in the bath, I thought I'd lost her. I thought she was gone. She looked so small and pale. And I know she thinks she's being a burden, I can see it in her face. But I just want to take care of her, I just want to help her. But I don't know how."

Helena leaned closer, placing her hand over Kate's which rested on her knee. "You're doing a great job."

Kate looked at her, in no way convinced.

"You know how long it took us to know there was something wrong the first time? Nine months. And that was just the self-harming. God knows how long she'd been struggling with the depression and anxiety before that. She became clever with it, hiding it so we never saw just how much she was hurting. Even now Mum doesn't know the true extent of what went on. They don't know about the self-harming. Seph would never tell her, she thinks it would be too much. I know this sounds strange, but for her to do it where you could find her…I think it could be her way of telling you. Like she's ready to admit that something's wrong."

"But I tell her all the time. That I'm there for her if she needs me."

"But that's not how Seph's mind works when she's in this place. I know it's hard to comprehend, but she's not thinking clearly right now. I can see it when you two are together, just how much she trusts you, and that's a big thing. She'll be worrying that this is too much for you to handle. She'll feel ashamed, and defeated, like everything she's done wasn't worth it, like she's let everyone down."

"How do I help her, Helena? I feel so useless. It's killing me just seeing her like this."

"You're doing everything right already. Some days she'll want to cry, some days she'll want to shout, other days she'll do nothing but stare into space, and they're the hardest. You need to just keep reassuring her that you're there. Listen to her, hold her, cry with her. Do all the things which you want to do anyway, all the things which come naturally, and you'll be fine." Kate looked up at Helena as she paused. "It's not going to be easy. But she'll come back out the other side. I'm confident she will because she has you this time."

"You think?"

"I know. And I know how hard it can be being in your shoes. So please, don't think you have to do it on your own either. If you need to talk, or cry, or just get an hour away from it all, my door is always open."

Kate gave Helena a watery smile. "Thank you."

"No, thank you. You have no idea what it means to know that my sister has someone like you looking out for her."

Seph turned when she heard the key in the door, watching as Kate walked in, head down, shoulders sagging slightly. She looked tired, Seph thought. But then she would do. Seph couldn't imagine Kate would have let herself get much rest while Seph was sleeping. She was in a world of her own, and probably wasn't expecting Seph to be out of bed. But she'd woken not so long ago, her stomach grumbling and making the need for food known for the first time in days. She'd panicked a little when she couldn't see Kate straight away, but the note left on her bedside table had softened it slightly, and she had made her way downstairs on shaky legs. After dropping her bag on the sofa, Kate finally looked up, surprise evident when she saw Seph standing in the kitchen.

"Hey. What are you doing up?" she asked, making her way over.

"I got hungry," Seph replied, shrugging.

Kate stopped in front of her, and Seph leaned into the contact as she brushed the hair back from her face, gently tucking it behind her ear. "Sit down," she said, steering Seph towards the table, "I'll make you something. I've just been to the shop on my way back."

Seph hobbled over to the table, her leg still painful and sat down slowly, cautious about pulling it open and causing it to bleed again. Kate walked past her, grabbing the shopping bags she had left by the front door, and walking back into the kitchen.

"Where did you go?" Seph asked, watching Kate switch on the oven, followed by the kettle, before stopping at the question.

"I went to see Helena."

Seph took a moment to process what Kate had said. Kate had been to see Helena? Kate wasn't in the habit of going to see her sister alone, which meant there was only one reason why she would now. That, coupled with the tension she could see in Kate's rigid body, as she stood with her back to her, only confirmed what Seph knew.

"Oh. Okay."

Kate spun, her face painting a picture of confusion. "Okay?"

"Yeah." Seph let out a long sigh, looking down as she picked at her fingernails. "I get that this isn't easy to deal with. So it makes sense you would need someone to talk to."

The sound of a chair moving across the floor, and the warm touch of Kate's hands over her own, stilling their movement brought her eyes back up.

"I'm sorry. I didn't want to leave you, and I didn't want to go behind your back, but I didn't know what to do and who else I could talk to about it."

"I know. You don't have to apologise. Most people probably would have walked away from this mess a long time ago, the least I can do is let you vent to my sister."

Kate leant forward, cupping Seph's cheek in her palm, and something about her touch made everything in her head a little less frantic.

"I'm not walking away. We'll get through this, yeah? Me and you, we'll do it together."

Seph nodded, more tears threatening to overwhelm her. She was grateful when Kate noticed, changing the conversation as she stood up and made her way back to the kitchen.

"You need to rest. So I thought, duvet day? I've stocked up on all your favourite snacks, I've got crisps, salted popcorn, sweets and cherry coke. I'm making bacon sandwiches for brunch and I thought tonight we could get pizza. I'll even let you be in control of the remote."

Seph couldn't help but smile. It was small and tired, but the first time she had felt like smiling in the past two days. And if she was honest, much longer.

"Sounds good. And you could probably do with the rest before you go back to work tomorrow." Kate had told her in her note that she had taken today off, but she was already secretly dreading tomorrow when she returned to the office.

"I've taken some leave."

"What?"

"I've taken some time so I can be around while you work through this."

"You're just worried I'm going to do something stupid again," Seph muttered, guilt flowing through her at the news that Kate wasn't going to work.

"No, that's not why," Kate replied while she made Seph a cup of tea. "You need some help. I mean...you need support to get through this. And you will, because you've done it before and I have faith that you'll do it again. But for the next couple of weeks, I want to be here to help you do that, in whatever way you need."

Seph couldn't find any words. She smiled again, this time a little warmer than before. She had a feeling that Helena had done more than just listen to Kate. Her eyes glistened with unshed tears; this time through gratitude rather than self-loathing or guilt. Kate walked back over to her, clearly sensing her emotions were close to getting heavy again, and wrapped an arm around her shoulders, pulling her close. Seph wound her arms around her waist, burying her face into her stomach.

"Everything else can wait. You're my priority now," she said, pressing her face into Seph's hair with a kiss.

Kate settled Seph on the sofa, covering her with a blanket after she complained of still feeling cold, then busied herself making the bacon sandwiches. She tried to make conversation with her, but after a few minutes Seph had gone quiet and Kate looked round to find her curled up in a ball, the blanket scrunched tight around her, staring into nothing. She sighed; the silence and empty stares were some of the hardest moments she observed. Helena was right, watching the woman she loved being so distant and empty physically made her heart hurt.

Plating up a small sandwich, Kate walked over to Seph. "Hey, you want to try and eat some of this?"

"I'm not hungry," Seph muttered, still staring into space.

"You need to eat, sweetheart. You hardly had anything yesterday, you'll make yourself ill if you don't eat."

"Maybe later. I just feel a bit sick right now."

Kate sighed. She knew as much as she wanted to push Seph to eat something, she had to tread carefully. It was a fine balance between being encouraging and being overbearing. One wrong move and she was scared she would push Seph too far.

"Okay, try again later. Are you still cold?" Kate asked, unsure as to whether the blanket gripped tightly around her was more for warmth or comfort.

"A little bit."

"Why don't you have a bath? It might warm you up?"

"Yeah." Seph sighed. "Can't be bothered to run one though."

Kate pushed up from the sofa, holding her hands out for Seph. "Good job I'm here then. Come on, let's get you upstairs and I'll run you a nice big bath, and you can have a soak."

Seph eased herself up slowly, wincing slightly as she moved her leg. She imagined it was now feeling tight and uncomfortable where it was starting to knit together. The exhaustion and lack of food made her unsteady on her feet, but Kate wrapped an arm around her waist, gently guiding her up the stairs. By the time she reached the top Kate felt a little more confident that Seph wasn't about to drop to the floor, and she left her sat on the bed to get undressed while she ran a bath. She busied herself running the hot water and adding some bath foam to it, making sure there were clean towels, even though she knew there were as she'd put some in when she cleaned it the other night while Seph was sleeping. Anything to stop her from staring at it too long and picturing Seph slumped in it, grey and shaking. She heard a noise behind her and turned to see Seph, holding herself up against the doorframe, a look on her face similar to what she imagined hers must have been like as memories clearly played across her face. She held out her hand, encouraging her forward.

"Come on, it's all ready," she offered softly.

Seph undid her dressing gown but Kate sensed her hesitation, and so moved in front of her, placing her hands on either side of the gown, gently pulling it open, and down off her shoulders, before taking hold of her hands and gently tugging her towards the bath.

"Will you get in with me?" Seph whispered, barely loud enough to hear. "I don't like not being close to you."

Kate stopped and looked round, her heart melting at the whispered admission for the need to be close. Even though it might be for entirely different reasons, she understood Seph's need. She stepped forward, cupping Seph's cheek and lifting her face slightly to see her. "Of course I will, baby. Get in, I'll be with you in a minute."

Seph sunk into the hot bath, hissing as the warm water washed over her thigh, the sounds causing Kate to look round and see the flash of pain across her face. But the moment passed, as she sunk lower into the water, and Kate saw her body slump once she was fully submerged. Kate quickly shed her clothes, leaving them in a pile on the floor, before urging Seph to sit forward so she could slide in behind her. She pulled gently on Seph's shoulders, letting her sink back against her chest, and something within her calmed at the solid weight of Seph's body against hers. Reaching for the sponge and some shower gel, she lathered it up, before gently beginning to wash Seph, taking care to be gentle. Once she was done, she followed with a handful of shampoo, massaging it into her scalp. She smiled as she heard Seph hum, feeling some of the tension in her body loosen and ebb away, before rinsing it all off. Once done, she guided Seph's head back onto her shoulder, still letting her fingers run through her hair.

"Feeling better?" she asked after a while, studying Seph's face as it relaxed, eyes closed and muscles slack with what she hoped was a level of contentment.

"Mmm."

They lay there for a few minutes, Kate continuing to soothe Seph with her fingers in her hair and gentle kisses on her temple, her other hand pushing the bath water over her exposed skin to keep her warm, moving across her body. After a few moments, Kate's hand hovered over her thigh.

"Your dressing is coming off. Will you let me clean it and re-dress it?" she asked timidly. The last thing she wanted to do was make Seph uncomfortable, especially now she was seemingly more at ease.

Seph nodded and Kate soaked the remaining adhesive off her leg, peeling the gauze back to expose it and gently wash it. Seph screwed her face up with pain when Kate gently pressed it to see if it had started to heal.

"Sorry, sweetheart," she offered quietly, lifting her fingers away when she was happy.

Seph glanced down, before quickly averting her gaze and grimacing. Kate caught the action and the look of shame which swept over her features.

"Don't look like that. It's okay."

"It's ugly." Kate heard the unspoken meaning behind the words. *I'm ugly.*

"Hey," Kate whispered, pulling Seph's face around towards her gently. "You're beautiful." Seph's eyes were still closed, and her chin cast downwards, doing everything she could not to look at Kate in their close proximity. "Look at me, Seph."

Seph finally looked up at Kate, her eyes glassy and threatening to spill their tears at any moment, breathing shakily.

"I think this," she gently stroked her fingers around the inflamed skin on her leg, "is beautiful. Just as I think this," her fingers moved to the healed raised scar which ran across the left of her stomach, "is beautiful. And these," this time, she stroked across the bunch of short, sharp scars which were etched above her hip, "are beautiful. Because they make you who you are. Don't ever be ashamed of who you are or what you've come through. I'm not ashamed of you, in fact I'm incredibly proud of you."

She kissed the tear which had escaped down Seph's face, tasting the salt on her lips. As she whispered her declaration of love against Seph's skin, Seph crumbled, sobbing again in Kate's arms until there was nothing else left.

CHAPTER FORTY-ONE

Kate sat back, sighing deeply and rolling her neck. She was stiff from sitting at her desk for the past couple of hours, but she was putting in the extra effort to catch up after being out of the office for the past couple of weeks. She was working hard and fast, determined that she wasn't going to have to work overtime to make up for her absence, because while she didn't regret the time she had taken to care for Seph, she also still wasn't prepared to be leaving her alone while she toiled at the office.

It wasn't that she didn't trust Seph, she did. She'd come on leaps and bounds considering the place she was at a few weeks ago. Long, slow conversations at all hours, whenever the urge to talk came upon Seph were had, Kate doing her best to listen and reassure her whenever her doubts became too much or her fear took over. After a few days, she broached the topic of Seph seeking out a counsellor again, either her previous one or a new one, and the idea hadn't been shot down immediately, which was a huge victory for them both. A few phone calls later, and Seph's old counsellor had given her an appointment, and extended the invitation to Kate as well. Kate had been reluctant to start with, not wanting to encroach and intrude on Seph's time with her, instead compromising that if Seph went to the first one alone, she would come to the next. And surprisingly, despite her own nerves and reservations about the situation, that session had gone well. Yes, it was exhausting for both of them, Seph especially, but something about just *seeing* her getting some help made everything a little bit brighter and more optimistic. But still, she missed not being near Seph, the worry that something would happen while she wasn't there always playing in her mind.

A knock at the door interrupted her train of thought, and she groaned silently. She had asked not to be disturbed, the less interruption the better as she tried to carve a dent in her workload.

"Yes?" she called out wearily, trying to temper down her irritation. She knew her secretary would only be disturbing her if she absolutely had to.

The door opened and Janice peered round sheepishly. "I'm really sorry to disturb you Kate, but Tim is here."

"Tim?"

"Yes. And usually I wouldn't bother you if it was anyone else but..."

"No. No, it's fine Janice. Send him through."

Kate stretched again, mentally preparing for whatever Tim had to say. Things had been fairly quiet on the divorce front recently, Tim finally seeing sense and agreeing to have the house valued and put on the market. She had wondered if her lunch with Cam and Meg had anything to do with it, as Meg had also seemed to be coming round to the idea that her parents were getting a divorce. Seph's involvement in her life was another matter which had not been broached properly, but Kate was fine with that at the moment. The last thing Seph needed right now was introducing her to her fiery, self-righteous daughter. But Cam, bless him, had not only asked about Seph every time they met up for lunch but also had floated interest in wanting to get to know her better.

"Kate?" Tim's voice brought her back into the room.

"Hmm? Oh sorry. Hi, Tim."

"Hi. I hope I'm not interrupting you, but I was in the area and thought I'd pop in to tell you that the estate agents have been in touch."

"Oh, okay."

"They've had an offer, it's a little below asking but...Kate, are you alright?" he asked, cocking his head to one side.

"What?" She wasn't expecting the question. "Oh, yes. Yeah, I'm fine."

"Are you sure?" He pulled out the chair on the opposite side of the desk, dropping down into it and leaning forward. "I hope you don't mind me saying, but you look exhausted."

Kate laughed. "Why would I possibly mind my ex-husband telling me I look rough?"

"Fair point. But, I know I've not always been the best husband, Kate, and I know you seem to think I only really appreciated you for the fact we made a good power couple, but that's not true. Even if our marriage wasn't perfect, I still care about you. And right now, you look like something's been going on. Is everything okay with...with Seph?"

"Wow." She leaned back in her chair. "Really took a lot for you to say her name then, didn't it?"

"Yeah, it did. But I said it anyway."

"What? So you can find out if things are going wrong for us? So you can say I told you so?" she snapped.

"No. Kate..." He slumped back in his chair, mirroring her stance. "I was asking because you look like shit and you never look like shit. Even when things were going wrong with us, you still kept face. I just don't think I've ever seen you this tired."

Kate let out a long exhale. "Sorry, Tim. I've just got a lot on at the moment and I took it out on you."

"That's okay. Want to talk about it?"

Kate cocked her head to the side, regarding her ex. "That's sweet, but I don't think you really want to hear my troubles."

"Not necessarily. I assume by that comment, it *is* something to do with Seph?"

"I..." She could feel her resolve waver, the emotion lodging in her throat and threatening to spew out at any moment. Why was she getting so emotional about this now? And in front of Tim of all people?

"Kate?"

"Hmm?"

"What's wrong? Why are you crying?"

Was she? She hadn't even noticed. Swiping her fingers across her cheek, she stared as they came away damp.

"I'm...I'm sorry, I don't..." Her voice wavered, and she could feel another warm tear roll down her face. Why was she so emotional all of a sudden? It wasn't as if she had been repressing her feelings about all of this, she'd been to Seph's latest counselling session for God's sake and spoken there, and on more than one occasion met up with Helena to talk. So why was she about to burst into tears?

"Talk to me, Kate. What's going on? Is something wrong with Seph? I know her father died not so long ago. Has something else happened?"

Of course Tim knew about Seph's father; she joined his firm not long after he had died, and it would make sense that she would have told him her reasons for moving firms to work closer to home.

"No. Nothing like that. It's nothing really—"

"Bullshit, Kate. You don't do this. You don't get upset like this, so don't give me that crap."

Kate had forgotten that the downside to being married to the same person for twenty years meant that at times they could read you like a book. She pushed off from her chair, turning her back on Tim, mis-placed anger rising in her chest that he had called her out. She felt his presence behind her as she stood staring out of the window, keeping his distance respectful but close enough that she could hear him when he spoke quietly.

"Look, I know I said some horrible, unforgivable things to her, and to you, but I'm not a total dick. If something's happened, it doesn't mean I'm so heartless that I don't care. About you or her."

"She's..." Was Kate really about to do this? It's like her mind had just decided to screw her inhibitions and concerns and just vomit out everything. "She's not been doing very well. In fact, she's really struggling. After her dad died, she was in a really bad place, and we'd just managed to get out of it, things were starting to look up but then..."

"She slipped again?"

Kate scoffed. "That's an understatement. And it was happening right under my nose and I didn't notice."

"People are really good at hiding things, Kate. If you didn't see, it's because she didn't want you to."

"Yeah. I know. But it doesn't make me feel any better, you know. I promised her that I'd be there and I feel like if I'd looked harder, if I'd been more attentive—"

"No. No, you're not doing this. And if she was here now she'd tell you the same. Kate, you are one of the kindest, most generous loving people I have ever known. I'm certain there was nothing more you could have done."

"Then why do I feel like this?"

"Because you love her. And it hurts to see the person you love hurting, especially when you feel helpless in stopping it." Tim stepped closer, wrapping his hands around Kate's upper arms and turning her towards him. "Remember when Cam was, I don't know, eleven or twelve, and he fell off his bike and broke his arm? God, I remember you were beside yourself for days, beating yourself up because you kept thinking about every possible scenario where you could have prevented it from happening. What if you'd been there? What if you weren't at work and he wasn't at your parents? What if you'd come home early, or bought him a different bike, or given him something different for breakfast that day? Every tiny little detail, whether they mattered or not, you second guessed. But the truth is Kate, accidents happen. Cam could have fallen off his bike and broken his arm whether you were there or not. And Seph could have got to this point, if you had seen it or not. A million different scenarios, and a million different choices, and you could have still ended up here. But the one truth I do know will never change is the fact that you looked after him, and cared for him, even to the point of driving him crazy. And you'll do the same for her."

Kate sat in the comfy armchair, tapping her foot nervously. She wasn't sure why she was here, but once Tim had left, she had picked up the phone and rang the number before she even realised what she was doing.

"Kate?" A soft voice called for her attention, bringing her back to the present moment.

"Sorry." She drew her gaze up from where she had been staring at the floor. "Sorry, I shouldn't have called you. I really didn't expect you to be able to see me so soon."

"It's fine, Kate." Gloria smiled, that warm, soft reassuring smile which Kate imagined every counsellor had. "I had a spare slot, so I was happy to offer it to you if you need to talk."

"I know but, well, I'm not your client, am I? This is meant to be for Seph."

Gloria shifted in her chair, leaning forwards a little. "What Seph is going through, it affects you as well. That's why I asked if you would like to attend a session together."

"But we're not together. I mean now, here. It's just me."

"No, but sometimes, the other person in a situation needs some time alone to talk about how they are feeling." Gloria paused. "It's not betraying her. To be here and needing to talk. It's perfectly fine. And I'm sure Seph would say the same thing."

Kate smiled, thinking back to when she had told Seph that she had been to see Helena.

"What are you smiling about?" Gloria asked.

"Seph did say exactly the same thing. A few weeks ago, when I first...when she..." Kate still struggled to say the words, the image they conjured too powerful to deal with. "I went to see her sister, and when I told her, she said it was okay, because she understood that I might need someone to talk to about it."

Gloria sat back in her chair, giving Kate a soft smile. "See? So there should be no guilt about being here. So why don't you tell me why you called."

Kate sighed, tipping her head back and looking at the ceiling. "My ex came to see me today. It was nothing big, just formalities about the divorce. But while he was there, he called me out for looking tired. And I don't know, something just broke, you know? All of a sudden I was crying and I don't know why."

"You don't?"

"I do. Of course I do. It was more like I didn't know why I was crying *then*, of all times. And in front of Tim, of all people."

"You were the one who found Seph, right? When she had self-harmed and had collapsed after her anxiety attack?"

Kate shivered at the words. "Yes."

"You said you spoke to Seph's sister about her depression? Did you tell her what had happened?"

"Yes."

"But did you tell her *exactly* what had happened?"

"I..." Kate paused, trying to recall her conversation with Helena. "I mean, she knows. But I didn't give her any details. I mean, why would I? It was hard enough to tell her about how bad Seph had got, I wouldn't ever tell anyone, let alone Helena, anything else. Why would I want to cause her that pain?"

"Kate, you are the only person who saw Seph that day. You are the only person who knows just how bad things had gotten for her."

"I...yeah, but, I mean it's not something you just tell anyone." Kate spat, confused as to why she felt angry at the statement.

"No. But because of that, I think you are holding onto it. And I think that is what is causing you to feel the way you do. When was the last time you slept properly, Kate?"

"You're starting to sound like my ex-husband now," Kate grumbled.

"Maybe," Gloria chuckled lightly. "But maybe there's something to be said for being with a person for years. Even if you fall out of love with them, even if you change, it doesn't mean that they don't see you anymore. So," she cocked her head to the side with a knowing look which Kate was quickly becoming irritated with. "when was the last time you slept properly?"

Kate sighed, resigning herself to being honest. Ironically, she was too tired to argue. "I don't know."

"Since Seph harmed herself?"

"No, I guess not."

"Why?"

"Because I'm worried. And...and I'm scared," Kate admitted quietly.

"Of something else happening?"

Kate nodded. "Yeah."

"And when you do manage to sleep? What happens then?" Gloria gently pushed.

"I...there's this dream I keep having."

"Would you tell me about it?"

Kate closed her eyes with a heavy sigh. She'd had the same dream nearly every night for the past three weeks.

Kate walked up the stairs. Each step seemed agonisingly slow, her legs heavy like lead. Her mind was willing her to move faster, but her body wasn't complying, instead dragging her slower and slower each time she imagined trying to reach her destination.

As she reached the top of the stairs and pushed open the door, her chest tightened, as if there was a belt wrapped around her torso and with each breath it constricted tighter, until her ribs dug into her lungs with a sharp pain. The pain reached a torturous peak as she stretched her arm forward to pull back the shower curtain, revealing Seph's body, crumpled and bloodied in the bath. Her lips were blue, and her skin grey, peppered with goosebumps from the icy water which cascaded over her naked body. One leg was bent against the side of the bath, while the other was bent underneath her at an excruciating angle. Her hand draped limp and lifeless over the edge of the bath, blood dripping from her fingers into a coagulated pool on the floor. Every inch of her body was covered with slashes, red, angry and inflamed, some starting to scab with dried blood, other oozing fresh bright scarlet life force, all devastatingly horrific to witness. Kate went to run forward, but something held her back, an invisible force which stopped her from reaching where she so desperately wanted, no needed, to be. Her arms flailed, in a frantic attempt to break free and propel herself forward, her lungs screaming as she gasped for breath and her vision blurring as tears streamed down her face. Suddenly, as she put all her weight behind trying to push forward, the invisible restraint gave way, and she fell towards the bath and the broken form of the woman she loved.

"Kate?" The voice broke through the fog which consumed her mind and she blinked her eyes open, finding Gloria sat forward towards her, holding out a tissue. She took it gratefully, her hands shaking, as she wiped away the tears which were rolling down her cheeks. She was thankful for the moment of silence which Gloria allowed her as she tried to compose herself, taking a deep breath to calm her racing heart.

"Sorry," she muttered quietly, somewhat embarrassed she had become so lost in her head she had momentarily forgotten where she was.

"Don't be. Kate, you witnessed someone you love very much, so depressed and detached from themselves, do something which was devastating. And you are the only one who saw it. Even if you were to tell someone about how horrific it was, the true magnitude would never be conveyed fully. But I do think you need to talk about it."

"To you, you mean?"

Gloria sat back in her chair with a sly grin. "Maybe. Maybe not. It's entirely up to you who you talk to. But considering you haven't spoken to anyone yet, and your reasons for doing so, maybe someone impartial who has no emotional attachment to you or Seph is best."

Kate paused for a moment, digesting Gloria's words. If she was honest with herself, she had known that she needed to tell someone the details about that day, but her devotion to Seph's well-being had pushed down her own needs.

But now she was starting to see some light come back into Seph's eyes, and she was finally letting her guard down. The wall she had so steadfastly built was starting to crumble. She was still annoyed somewhat at the fact it was her ex-husband who had dealt the first blow to the weakening structure. But the fact remained that it had been, and if it wasn't him it would have been someone else. But maybe the fact it was Tim, and her confusion as to why, was what led her to Gloria. If it was anyone else, Helena or Sarah for example, then she wasn't so sure she would have made the call earlier.

"If...if I did want to speak to someone, can it be you? Or is that a conflict of interest for you?"

"It can be me," Gloria answered honestly. "But you have to remember that patient-doctor confidentiality is still a thing, even if two of the patients are in a relationship. I wouldn't reveal anything that Seph says about you, just like I wouldn't reveal anything you said about her."

Kate nodded. "I understand. I just think I would be more comfortable talking to someone who already knows some of the details."

"I understand that completely. How about we look and see when we can next get together?" Gloria asked, standing as she went to get her diary from the desk in the corner,

"Yeah." Kate breathed, a feeling of relief flooding through her for the first time in weeks.

Chapter Forty-Two

Seph walked down the stairs, her hair still wet from the shower, wearing a fresh pair of joggers and a loose t-shirt. It wasn't entirely a case of climbing into her comfy clothes at the end of the day; she'd spent the best part of the last few weeks in some variation of the outfit. But this afternoon she had been out with Helena and Millie, and it felt good to be in something a little more relaxed than her jeans.

Walking into the living room, she saw Kate sitting on the sofa, legs curled under her, elbow propped on the arm. She'd been distant since coming home tonight, quiet while she was eating her dinner, and she knew something was on her mind. Rounding the sofa, her thoughts were confirmed when she found Kate staring into space, her thumb in between her lips as she nervously bit at the skin.

"Kate?" Nothing. Kate continued to stare in front of her. She repeated herself, this time a little louder. "Kate?"

The second call broke her out of her reverie, and she looked round, almost shocked to find Seph standing in front of her.

"Everything okay?"

"Yeah. But I was about to ask you that."

"Oh. Oh, I'm fine."

Seph sighed deeply. She knew what this was about. Kate worried enough about putting Seph under any more stress, and after her recent episode, she was fairly sure that Kate held herself responsible. She moved forward, sitting down beside Kate. "Kate, I know something's bothering you. What is it?"

"It's nothing. Sorry, it's just been a long day."

Kate went to stand, but Seph wasn't going to allow her to just brush this off. She'd never seen her so distracted and distant and she really didn't like it. Whatever she was turning over in her mind must be big, something consuming and heavy. She could see it in the way her shoulders were slumped, the dull lifeless look in her usually warm eyes. It scared her seeing her so far removed from her usual self. As she stepped past, Seph reached out and wrapped her hand around her wrist, stopping her in her tracks.

"Kate," she said softly, almost pleading.

She could see the rise and fall of Kate's shoulders as she took a deep breath, her head dropping. "Seph, I..."

"Please. Talk to me. I know why you won't, I know why you think you can't, but this won't work if you decide the best way to stop me from struggling is just to shut me out."

"I'm not shutting you out."

"You're not opening up to me." She sensed Kate tense underneath her hold. "You know the thing which got me in this place was me not opening up. Not talking about what was going on with me because I was worried you had too much to worry about in the first place. You're doing the same. Your intentions are good, but it's exactly the same. And I'm trying my best to get myself out of that habit, but how am I meant to do it when you are doing the same to me? How are we meant to be honest with each other, if you won't talk to me?"

Seph let the question hang in the air between them. Apart from the conversations which they'd had after her therapy sessions with Gloria, it was probably the most that Seph had spoken about her recent spiral willingly. Kate turned slowly, and Seph's breath hitched when she clocked the tears which were streaming down her face.

"I'm sorry."

"Don't be sorry." Seph stood in front of Kate, wiping away the tears. "Just tell me what's wrong."

"I've been having nightmares."

"Okay." Seph nodded slowly. "About what?"

"You. Not...not being here."

"Not being here? Where have I gone?"

"No. I mean...after...I find you. In the shower. But I'm too late."

Realisation dawned on Seph like a sledgehammer. A lead weight settled in her stomach, a feeling of nausea forcing its way up her throat.

"Babe, that's not what was happening, you know that right? I didn't...I wasn't trying..."

"I know. I know you weren't. But...I'm just struggling with getting that image out of my head. And I'm not blaming you, I'm not saying it's your fault, it's just..."

Seph could tell that Kate was struggling to articulate what she wanted to say. She dropped down onto the sofa, pulling Kate with her and wrapping her arms tights around her shoulders. "I'm sorry that my actions have made you feel this way. When I'm in that place, I can't comprehend that anyone else cares for me enough to be affected by my actions."

"I never thought that it would get that bad again. I never thought anything would be as devastating as when I first saw you when I came back here that day after the party."

"I know. I was just so scared about slipping again. I felt like a failure for not being able to cope, and I thought you would see it and realise it was all too much and leave again. I wanted to support you, just as you have done for me, with everything that was happening with Tim." Seph dropped her head, speaking quietly. "I didn't want you to feel like this was all one-sided. Like I was a burden."

Seph felt Kate move, before a warm palm cradled her face and pulled it up to meet Kate's gaze. "You are never a burden. And I know accepting that is nowhere near as easy as me saying it, but please, promise you'll try to remember it."

"I'm trying. Gloria tells me the same, and I'm working on it. It's been the default for so long for me, it's a hard habit to break, you know?"

"I understand, baby."

They sat there for a second, Seph enjoying Kate's thumb rubbing repetitive patterns across her cheekbone, before squeezing her closer again into her body.

"So what are we going to do about these nightmares? Is there anything I can do to help?"

"I...I've actually been seeing Gloria about them."

That wasn't the response Seph was expecting. She never thought she would hear her girlfriend was also seeing her counsellor. A warm sense of pride at Kate's proactive action filled her chest, mixed with a strange sense of something she couldn't place at her own inability to be as brave and do the same. *No, you're working on that. It's not a weakness*, she reminded herself. Her silence must have been misinterpreted by Kate though as she continued to talk.

"I'm sorry if you feel like I'm stepping on your toes. Or that I've been hiding something from you. I just wanted to see what she had to say really before telling you. But I can find someone else to talk to if you—"

"No!" Seph stopped her. "No. I don't mind at all that you're speaking to her. I'm happy that you are talking to someone about your nightmares. If this is what you need, then I would never begrudge you that."

"And you don't mind that it's Gloria?"

"Absolutely not. If she works for you, then it's fine by me." Seph sighed, relief flowing through her at the fact she now knew what had been troubling her girlfriend these past few weeks. "I'm done with each of us blaming ourselves for things which go wrong. This year has been one of the hardest of my life. But it also had some of my happiest moments. And each and everyone has been with you. Through my darkest times, you have been there guiding me through. And I promise to do the same for you. But we need to do it without the past hanging over us. Move on with me, Kate. Let's draw a line under the past year and move on together. Work through our stuff *together*."

Kate looked up and smiled at Seph, pressing a chaste kiss against her lips. "I'm right there with you baby, I promise."

Chapter Forty-Three

*F*ive weeks later

Seph breathed deeply, her foot tapping involuntarily underneath the table. This is what she needed. To be out. To be around people. Okay, maybe this was a few too many people, but they had been lucky enough to snag a booth in the corner, hidden slightly from the crowds and it eased her worries slightly. That and the warm hand which slid onto her knee, squeezing it gently to stop the foot tapping.

She turned and smiled at Kate. "Sorry."

"It's fine. You okay?" Kate asked, leaning in close so she could speak softly in her ear, preventing them from being overheard.

"Yeah."

"We can go—"

"No. No, this is good. I need to get out more."

"Okay, but if you need to—"

"I'll let you know."

Seph smiled again as Kate leaned in closer, brushing her lips gently against her own. Seph relaxed further, the kiss washing away some of the tension, knowing she was safe with Kate. If she needed, Kate wouldn't hesitate to sweep her out of any situation which made her feel uncomfortable.

"You two are so cute together."

Seph pulled back from Kate, blushing slightly at the fact they had been interrupted. She'd almost forgotten about the invitation Anna had extended months prior, for her and Kate to go out with her and her boyfriend. But Anna had reached out while she had been off work recently, and the two had got talking more. Seph had appreciated the effort she took, asking if she was okay, but not pushing too much to find out what was wrong. Kate encouraged her to talk to Anna if she felt comfortable, but not pressuring her to reveal anything she wasn't ready to say. Seph took the leap a few weeks ago, asking if Anna wanted to come for coffee. Something small, something in an environment she could control. And it had done her good. She felt some sense of relief at just talking to someone, not about her issues, not about what had happened, but just about everything else mundane and ordinary. Anna, it seemed, had felt the same, returning the invitation the next week. When she had brought up the idea of going out again, for lunch and drinks, Seph had initially panicked. But both Anna and Kate were understanding, and this morning while she was getting ready, she felt excited at going out for the first time in a long time. Still, she wasn't planning on getting caught kissing Kate so publicly.

"Are you embarrassing people again?" Anna's boyfriend Darren slid in the booth behind Anna, placing their drinks on the table. This was the first time she had met Darren, but he was as lovely as Anna, and they had all gotten on easily from when they first arrived.

"Not intentionally." Anna smiled at Seph. "It's just nice to see them so happy. When I've been at the house, Kate always makes herself scarce"

"That's just so you two can talk without me hanging about. It's nice that we can all come out together though." Kate clarified, smiling at Anna.

"Yeah. I'm sorry it took so long though. Maybe now, we can do it more often."

"Yeah, we'd like that. Wouldn't we, Seph?"

Seph smiled. "Yeah, actually."

"Oh, wow." Anna laughed, "I didn't realise that you were so worried about seeing me outside the office!"

"No! No, it's just—"

Anna leaned over the table, placing a reassuring hand on Seph's. "I got it, I was only messing." The last coffee date they'd had, Seph had opened up a little to Anna about why she had been off work. Anna had listened without judgement, before giving her a huge hug. And then they carried on talking about something completely different. Her acceptance of Seph as she was had lifted a weight from her shoulders, and only made her feel more confident in coming out this afternoon.

Once again, Anna did what Anna was so good at, quickly and effortlessly diverting the conversation onto something more pleasant and neutral, and as the next hour or so passed, Seph relaxed even further. Seph could feel the warmth of Kate's body from where her thigh was pressed against her, and she trailed her fingers across it, unable to resist from touching her. She looked amazing in skinny jeans and a loose, sheer black top which hung off one shoulder, and as time passed, Seph was finding it harder not to just lean over and place kisses down the length of her neck. That's before she even thought about the knee-high black boots she was hiding underneath the table. A break in conversation as Anna left the table gave Seph the perfect opportunity to lean in close.

"You look amazing today, by the way."

Kate gave her a smile which was so wide it had to have ached. "Thank you."

"I know I haven't been in the right place to say it much recently, but you're gorgeous." Seph watched as Kate's eyes fluttered closed, her breath ghosting across her cheek. Seph could smell Kate's perfume, a scent so distinctly her, it still sent her stomach flipping.

A cough from behind them broke them out of their bubble, and Seph looked up, already prepared for Anna's teasing.

"Hi."

Fi was the last person she expected to bump into. Most likely because she hadn't given her supposed friend much thought recently, her silence now spanning months. Seph swallowed, her jaw clenched tight as she forced back the feelings of anger and disappointment which threatened to spew out. Her silence lingered, and she knew Kate was curious as to who was addressing them, but she didn't feel like niceties were appropriate.

"I-I thought I saw you earlier, but I wasn't so sure. You've changed your hair."

"Well, it has been four months." At the mention of how long it had been Fi looked down sheepishly. "What do you want, Fiona?"

At the mention of Fiona's name, she felt Kate stiffen beside her, the hand which rested on her thigh squeezing once again in a silent act of support and strength.

"How are you?"

"How am I?" Seph was incredulous at the generic question, but then what did she expect Fi to say? She'd long since given up imagining how this conversation would go. "Just fine, thanks."

"Are you going to introduce me?" Fi asked, gesturing towards Kate.

Seph scoffed. She couldn't imagine that Fi had forgotten Kate's name, after all she was the reason that they hadn't spoken to each other for months, but Fi's assumption that hers and Kate's relationship hadn't lasted irritated her. She had so little faith in them, but then she'd not stuck around to find out much about Kate, or what they were like as a couple.

"This is Kate."

Fi looked shocked. "K-Kate? As in—"

"Yeah." Seph cut her off. "You know what Fiona, this isn't the time or place. You can't expect me to just be civil to you after you've ghosted me for the past four months."

"I'm sorry."

"If you were really that sorry you wouldn't have waited to see me." Seph clocked Anna and Darren coming back over to the table. "Now if you don't mind, I'm out with friends."

Seph turned back to the table, disregarding Fi and abruptly ending the conversation. She heard her inhale, as if she was about to say something, before clearly changing her mind and walking away. Closing her eyes, she breathed through the emotions which were rising within her, determined not to let them pull her under, before feeling Kate lean into her.

"I'm so proud of you, baby," she whispered.

Chapter Forty-Four

Kate looked up from where she was standing next to the stove, pausing mid-stir as there was a knock at the door. Leaving the spoon in the simmering sauce she was making for her and Seph's dinner, she wiped her hands before making her way to answer it, expecting Helena, or maybe even Cam. Her face set hard as she opened the door to a surprised looking Fi.

"Oh, hi. I didn't realise you'd be here."

"I live here," Kate replied matter of factly. *Another thing you'd know if you bothered to call Seph*, she thought.

"You...live here?" Fi seemed confused by the revelation, but Kate had no sympathy for her or for her lack of knowledge.

"Yes. What do you want Fiona?"

"Is Seph in?"

Kate sighed. "I don't know if she wants to see you."

"Can you tell her I'm here? I need to speak to her."

"You don't get to be the one who makes that decision anymore, Fiona. You don't get to decide now's the time to talk after so long of staying away."

"Please, Kate. I just want to talk."

"Why should she talk to you?"

"Because I'm her friend."

Kate stared open-mouthed at Fi's comment. Even she could tell that Fi didn't entirely believe that anymore, uncertainty lacing her words, but had she really tried to just claim that she was Seph's friend?

"Her friend?"

"I know I've not been around. And I know that I should have been in touch sooner but—"

"If you were her friend," Kate interrupted, quietly seething with rage. "If you were her friend, where were you when she quit her job? When she was terrified of being in a new relationship? Where were you when she started doubting herself? As her friend, where were you when she was shaking and crying with anxiety on a daily basis? Or when she spent three weeks hardly leaving the house after I found her, barely conscious in the shower, with a razor blade in her hand and her leg torn to shreds? As her friend, where were you through all of that?"

"I-I didn't know."

"No. You wouldn't. Because you walked out on her, without listening to her, without thinking about what it was doing to her. She was terrified about telling you, and you just confirmed all her worst fears."

"I'm sorry. I..."

Kate could see the tears forming in Fi's eyes, but she didn't care that her words had upset her. She'd long given up caring about what Fi thought, but she had imagined what she would say to her if she ever met her time and time again. While she didn't care if Seph never wanted to see Fi again, she also would support her if they did try and rebuild their friendship. However to do that, first Fi had to know the true extent of what had happened. And Kate was more than happy to let her know.

"I'm not the one you should be apologising to. It wasn't me who needed you."

"If I can speak to her. Maybe I can apologise, try and make it up. Please, Kate. Can you talk to her, ask if she'll see me. Just for five minutes."

"Five minutes? You expect months of radio silence to be made up in five minutes?"

The third voice in the room surprised them both. Kate turned around to see Seph standing at the bottom of the stairs, too preoccupied with giving Fi a piece of her mind that she hadn't heard her come down. She leant against the wall, arms folded across her chest defensively.

"No. Of course not. But Seph, please, I just want to talk to you." She made to step towards her, her path still blocked by Kate.

"Why?" Seph asked.

"What?" Fi looked confused, as Kate looked back at her.

"Why? Why do you want to talk now?"

"Because—"

"If you hadn't seen me yesterday, would you be here now? Or is it just guilt?"

Fi looked down at her shoes, looking even more uncomfortable at Seph's question. "Probably not. And yes, I feel guilty. I was so angry at you, Seph. When you told me, I felt just like I did when I found out about Rob. I let that anger take over, to the point where it was just irrational and unfounded. But by the time I realised, I'd left it too long, and I didn't know how to try and talk to you again."

"So what? You just hoped to bump into me somewhere and we'd carry on like nothing happened?"

"No, of course not. I...I just saw you there yesterday, and realised I was being an idiot. I'd never have forgiven myself if I had the opportunity to speak to you and *not* taken it."

"Seph?" Kate had watched silently as the two former friends had spoken, proud of Seph for speaking out and not letting Fi just walk back in. But she was also wary that Seph was still tentatively healing, and she didn't want her to push too far too soon.

"We can talk." Fi went to take a step forward, but stopped when Seph carried on. "But not today. I'm tired and I don't know what I want to say to you yet. I'm angry at you, for just disappearing on me and not giving me the chance to explain to you. But I also know how hard it is to put yourself in an awkward situation. Text me, and maybe we can go for a coffee or something. Start to work things out."

Seph walked towards the lounge with two steaming mugs of hot tea. She paused, taking a moment to watch Kate. She was sprawled the length of the sofa, her head propped up on one of the cushions, with one hand behind it, the other holding a book which rested on her chest. It was these moments of quiet domesticity which Seph appreciated the most. She made her way over to the sofa, placing their tea on the coffee table before sliding herself alongside Kate, balancing herself in between her body and the edge of the sofa. She anchored herself with an arm around her waist and by tangling her legs in between Kate's resting her head on her shoulder. She nuzzled her face in, giving her a squeeze before relaxing completely.

"Hey you. You okay?" Kate asked, looking up from her book.

"Mmhmm."

"What's this for then?" she asked, laying her book down on her chest, the hand behind her head coming to pull Seph in even closer.

"No reason. Do I need one?"

"Never need a reason for a snuggle, baby."

Seph let herself revel in just being wrapped up with Kate, hearing her heartbeat underneath her ear, her fingers tracking idle patterns across her hip where her jumper had ridden up slightly.

"Thank you," she spoke into the comfortable silence, "for what you said to Fiona."

"I didn't realise you heard it."

"I heard most of your conversation. I was on the stairs but I was still unsure whether to talk to her or not. But thank you."

"There's no need to thank me. I'll always stand up for you, you know that."

"I know, and I'm glad, because I don't think I'd have been brave enough to tell her everything."

"I know I probably was out of line."

"How?" Seph pushed up so she could see Kate's face, confused as to what she meant.

"Because...well, because she didn't know that you used to self-harm, and I told her that you had. That wasn't my information to tell her and I'm sorry."

"I hadn't even thought about that..."

"I was just so angry at her. When you first told me about her walking out and the reason why, I understood, but then as she kept ignoring you, I could see how much it hurt. She wouldn't even answer your calls, when all you needed was a friend to speak to. When she came to speak to you yesterday, and I realised who she was, I was gobsmacked she even had the nerve, but then to act all sheepish and shy...it took all my will-power not to say anything there and then. So then when she dared to turn up this morning, I just lost it." She stopped when she realised Seph was smiling at her. "What?"

"Nothing."

"You're smirking. What's so funny?"

"It's sweet how you get all *knight-in-shining-armour* for me. And a little bit sexy."

"You're an idiot." Kate laughed as she nudged Seph playfully.

"Yeah, maybe. But I'm your idiot and you're stuck with me."

"Wouldn't want to be stuck with anyone else."

Chapter Forty-Five

"Hello, you two," Maggie greeted Seph and Kate, kissing both on the cheek, "Sorry I haven't had the chance to stop and talk to you properly. Everything's been a little crazy, and obviously your father hasn't done much at all in the way of organising and helping."

Seph smiled. Maggie had spent months organising David's retirement party. Kate, and now Seph, visited them regularly, and had been receiving routine updates on every visit about what was the latest piece to be planned, or what had gone wrong or changed since the week prior. And for all her complaining at the lack of involvement David had, Seph suspected that Maggie preferred it that way, and was in her element organising such an event.

"It's fine, Mum, you've done a fantastic job. Everything looks great."

"Thank you, darling. But I do have an ulterior motive for coming over. Your dad's asked if you can find him, apparently he has someone he wants you to meet."

"Oh, great. Just what I want to do, network."

"I know, I told him. But you know what he's like. I think it's some old law school friend who he's been gushing to about you. Just pop and say hi, please?"

"Fine." Kate turned to Seph who had been watching the interaction, smirking somewhat at Kate's mild irritation at her father. It reminded her of what her and her own father were like, constantly annoying each other but with an underlying tone of love. "Will you be okay if I just disappear for a few minutes? I won't be long."

"Yeah, I'll be fine."

Kate leant in closer. "Are you sure?"

"I'll be fine. Go on, go speak to your dad. I'll just stay here with your mum."

"Absolutely. You haven't brought Seph round to see us in far too long, we need a good catch up."

Seph watched as Kate hesitated again, before walking off, still throwing a glance over her shoulder as she did so. Kate had barely left her side all night, and Seph had to wonder what was going on. Something seemed off with her, like she was on edge, and it was a side which she'd never really seen before.

"Is Kate alright?" Maggie asked, also watching Kate from across the room.

"I...I don't know. I thought maybe I was just imagining things, but she does seem a little tense tonight."

"Everything okay with you two? Tim hasn't been causing any more trouble has he?"

"No, actually. The house sale has been going through fairly smoothly, I think they might have a completion date soon. Everything is fine. As far as I'm aware."

Seph watched as Kate turned from the conversation she was in across the other side of the bar, flashing her smile when she noticed Seph looking at her. Seph couldn't help but smile back, warmth filling her chest at the sheer amount of love which she felt from one look.

"You know, I don't think I've ever seen Kate as happy as she is right now." The words hit Seph like a brick, and she wasn't sure how to respond to them. She let her head hang for a moment, taking in what Maggie had just said. "In my opinion, and I know that's not worth much, you two were made for each other. You absolutely made the right choice, even if it wasn't easy."

"Thank you. And actually, it means a lot. I was terrified of being judged by you when I first met you. I thought no one would see past the woman who broke up Kate's marriage."

"Oh, darling," Maggie wrapped an arm around Seph's shoulders, giving her a small squeeze, "I hope you know by now that that's not how we think. It's no secret and I'm sure Kate's told you that as the years went on, we weren't Tim's biggest fans. We could see just how much he relied on Kate, and he became brash and bullish. As he got older his youthful over-confidence quickly turned into arrogance. Sometimes I wish I'd said something sooner, to save her so much stress. But then, everything happens for a reason, and if I'd told her sooner, maybe she'd have never met you."

"Maybe." Seph looked over the room again, grimacing when she saw Meg make her way towards her and Maggie. "Oh great."

Maggie followed Seph's line of sight, clocking her grand-daughter as she came nearer. "Is she giving you grief?"

"That would involve her actually speaking to me."

"I thought she and Kate were getting on better now?"

"Yeah," Seph sighed, "and I'm happy that they are getting along better. But she won't come to the house, and I think it's frustrating Kate that she won't make an effort to meet me."

"Ah. Hold on, here she comes."

Seph plastered on a smile as Meg arrived in front of them, but it quickly fell as she angled her body away from her, effectively dismissing her from the conversation she was about to start.

"Gran, have you seen Cam? I need to speak to him."

"No. Aren't you going to say hello to Seph?"

Meg barely turned her head, taking a fleeting, scathing glance at Seph beside her. "Hi."

"Megan, a word, please." Maggie gripped Meg's arm, firmly guiding her away from Seph and into a corner. Seph couldn't help but watch the interaction, curious as to what the conversation was. She had never seen Maggie look so...angry? Her body was tense, leaning into Meg's personal space, clearly telling her grand-daughter something in a way only a grandmother could. Meg looked down at her shoes, a sheepish, chastised look on her face which Seph had never seen before. Granted, interactions between them had been few and far between, the odd moment when Seph had been to Kate's office and Meg had been there. And that one time when Cam had driven over to try and get Meg to come for dinner, which had resulted in a blazing row between the two siblings on the street. That was a fun day for her neighbours to witness. Even when Kate was on the phone to Meg, she could hear her snappy tone through the speaker whenever anything to do with Seph or the divorce was mentioned. Which was still a considerable amount considering Meg was supposedly coming around to the idea of her parents separating. But now, standing in front of her grandmother, was a shadow of the young, fiery, forthright woman Kate had painted a picture of.

Meg turned from where she was standing, starting towards Seph, Maggie following closely behind. Seph averted her gaze to hide she had been watching.

"I'm sorry for being rude just now."

"Oh. Umm, that's okay." Seph wasn't entirely sure what to say. Of all the things she was expecting Meg to do, apologise was not even on the list.

"No, it's not, Seph. Meg was out of line, and while I appreciate you wanting to keep the peace and make things smooth for Kate, Meg had no right to behave the way she did to you," Maggie interrupted.

"Oh, well, I appreciate the apology. But your grandmother's right, I am accepting it to keep things easier for your mum." Seph opened her mouth to say something further, snapping it closed when she changed her mind. Maggie, as astute as ever could see what had happened.

"Say what you want to say, Seph. Meg needs to hear it."

"I—" Seph closed her eyes. She wasn't sure if she wanted the potential backlash from speaking her mind, but then again, maybe Meg needed to hear it from someone else. She just wasn't sure if that person was her. What could she say which everyone hadn't said already? And why would hearing it from her be any different? If anything she would be less inclined to listen to her. But then she remembered what Kate had said to Fiona, how she had said the things which Seph was too afraid to say. "Your mum's the greatest person I've ever met. She's kind and generous and loving like no-one else. And she's helped me out of the darkest hole in a way no-one else could. But the resentment you hold towards her is killing her, Meg. She's not asking for happy families, she's not wanting us all to get along all of the time. But she does wish that you would give me, *us*, a chance. I know you see me as the person who destroyed your parents' marriage, and to some extent you're right—"

"Seph—"

"No, Maggie. She's right. Whatever the state of your parent's relationship before I came along, I was the catalyst for that ending. But you have to believe me when I say that was never my intention. I just...I fell in love with your mum. And I'm sorry that you and Cam got hurt in the process. But you're not the only ones. Your mum got hurt too. And she's hurting now, knowing that you feel the way you do about her."

"I don't hate her. If she thinks I do—" Meg's voice wavered.

"She doesn't think you hate her, Meg. She just wishes that things could be better between you again. And while you refuse to acknowledge me and our relationship, that's always hanging over her. She puts on a brave face, but I see it, and it hurts to see her so troubled by it."

"I didn't realise that it was bothering her so much. I thought now we were speaking, maybe things were getting better."

"I think she's worried that if she says anything, it will ruin everything again. So she just keeps quiet. But you have to know that I'm not planning on going anywhere, and I'm fairly sure your mum feels the same."

"What can I do? I don't want her to feel like this."

Seph could see the tears welling in Meg's eyes, a far cry from the arrogant young woman who she had come to hear about so often. Instead she looked like a young child, devastation in her features. She took a step forward, placing a gentle hand on Meg's arm.

"Just...maybe make more of an effort to acknowledge it. It doesn't have to be big, just take it into consideration when you next speak to her."

"T-thank you. No-one's really told me that before. Cam says stuff but, I don't know, I don't always listen to him because I'm used to him just being my annoying big brother, you know?"

"Oh, trust me I know." Seph's mind flipped back to all the times when she ignored Helena's ranting when they were younger.

"Maybe I should go see her." Meg turned around to find Kate. "Oh, where did Gran go?"

"No idea," Seph said, equally as confused as to when Maggie disappeared. "Go find your mum. Last I saw, she was being pestered by your grandfather, so no doubt she'll be happy with the interruption."

"Okay." Meg turned to leave, pausing as she did. "Thanks, Seph. I'm sorry I've been such a bitch about it all."

"Go find your mum."

Len

Kate immediately spotted Seph, sitting alone on one of the benches which surrounded the large ornamental lake which sat in the middle of the hotel grounds. A flare of panic shot through her at why Seph was sitting alone in the dark, but she tamped it down, approaching her from behind. Once she reached her, she placed a gentle hand on her shoulder. Seph jumped at the unexpected touch, her body instantly relaxing when she turned and saw Kate standing next to her.

"Hey you." She smiled up at Kate, her nerves settling a little more at the sight.

"Hey. What are you doing sitting out here on your own?"

"Got a bit warm in there. Thought I'd grab some fresh air."

"Mmm." Seph seemed honest in her reply, but Kate was still uncertain. She slid onto the bench next to Seph, shuffling up close and wrapping her hand around her arm. "Are you having a good time?"

"Yeah, are you?"

"Yeah." Kate exhaled deeply. Although it was nice to be out with Seph, she couldn't rid the nervous dread which had been sitting in her stomach all evening.

"Kate?"

Kate turned to look at Seph. "Yeah?"

"What's wrong?"

"Nothing," Kate quickly answered. Maybe a little too quickly.

"You're a terrible liar." Seph smiled, and tucked a piece of hair which had fallen from her loose up-do behind her ear. Kate's eyes fluttered closed at the gentleness of Seph's touch. "You've been tense all evening. Like something's worrying you."

Kate smiled at Seph's perceptiveness. From the first moment they had met, it had always amazed her how Seph knew exactly what Kate was thinking, what she was feeling, better than anyone had ever done.

"I guess I've just been a bit nervous about tonight, you know? You, being here, with all these people."

"I'm fine, I would tell you if I wasn't. You know that, right? I would tell you."

Kate did know that. She understood why Seph had hidden her previous spiralling thoughts from her, but they had both gained a lot from going to see Gloria. Mainly the importance of not thinking that they were a burden on the other when they were struggling. They'd learnt and accepted, over many long nights of talking and crying, that in order for things to move forward between them, they needed to not be afraid of telling the other what they were feeling. That the other always had time to listen. To understand. To love each other in the most basic, human way possible.

"I know. I guess tonight just reminded me a lot of last time." Kate felt the emotion suddenly rise up her throat, choking her words. "Of that night."

Seph ducked her head and caught Kate's gaze which had been fixed firmly on something in the lake. "Not everyone is Lynne Williams."

"I know. But I love you so much and I just worry. I can't help it."

"You're allowed to worry. *I'd* be worried if you didn't. But I'm also allowed to tell you when it's for no reason, right? And tonight, I've had a lovely night."

"Okay." Kate pressed a soft kiss to Seph's lips, lingering a little as she took in the feel of her mouth against her own. As she pulled away, she rested her forehead on Seph's. This woman was everything to her, and she couldn't believe she had ever been so stupid to think that she could have lived without her. God, her heart ached for the sheer love she had for her, and it only grew every day. She savoured the moment they were in, just sitting in the dusky, early summer air, only the sounds of the crickets in the grass around them and the faint music which drifted out from the dancefloor.

"So the weirdest thing happened earlier. Meg came up and apologised to me, and suggested we all go for coffee next week," Kate said, finally disconnecting from Seph.

"Yeah? That's great."

"Yeah. What happened? She said she'd been talking to you earlier and that she actually found you quite nice."

"Well, there's a compliment!" Seph chuckled softly.

"Coming from my daughter? It really is. What did you say?"

Seph shrugged. "Nothing really. It was more your mum than me."

"But you did speak to her?" Kate asked, an eyebrow quirked.

"Maybe a little. I just told her the truth." Kate got the impression Seph was downplaying whatever it was which she had said.

"Which was?"

Seph looked up at the sky, clearly thinking about the conversation she'd had with Meg. "That you were unhappy because of the distance between you two. And all you wanted was for her to be a little more open and understanding to accepting who you are now."

Kate was a little stunned. She knew that Seph would defend her, would always look out for her, but she never thought she would speak so openly and honestly to her daughter.

Kate ghosted a gentle kiss on Seph's cheek, before resting her head on her shoulder. "Thank you."

"Any time, gorgeous." The music drifting across the gardens changed, something a little slower signalling the beginning of the end of the night as everyone and everything began to wind down. "I love this song," Seph mumbled into Kate's hair.

Kate listened carefully, not really previously paying attention to the song which was playing, just recognising it when Seph shifted underneath her and stood up.

"Where are you going?" Kate asked, perplexed. She was enjoying having some time with just the two of them and wasn't ready to go back to the hustle of the main party.

"Nowhere." Seph held out a hand. "Dance with me?"

Kate's face broke into a wide smile, and she wrapped her fingers around Seph's, standing in front of her. A warm arm instantly came to wrap itself around her waist, the other hand still holding onto her own. Kate leant into Seph as they began to sway together, softly serenaded by the sound of Lady Gaga's *Hold My Hand*.

"I think this song is very fitting for us," Seph said, as Kate felt her tighten her grip and pull her closer. The feel of Seph's body so close to her own, pushed up against her as if they were almost one entity sent a shot of love and arousal through her. God, this woman was everything. She let herself just exist in the moment, savouring everything which Seph was; the feel of her palm on the small of her back, the pressure of her cheek against hers, the way her chest moved with every breath. In this moment, she was the happiest she had ever been.

The song drew to close and Kate lifted her head, placing a kiss to Seph's lips. She lingered, not wanting to sever the contact, just happy with the feel of her lips pressing against Seph's. Until she felt Seph flick her tongue out, just enough to tease her bottom lip. It was fleeting, but even the minuscule touch sent a flare of arousal straight between her legs. This woman could always turn her on with the simplest of touches. Seph captured her lips fully, her kiss hungry, and at that moment, Kate knew Seph felt it as well, that spark, the need to feel each other's skin against their own.

Kate kissed her back, full of hunger and fervour, moaning when Seph un-linked their fingers and slid them into her hair, pulling her closer. She couldn't escape, and she never wanted to, her mouth instead devouring Seph's with every ounce of passion her body contained. Biting down gently on Seph's bottom lip, she pulled back slightly, tugging with her teeth, teasing a sinful moan from the very core of Seph's body, her lace underwear soaking with the sound. She broke away, taking a second to study Seph, her chest heaving and breaths coming out in ragged pants, relishing in the fact she could reduce her to such a state with so few actions.

"Take me home," Seph whispered against her lips as she went in for another kiss.

Chapter Forty-Six

T he stillness of their bedroom sent a wave of calm across Seph's body, her skin tingling with the anticipation of touching Kate. They'd been here before, that tentative first time after life had thrown them a curveball, but despite all her reservations, her fears and doubts about herself, she was more than ready to take this step. To give herself wholly over to the woman who stood in front of her, and had been standing there for months.

Kate's fingers ran tentatively down Seph's, gripping her fingertips loosely. Seph could sense the hesitation in her actions, the last time they'd had sex ending with Seph pulling away. And then, everything happened. But this time, there was no underlying anxiety, no uncertainty, no spiralling thoughts she had to push to one side. There was just her and Kate, and the rest of their lives in front of them.

"If this is too much—" Kate started.

Seph surged forward, taking Kate's lips in a passionate kiss, conveying all her love and certainty through her lips. Kate melted under the touch, her fingers linking tighter in their hold. Seph let her free hand slide over the subtle curve of Kate's hip, feeling the lace of her dress underneath her palm. God, she had looked amazing tonight. She had been stunned the moment she had seen Kate in her dress; black satin clinging to every slight curve of her hips, stopping mid-thigh, the strapless bodice accentuating those delicious collarbones that were begging to be kissed. Flowing down from her waist, a black lace skirt trailed down to the floor, teasing just enough of her legs through the sheer fabric to show where the dark satin stopped and her pale perfect skin began, all the way down to those killer heels which Seph just knew were hidden under there.

She was fucking exquisite. And hers. She couldn't wait to unzip her dress, and discover every inch of perfect skin.

"You look amazing in this dress," Seph told her, "but I really can't wait to get it off you."

As her fingers found the hidden zipper at the back, dragging it down to release the corseted top, Kate tugged her fitted t-shirt out from the waistband of her trousers. She was unable to appreciate the look of Kate once her dress pooled to the floor immediately, as Kate pulled the shirt over her head, dropping it to join her own clothes, before quickly moving onto the belt of her ankle grazer chinos. Seph leaned into Kate, trailing hot kisses down her neck, her hands feeling the soft skin of her waist, and dancing across her back. Dipping her head lower, she mouthed over the black lace of her bra, feeling her nipples harden underneath her touch, straining against the fabric.

"T-take it off, Seph," Kate pleaded, Seph's hands instantly finding the clasp and popping it open. She let it fall to the floor, before her mouth wrapped around Kate's nipple again, lathing it with her tongue. Kate's hands abandoned Seph's hips, instead her fingers twisting through her hair and holding her close to her breast. While her mouth paid attention to Kate's breasts, her fingers teased down her thigh, and she could feel the goosebumps scatter across her skin. Seph walked them back towards the bed, sitting Kate down, but suddenly stopped from following her with a hand to her chest.

"Undress? I want to see you," Kate asked, her eyes hungrily raking over Seph's body. Seph didn't hesitate, the look Kate was giving her filling her with a confidence she had never experienced before, instead finishing what Kate had started, and kicking her trousers off. Her own underwear and bra followed quickly, before Seph peeled Kate's black lace briefs off. She crawled onto the bed, Kate laying herself down, gasping as she slipped her thigh in between her legs and feeling the full extent of Kate's arousal. Kate caught her in another searing kiss, moaning into her mouth as bare skin touched skin in every conceivable place.

"Fuck," Seph whispered, overwhelmed by the feeling of Kate's nipples brushing against hers, the way her leg slid against her wet sex. She rocked her hips and Kate gasped, before wrapping her hands around Seph's backside and pulling her in tighter.

"Mmm, that feels..." Kate groaned, unable to finish what she wanted to say. "But I want to feel you."

Seph gasped as Kate's hand moved, slipping through her own wet, slick lips, teasing her clit. She braced herself on her arms, rocking into the touch, desperate for more than the teasing swipes which Kate was giving her. She watched a sly smirk spread cross Kate's face, the woman beneath her knowing just what she was doing to Seph. And then, her eyes slammed shut as she was filled with one, and then two fingers.

"Fuck! Yes, Kate."

"Oh, baby," Kate encouraged, and Seph let herself go, repositioning herself so she was straddling Kate's hips as Kate slipped another finger in. "Fuck, you look incredible."

Seph rode Kate's fingers, feeling her other hand come up to grasp at her hip, encouraging her to move harder and faster. Her own hands splayed against the soft flesh of Kate's stomach, running over taut muscles as she thrust harder into Seph. She groaned, a sinful moan which filled the room as Kate hit that perfect spot which would send her falling over the edge. Tracing her hands down, over her thigh, she reached behind her, wanting to make the woman beneath her come just as hard as she was sure she was going to, coating her fingers in her slick arousal before thrusting them in Kate.

"Shit! Seph!" Kate shouted, her own rhythm faltering as she adjusted to the feeling of Seph filling her, before matching Seph thrust for thrust.

"Shit, I'm close," Seph panted, feeling the sweat trickle down her back, another rush of arousal coating Kate's fingers.

"Me too, baby."

I know, you're so tight." Seph looked down at Kate, her eyes screwed closed, pleasure painted on every inch of her beautiful face, flushed and glowing. Right now, she looked more beautiful than she had ever seen her, and an overwhelming flood of love for her washed over Seph. She pulsed around Kate's fingers, and she knew that she had felt it too, Kate biting down on her lip. "Come with me, Kate."

Seph rocked against Kate, her orgasm rushing through her, followed shortly by Kate's as she moaned, long and deep, riding every wave Seph's fingers granted her, before slumping, boneless and limp against the bed.

Slipping out of her, Seph draped herself over Kate, equally as spent and exhausted, but buzzing with every aftershock which coursed through her body.

"That was...fuck," Kate murmured, turning her head and placing a kiss against Seph's temple.

"Yeah." Seph laughed, equally as lost for words.

Seph could feel the racing beat of Kate's heart underneath her cheek, and she closed her eyes, listening to its thunderous *thud-thud, thud-thud*. *That heart belongs to me*, she thought, and with it, the love it continuously and unconditionally gave her. She finally felt like she had weathered the storm she had spent so many months fighting.

CHAPTER FORTY-SEVEN

Kate placed two cups of coffee down on the bedside table with a gentle clink, before sliding back under the duvet next to a still-sleeping Seph. She shuffled down under the covers, feeling the ache which was settling in her muscles and smiling to herself. Last night was incredible, not only the sex, but for cementing their path forward together as a couple. Kate felt as if all the barriers were broken now, nothing in between her and Seph. Seph rolled over, the duvet falling and exposing her perfect breasts. Nothing in between them, literally and figuratively.

Bright blue eyes slowly flickered open and instantly a soft smile spread across Seph's face.

"Morning," she said, her voice gravelly with sleep.

"Morning. Did you sleep well?"

"Yeah." Seph stretched her arms up, drawing attention to her naked chest and Kate couldn't help but take another long, appreciative look. Seph quirked an eyebrow. "See something you like?"

"Very much so," Kate replied, as she leant in and gave her a good morning kiss which took her breath away. Once she'd broken away, Seph rolled over, tucking herself into Kate's side, her head resting on her chest.

"What do you fancy doing today?" Seph asked, humming as Kate ran her fingers across her undercut, scratching at her scalp.

"Can we not just do this?"

"Mmm, don't have to convince me of that idea."

"If you'd told me that night that over a year down the line we'd be laying here together like this, I'd thought you were crazy."

"Yeah, me too."

"You know," Kate started, smiling as Seph pressed a kiss onto the curve of her breast, squeezing her closer with the arm draped around her waist. "That night, I couldn't wait to see you again. I didn't know why to begin with, or at least wouldn't admit it to myself, but I was like a giddy teenager getting ready for dinner. It took me at least twenty minutes longer than usual, and I was nearly late."

Seph looked up, playful surprise painting her features. "You were not!"

"I was. I think I changed what I was wearing about four times and kept faffing with my hair. It had been twenty years since anyone had remotely made me feel like that, and it terrified me."

"I didn't know that."

"Yeah. I was a forty-eight-year-old woman who was getting butterflies at the thought of seeing a pretty girl. I had to give myself a bit of a talking to before I left the room, tell myself to get a grip. But then when I saw you at the bar, that all went out the window." Seph laughed again, and Kate felt her sink further into her side. "You looked amazing in these skinny black jeans and leather boots. I'm not going to lie, I totally checked you out as I walked up to you. You looked so sexy. God, I was so frustrated when I got back to my hotel room that night."

"I'm sorry you were left so wound up."

"Don't be. It would have been totally different if we'd have done something that weekend. I already knew at that point you deserved more than just some weekend fling or to be lied to. That's why I told you the truth. Besides, it was worth the wait."

"Yeah, it was," Seph answered softly, her eyes fluttering closed as Kate's fingers stroked across her cheek. "And since we're doing confessions, the four costume changes must have worked. I remember clocking a sneaky look at your cleavage as you sat down."

"Oh, all the secrets are coming out now!" Kate chuckled.

Seph playfully pushed Kate in the ribs, tickling her and causing a playful squeal. "Is that coffee I smell?"

"Yeah, hang on." Kate sat further up, leaning over to her bedside table to pass Seph her coffee. She paused, a thought running through her head as she stared at the piece of furniture, before her hand reached for the drawer.

"Seph..." she said quietly. "I've got something I want to ask you."

"Hmm, sounds ominous," Seph replied distractedly. That was until what Kate was holding in her hand registered in her brain.

Kate tried hard to still her tremble, as the slightly battered red box with gold trim shook in her hand. Nestled within it on cream padding, was a silver band, slightly thicker than most women's rings, but wide enough that it still looked feminine. It was also wide enough to accommodate the stunning deep red stone which was half inset into it, flanked either side by a single smaller clear stone. She cleared her throat, trying to find her voice which had decided now was a good time to do a disappearing act.

"Not ominous at all. Hopefully."

"What..." Seph drifted off, unable to finish her sentence.

"I was going to wait a while, at least until the divorce was finalised. But just now, I realised, what was the point of waiting? I want to ask you right now. I want to *marry* you right now. I mean, we've not even discussed marriage, I don't know if it's something you've even considered. And if it's not, then that's fine, but I'd still be asking you to wear the ring as a sign of my commitment to you. Because I love you, and that's not going to change because of a bit of paper. Can you say something soon, please? I'm getting worried and really aware that I'm rambling."

"Yes."

Kate heard the word but couldn't comprehend it in her brain. Did Seph just say yes? To marrying her?

"What?"

Seph looked up from where she had been staring at the ring, her eyes brimming with tears which were quickly mirrored by Kate's.

"Yes. I'll marry you."

Kate pulled Seph close by her face, cupping her cheeks and bringing her in for a long, slow kiss which was filled with everything she wanted to say. *I love you.*

I'm with you. I'm not leaving. You are my forever. As she broke away, she rested her forehead on Seph's, not wanting to be out of her proximity for any longer than she had to be. Her heart was pounding, from the adrenaline of asking, and equally from receiving Seph's answer. She hadn't imagined it. She hadn't misunderstood it. Seph wanted to be her wife.

"I love you," Kate said, brushing a tear from where it had slid down Seph's cheek.

"I figured you might not want to get married again. So I never wanted to ask you. In case you said no."

"Maybe if things had been different for me, I wouldn't. But I don't know, I think I always knew it was you." Kate laughed, heartily and deep as a memory danced across her mind. "Mum was right."

"About what?"

Kate let go of Seph's face, reaching over to pick up the box which had been left on the bed, holding it in between them. "About a week after you first met them, I was over there and she gave this to me. It was my grandmother's engagement ring, she'd given it to Mum years before she died, and Mum had just kept hold of it, never really knowing what to do with it. So she gave it to me, saying maybe I might have someone I'd like to give it to. I told her it was too early to think about marriage, but she insisted that I keep it. She said she had a feeling. I bloody hate that she's right all the time."

"It's beautiful," Seph mumbled, clearly overwhelmed by the gesture and the story. "Are you sure?"

"Sure of what?" Kate asked, confused. Surely asking Seph to marry her couldn't hold any doubt about how committed she was to her.

"About giving me your grandmother's ring?"

"Absolutely. She would have loved you. I sometimes think about how much trouble you two would have got up to if she was still here." Kate paused, smiling to herself at the thought. "Would you like to try it on?" Seph looked up at Kate for the first time since Kate had started recalling the story of the ring, wide-eyed and shocked like *that* was the most important, life-altering, surprising question of the whole exchange.

"Can I?"

"Of course. I hope it fits, I had to stealthily measure one of your other rings to try and guess the size in case it needed altering."

Seph laughed, the emotion she was trying to suppress bubbling up in the back of her throat and threatening to take over. Kate took the ring out of the box, taking Seph's hand in hers.

"You're shaking."

"Not everyday you get proposed to," Seph muttered in explanation.

"Guess not. Never thought it would be nerve-wracking for you as well as me." She brushed her thumb across the back of her hand in a silent act of calming reassurance. "I love you. More than I've ever loved anyone, and..." Kate's voice broke again, fresh tears of joy rolling down her face. "And I can't do a big speech because I'll sob like a baby throughout it. So, will you marry me?"

"Yes."

She slid the ring onto Seph's finger, before curling her hand around the back of her neck and pulling her in for a searing kiss. She could taste the salt of her own tears and Seph's as they mingled together. Their kiss naturally slowed to something altogether more sensuous, long and lingering against each other's lips until Kate pulled away to take in a deep breath, resting her forehead against Seph's.

"I love you."

"I love you, too."

They looked down at their joined hands, Kate brushing her thumb over the ring which now had its home on Seph's finger, admiring how it looked, how it fitted so well, like it had always meant to be there.

"Beautiful." She smiled, looking back up at her fiancee.

EPILOGUE

Eighteen months later

Seph looked around the dancefloor, smiling as she watched her friends and family mixing together. It hadn't been a big, fancy affair, but for her wedding day, it had been perfect. *My wedding day.*

She'd probably had a moment every day since Kate had asked her to marry her where she doubted herself, where she had thought she must have been imagining it, but no, Kate had proposed, and now here they were. Wife and wife. She had honestly never considered this was how her life would turn out, but she was happier than she could ever remember being. On the whole, she could honestly say that the past twelve months had been some of the best she'd ever had. Her mental health was good, her sessions with Gloria now much more of a check in than anything else and only once a month, her job was going well, and she had even cautiously built her friendship with Fiona back up to the point where she had come today. Kate and her had even found time to take that holiday to Portugal that they'd both been dreaming about for so long. She couldn't help the grin which spread across her face as she remembered when she saw Kate in that black and gold bikini. Or how she had removed said bikini in the hotel room shower, dropping it to the floor as she sank into her.

"There she is! I wondered where you'd got to." Her sister's voice broke her out of her daydream and she felt herself flush at being interrupted thinking about Kate in such a way. "I don't want to know what that smirk is for."

"No. Best not. Everything okay?"

Helena smiled at her little sister, draping an arm across her shoulder. "Everything's perfect. My little sister's got married, what more could I want?"

"Thanks for stepping up today. I couldn't imagine anyone else doing it."

Helena had sobbed for a solid ten minutes before giving an answer when Seph had asked her to be her best man. Finally when the tears had subsided, she had been hauled into a snotty, bone-crushing hug as she agreed.

"It was an honour. Kate was looking for you."

"Everything okay?"

"Yeah. Think she just wondered where her wife had gone." Seph couldn't hide a smile. *My wife.* Helena saw it, grinning herself. "Sound's good, doesn't it?"

"Sound's perfect. But now," Seph placed a kiss on her sister's cheek, "I better go find *my* wife."

It didn't take long for her to locate Kate, her body and mind instantly managing to sense where she was, like a homing beacon calling to her. She took another look as she approached where she was standing with Meg, in awe at how beautiful she looked. When she had first seen her walking down the aisle towards her, she had literally stolen her breath away. The ivory gown she had chosen had a sweeping neckline, and hugged her all the way down her body, before flaring with a silk train out behind her. The top half was covered in delicate lace appliques, the lace also running down her arms. But when she turned to give her bouquet to Meg, who had agreed to be her bridesmaid, she had nearly passed out at the sight of her naked back, the hemline plunging all the way down to the dip in her spine. Now, once again with her back to her, Seph was struggling with the overwhelming urge to take Kate off to a private room and make love to her, running her tongue across the skin on show.

Clearing her mind, she coughed lightly to gain Kate and Meg's attention, smiling innocently as they turned around.

"Hey, there you are," Kate greeted her as she leant in for a kiss. Seph lingered at the contact, humming slightly at the slow manner at which Kate teased her tongue across her lips before pulling back.

"Urgh, you two are sickening," Meg said, grimacing.

"I'm sorry if your mother is embarrassing you by kissing her wife on their wedding day," Kate said playfully. The relationship between Kate and Meg had improved vastly over the last year, Meg now a regular visitor to the house for dinner. Seph was even able to call on her for wedding advice when she was planning certain things which she wanted to keep hidden from Kate until the big day. When she had agreed to be Kate's bridesmaid, it had seemed like the final piece of the puzzle had fallen into place.

"Yeah, well. I guess I can forgive you just this once. But after today, you better keep the PDA down to a minimum," Meg joked, giving them both a stare.

"We'll try Meg, just for you. But until then..." Kate leant in giving Seph another kiss.

"Ew, Mum! I'm off."

Kate and Seph both laughed as they watched Meg disappear into the crowd, before Seph turned to Kate. "Helena said you were looking for me? Everything okay, babe?"

"Everything is more than okay," Kate replied, turning and wrapping her arms loosely around Seph's waist. "Just wondered where my gorgeous wife was."

"Just went and mingled for a bit, then stood watching *my* gorgeous wife from afar."

"She must be a very lucky woman to be married to you."

"Oh, I'm the lucky one," Seph said, pulling Kate in close, her fingers dancing down Kate's spine. "Have I told you yet how amazing you look in this dress?"

"Once or twice, maybe," replied Kate with a smirk.

"Is that all? Well then, I better start upping my game," Seph pressed a kiss just below Kate's ear, feeling the hairs on her body stand to attention. "Or maybe I should just show you later."

Kate padded across the thick, luxurious carpet of their honeymoon suite towards the ice bucket which she had ordered up to their room, pouring herself and Seph a glass of champagne. Her feet ached from standing most of the day in heels, but it was a feeling she wouldn't trade for the world. Because that standing included when she was at the altar, saying her vows to Seph. And now they were back in their room, Kate out of her exquisite wedding dress and wrapped in a silk robe, she could finally let that sink in. Seph...was her wife.

She heard the door to the ensuite open behind her, turning to see Seph walking out. She'd unbuttoned and untucked her shirt and waistcoat, letting them hang loose, her sleeves rolled up from earlier in the night. When Kate walked into the room earlier in the day, to find Seph standing waiting for her in a stunning burgundy three-piece suit, paired with a black shirt, her heart raced. In her lapel was a single cream rose which matched her dress, and Kate's own bouquet of cream roses was mingled with claret calla lilies which perfectly paired with Seph's suit. It was those little details, which she loved most about today. She hadn't known about Seph's suit choice, only knowing that they had chosen the colour scheme together and thinking it would carry through to the reception, the invites and place cards and table dressings. She had no idea that Seph had chosen a suit which matched as well. But she had known, from the moment she saw her, Seph had chosen the suit with Kate in mind; it perfectly fitted her, every curve of her body accentuated by the cut, it's sole intention to drive Kate wild. But now, seeing her wearing it loose and open, relaxed in her company, it was even sexier as it teased what lay beneath. Snapping herself out of her daydream, she stalked over to Seph, holding out one of the champagne flutes. As soon as her hand was free, she curled it around Seph's neck, pulling her in for a passionate, lingering kiss.

"Happy wedding day, Mrs Earnshaw-Graves," she whispered against Seph's lips.

"Mmm, that sounds good."

"It does, doesn't it?" She clinked her glass against Seph's. "To us."

"To us," Seph repeated, taking a sip. Kate watched intently as Seph's throat bobbed when she swallowed, the urge to kiss down that slender neck almost too much to resist.

"You looked incredible today," Kate said, the fingers which were around Seph's neck coming forward to play with the collar of her shirt, teasing the skin which lay beneath it. "This," her hand ran down the front of Seph's open waistcoat, brushing over her breast as she did so, "is my favourite of all your suits."

"Mmm, I thought you might like it," Seph muttered, as she leant in closer and brushed a kiss over Kate's pulse. Kate melted under the gentle caress of her lips as they trailed down her neck, reflexively tipping her head back to expose more to Seph. "But you, my God, I wanted to make love to you as soon as I saw you in that dress."

"Well, you haven't seen the final part of the outfit yet," Kate replied, taking a step back. Placing her glass down on the dresser, she slowly untied the belt of her robe, slipping it off and throwing it onto the chair in the corner of the room. She smirked as Seph's mouth comically dropped open, the way her eyes raked across her body fanning the flames which had sat low in her belly all day.

"Fuck," Seph uttered, taking in the sheer hold up stockings with ivory lace at the thighs, the matching lace of her panties and no bra. She couldn't wear one with her dress, and she had considered putting one on to complete the look for tonight, but she thought that Seph would appreciate the sight of topless Kate when she revealed herself. The way her pupils dilated when her eyes reached her breasts, her nipples already hard and begging to be touched confirmed Kate had made the right decision. Seph stepped forward, her mouth capturing Kate's with a hungry kiss full of love and want. Her mouth trailed down Kate's neck, eliciting a delighted hum as she did so, her tongue dipping in the valley of the collarbones that Kate knew she found sexy. Kate threaded a hand through Seph's hair, its loose beach wave still sitting perfectly even after all day, and pulled her back up, crashing their lips together once again.

"Fuck, you're driving me crazy," Kate muttered.

Just as she went in for another kiss, Seph pulled away, dropping to her knees and smoothed her hands over the soft skin of Kate's legs. Kate's eyes fluttered closed as she imagined the path they were taking from what she could feel. She felt Seph place soft kisses on the side of her knee, working her way higher, her thumbs grazing the edge of her lace panties, feeling how soaked she was. It drove her wild, and it took everything she had within her not to just drop to her knees and push Seph onto the floor.

Before she lost her resolve, Seph appeared in front of her, her hands gripping Kate around the waist in firm hold, walking her back towards the bed.

"You might want to lay down. I can feel you shaking." Seph wasn't wrong, her legs had been close to giving out the moment she looked down to find Seph on her knees in front of her. Kate sat down on the bed, pushing herself backwards and resting on her elbows, a sly grin on her face. Seph stood, her gaze hungry, and it ignited every nerve ending in her body. "God, I don't know where to start with you."

"How about you finish off what you started a minute ago," Kate said, her voice deep and husky with desire as she let her legs drop open.

Seph's breath hitched at Kate's invitation, instantly dropping to her knees and prepared to give her everything she desired. This time she didn't tease, didn't edge her along, and for that Kate was grateful, the ache she had for her wife too great to hold out. She watched as Seph's fingers brushed across the waistband of her panties, hooking her fingers underneath them and dragging them down her legs, before her thumb pushed against Kate's swollen clit. Kate's head dropped back, a moan falling from her lips as Seph finally gave her what she needed. When Seph's tongue followed, swirling round her clit, tasting Kate as she writhed underneath her, her eyes slammed shut. When she grazed one particularly sensitive spot, Kate's hips jerked, and she felt Seph's arm pin her in place, her blunt fingernails digging into the flesh of Kate's thigh with a delightful sting. Everything around her disappeared, only the feel of Seph between her legs, the way she was tracing delicate random patterns across her clit with the tip of her tongue, the only sound her own moans as she felt herself climb higher and higher. Then, she felt Seph's tongue dip lower, pressing against her, teasing her before pulling away, and she needed Seph inside her like never before.

"Fuck! Seph...please."

The sound of Kate begging must have had an effect on Seph as she felt her moan against her, the vibrations travelling through her body. Pushing herself up on shaky elbows, the sight of Seph's head buried between her thighs sent another wave of arousal through her. Glancing to the right, she spotted the reflection of them in the mirror, and for a moment, she wished she'd taken the time to undress Seph, so she could see her beautiful body as she made love to her. Then she focused on what she *could* see and hear; the way Seph's hips were subtly rocking, the soft huffs of frustrated tension as she licked around her sex, the tension in her hand as it gripped onto Kate's thigh. Seph was desperate, and she imagined she was soaked.

"Touch yourself for me," Kate said, her voice hoarse with her own arousal.

Without hesitation, Seph's hands fumbled with the button on her trousers, then disappeared beneath the waistband, her movements stuttering for a split second as she obviously ran her fingers over her own clit. The moan she released at the touch vibrated through Kate. Seph was so close already, Kate could tell, but Seph didn't falter, and almost with a renewed vigour, she slipped her tongue inside Kate and started to thrust. Kate's reaction was instantaneous, her hands shooting to grab at her hair, holding her in place as her hips rocked into her face. She could feel herself tighten around Seph's tongue, and with a final press and a circle of her thumb across her aching clit, Kate felt herself come as she roared into the room, with a never before known intensity. Through her own haze she heard the moment seconds later when the coil within Seph snapped, her own orgasm pulsing through her body, and almost passing into her. She shook as Seph slowed, easing them both through it, before slipping her hand out of her trousers, and running her hands back up Kate's calves, dropping gentle butterfly kisses across her sensitive sex. Kate's grasp on her hair loosened, and she opened her eyes to see a flushed but beautiful Seph leaning over her.

"Fuck," Kate whispered, "I think you've just killed me."

Seph chuckled, before leaning down, kissing her, dipping her tongue into her mouth, Kate moaning at the taste of herself. "Mmm, you looked so fucking amazing."

Kate took her bottom lip in between her teeth. "Hmm, so did you. I just wish I could have seen it properly, I bet you look so good fucking yourself." She felt Seph shake above her, as she closed her eyes.

"Kate..."

Kate smirked at Seph's response, the way she involuntarily rocked her hips into her. She took advantage, rolling them both over until Seph was pinned underneath her, her hands wrapping around her wrists holding her in place.

"Now I believe I have the absolute pleasure of taking this suit off your gorgeous body, and making love to my wife."

A beaming smile crept across Seph's face at her words. "Say that again."

"What? What does *my wife* want me to say again?" Kate repeated, knowing exactly what Seph wanted to hear. She leant down, pressing a kiss to Seph's lips, matching her smile as she did so.

"I love you," Seph whispered, chasing Kate's mouth as she pulled back.

"I love you too, baby," Kate replied, sincerity lacing every word, as her fingers trailed through Seph's slick heat. "And this is just the beginning."

ALSO BY AMI SPENCER

Broken

About the Author

Ami Spencer has always been writing in some way or another, but it wasn't until long, lonely night feeds with their second baby that they started to take it seriously.

Originally from Norfolk, they now live just outside Halifax, with their partner, two children, dog and cat, both of which can regularly be seen on their Twitter feed, impeding them in some way from writing.

When not working, writing or child-wrangling, they can usually be found reading (either as a beta reader, or indulging in Thasmin or Talder fanfiction), binging their favourite boxsets (Doctor Who, The West Wing, Motherland: Fort Salem to name but a few) or partaking in a gin and tonic.

As for their writing, they love to write (and read) about sapphic love set amongst the struggles of real life; they are currently working on ideas dealing with topics such as depression, autism and coming out as non-binary.

You can find them on their social media;

Twitter: @aspencerwriter

Facebook: amispencerwriter

Instagram: @aspencerwriter

As an independent author, reviews mean everything! If you enjoyed this book, please feel free to leave a review, or shout about it on social media! Thank you!

Ami x

Printed in Great Britain
by Amazon

17836605R00195